THE HAUNTING OF
WINCHESTER MANSION

ALEXANDRIA CLARKE

A FRESH START

Bailey and Bodhi: Flipping Out

We're on the move again! If you're an avid reader of this blog, you already know that Bodhi and I just finished renovating an adorable beach house in Fort Lauderdale. (If you're new to Flipping Out, click here for before and after pics of our favorite projects!) It was a doozy, but we learned so much. For instance, I now know that I would never want to live in Florida. First of all, it's hot. Secondly, it rains a lot. What kind of propaganda is the "Sunshine State" feeding us anyway?! But the weather doesn't compare to the third thing I learned: sinkholes are the monsters under your bed. Literally. A Jacuzzi-sized crater opened up in the room we were sleeping in and swallowed our mattress whole. Thankfully, we weren't at the house when it happened. Check out the full story (and terrifying photos) of our sinkhole struggle in my February entries. Anyway, we went into this project thinking it would be a quick flip. Instead, we spent a lot of money and a lot of time repairing the foundation of the house, which will *definitely take a toll on our net return. Seriously, everyone. Fear the sinkhole.*

On a more cheerful note, the sinkhole house is now on the market! Don't worry; it is now sinkhole free. We made sure of that. If you love a searing sun, ravenous mosquitos, and hurricane-force winds, this beach house is perfect for you. Okay, fine. I'll admit it. Florida is pretty great in some ways. The sunsets are straight out of a cruise commercial, and let me tell you, it's pure paradise knowing that when you wake up, you can throw on a bikini and head out to your backyard... because your backyard is the beach! If you're interested, click on the links below for pictures, a virtual tour, and pricing.

Now that the beach house is waiting to be sold to a happy owner, Bodhi and I are in search of a new property together! You know the drill, people. We love a challenge, so drop a message in my inbox if you have an idea in mind for our next project!

UNTIL NEXT TIME!
  Bailey

I ATTACHED a photo of Bodhi and I posing proudly in front of the completed house, clicked the link to publish the new blog post, and lay back on the cool tile floor of our tiny apartment. I stared up at the stucco ceiling. The leak in the corner of the living room had started dripping again, staining the cheap white paint with a tinge of garlic yellow. I sighed, tilting my head toward the sliding glass doors. The vertical blinds were broken, and Bodhi wouldn't bother to repair them. Outside, the pouring rain blanketed our usual view of the complex's algae-infested swimming pool in a monochrome gray sheet. The fan palm on the patio folded sadly under the weight of the water and wind, its leaves bent like broken fingers against the concrete in a feeble attempt to hold itself up. Thunder drummed in the distance, and every few minutes, a flash of lightning illuminated the small apartment with a ferocity that went unchallenged by the weak lightbulb of the overhead fan. My own face peered back at me from the reflection in the glass door: tanned, freckled cheeks, chin-length light brown hair, and hazel eyes that used to have a little more sparkle in them. Without sitting up, I reached for the nearby plastic trash can and relocated it to catch the steady plop of rainwater from the ceiling.

Thankfully, our living situation was temporary. We had moved out of the sinkhole house a few days ago. The apartment was a go-between, a shelter from the rain while we decided where to go next. With any luck, it would be someplace dry. Phoenix, maybe. Or Las Vegas. I was always impatient between projects. In theory, moving to a new city every few months and living out of half-built houses seemed appealingly bohemian—especially toward the end of the renovations when the houses we flipped really started to come together—but I had developed the poor habit of forgetting what life was like during the hiatus between projects. Without the distraction of blueprints, construction crews, and the eccentric catharsis of filling one of those massive industrial dumpsters with the guts of an old house, my mind tended to settle on things that I didn't want it to settle on. Like why it took Bodhi an hour and a half to bring home Chinese food from a restaurant that was five minutes away.

My laptop chimed from its perch on the cardboard box that currently served as our coffee table. Someone had already read and responded to my newest blog post. I closed my eyes, listening to the rain pitter patter on the roof. I liked to wait until my inbox was full. Then I went through all of the messages at once. It was a process I had learned at the beginning of my journey into blogging. I used to read an e-mail, get distracted by a new message, and never get back to the old one. I missed some great opportunities that way, including a historic property in Boston that had apparently belonged to one of the Founding Fathers and an old fire-house in Brooklyn that would have made the most fabulous apartment. Nowadays, I spent hours poring through my inbox and real estate websites. The best properties weren't easy to find, but I had a knack for unearthing a good deal.

I heard the key turn in the deadbolt, followed by Bodhi's familiar grunt as he shouldered open the door. It regularly stuck to the frame, a result of the humidity levels in Florida. The ever-thickening air was another reason to get out of town as soon as possible. Water cascaded off of Bodhi's raincoat as he trekked inside, leaving a trail of puddles from the door to the living room. At some point, the wind had caused his hood to abandon his head. With each hand occupied by a paper bag full of Chinese food, he had no way of pulling it back into place. His mane of black curls was plastered to the olive skin of his face, and though his forehead crinkled, a sure sign of grumpiness, a glimmer of longing dared to flash inside me at Bodhi's appearance. It was a memory of a feeling, a tiny spark of hope before it flickered out, extinguished by the careless way Bodhi dumped the food on the floor. A plastic container of wonton soup escaped from the paper bags, rolling across the tile and settling against my bare foot. Bodhi shook out his hair, showering me with rainwater.

"Bodhi, my laptop!"

"Sorry. Why are you lying on the floor?"

"It's not like we have any chairs."

He meandered into the bedroom and returned with two pillows, plunking them down on either side of the cardboard box. "Welcome to Southeast Asia."

"I suppose that's appropriate," I grumbled. I wedged one of the pillows beneath my butt and opened the wonton soup.

"China is in East Asia, actually."

"Don't people sit on the floor in China too?"

"I've never been to China," he called, disappearing into the bathroom.

"I know." I set my laptop aside, made a grab for the damp paper bags, and reached inside for the first plastic container. It was scalding hot. I hissed, retracting my hand to suck on my burnt fingers.

Bodhi emerged from the bathroom. He had stripped out of his soaked clothing and down to his boxers. A blue-and-white towel was draped over his damp shoulders. I steeled myself, biting my lip. I told him ten times a day not to pilfer the pool towels. The apartment complex was anal about it. We had already been charged additional laundry fees.

"Everything okay?" he asked, scrubbing his hair dry with the pool towel.

"It's hot."

"Go figure."

He sat opposite me and gently toppled the bag, spilling the contents across the surface of our cardboard table in a messy jumble. Carefully, I righted each container. Bodhi handed me a pair of chopsticks and a two-liter bottle of soda.

"Cups?" I asked. He shook his head. I unscrewed the cap and took a swig from the bottle, crinkling my nose. The carbonation made my eyes water.

As Bodhi sifted bourbon chicken into a container of egg fried rice, he gestured with his chopsticks toward my open laptop. "Any luck?"

"I just posted the new blog entry a few minutes ago."

The e-mail feature chimed three times in a row.

"Sounds promising," said Bodhi. "Why don't you check it?"

"I like to see the messages—"

"All at once," he finished. "Yeah, I know."

"Plus, I'm eating." I dipped a spring roll into a dollop of duck sauce and took a liberal bite.

"Fine."

But when silence fell and the crunch of the spring roll's crispy exterior between my teeth echoed to the far corners of the miniscule apartment, I relented. I dusted off my hands and drew my laptop toward me.

"Crap. Crap. Crap," I declared, flipping through the first few property suggestions with practiced ease. "Too expensive. Too ugly. Too Stepford Wives."

"Hang on. Go back," said Bodhi. "What about the blue one?"

"It's in Detroit."

"Hard pass."

A notification for a new message popped up. I squinted at it. The thumbnail showcased a sizeable home nestled between brilliant green trees. In the lower left hand corner of the photo, sparkling reflections of the sun glinted off a body of water. I clicked on the e-mail.

"That place is for sale?" asked Bodhi. He leaned forward to get a better look at the picture, but the cardboard box caved in beneath the weight of his elbow, and the food containers slid inward. Quickly, Bodhi sat up straight, popping the box back into place from the underside.

I flipped through the pictures attached to the new e-mail. This house had potential. It was immense compared to the properties we usually tackled, but it would be an easy renovation. From a cursory glance, the house was in decent shape. Its only flaw was that it had been built well over twenty years ago. For real estate these days, it was severely outdated.

"Well?" Bodhi prompted.

6

"Just a minute. There's a message attached."
I read it out loud:

DEAR MS. TAYLOR,

I RECENTLY DISCOVERED YOUR BLOG, and I think you would find great interest in a property in my possession. It has been vacant for quite a few years, and I fear many critters have taken up residence in the meantime, but other than that, the house is in admirable condition. I have no use for the house myself, and I've simply tired of the responsibility that comes with owning such a stagnant piece of land. As such, I'm willing to come down as low as possible on the price. If you are interested, please let me know as soon as it is convenient for you.

COURTEOUSLY,
   Milo Holmes

"WHERE IS THIS PLACE?" Bodhi asked, squinting at the mountainous scenery in the background of the exterior shots.

I double-checked the listing. "Some tiny town called Black Bay. It's in Washington."

"You know it rains like hell in Washington too, right?"

"It might be worth it, if he means what he said about the price."

He ate the last bite of my abandoned egg roll and dusted his hands off. "I have to admit I'm interested, but it seems too good to be true. A house like that? Something has to be wrong with it if he wants to sell it for so little."

"What if we don't bite and end up letting another great opportunity go to waste?"

Bodhi tipped his head back, swishing soda in his mouth. He was thinking. The veins in his neck—his lifelines—stood at attention. He swallowed. "Can you do a little digging? This Milo fellow. Ask him for more information."

It was as close to a consensus as we were going to get at the moment. I wrote a short reply to Milo Holmes, requesting additional information. At the bottom, I left my cell phone number, signed off, and hit send. As the e-mail application *swoosh*ed, the familiar anticipation of acquiring a new property settled in. I tapped my chopsticks rapidly against the cardboard box to get the jitters out.

Bodhi trapped them beneath his own chopsticks then lifted a piece of bourbon chicken to my mouth. I almost veered away, thrown by this rare display of affection, and studied the man sitting across from me. He was familiar but blurry, like I was looking at him from beneath the depths of the murky water in the community pool. This was an older version of Bodhi, a more playful version that hadn't made an appearance in quite some time. I missed this version.

I ate the chicken. I saw the ghost of his smile. My cell phone rang.

2

WELCOME TO BLACK BAY

*B*odhi hated Washington.

He declared his hatred over the anguished groan of the landing gear deploying from the belly of our cramped plane as the pilot lowered us through Seattle's dreary atmosphere, aiming for the SeaTac airport. As the ground rushed up to meet us, the muscles in my stomach clenched. Landing was the worst part of flying. It was the idea that you could make it all the way to your destination, the safety and solidity of the tarmac teasing you from the view outside the diminutive oval window, and still die in some inexplicable calamity that befalls the aircraft in the last five minutes of flight. That would be infinitely more tragic than dying during a fatal take-off procedure. At least if you bit the bullet during take-off, you hadn't spent the last few hours of your life with your knees crammed against the vinyl seat in front of you, eating stale peanuts and breathing recycled air within a glorified tin can as your husband reads SkyMall with a level of concentration unwarranted by such expensive and useless materialism. In any case, Bodhi's immediate animosity toward Washington State did not do any wonders for my aching low back, full bladder, or general anxiety.

His seat belt loosened as he leaned across me to peer out of the window. "Have you ever seen a place this gray? It looks like a painting I saw in the Tate Modern once. Giant canvas —must've been at least eight feet tall—and the artist covered the entire damn thing in one shade of gray paint. Who does that? How is that art?"

"The trees are green." Anything to get Bodhi to shut up about the painting.

"If you can see them through the clouds."

I didn't care about the clouds. They were a safe haven compared to the apartment in Florida. One bedroom. A full-sized mattress. Innumerable accidental touches followed by hasty awkward apologies. There was an inch and a mile between us.

Milo Holmes's first phone call was a blessing, as were the following ones. It was the easiest buying process I'd experienced thus far. Milo was polite yet persistent. I had offered him a price that was borderline disrespectful, but he hadn't blanched. On the contrary, he insisted on taking care of everything from drafting the closing papers to supervising the inspection. He had walked me through each detail over the phone, tirelessly e-mailed me copies of the paperwork, and shortened the entire process by at least fifty percent. All that was left was for Bodhi and I to make an official site visit. If everything went to spec, the house in Black Bay would be ours to rebuild.

Blissfully, the plane touched down without going up in a fiery inferno. We deplaned, picked up our bags, and rented a car from the airport. The drive to Black Bay was quiet save for the navigation application on Bodhi's phone barking out directions. I rested my forehead against the window, watching the trees, which in fact were not gray, blur together as they rushed by.

"There it is."

The car crested over a hill. Black Bay lay before us, a quaint town nestled at the base of an enormous bluff. It spread out delicately and in tremendous hues, as though someone had painted the entire scene in watercolors. Nature remained greatly undisturbed here. The residents of Black Bay had taken care to build their houses and businesses between the reaches of the tall trees and flowering plants. The bay itself curled around the town in a tight hug. Despite the cloud cover, the bright blues and whites of windsurfers and sailboats drifted languidly about, a stark contrast to the navy background of sparkling water. We passed a weathered sign with chipped paint as the car trundled toward the main street: *Welcome to Black Bay - Population: 7324.*

"It's quite colorful," Bodhi admitted, letting off the gas to cruise down the hill.

The main street was rife with activity. Women shopped in boutiques, men chatted amiably on street corners, and children laughed as they flew kites past a fountain in the town square. The marina was busy too. Fishermen hauled in their catches from the early morning while teenagers played catch or lounged on the docks, dangling their bare feet over the water. It was a Saturday, and it seemed all of Black Bay wanted to spend their day in the summer breeze.

Bodhi drew to a stop, gesturing for a gaggle of high schoolers to cross the road in front of us. "What time did you say we were supposed to meet this Milo guy again?"

"Eleven o'clock."

It took less than ten minutes to drive from one end of Black Bay to the other. The far side was quieter, more subdued, as though the thick forest ate sounds and swallowed them deep in its belly. A narrow road invited us into the misty retreat of the overlooking rock. I craned my neck, peering through the windshield. Somewhere above, our potential property loomed, but the only hint of its existence was the faint outline of a widow's walk, barely visible through the thickening fog. Still, the familiar flutter of anticipation spun in my stomach.

The car climbed up the slender street, winding back and forth through the trees until the land leveled out. As the house appeared in full view, I inhaled sharply. The plethora of pictures Milo had sent me hadn't done it justice. The coastal home's design might have been outdated and its derelict exterior run down by years of saltwater erosion and constant rain, but its soaring columns, grand doorways, and multiple wooden decks were breathtakingly gorgeous. I stepped out of the car before Bodhi put it in park, planted my hands on my hips, and took in the sights.

"How do you like it?" a voice called.

From the side yard of the house emerged a tall, lean man in jeans, deck shoes, and a tan windbreaker. He was a few years younger than me and Bodhi, in his late twenties maybe, with fierce blue eyes and fair hair so sundrenched and windswept that he would not have looked out of place in a J. Crew catalogue. He jogged toward us and offered a tanned, calloused hand.

"I'm Milo," he said. "You must be Bailey."

"That would be me." I grasped Milo's warm hand in my own. "Your house is beautiful. This is my husband, Bodhi."

Bodhi shook Milo's hand as well. "Aren't you a little young to own a property like this?"

Milo chuckled. It was a deep, low sound, a man's laugh that didn't match his boyish appearance. "Probably. Would you like to see inside?"

With a bounce in his step, Milo led us to the front doors. They were unlocked. Apparently, there was no need to worry about break-ins. After all, the house was alone on the bluff. The rest of Black Bay's suburbs, if you could call it that, was interspersed in the town below.

"The original owner's things are all still here," Milo explained, swinging the double doors wide to reveal the foyer and living room.

The house was fully furnished and decorated. Every surface—polished wood tables, an outdated stereo system, a collection of porcelain horse figurines on the mantle—was blanketed with a layer of dust. There was a palpable stillness in the house, as if it had gone undisturbed for so many years that it no longer remembered how to interact with living creatures. Our entrance stirred the dust particles. They danced through the sunbeams streaming in from the front door, swirling about like a welcoming shower of off-brand confetti.

I trailed my fingers through the grime of a narrow table by the door, pausing to examine the contents of a small crystal tray. Car keys. I picked them up, dangling them in Bodhi's direction. "I don't suppose the car comes with the house, does it?"

Bodhi snatched the keys and put them back in the tray. "Don't, Bailey."

Milo remained on the threshold, a silhouette framed against the white sun of the late morning. "I know it's a little odd," he admitted. "The house was put up for auction several years ago. My father bought it originally. No idea what he wanted to do with it. Anyway, when he died, he left it to me."

I crossed the living room, the lush carpet muting my footsteps. A cashmere throw blanket was tossed casually over the arm of a dark leather sectional, as though someone had just been here watching something on the bulky, big-screen television. A grandfather clock lorded over the room, both hands still and silent. In the far corner, a grand piano posed proudly with a yellowing booklet of sheet music open on its shelf.

Tentatively, I touched a rigid page. "Claire de Lune. Debussy."

"You can do whatever you want with the piano," Milo said. "And the furniture. Sell it, trash it. I don't really care. We meant to have an estate sale, but it never happened."

"What a waste," I murmured. "It's so beautiful." I pressed a key on the piano. A shrill note punctured the stagnant air. I winced. "Out of tune, but beautiful."

Bodhi crossed his arms, gazing up at the exposed wooden beams of the living room. The crinkle in his forehead appeared. He was contemplating the possibilities, mapping out potential changes in his mind for renovations. "Where's the kitchen?"

Milo pointed. "Through there."

Bodhi ventured off. His voice echoed into the living room. "Bailey, we could knock out the wall and open this entire room up."

"Okay!"

Milo massaged one of his hands with the other, anxiously kneading the muscle between his finger and thumb. "Does that mean we can officially close today?"

"It means we'll have a look at the rest of the house." Bodhi poked his head in from the adjacent room. "If you don't mind."

"Be my guest."

Bodhi wandered off. He was that type of person. He preferred to explore alone and at his own pace, which often left me to kindle a conversation with the seller about the remainder of the closing process.

"Would you like the grand tour?" Milo asked. He indicated the wide staircase stationed beyond the foyer, its intricately carved balustrade ascending into a Cimmerian second level.

"Actually," I countered, "I'd love to see the view."

With an athletic fluidity, Milo altered his path and ushered me through the snug kitchen and out a back door. On the decrepit wooden deck in the backyard, I didn't know where to look first. The house had a spectacular garden. It was wild and overgrown, but at one point, it might have been the pride and joy of whomever had lived there. The view beyond the garden caused the warm summer air to catch in my throat. To the right, the dense forest resumed, cloaking the steep ascent in swarthy green. To the left, the bluff dropped off suddenly, leaving nothing but open air. Sea spray ricocheted up from below. The sun dyed the clouds pale yellow and pink, like pastels painted across the sky. I opened my arms wide and took a deep breath.

"Nice, isn't it."

It wasn't a question.

"Heavenly," I agreed. Milo stared wistfully out at the water. "Seriously, Milo. Why would you want to sell this house?"

"I don't find Black Bay quite as idyllic as the everyday man."

"Ah, yes. I can see why. Horrible place."

The massive deck creaked and groaned as he walked toward the edge. "This house is too big for me anyway. What am I going to do with four bedrooms?"

"Four bedrooms." I looked up at the second level of the house, musing. From one bedroom in Florida to four in Washington. Bodhi and I would hardly cross paths in our spare time.

"And an office, a library, a wine cellar—"

"I didn't realize I was buying Jay Gatsby's house."

Milo winked at me. "All that's missing is the American

Dream."

"Isn't it always?"

We fell silent. The wind whistled over the rocks. Below, the waves crashed against the bluff. I wondered how Bodhi was getting along. The final leg of our short journey was in his hands. If he decided the house wasn't worth it, it was back to holing up in whatever hotel room or inexpensive apartment was available. At least a town like Black Bay was bound to have a pretty bed and breakfast with a view of the water for us to stay in. If the house fell through for some unpleasant reason, I had found a backup property in New Mexico, but as I gazed across the water, I desperately hoped for Bodhi's approval.

"It's not that big, really," Milo said. He looked at me. "As Gatsby's mansion, I mean."

"If it was, we wouldn't be here." The wind blew hair into my face where it stuck to my lips. I brushed it away, bristling. There was no graceful way to spit hair out of your mouth. "Bigger houses are harder to flip. There's more work to be done, and they're less likely to sell. We're going out on a limb for this one."

"We can knock a little more off the price if that will help," Milo said.

A hint of doubt colored the short distance between us. "Is there something you're not telling me?" I asked. "Most people would do their damnedest to wring us dry on a house like this."

"Like I said, I inherited this house," Milo answered. "I don't lose anything by selling it. I don't want the responsibility. It's been a thorn in my side already, and I don't need an extravagant wad of cash to get out of Black Bay."

"Are you moving?"

"As soon as possible."

He tucked his hands into his jeans and hunched his shoulders against the wind. Even though it was early June and summer was in full swing, the breeze was cool enough to ruffle the sleeves of his windbreaker. I rubbed my palms together, watching Milo out of the corner of my eye. He bounced on the toes of his deck shoes, his calves bulging against his jeans. It wasn't anxious per se. It was more like he didn't realize he was doing it. His heels tapped against the rotting wood of the deck. Tap, tap, tap. Like a determined woodpecker.

"What's not to like about Black Bay?" I asked him.

"Who said I didn't like it?"

I made a face. "You did."

"I don't hate it."

"Okay."

We were quiet for another minute.

"But why don't you like Black Bay?" I asked again. "I'm sorry to badger you. It's just—I do a lot of research before we buy these houses, you know? We have to make sure we don't purchase some place in the middle of nowhere. Black Bay checks out. Low crime rates, good job opportunities, highly rated schools, great local culture—"

"Bailey!" Bodhi's voice floated out from somewhere above. The wind carried it down to us then swept it over the edge of the bluff.

We turned. Bodhi stood on a smaller deck that protruded from the second floor of the house. He leaned over the railing. "This is the master bedroom! Can you imagine?"

I gave him a smile and a thumbs-up. "What do you think?"

"I think I'm excited to get started. How's it going down there?"

He wasn't asking about the view. He was referring to my conversation with Milo.

"We're still talking," I called up to Bodhi.

"Talk faster. Demo and reno!"

"Demo and reno," I said back. With a grin, Bodhi retreated into the master bedroom.

Milo lifted an eyebrow. "What's demo and reno?"

"It's what I call demolition and renovations on my blog," I explained. "It's clever. It rhymes. Kind of. People like that. I thought you read it?"

He ducked his chin into the front of his windbreaker like a shy tortoise. "Honestly, I came across your blog during a web search. I mostly looked at the pictures. It's pretty impressive what the two of you can do."

"Thanks."

Bodhi emerged into the backyard, interrupting Milo's praise. He stomped heavily on the wooden deck. "This will have to go. And the railing on that second level is falling apart. I'm thinking glass panes instead. Modernize the place, you know? Open spaces, big windows. Maybe an industrial kind of vibe. What do you think, Bay? You're the one with the designer's eye."

"I could see that happening. We'll draw something up together."

Bodhi joined me and Milo, but unlike us, he didn't look out at the view. He draped a heavy arm across my shoulders, turning me to face the aging house. I rounded forward, compensating for the extra weight. "Everything check off?"

Bodhi nodded, tucking me into his side. "I'm ready to close if you are."

"I'm ready."

Sunlight glinted off Milo's eyes—just like the water below, they shimmered bright white and blue—as he smiled. "I'm glad this all worked out."

"As am I," I said, ducking out from under Bodhi's arm. "Milo, would you like to join us in town for lunch? We wouldn't mind a local's perspective."

"Thanks, but I'll pass," he said. "If you like, I can expedite the closing process. I just need a little time to do so. Meet me back here around two?"

"Perfect. Before you go, will you do us a favor?" I opened the camera app on my phone and handed it to Milo. "Will you take a photo of us in front of the house? I need one for the blog."

"Absolutely."

I stationed Bodhi at the corner of the deck, hoping that Milo could capture both the house and the horizon in the photo. Milo trampled a rose bush searching for a good view-point, chewing on his lip as he tilted the phone this way and that for the best angle.

"Ready?" he called across the yard.

We moved robotically. I linked my arms loosely around Bodhi's waist. He perched his chin on top of my head. I smiled, working to extend the expression to my eyes. Bodhi smiled, the muscles of his jaw rustling my hair. The phone faked a camera noise. We drew apart.

"One more for safety," Milo called out.

Back toward Bodhi. Click. Away from Bodhi. Sigh.

Milo bounded up to the deck, holding out my phone. "There ya go. And—" He reached into the pocket of his jeans, extracting a single key. "There's that. Feel free to get comfortable. I don't mind. I'll meet you back here. Oh, and by the way, if you don't want to drive to town, there's a pathway around the southeast corner of the house. It's a nice walk. Twenty minutes or so."

"Sounds great."

With a curious sense of finality, Milo dropped the lonely silver key into my palm. It lay against my skin, cold and still like a dead sardine. My fingers curled around it, clutching at the American Dream.

3

SANCTUARY

*I*f possible, Black Bay was even warmer and more welcoming on foot. By the time Bodhi and I reached the center of town, most of the clouds had cleared out, leaving a radiant sky with a few decorative wisps of cotton candy. I shed my jacket, tying it around my waist. In Fort Lauderdale, my shoulders had burned and peeled so many times that I'd started wearing long-sleeved, UV-protection shirts outdoors. In contrast, the subtle affection of Black Bay's sun tickled my tanned, freckled skin with such ardor that I cuffed my jeans and rolled the sleeves of my T-shirt up as far as they would go.

Beside me, Bodhi shone with a fine coating of perspiration. It tugged at his dark curls and highlighted the angle of his cheekbones and called attention to the hollow at the base of his throat. The golden sun flirted with his golden irises. I caught his index finger in mine and squeezed. That we could handle.

The high street swept us up with an enviable ease. The breeze from the bay played with my hair as we strolled past a grocery market advertising locally grown produce, farm fresh meats and cheeses, and an abundance of other enticing items. We paused, chuckling, to allow a gaggle of children playing tag pass by, then continued on our way, glancing into the bright, welcoming shop windows. There were no chain restaurants here, no looming supermarkets or wholesale stores. The businesses were small and crowded. One storefront boasted homemade ice cream and cookies. A used bookstore advertised two for one classics. There was even an archaic office for the local newspaper, the *Black Bay Banner*, a new edition of which was published every other Sunday.

The locals themselves were infectiously joyous as well. They smiled or tipped the brim of their hats at each other, pausing to chat or say a quick hello in doorways or on street corners. Everyone seemed to know everyone else.

"Beautiful day, isn't it, Joyce?"

"Sure is, Bobby. Say hello to your wife for me, will you?"

In fact, the locals were so familiar with each other that mine and Bodhi's presence in town almost seemed to elude their understanding. Though they met my gaze with the same polite smiles they afforded their neighbors, there was a vague impression of confusion in each passing glance. Black Bay, however amiable, was not accustomed to new faces.

On the corner of the cross section at the town square, the warm aromas of fresh coffee, sizzling sausage, and cinnamon scones wafted from the open doors and windows of a bustling cafe called Sanctuary Coffee House. I tugged on Bodhi's finger.

"I smell hotcakes. And real maple syrup."

"Sold," he said, steering me inside.

The Sanctuary was a popular place. There were no tables available, so Bodhi and I settled in on two bar stools at the counter, squeezing between an elderly gentleman who smelled faintly of fish and a high schooler immersed in a bruised copy of *Catcher in the Rye*. I hummed contently as the cappuccino machine happily pulverized fresh coffee beans and tapped my fingers on the countertop in time with the upbeat acoustic guitar music emanating faintly from the overhead speakers. Soon, a middle-aged woman in a denim shirt and a green apron sidled toward us. In a practiced move, she filled two glasses with ice water, garnished them with lemon, and slid them across the counter.

"Everyone in town must be getting a load of you two," she said with a warm smile.

"Why's that?" Bodhi asked.

She tightened the bright red bandana that held her shock of blonde hair away from her face. "Beautiful new couple? I'm surprised Pam hasn't whisked you away for a photo shoot already."

"Sorry, but who's Pam?"

The woman set two menus next to our waters, each one emblazoned with the Sanctuary's signature swirly font and a depiction of a fierce eagle eye. "Pam Lopez. She's the editor of the Black Bay Banner. Not a lot of news to print in such a small town, you know? She loves newcomers. Newcomers are news."

Bodhi tugged his stool closer to the counter and sipped his water. "As much as I'd hate to disappoint Pam, we probably won't be here long enough to warrant front page news."

"No? Just passing through?"

"In a way," I filled in. "We flip houses. We've just bought the house up the road."

The woman blinked. "The Winchester house?"

"If that's the one on the bluff."

"With the widow's walk?"

"Yes, ma'am."

"Oh."

She pursed her lips. Bodhi and I exchanged loaded looks.

I shuffled closer, raising my voice to be heard over the buzz of the cafe. "Is there something wrong with that house?"

"No, not at all! It's just been empty for years."

"What happened to the owners?" asked Bodhi.

A server dashed by, balancing a tray of salads and sandwiches on his shoulder. The woman made room for him before answering Bodhi. "He's a strange fellow. Doesn't come into town."

"Milo, you mean."

"Is that his name?"

"You didn't know?"

She shook her head. "Like I said, he's a bit off-kilter. Never even seen him in person. But where are my manners?" She wiped her hands on her apron and shook one of mine. "My name is Ava."

"I'm Bailey," I said. "This is Bodhi."

Ava beamed, patting Bodhi's hand affectionately. "Welcome to Black Bay! And to the Sanctuary. Best coffee in town, roasted right here on the premises. Then again, I own the place, so I'm a little biased. Can I get you something else to drink?"

Bodhi flipped over the menu, perusing. "I'll have a cold brew."

"Sweetened?"

"Sure. Bailey?"

"The cappuccinos smell amazing," I said.

"A cappuccino and a cold brew coming up."

As Ava drifted away, busying herself with our drink order, Bodhi pivoted toward me. "Okay, is it me or was that a little weird?"

"I thought she was nice."

"Nice, sure. Still weird."

I unfolded my menu. Though it was lunchtime, the

column of breakfast food drew my attention. "It's a small town, Bodhi. Don't be so judgmental."

"I'm not. And who are the Winchesters?"

A swell in conversation near the door of the Sanctuary turned my head. A stout man with a full beard had entered the coffee shop. There was nothing remarkable about his appearance, but he was greeted with enthusiasm by every person within shouting distance. He was of average stature but broad and muscled throughout his shoulders and chest. He wore faded jeans, workman's boots, and a white T-shirt. His age only showed in the crinkles at the corners of his eyes and the salt-and-pepper of his beard. He swept off his baseball cap, revealing an impressive amount of voluminous, solid gray hair, and tipped it in acknowledgement of the Sanctuary's effervescent patrons.

"Mayor?" I guessed in an undertone to Bodhi.

"Local drug dealer," he joked. I elbowed him, suppressing a laugh.

"One cappuccino," said Ava, reappearing with a steaming cup. "And one cold brew. Anything to eat?"

"Whatever they order, put it on my tab," boomed a voice. A meaty hand clapped down on my shoulder as I glanced up. The mayor, for lack of a better word, had approached us from behind. He grinned at me and Bodhi, displaying a spirited smile. "I heard through the grapevine that Black Bay had visitors. Least I can do is treat you to a meal."

Bodhi shrugged out from under the man's weighty grip. "That won't be necessary—"

"I insist." He took a few dollars from his back pocket and offered them to the nearby high schooler. "Budge up, if you don't mind, darlin'."

The younger girl bounced off the stool without argument, tucking *Catcher in the Rye* beneath one arm. "Thanks, Ethan. See you at the sailing competition tomorrow?"

The man winked. "Wouldn't miss it."

As she bounded away, the man hoisted himself on her vacated stool. "I wasn't kidding, you know. Order something to eat. It's on me."

I took the bait, asking Ava for a platter of hotcakes and eggs. Bodhi followed suit and ordered a roast beef sandwich. As Ava placed our order, the man dumped several packets of artificial sweetener in a gargantuan glass of iced tea.

"I'm Ethan, by the way," he said, stirring his beverage with a plastic bendy straw. "Ethan Powell. I run the lumber mill south of here. And the nearby warehouse. And a few of the businesses in town. But I'm getting ahead of myself. I passed by the *Banner* and Pam Lopez said there's a new couple in town. Bailey and Bodhi, is it? My grandfather had a dog named Bodhi."

"Word sure does travel fast here," said Bodhi.

"Small town, sir. People talk."

"We're renovating the house on the bluff," I explained again.

"The Winchester house?"

Déjà vu. As Ethan's deep voice resonated across the cafe, a few customers looked up from their coffee cups. I nodded. "That's the one."

Our food arrived. I slathered maple syrup across the hotcakes and took a bite. Like the rest of Black Bay, breakfast was heavenly too.

Bodhi plucked out the toothpicks that held his sandwich together. "Who are the Winchesters?"

"Who *were* the Winchesters," Ethan corrected, shaking his head. "Tragic, really. You have to know the history first. Twenty-odd years ago, Black Bay was suffering. Our town always relied on timber and fishing, but with better technology and bigger companies moving in, a lot of our factories and mills were being shut down. It was bad. A lot of locals lost their jobs or went bankrupt. People moved out to the cities for more opportunities, and Black Bay felt like a ghost town for a while."

I swallowed another bite of my hotcakes. "Looks like it's doing all right now though. What happened?"

Ethan bowed his head politely. "The Winchesters happened. They built that house of yours. Beautiful family. Two great kids. Christopher Winchester was a businessman, but not a deplorable one. He consolidated what was left of the businesses in Black Bay. Saved the small-town economy, you know? And he worked real hard with the locals to restore Black Bay without sacrificing our own ideals. Top-notch fellow, really. His wife Elizabeth was lovely too. She kept morale up. Started a book club and volunteered for whatever cause needed her most."

Through a full mouth, Bodhi mumbled, "What was so tragic then?"

Ethan's eyes darkened, as though one of the clouds from earlier had suddenly appeared inside the cafe. "They died. All four of them. Boat accident."

The sandwich dropped from Bodhi's hand. I choked on a sip of my cappuccino, my nose dipping into the foam. My heart ached. It was as though someone had reached into my chest, wrapped my organ in their fist, and squeezed. Bodhi's calloused palm found my knee. I stared down at it, focusing on the heart-shaped birthmark on the back of his hand.

"It's their house," I murmured to Bodhi.

"We can bail," he offered. He kept his head bowed, his back turned to Ethan in an illusion of privacy. "We haven't signed the papers. We can just go."

I dropped my forehead into my hand, shielding my eyes. The coffeehouse was too loud, too busy. Voices called, plates clanked, machines whirred. The hotcakes smelled too sweet.

26

My stomach heaved. Everyone was looking. Was everyone looking?

Ethan stood on the leg of his stool to peer over Bodhi at me. "Everything all right?"

"I've got it," said Bodhi firmly. Ethan sat down. Bodhi rubbed my back. "Bailey?"

"We should stay," I whispered. I cleared my throat and spoke up. "We should stay. It shouldn't— it's fine. We should stay. The house is too gorgeous."

"Are you sure?" Bodhi asked.

"I didn't mean to upset you," Ethan interrupted before I could answer. "The Winchesters passed a long time ago. No one in town is going to fault you for buying their house."

"That's not it," Bodhi said.

"I'm sorry. I don't understand—"

"It's fine," I said again, this time louder. I wiped the cappuccino foam from my nose. Smiled at Bodhi. Smiled at Ethan. "It's no big deal. Thank you for your concern, Ethan."

Ethan offered me a napkin, which I used to mop the sticky sweetness of maple syrup from my fingers. "Sure, darlin'."

I pushed my plate away. My appetite had abandoned me. I resented it. The hotcakes lay sad and half-eaten. I rotated the plate so that only the untouched part of the stack was visible to me.

Bodhi had stopped eating too, instead rubbing my back in slow, comforting circles. I pointed to his sandwich. "Finish that. I know you're still hungry."

"Are you sure?" he asked again.

"Of course." I cleared my throat once more. "So, Ethan?"

"Yes, ma'am?"

"I couldn't help but notice you're pretty popular around here."

As if in example, a small child trundled by with a sippy

cup full of orange juice and called up to the bar stool. "Hiya, Mister Powell!"

Ethan grinned and waved before returning his attention to me. "I grew up here," he explained. "The lumber mill was a family business, see? It was my grandfather's then my dad's. I would've lost it all if it weren't for Christopher Winchester. He did so much for Black Bay. Ever since he passed, I like to think it's my duty to take care of the town. Someone's got to, you know?"

It made sense. Ethan Powell was the unnamed father of Black Bay. In my opinion, every small town needed someone like him to keep things running smoothly. Otherwise, the close quarters and local gossip was bound to come to a head at some point.

Bodhi dusted his hands off on his napkin. "We're going to need some guys to help us out with the construction up at the house. Do you know of anyone who needs work?"

"You've asked the right man." Ethan finished off his iced tea then tipped back the glass to chew on the ice cubes. As he crunched, he said, "I got a bunch of guys who're always looking for a couple extra bucks. Just say when."

"It won't be right away," Bodhi answered. "I need to do some work on my own first. Draw up the plans. We haven't even signed the closing documents yet."

"Speaking of which," I said, checking my watch. "It's one-thirty. We should head back up to the house soon."

"I've kept you. My apologies." Ethan waved Ava over, lumbering off his bar stool to extract his wallet from his back pocket. He handed a twenty to Ava and a business card to Bodhi. "Call me anytime. And not just for construction work. If you need anything at all, feel free to let me know. I was serious about looking out for the people of Black Bay. Even if you're only around for a couple of months, I'm here for you."

I stood up and patted Ethan on his broad back. "Thank you for that, Ethan. And for lunch."

"Anytime, darlin'. Take care now."

Bailey and Bodhi: Flipping Out

SO THIS IS the first time Bodhi and I have ever participated in a private sale, and I have to admit, there's a certain finesse to it. Our new buddy, Milo, had prepared all of the necessary documents in advance, which we signed in mere minutes. What a relief! There was no hassle. No last-minute negotiations. No real estate sharks or loan officers. If only every transaction we made was as simple and stress-free as the one for the Winchester house.

Yes, ladies and gentleman, our new house officially has a name, but unlike The Pit in Fort Lauderdale (jk!), our project had already been christened before we arrived in Black Bay. The Winchester House. Sounds regal, doesn't it? It looks regal too. It's not a palace by any means, but the Winchesters were definitely blue-blooded. This place has a ballroom. A ballroom! Okay, so it's more of a big, empty hall, but you could absolutely hold a modest ball in there.

And did I mention the view? Right now, Bodhi and I are sitting out on the deck of the master bedroom, drinking wine and watching the sunset. Talk about ridiculously romantic. It's literally all ocean and mountains here. The sky is purple. PURPLE. Don't worry, I'll attach pictures.

EAT YOUR HEARTS OUT, flippers.
Bailey

. . .

I UPLOADED the pictures from my phone to the new blog post, including the one of me and Bodhi outside on the lower deck. I zoomed in on it, studying our expressions. As long as my followers didn't look too closely, no one would notice how our bodies didn't quite connect at the center. Or how, despite my best efforts, my smile faltered around my eyes. I zoomed out, uploaded the picture, and published the post before I could second-guess myself.

After our meeting with Milo, we had spent the rest of the day tidying up what we could of the Winchester house. It was a good thing the family had left an entire cabinet full of cleaning supplies. Even better, the 90s-era vacuum cleaner still worked. My afternoon consisted of the simple yet daunting task of ridding the house of its thick layer of dust. I emptied the vacuum bag at least ten times, covering my nose and mouth as it coughed ashy clouds into the trash can. My dedication lasted long enough to clean the kitchen, one bathroom, and two of the upstairs bedrooms. The rest, I planned on tackling during the next few days.

For now, I sat on the bare mattress of the king-sized bed in the master bedroom. The sky really was purple, a light lilac hue near the surface of the water that stretched up into a dark plum color before conceding to the twinkling stars. Beyond the open French doors, Bodhi propped himself up against the railing of the second story deck. He gazed out across the open ocean with a bottle of beer—some kind of local brew that we picked up at the market on our way back up to the bluff—perched nearby. The fabric of his shirt danced in the breeze. It rode up above his jeans, revealing a stretch of his tanned back and a strip of paler skin at his waistband. As though he could feel my eyes on him, he turned away from the water.

"You okay?"

I nodded.

"All done with the blog post?"

Another nod.

He yawned, stretching his arms overhead as he came inside. "I know it's early, but I think I'll head to bed. Flights always wear me out."

"Can you close and lock the doors please?"

He eased the stiff French doors shut and pulled the curtains over the windows.

"Night."

He paused as he passed me. There was a barely noticeable stumble in his step as though he thought about kneeling down to kiss the top of my head. He didn't though. He walked away. I watched his reflection on the screen of my laptop. At the door of the bedroom, he looked over his shoulder at the space left beside me on the massive bed.

I waited.

Bodhi left. I rolled my shoulders out, realizing how tense the muscles in my back had been while he'd considered his sleeping arrangement. I closed my laptop, no longer able to look at the happy crap I'd posted on the blog. It was all a farce. The only time Bodhi and I shared a bed these days was if we had no other options, ergo the apartment in Florida. It was easier on all parties involved if we slept in separate rooms. That was why I had made sure to clean two of the upstairs bedrooms. I needed space.

As soon as Bodhi was out of sight, I stripped off my jeans, too tired to root through my poorly packed suitcase for a pair of pajamas. The purple tinted light of the beckoning evening filtered through the diaphanous white curtains, casting a lavender glow across the plush carpet. I fell onto the bare mattress of the king-sized bed and stretched diagonally from one end to the other.

Flights didn't make Bodhi tired. He loved them. Before we met, he traveled to whatever country struck his fancy, worked unpleasant jobs to pay for his room and board, and owned a grand total of five shirts. When he was on the ground, he talked incessantly about how he missed the "in between" feeling of being in the sky.

I stared at the ceiling. The Winchesters did not believe in stucco ceilings. It was smooth, painted a creamy off-white that reminded me of French vanilla ice cream. I closed my eyes. Purple skies and empty airplane aisles and French vanilla ice cream floated through the darkness behind my eyelids.

I woke with a scream lodged in my throat. It was stuck there, bubbling. I couldn't breathe. I was drowning. Or I had been.

A gust of wind brought me to my senses. The bedroom was dark. I unfurled my fists. My fingers were cold, but my palms were damp and warm. I had dug my fingernails into the flesh there, drawing blood. Another breeze swept through the room, chilling the layer of sweat on my body. I shivered and looked up.

The French doors were open, the black night beyond luring me into its depths.

4

THE HOUSE ON THE BLUFF

*A*t dawn, the woods around the Winchester house came alive. Through the glass panes of the windows, I heard the happy whistling of waking birds, the rustle of the ocean breeze through the leaves on the trees, and the subtle, ever-present hush of waves kissing the rocks below. The French doors to the balcony were closed. I propped myself up on one lonely pillow. Last night's disruption slipped away. It was like holding a memory in a sieve. Remnants lingered, but the details were flushed out. It could've all been a dream, but the crescent-shaped grooves and dried blood in the palms of my hands said otherwise.

I was no stranger to nightmares. They were my closest acquaintances these days. As soon as I drifted off, they came for me. I fought it at first. I quit drinking coffee for a while, participated in sleep studies, and went to therapy. Bodhi tried to help too. He held me or supervised me, but he never woke me up. For some cosmically ironic reason, waking someone from a night terror was considered a no-no. I never understood it, but I had accepted it. Now I greeted my dreams as co-workers: *Hello. I see you. I accept you. Let's get this over with.* And in the morning, I left the terror to linger in the space between the fitted sheet and the duvet cover.

Downstairs, Bodhi was already awake. He was a morning person. He rose and set with the sun. I padded softly into the kitchen in socks to find him sitting cross-legged on the counter, a mug of instant coffee between his hands. He had opened the window above the sink, and as he gazed toward the lightening horizon, his back rose and fell with each rhythmic, lengthening breath. I lingered in the doorway. Bodhi alone was a foreign species. As soon as he was aware of other people, his shields went up. I savored the rare opportunity to see him unprotected.

I stepped heavily into the kitchen, rewarded with a loud creak from the aging floor. As Bodhi turned, I over-exaggerated a yawn. "Morning."

"Hi. How'd you sleep?"

"Well enough."

"Even with the—?"

I looked down at the linoleum. "Mm-hmm."

"Good. Coffee?"

"Please."

He hopped off the counter, opening a cabinet beside the quiet refrigerator. It was stacked with ceramic mugs in various earth tones. Bodhi caught my eye as he reached for one the same color as the blue-gray ocean outside.

"It's weird, isn't it?" he asked, rinsing dust off the mug in the sink before filling it with hot water from a kettle on the stove. "Time forgot about this place. The mugs. The kettle. There's an entire set of fine china locked away in a display cabinet in the dining room."

"Please tell me you didn't find the coffee here too."

He cracked a smile. "No, I walked into town earlier this morning. Picked up some fresh biscuits too. The bakery even had clotted cream and homemade jam."

"Wow."

The mug passed from his hands to mine. He lifted a paper bag on the counter. "Would you like one?"

"Maybe later."

"Okay."

There was a fleck of dust floating in my coffee. I picked it out. Took a sip. Wrinkled my nose. Instant coffee might have done the trick for Bodhi, but to me it tasted like dirty water. I set aside the mug, wondering if its previous user would gasp in horror at the thought of it holding anything other than the highest quality whole bean brew. Something told me the Winchesters woke up to their coffee made for them.

"What are we supposed to do with all of this stuff?" I asked Bodhi. "Milo doesn't want it, and it seems like such a waste to throw it all away."

"Donate it?" suggested Bodhi.

"That piano is Steinway and Sons. Those things cost about as much as some of the houses we've rebuilt."

"Then sell it. We could use the extra cash. Milo doesn't care, remember?"

"I don't know. It feels wrong. I can't explain it."

Bodhi kicked himself up onto the counter again, the heels of his bare feet bouncing against the cabinet doors. "The sinkhole house had an entire collection of vintage surfboards."

"Yeah, but the owner came back for them, remember?"

"I think it's safe to say that the Winchesters won't be back anytime soon to collect their stingray."

"Steinway."

"Right." He dipped his finger into the open jar of jam. "It's going to take us forever to clear out this house. We'll have to work the house section by section. That will give you time to figure out what you want to do with Mr. Stingray over there."

There was a flash of teeth. He was pulling my leg. "I guess since we didn't get the opportunity to name the house, we'll have to settle for branding the piano."

"It does have a nice ring to it."

"Mr. Stingray it is."

Bodhi offered me the jam jar and a spoon. I took a bite. "Apricot?"

He nodded, licking a rogue dollop of jam from his pinky finger. "They're in season. What are you planning today? I called Ethan Powell earlier, and he wants to meet with me."

"For what?"

"He's already recruited a couple guys to work on the house. Carpenters and such. I figured I'd check them out. Plus, he said he would take me on a tour of the lumber mill. It was refurbished a few years ago, so he knows the town's guidelines for this kind of stuff."

"Wouldn't the guidelines for houses and lumber mills vary a bit?"

"It's still nice to meet someone who knows the process," said Bodhi. "He's got connections, this guy. We shouldn't run into any problems. Remember that lake house in Tahoe with the jackass next door?"

"Vividly."

"Knowing a guy like Ethan Powell helps us avoid confrontations like that."

I lifted my mug. "To Ethan Powell."

Bodhi clinked his glass against mine.

"Hey, Bode?" I ventured carefully. "Don't forget to lock up at night, okay?"

Coffee sloshed over the lip of his mug as he set it down on the counter. "I did."

"I saw you close the French doors, but I don't think you locked them."

"Bailey, you asked me to lock the doors, so I locked the doors."

"Well, they flew open in the middle of the night, so I'm not sure you did."

He stared at me, quiet. His eyes, usually a rich amber, looked black beneath the shadow of his messy curls.

I swallowed hard and lowered my gaze. "Maybe the lock's busted or something."

"I'll check it later."

I sipped my instant coffee and instantly blanched. In my periphery, Bodhi rolled his eyes. "I think I'll stay here today," I announced. One more sip. Tight lips. No flinching. "I want to get to know the house better. Take pictures for the blog, sketch out some ideas, clean a little more."

His cell phone chimed a reminder tone. "That's for my meeting with Ethan," he said, dropping from the counter and sliding into his shoes. "You're staying here then?"

"Yeah."

"Fine. Have you seen my keys?"

"You left them on the counter."

"They aren't there."

Any excuse to abandon the acidulous beverage. I left my mug of seawater on the kitchen counter and joined Bodhi in the living room. He checked behind the sofa cushions, but I spotted his keys right away. They were in the crystal tray on the table by the front door, nestled carefully next to the twenty-year-old car keys that I had found yesterday.

I rescued Bodhi's set, jingling them overhead.

He made a grab for them. "Where were they?"

"In the tray."

"Don't put them there. It's weird."

"I didn't put them there."

"I left them on the counter, and only one of us sleepwalks."

Before I could reply, he briefly kissed my forehead and left through the front door. I heard the rumble of our rental car firing up. When the hum of the engine faded down the hill, I took a biscuit from the kitchen and went back upstairs. With Bodhi occupied, the house was mine to explore at my leisure.

Yesterday, I investigated the first floor. Like Milo had said, the house had more than enough rooms to entertain. Beyond the kitchen and dining room, there was an office with a mahogany desk, a high-backed chair, and a velvet pool table. The next room over was a modest but extensive library, the spines of the books faded by the sunlight from the window. The ballroom—or whatever it had been—was the only one empty of furnishings. At the end of the hallway, an unmarked door hid a set of stairs that led down to the basement. I assumed the wine cellar was down there, but the swinging lightbulb flickered and died when I coaxed the switch upward, so I left the depths of the Winchester house to explore another day.

The second floor was mostly bedrooms and bathrooms. Bodhi had laid his suitcase out in what appeared to be a guest room, with generic decorations and no personal touches, but when I swung open the door to the next stop on my exploration, my stomach heaved at the sight.

A four-poster canopy bed dominated the room, framed between two curtained bay windows. A stocked bookshelf attempted to contain a collection of literature that looked as though it had been pilfered from the library downstairs. The books were stacked haphazardly, placed at any angle to fit chaotically within one another like a bizarre game of Tetris. The wardrobe was open, revealing racks of evenly spaced hangers. They clung to cashmere sweaters, polo shirts, tennis skirts, and elegant dresses that were fit for high tea. A pair of riding boots peeked out from beneath a pile of discarded laundry. The room blatantly belonged to a girl—a young one, I assumed at first—but an open copy of Simone de Beauvoir's *The Ethics of Ambiguity* in the original French lay spread-eagled on the dusty duvet. How many teenaged girls made a habit of dabbling in foreign existentialist literature?

I left without touching anything. The Winchesters' possessions had gone undisturbed for twenty years, and I wasn't ready to change that quite yet. I took a picture of the room for my blog and moved on. At the next door, I braced myself, anticipating what I might find on the other side. I turned the handle.

And screamed.

A parade of rats scurried out from under the bed, their devious little fingers whisking across the hardwood floors as they disappeared into an open vent in the wall. I pressed a hand to my chest, urging my lungs to work properly again. Rats were easily taken care of—Bodhi and I had dealt with them at a number of properties—but no matter how often we came across them, their beady eyes and sharp teeth never failed to set my pulse racing.

The rats' room had previously hosted a high school athlete. Black and gold posters, emblazoned with *Black Bay High School: Golden Eagles*, adorned every wall. A collection of trophies—football and track—stood in formation along a shelf by the door. A small work desk, covered in ancient issues of *Sports Illustrated* and *Car and Driver*, looked like it had rarely been used for homework. I tiptoed over the threshold and reached for the nearest trophy.

"Forgive me," I muttered to the tiny, faceless gold man. And then I chucked the trophy toward the bed. It thunked to the floor. All was quiet. No more rats.

Gingerly, I knelt down, lifted the red plaid duvet, and peered under the bed. It smelled atrocious, and it was no wonder why. The rats had made themselves comfortable amidst a pile of yellowing football pads and cleats. I withdrew, holding my breath, and took another picture for the blog. I could edit out the rat droppings later.

In the hallway, I skipped the last door. My heart—and nose—could only take so much. Craving fresh air, I went downstairs, out through the back door, and into the garden. As I pushed through a thicket of high grass and weeds, working my way toward the edge of the bluff, wild rose bushes snagged my T-shirt. The fluffy tendrils of dandelions took to the wind when I passed by, tickling my nose. I looked up at the sky. The garden could swallow me, and I would let it. Let the vines hug me into the ground. Let the flowers flourish in my pores. As long as I had a view of the stars at night, the earth would hear no complaints from me.

I stopped twenty feet short of the bluff. There, a delicate tree in full bloom undulated in the breeze. It was a plumeria tree, with shimmering flowers as pink as a hummingbird's throat. It would not have been unusual aside from two things. First of all, plumerias were a tropical flower. I had seen them in Florida and Hawaii, but plumerias weren't likely to fall in love with Black Bay's dreary climate. Secondly, though the rest of the garden was wild and overrun, the plumeria tree looked as though it had been carefully tended to. The weeds did not snake up its trunk to smother the flowers, and its silky scent, reminiscent of coconuts, wafted unhindered across the sole patch of neatly trimmed grass.

I approached the plumeria tree, plucked a bloom, and held it beneath my nose. With one hand on the trunk to steady myself, I stepped as close to the edge of the bluff as I dared. There was no fence, no barrier between me and the open air. The horizon boasted a solid, straight line, a peaceful dichotomy of sea and sky. I looked down.

Below, the water was far from tranquil. Waves gathered

farther out, collecting energy as they rolled inward. White-wash erupted as the rock interrupted each curl's path, a violent surge of static that intensified with every ill-timed swell. The stone at the base of the bluff was jagged and raw. It split the waves to pieces without remorse.

My head swam. The water swam. No, that wasn't right. It was the effect of my relaxed vision, the separation of body from mind. The water and rocks were alive. Awake. Breathing. Mortal. I stepped forward.

"Bailey!"

My shirt tightened against my throat as someone took hold of the fabric and yanked me away from the bluff's edge. I woke from my stupor, spinning on my heel.

Milo, his blue eyes wide and burning, stood in the garden, his fingers still outstretched, reaching for me. For something that wasn't there.

"What are you doing?" he demanded.

I feigned innocence. "Looking."

"Looking? You were about to step off!"

"Oh, please."

I brushed by him, but he followed along after me, navigating the fickle garden with practiced dexterity.

"Wait, wait," he said. "Hey, I'm sorry, okay? The winds up here can be rough. It's not safe to stand that close to the edge."

"I wasn't that close."

"Look, if you need someone to talk to—"

"I don't."

"Okay, but if you do, I'm around."

Milo trekked diligently after me as I stepped onto the deck. I whirled to face him. "What are you doing here anyway?"

"I just wanted to know how you guys were settling in."

"We're fine, thanks."

The wind blew his hair into his eyes. He squinted across the deck at me, sweeping a hand through his blond locks to tame them. "What usually makes you feel better?"

"Excuse me?"

He indicated the bluff's drop-off. "At times like this, what makes you feel better? I like thinking about the future. Where will life take me? Where will I go? There are so many places I haven't explored. Machu Picchu. Easter Island. Las Vegas. That's a dream of mine."

He babbled like a brook, a constant stream of words.

"I have no idea what you're talking about," I said, turning away from Milo to march into the kitchen. To my dismay, he followed me like a persistent puppy.

"Sure you do," he said. "I know what depression looks like, Bailey. I know what suici—"

"Cold water," I blurted out. Milo fell silent. "A tall glass of cold water. Freezing, really. I have to be able to feel it, like it's flushing out the rest of me."

Milo opened a cabinet next to the sink, drew out a clear glass, and set it on the counter. His fingers brushed the back of my hand. "Good?"

I took the glass. "Good."

"Good," he said again. "I'll let myself out."

I waited until the front door closed again before unclenching my other fist. The plumeria bloom fell to the kitchen floor, its petals crushed and broken.

BODHI RETURNED in the early evening with takeout from an Italian restaurant in town. We ate chicken parmesan and drank wine out of the Winchesters' cups on the big seat of the bay window in the living room.

"How was your meeting?" I asked Bodhi.

"It went really well," he said, pausing to wipe marinara

sauce from his chin. "Ethan's going to be a real asset. His guys are great, you know? Smart and hardworking. Honestly, it's been a while since I've been this excited to get started."

"I'm so glad."

"What's on your mind?"

I sipped from my wine glass. "What do you mean?"

"For the house. Any ideas?"

"Oh. Well, I think we should keep the bay windows."

"Agreed," he said. "Some of them anyway. The ones upstairs. This one might have to go. I think we should open up the entire first floor and install those massive sliding glass doors. That way, you have a view of the bluff no matter where you stand."

"Open floor plan?"

"Exactly." He jabbed his fork in my direction for emphasis. "At least for the kitchen, living room, and dining room. I haven't decided about the rest of the first floor yet."

I speared a piece of chicken. "What about upstairs?"

"I quite like how cozy it is up there, actually," Bodhi said.

"Me too. Have you been in those other rooms? The Winchesters' kids' stuff is still there."

He tore a slice of crusty Italian bread in half, decorating the windowsill with a shower of crumbs, but paused before sweeping it through the sauce on his plate. "Oh?"

"Yeah."

"I can clear those rooms on my own," he offered. "You don't have to—"

"No, it's fine," I said. "Really. It just… got me thinking."

"About?"

My wine glass was empty. I reached for the bottle. "About how Black Bay might be the perfect place to raise a family."

Bodhi stiffened. "What?"

I poured the wine and swirled the contents of my glass, keeping my gaze on the tiny bubbles that popped and fizzled in the alcohol. "I don't know. Don't you get tired of moving so often? I want a home. A place to be."

"I thought you didn't mind moving around."

"It was adventurous and fun when we were younger, Bodhi. Now it just feels like we're running away."

"From what?"

"You know."

He shoved his unfinished plate away. "No, Bailey. I don't know. Please enlighten me."

I gambled a glance in his direction. It was like looking into the barrel of a roulette revolver and knowing that the bullet had just clicked into place. "I just thought, maybe, if we were on the same page—"

"I heard you screaming in your sleep again last night."

I closed my eyes. "You did?"

"Yeah. And I'll make you a deal."

"What kind of deal?"

He leaned across the window seat, gently tipping my chin up so that I would look him in the eye. "When you stop screaming in your sleep, we'll try again."

I jerked out of his grasp.

He picked up his plate, cleaning up the rest of our meal. "Otherwise, I don't want to hear about it. We've been in Black Bay for a grand total of two days. It's probably not as perfect as you think it is. Not to mention, even if I did want to think about what you're thinking about, this house is far too big for us. We couldn't afford the upkeep…"

I stopped listening as he disappeared into the kitchen. We avoided each other for the rest of the evening. I perused the small library, collecting a few books to read before bed, but I ran into Bodhi in the hallway outside the bathroom. He had just showered, and the sharp scent of his lemon-coconut bar soap lingered in the steam around his body. Without thinking, I reached out and trailed the tips of my fingers across his damp forearm and over his bicep.

He pressed me to the peeling wallpaper. The chair rail molding dug into my lower back as he kissed me once on the lips. The old books dropped to the floor. I slid my hands up to his shoulders. Then, before I even opened my eyes, he vanished into the guest room. Cold and empty, I picked up the books and slipped into the master bedroom, but when I made to stack the titles in alphabetical order on the bedside table, I paused.

A tall cup of water sat centered on a marble coaster. Beads of condensation pooled on the glass, dancing in the low light of the table lamp.

5

PRIORITIES

Bailey and Bodhi: Flipping Out

*T*he day has come! It's been a few weeks since we arrived in Black Bay, Washington, but we are almost ready to start Demo and Reno. It's taken us a little longer than usual to start clearing out this house, but if you checked out my pictures from a few days ago, you'll understand why. This place is basically the Winchester Family Museum. No one's touched it for twenty years, and in some ways, it feels like we're committing some kind of sin against nature by disrupting it. It's borderline macabre.

Anyway, we still don't know what to do with all of the Winchesters' stuff. Some of it couldn't be saved. We threw out an entire rat-infested bedroom set, and don't even get me started on the rotting pool table we found in the office. It practically disintegrated when we tried to move it. On the upside, there are a lot of beautiful things in this house that were relatively well-preserved. Bodhi and I have decided to list whatever's in decent shape. If you're interested, click the link below for our eBay page. I'm talking *a top-of-the-line cappuccino machine, several boxes of cigars that smell damn good, and a bunch of sporting equipment too. We really need to get rid of it, so everything is priced rather reasonably. Please help us!*

Tomorrow, we tackle the beast that is the attic. It looks like the Winchesters used it for storage, so I can't wait to find out what we'll unearth up there. I'm still keeping an eye out for the pesky and elusive family of rats that lives in the walls. Stay tuned, flippers. It's bound to get crazy.

WITH LOVE,
   Bailey

THE WINCHESTERS' attic was hot, stuffy, and without openable windows. To make matters worse, it was jam-packed with whatever the Winchesters had deemed unnecessary for everyday use, from cardboard boxes full of old photo albums to file cabinets to Christmas decorations. There was hardly room to walk, let alone work, and the steep, narrow staircase from the attic down to the second floor was a hospital trip waiting to happen. I had already stumbled twice, but it was near impossible to watch your footing when your vision was obscured by boxes of place settings and doilies. Bodhi, who was usually the level head in scenarios like this, lost it around mid-morning. He stormed down the stairs, drenched in sweat from head to toe, brandishing a hammer and threatening to light the entire house on fire. Thankfully, his case of the vapors was likely a result of dehydration because as soon as I cajoled him into drinking a full bottle of water, he returned to himself. We took a quick break—I had bought homemade ice cream sandwiches in town which were the perfect remedies for our woes—then headed back up to the infernal attic.

"Business papers?"

"Trash."

"A box of deflated footballs?"

"Trash."

"Oh, God. This one's full of sock puppets."

"Definitely trash. What kind of kinky shit were the Winchesters into?"

"They had kids, Bodhi."

Little by little, we made headway. By late afternoon, when the sun had sunk low enough to stop baking us like sticky hotcakes through the roof of the house, we could almost see the attic floor. I opened up yet another cardboard box. It was full of Styrofoam peanuts. I sifted through them, my fingers connecting with some kind of circular ring. I hooked my pinky around it and gently tugged upward.

Out came a baby mobile. It rotated serenely as I shook it free of the peanuts. The ornaments were tiny whales, hand-blown from different shades of blue glass. The sun refracted off of them, and they twinkled in the light, winking at me as they swam in their infinite circle. I smiled, wondering what lucky baby got to sleep under such a beautiful piece of artwork every night.

"What the hell is that?"

Bodhi stood at the top of the stairs, wound up like a spring. He stared at the baby mobile, but his eyes were blank. Dead. Or furious.

"It's a baby mobile."

"Throw it away."

"No, it's handmade!"

"I don't care," he said. He remained rooted in place, as if the sight of the mobile had paralyzed him. "Throw it out, Bailey."

I lowered the whales back into the box of peanuts. "That's such a waste. We should add it to the eBay page."

"I said throw it out!"

His voice boomed through the attic, rattling the window panes. My mouth dropped open. In all the time that I had known Bodhi, he had only raised his voice at me three times. Four, now.

"Fine. *Fine*. I'll throw it out, Bodhi."

I made sure the glass whales were securely nestled in the peanuts before folding the top in and popping one corner beneath the other. Then I carried the box to the pile of junk we had labeled as our trash pile and delicately set it next to a cracked laundry basket full of hand-me-down clothes.

"There," I said. "Are you satisfied now?"

He said nothing but finally moved, shuffling toward the opposite end of the attic to resume his task. I kept an eye on the box of peanuts, and that night, when I was sure that Bodhi was asleep and oblivious in the guest room, I snuck up to the attic, rescued the mobile, and hid it in the closet of the master bedroom.

When Bodhi finally deemed the kitchen and living room fit for demolition, Ethan Powell's crew of construction workers showed up in full force. The low roar of voices and the buzz of machines punctuated the walls of the master bedroom one morning before the sun had crested over the horizon. I lay in bed, listening to the machinery overpower the natural hum that usually accompanied my mornings and examining a scar that encircled my right thumb. Years ago, Bodhi had rushed me to the hospital after a run-in with a circular saw. Everything had turned out all right, but after that, Bodhi was hesitant to let me within five feet of anything with a blade. Once the heavy-duty construction work began, I steered clear of the site. I had plenty to do—there was more than enough of the Winchesters' possessions left to keep me busy —but the barrage of noise outside was already giving me a headache.

The town itself had gone vastly unexplored for the past few weeks. We had spent the majority of our time in Black Bay laboring in the house. It was easy to throw myself into the dirty work of it all. Ripping up carpets, scraping wallpaper off, and digging through drywall was cathartic in a way. Destruction was simple; rebuilding was hard. We were so caught up in the demolition that we only ventured into town if we needed to. Nevertheless, we were still the hot topic of Black Bay. Whether I was picking up materials at the hardware store or swinging by the Sanctuary for lunch, the locals stopped me to chat. Everyone wanted to know what was going on up at the Winchester house. Usually, I slipped out of the conversation by jotting down the URL of *Flipping Out*.

I used the morning to catch up on the blog. Ever since the first night I'd contacted Milo, my followers had been more active than usual. Direct messages and e-mails overflowed my inbox every night, and I was finding it hard to keep up with it all. It was a double-edged sword. On one hand, the blog was one of our best sources of revenue. Not only did we profit off the advertisements in the sidebars, but *Flipping Out's* followers were keen to buy up the items from the house that we had listed on our eBay page. On the other hand, it was getting more and more difficult with the number of eager fans to please. They weren't just interested in the house; they were interested in me and Bodhi. I did my best and posted a myriad of photos, but there were only so many times I could sneak a candid picture of Bodhi sweating through his T-shirt as he pried up loose boards in the backyard deck before he realized what I was doing.

"Take pictures of yourself," he'd say, pushing his damp curls away from his forehead.

"Our entire website operates on our happy couple vibe," I'd argue back.

Whatever the circumstance, working on the blog was slowly beginning to eat away at me. At this point, it felt like I was running mine and Bodhi's ad campaign rather than actively participating in the renovations for the house. Bodhi's attitude continued to spiral downwards. Ever since the baby mobile incident, we rarely spoke unless it had to do with joists or sliding glass doors or electrical wiring. At night, I held my breath when I heard his footsteps in the hallway and let out a sigh of relief when they faded toward his own room.

Shortly before noon, I waved goodbye to Bodhi and the rest of the construction crew and walked into town. For once, I had no errands to run, and the white tips of the waves in the bay below coaxed me down from the tension at the house. I wandered into one of the cute boutiques, bought a scoop of mint chocolate chip at the ice cream shop, and steered a mini remote-controlled sailboat around the fountain in the square, laughing as a devious seven-year-old crashed his boat into mine.

I walked south. Ethan Powell's lumber mill loomed in the distance. I considered stopping by to ask Ethan if he'd give me a tour—at least it would fill a few hours of my day—but the sign of a nearby restaurant caught my eye. The name, Lido's, sounded familiar to me, and my stomach was grumbling in protest, so I headed inside and slid into an empty booth. A waitress, wearing jeans and a black T-shirt with Lido's stamped across the front in white font, strolled over with her order pad.

"Bailey, right?" she asked. "What'll it be?"

"Just a soda, please."

"Eating lunch? Got a fried fish special."

I perused the menu for a brief moment. "Fried fish sounds great."

"Back in a mo'."

As she ambled off, I looked around Lido's. It was a bar and grill of sorts, with big windows in the back that opened up to the bay and even bigger television screens to display whatever football or baseball game was being broadcasted in that moment. Along the wall, there were dozens of group photos. Apparently, Lido's was in the business of sponsoring Black Bay's high school football team as well as the Little League. A trophy case at the far end of the bar displayed an oversized MVP award, along with a framed photo and a plaque too far away for me to read.

The door to Lido's swung open, and as soon as Ethan Powell walked in, he noticed me sitting alone in my booth. I waved jovially.

"Hey there, darlin'," he said with a grin. "Mind if I join?"

"Not at all."

"Where's that husband of yours?"

"Working on the house," I said. I lifted my disfigured thumb. "I was banned from the heavy-duty stuff a few years ago."

Ethan winced appropriately at the odd angle of my finger. "Can't see why."

The waitress reappeared and set a glass of soda in front of me. "Hi, Ethan. Wanna order something?"

"An iced tea and a burger, my dear."

"Coming up."

I sipped my soda through a straw, rotating the glass around until I realized why the Lido's logo had looked so familiar to me. The water glass that had appeared on my nightstand that first night—the one that I'd made a habit of refilling before I went to bed—was identical to the one that sat in front of me now.

"Hey, Ethan."

"Yes, ma'am?"

"Did the Winchesters ever come to this restaurant?"

"Every Friday night, after the big game. Why?"

I held up the glass. "We have one of these up at the house."

Ethan's eyes crinkled as he chuckled, as though he had remembered a fond memory. "That would've been Patrick's doing. He and his buddies were always nicking stuff from businesses in town. Bit of harmless fun."

I thought of the room full of football paraphernalia at the house. "Patrick. He was their son, right?"

"Yes ma'am. Black Bay's true MVP. That trophy over there is his. Wanna take a look?"

Together, we slid out of the booth to approach the trophy case. The plaque read: *In Loving Memory of Patrick Winchester, 1979-1996.* Below, there was a quote from Thomas Campbell.

"To live in hearts we leave behind is not to die," I read aloud.

"Seventeen years old," said Ethan, shaking his head. "He was the town's golden boy. Good grades, good manners, and a hero on the football field."

I leaned in to get a closer look at the framed photo. It was a group picture—similar to the ones that hung on Lido's walls—of Black Bay High School's Golden Eagle football team, each of the athletes smiling ear to ear.

"Which one is Patrick?" I asked.

But before Ethan pointed, I knew that Patrick Winchester was the grinning towhead of a boy kneeling between his teammates at the exact center of the faded photograph. His hair was a mess, as though Patrick had removed his helmet and tucked it beneath his arm just prior to the photo, and sweat smeared eye black across both of his plump cheeks. He looked familiar in that way all notable quarterbacks of high school football teams looked familiar. Patrick was the epitome of the all-American boy, and from the looks of Lido's shrine, all of Black Bay missed his boyish buoyancy.

"They lost the championship the following year," Ethan said. "It would've been Patrick's senior year. I think his death traumatized every boy on that team. A collectively broken heart. They just didn't have it in them after that."

"You said he died in a boating accident?"

Beneath Ethan's bushy beard, a noticeable frown appeared. "Yes ma'am. I know you're not too keen on the subject though. I don't mean to upset you."

It was then I realized that a silent tear had tracked down my cheek. I wiped it away with the back of my hand. "I'm all right. Just curious. Do you mind telling me what happened?"

Back at our booth, the waitress had delivered my fried fish and Ethan's sky-high burger. As we dove in, Ethan explained about the Winchesters between bites.

"The Winchesters loved sailing," he said, offering me an onion ring. "They had a beautiful boat, the biggest one in the marina. They were out on the bay every weekend. Christopher and Elizabeth were gracious people. They liked to take the locals out for a spin every once in a while. Patrick and Caroline used to compete in the races with their own boats. They were all very well-acquainted with the water."

I dipped a fork full of fish into a ramekin of tartar sauce. "Then how did everything go so wrong?"

"No one really knows," Ethan answered. "No bad weather. No rough waves. The Winchesters took their boat out on their usual weekend family trip. Next thing we knew, they'd crashed against the rocks right beneath their house."

My stomach lurched as I remembered the ethereal feeling of nothingness near the plumeria tree. "Against the bluff?"

"Yes ma'am. It was suspicious to say the least. Everyone

knows it's not safe to sail around there. We never quite figured out why they went up that way."

I sipped my soda, letting the carbonation distract me from the nervous churning in my gut. "Who found them?"

"Retired member of the Coast Guard," said Ethan. "Sam Williams. He works in the lumber mill now. But he didn't find everyone."

"What do you mean?"

"Christopher and Elizabeth were still aboard the wrecked boat, in a manner of speaking, but the kids' bodies were never recovered."

"Oh."

He paused in lifting the last bite of his burger to his mouth. "I've upset you again."

"No, it's just… rough, you know? To bury a child to begin with is tragic. To bury two? And in empty caskets?"

"You can't imagine." Ethan wiped mustard from his fingers with a paper napkin. "The town was in pieces. Took a while to put everyone back together again."

I pushed the remnants of my half-eaten meal around my plate. A familiar weightlessness lifted my mind from my body as thoughts of how the Winchesters' last moments together as a family had gone. Did they see the crash coming? Or did they die happy and oblivious to the inevitable calamity?

Despite my protests, Ethan picked up the check again. As we exited Lido's, he patted me on the back. "Can I walk you back to the house, darlin'?"

I looked up, squinting in the sunlight to see the kindness in his eyes. "No, I'll be fine. Thanks, Ethan."

But as we parted ways, Ethan to his lumber mill and me toward the center of town, I found myself dreading the walk back up the bluff. Bodhi would still be working, and there-fore, he would still be stoically ignoring me. The day was young, and it begged to be filled with plans that involved something other than silently arguing with my husband. Making up my mind, I dialed a number on my phone and waited for the other end to pick up.

"Hello?"

"Milo? It's Bailey."

Immediately, his voice brightened. "It's nice to hear from you! How have you been?"

"Good, good," I insisted. "Listen, I was wondering. Would you like to meet for coffee at the Sanctuary?"

"Is there something wrong with the house?"

"Not at all. But Bodhi's busy, and I don't really know many people in Black Bay. I just wouldn't mind the company."

There was a pause on the other end of the line. "I'd love to meet you, but I don't care to walk into town unless I have to."

"Do you have somewhere else in mind?"

"I thought you'd never ask."

6

UPHILL, DOWNSTAIRS

I waited for Milo at the top of the southeast pass, keeping to the shadows of the ever-thickening forest. Beyond the trees, the ruckus of construction continued, but the pops and bangs of work were dulled by the woods' natural soundproofing. I spotted Bodhi standing on the roof of the Winchester house, prying shingles off and inspecting whatever was underneath. His white T-shirt clung to his broad shoulders as he chucked garbage into the dumpster below. From this distance, it was easy to pretend that Bodhi was ten years younger. We were naïve and carefree then. I'd barely met Bodhi, but he so enraptured me with his nomadic bohemian lifestyle that I'd foregone my senior year of college to backpack through Nepal with him on a quest to trace his ancestry. Life was simpler then. It had to be when you carried all of your possessions on your own back. Maybe it was the effect of getting lost on a foreign continent or maybe it was because I'd never connected with anyone before Bodhi, but it was in Nepal that I realized love was a falcon. It dove headfirst, furiously and without caution, but no one ever warned me about what would happen when it finally hit the ground.

"Bailey?"

Milo's mellow tone roused me from my reminiscence. His shock of sun-bleached hair played in stark contrast against the dark trees. His usual deck shoes were absent, replaced by a sturdy pair of hiking boots.

"Are you all right?" he asked.

"Yes. No."

He scanned me from head to toe. "Well, which is it?"

"I'm not sure."

"Do you want to talk about it?"

I thought of Bodhi, the silent sufferer. He did not talk, so neither did I. "Not particularly. Just forget it. Where's this place you told me about?"

Milo pointed above us, where the rock careened skyward at a declivitous angle. "Onward and upward."

"You're kidding."

His daredevil grin assured me that he was not. For half an hour, Milo led me from the path, boosted me over obstacles in the terrain, and clambered through shrubbery to carve an unencumbered route for me until we sat in a crevice chiseled out of the highest part of the bluff. The little grotto lorded over the ocean and the house. From this height, Bodhi and the other workmen were faceless pawns on a chessboard, and the house itself looked like a model. I pressed myself against the rock, simultaneously riveted and horrified by the steep drop, and ignored the chill of damp dew against my shoulder blades through the thin cotton of my T-shirt.

"Don't worry," Milo said, tucking his knees into his chest. "There's an overhang just below us. I've fallen off here before."

"*You have?*"

"Yup." He peeked over the ledge, precariously close to the

edge. "The trees caught me on the way down. Other than a few scrapes and a fractured wrist, I made it out okay."

"How did you find this place?"

"I have a bad habit of exploring without thinking of the consequences."

The construction equipment in the yard looked like toys that a child had forgotten to put away after playtime, bright yellow sunshine spots amidst a gloomy green background. On the roof, Bodhi ran the show, shouting orders and wiping his brow as I reclined lazily above.

"So what's bothering you?" Milo asked.

"What makes you think something's bothering me?"

"Just a hunch. Also, it's pretty obvious. You get a crinkle between your eyebrows when you're upset."

"You're annoyingly perceptive."

"It's a gift."

I sighed, rubbing my arms to warm myself up. Our hideaway was sheltered from the sun, and in the shade of the rock, the breeze flirted coolly with my skin. "Did you know about the Winchesters?"

"Everyone knows about the Winchesters," Milo replied matter-of-factly. "What about them?"

I chewed on my bottom lip, thinking. "This is going to sound insane."

"I've probably heard worse."

I glanced at Milo. He watched me attentively. There was no expectation in his expression, no obligation for me to speak. Maybe that was why I admitted my morbid thought so easily to him.

"I think I'm jealous of them."

There was a note of surprise in his voice. "Jealous? Of dead people?"

"I mean, I don't envy their current state or anything," I added hastily. The kink in Milo's eyebrow spoke of judgment, even if his voice didn't. "I just think that, if they had to die, at least they died all together. Other than the rest of the people in town, there was no one to mourn them. No family at least. To be left over—to be the survivor—hurts worse than being the person that leaves everyone else behind."

"Are you speaking from experience?"

I didn't answer. Instead, I closed my eyes, letting the rush of wind fill my ears like the calming static of white noise. It drowned out Milo's even breaths, but I felt him beside me all the same. He was quiet and pensive, and as the time stretched out between us, he remained blessedly silent.

"TRUTH OR DARE."

"Dare."

"I dare you to go into Patrick's room and steal a pair of his boxer shorts."

"Ew, gross. I'm not stealing my brother's underwear."

I turned over without opening my eyes, plumping the pillow beneath me. The whispered conversation carried on, punctuated by occasional outbursts of giggling.

"You said dare!"

"That's because if I said truth, you'd ask me about who I like at school again."

"Just admit you're crushing on Alex."

"I said dare!"

"Fine, I dare you to admit you're crushing on Alex."

The voices flitted in and out of my dreams, floating hazily along like smoke in a summer breeze. I fixed the pillow over my head. My kingdom for a dreamless sleep.

The tropical scent of plumerias washed over me, so overwhelming that it was as if the tree from the backyard had inexplicably relocated to the master bedroom. In reality, the

French doors had probably swung open again. Blearily, I opened my eyes.

Blue glass whales revolved above my head, twinkling like shooting stars in the dimly lit room.

I stared at the baby mobile suspended in midair. I had not taken it out of the box. I had not even taken the box out of the closet. Yet here it was, dangling just a few feet above me with no visible means of support.

Suddenly, whatever was holding the mobile in place snapped. The whales nosedived, careening toward my face. I shrieked and wrenched the duvet up over my head.

The mobile never landed.

I woke with a start to the sharp rap of knocking on my bedroom door.

"Bailey?" Bodhi called out. "Are you all right? It's eleven o'clock. You've been asleep for ages."

Sunlight touched every corner of the room. I squeezed my eyes shut, watching red and orange flashbulbs dance behind my eyelids. It had all been a dream, from the murmured conversation to the smell of the flowers to the whales in the air, but when I swung my feet out of bed, my heart stopped.

The baby mobile lay in a heap on the floor, unbroken but tangled.

"Bailey?" Bodhi called again. "I'm coming in."

"No!" I gathered up the fallen mobile and carried it to the closet. The box of peanuts had tipped over, spilling Styrofoam across the floor. Hastily, I swept the peanuts up with my hands, replaced the mobile in its box, and closed the closet. Not a second later, Bodhi inched the door open, peeking in through the small gap.

"What's going on in here?"

I stood guard in front of the closet, pulling my long T-shirt down to cover my bare thighs. Bodhi's eyes flickered downward, noting my discomfort, but he didn't comment on it.

"Nothing," I said.

"It's eleven o'clock."

"I heard you the first time."

Bodhi opened the door fully. He was already sticky with sweat. As he surveyed the bedroom, he asked, "Have you been moving the construction equipment around?"

"Yeah, I took the forklift for a joyride actually."

"That's not what I meant."

I dragged a pair of running shorts out of my suitcase and tugged them on. "I don't know what you mean," I said. "I've tried to stay out of the way. Do you need help with something?"

"Not yet. We were going to start taking the tiling up in the kitchen, but we can't find the jackhammer. And all the shovels have gone missing."

"I didn't touch them, but I'll help you look."

After pulling on a pair of dirty sneakers, Bodhi and I swept the house from top to bottom for the missing equipment. The construction crew had been working since dawn, preparing the first floor for renovations. I nodded politely to each of the men Ethan Powell had provided to us. In the past few weeks, I had grown more familiar with their sunburnt, weathered faces than that of my own husband. Unfortunately, none of them had any idea as to where the jackhammer and shovels had gone either.

"Do you think someone stole them?" I asked Bodhi, out of earshot of the other workers.

"Why would anyone do that?"

"I don't know. They could sell the jackhammer. Make a quick buck."

Bodhi looked over my head to study the crewmen. "I can't

see any of them doing that. Ethan pays them well, both here and at the lumber mill."

"The only place we haven't looked is the basement," I said. "And I haven't been down there since we relocated all of that junk from the attic."

"Neither have I. I suppose we should check it out just in case."

Armed with a pair of flashlights to combat the murky depths of the basement, Bodhi and I tentatively crept down the creaky stairs and into the labyrinth below. I felt for each step with my toes before placing my weight down. The basement had gone untouched. After our struggles in the attic, Bodhi and I had decided to leave the worst for last. Maybe it was the lack of light, or the stacked relics of the Winchesters' past fortune, or the musty scent of the stagnant air, but neither one of us trusted the basement's eerie vibes enough to work alone down here.

"There," I said, sweeping the beam of my flashlight across the only part of the basement floor that wasn't obscured by filing cabinets or ancient sailboat accessories.

"What the—?"

Five shovels and the jackhammer had been laid out in a neatly organized line, one right next to the other, across a wide patch of concrete a few shades lighter than the rest of the house's foundation.

"Really, Bailey?" Bodhi wedged his flashlight beneath his armpit so that he could haul the jackhammer upright.

"What?"

He shouldered past me, grunting as he lifted the jack-hammer up the first couple of steps. "You seriously need to get your sleepwalking habit under control."

My lips parted in awe. "Do you actually think I got up in the middle of the night, pilfered a bunch of shovels and a jackhammer from the yard, and lugged them down to the basement all while I was dead asleep? Bodhi, I can barely lift the jackhammer on my own."

"No one else would've done something this weird," Bodhi countered. "Get some help, Bailey. And bring those shovels with you."

I did as asked. Outside, I arranged the five shovels in the front yard end to end, carefully recreating the pattern from the basement. But when I stood back to admire my handiwork, the blatant pettiness was so overwhelming that I kicked each shovel out of line before going back inside.

AROUND LUNCHTIME, I sat in the window seat of the master bedroom with my laptop perched on my knees. The screen had gone to sleep. For a while, I'd been researching the area in and around Black Bay. Though it would be several months before we finished renovating the Winchester house, it couldn't hurt to get to know the market for when we finally put it up for sale. It would be my biggest challenge yet. Black Bay drew the attention of modest families with modest incomes, and those were not the type of people that would be interested in buying a miniature mansion. Then I'd gotten distracted and searched the common symptoms of sleep-walking, but when I pulled up a web page detailing the link between sleepwalking and post-traumatic stress disorder, I quickly clicked out of it. I had been staring out of the window at the plumeria tree in the distance ever since.

Footsteps passed by in the hallway outside the bedroom, but I ignored them. I hadn't spoken to Bodhi since hauling the shovels up from the basement, and I strongly suspected that he had no interest in speaking to me either. However, when a loud banging noise reverberated through the wall from the room next to mine, I wondered what the hell Bodhi was doing upstairs. The renovation plans were only finalized for a certain section of the first floor. He had no business working on one of the bedrooms without consulting me first. The banging paused for a moment then continued in full force. I closed my laptop, set it aside, and stormed from the bedroom.

"Bodhi, what the hell—?"

I threw the door to the adjacent bedroom open. It ricocheted off the wall with a disruptive smack. Bodhi was nowhere to be seen, and the banging noise ceased as soon as I set foot in the bedroom. This was one of the rooms that we hadn't had the chance to comb through yet. The canopy bed, full closet, pale pink wallpaper, and stacked books remained as a reminder that this house did not and probably would not ever feel like it belonged to us.

The banging returned in full force, emanating from the seat in the bay window, directly above an air vent that I knew the rats were so fond of traveling throughout. With bated breath, I crossed the room. The drumming quickened and crescendoed with every step that I took, but when I lifted the cushioned seat below the window and immediately jumped back in anticipation of whatever lay trapped inside trying to get out—

All was quiet. The storage area was free and clear of anything alive. There was no explanation as to what had been banging on the underside of the seat. When I gathered my courage and peeked inside, half-expecting to see a rabies-crazed raccoon, I instead found an assortment of leather bound journals arranged in neat stacks. I reached in, my fingers grazing the cover of the topmost notebook.

A shrill scream pierced the air, resonating from somewhere outside. The window seat slammed back into place, nearly trapping my hand as I drew the diary out. I spun on my heel, dashed out of the room, and down the stairs to the first floor. My heart hammered against my rib cage as I raced through the reasons for a scream like that. Someone was injured—there was no doubt in my mind about that—but what had happened? Was it Bodhi's vocal chords stretching to make that awful sound?

Except on the first floor, the construction crew was nowhere to be seen. The jackhammer lay abandoned near a pile of jagged tile pieces and on a sticky note on the dusty countertop, Bodhi's handwriting told me that they had gone into town to get lunch.

Another scream tore into me like a shard of glass, this time echoing from beyond the basement door. I sprinted down the hallway, wrenched the door open, and stumbled into the darkness, fumbling with my cell phone. I dialed 911 as I blindly took the stairs, but the line never rang. I should've known that the service in the basement was spotty.

The next scream chilled my blood. I clapped my hands over my ears. So close. As if the victim was standing beside me. In the murky gloom, a hunched figure lurked near the bottom of the stairs.

"I'm here!" I called. The splintered stairs bit at the soles of my bare feet, but I didn't slow my pace. On the last step, something caught around my ankle. I yelled as I fell forward, my own voice mingling with the prolonged, terrified wail. I threw my hands out to break my fall, but my knees hit the concrete foundation first, sending a shock wave of pain through my bones.

All at once, the screaming stopped. The overhead light—a dirty fluorescent tube that had stoically refused to cooperate with me and Bodhi in the recent past—flickered on. The basement quivered beneath its oscillating gleam, still and silent.

I pushed myself to my feet with a groan. Blood ran down both of my knees, dripping onto the concrete in desultory patterns. I scanned the room carefully for movement of any kind. "Hello? Who's down here?"

Not even a rustle.

During the fall, the leather-bound journal had escaped my grasp. It waited with its pale pages spread and exposed until I knelt to scoop it up again. I sat down on the bottom step, resting my forehead on the glossy leather cover.

No one was screaming. No one ever had been. I shook my head, wondering how much sleep deprivation could interfere with day-to-day life. Maybe Bodhi was right. Maybe I did need help.

Apparently, my auditory hallucinations were far from finished. Overhead, the doorbell chimed. Three low, long, gong-like tones, muffled but discernible, echoed through the house and down to the basement. My eyelids fluttered shut. The doorbell didn't work. I was sure of that. Bodhi had moaned about replacing it. I had suggested that we install an intercom instead.

That conversation happened. I swore to myself it did. I swore to myself that both Bodhi and I had tried the dingy doorbell button, only to be met with silence.

Above, the sepulchral tones knelled again.

7

MUSIC OF THE NIGHT

*W*hen I answered the front door, Ethan Powell smiled in greeting before his gaze wandered south to the ragged skin of my knees. His brows knitted together in worry.

"Dear Lord. What happened to you, darlin'?"

"Took a spill. Did you ring the doorbell?"

"Yes. Why?"

"We thought it was broken."

As I waved Ethan inside, I caught a glimpse of myself in the hallway mirror. The woman staring back was unfamiliar. Gaunt. Drawn thin. As though an artist once known for graceful, unbroken brush strokes had used a cheap mechanical pencil instead.

"Let me look at those knees," said Ethan, leading me through the living room. "Thought I'd stop by and check out the house. See how you and Bodhi are coming along. Good thing I did. Look at that kitchen!"

He gazed with wonder at the demolished wall between the kitchen and the living room, treading carefully amongst the debris.

"Bodhi's not finished," I said. "Obviously."

"How long do you think it will be until it's all done?"

Ethan patted the countertop beside the kitchen sink. I hopped up, rolling the hem of my shorts away from the bloody mess as Ethan ran a clean dish towel beneath the steaming stream of tap water.

"This is our biggest project yet," I said. "Usually, it takes us anywhere from four to eight months to completely renovate a house, but who knows? We could be here for a good year."

He dabbed tenderly at my shredded skin, cleaning dirt and dust from the wounds. "How do you and Bodhi decide what to do with the renovations?"

I sighed, massaging the bags beneath my eyes with the pads of the fingers. "Depends on what sells, the trends in the housing market, et cetera. Lots of research. Bodhi handles the construction side of things. I focus on design and real estate, so we don't clash often."

Ethan wiped off my shins methodically. Professionally. Perhaps he'd dealt with similar injuries at the saw mill. Perhaps he'd dealt with worse.

"That's lucky," he said. "You got a first-aid kit, Bailey? These knees are going to need some bandages."

"Under the sink."

He fished around in the kit, extracting a roll of gauze and a tube of antibacterial ointment. In a few minutes, he'd expertly wrapped my knees in the clean white bandages. As he rinsed off the bloodstained dish towel in the sink, he gestured to where my left hand rested on the countertop. "Whatcha got there?"

The leather journal was pinned beneath my fingers. I had carried it like a torch from the basement, taking comfort in the texture of its weathered cover. I showed it to Ethan. "Someone's journal. I found a bunch of them in one of the upstairs bedrooms."

Ethan patted his palms dry on the thighs of his jeans. "May I?"

"Sure."

He flipped through the first few pages of the diary, his beard bristling as he combed the contents, then shut it swiftly. "Hmm."

"What is it?"

"It's Caroline's personal diary."

"The Winchesters' daughter?"

"Surely," he confirmed. "I can't say I feel comfortable reading them. It's an invasion of privacy. You said there were quite a few of them?"

"I found a whole stack of them in the window seat of her old bedroom."

"I can take them," Ethan offered, tucking the journal into the back pocket of his jeans. "I'm sure you're uncomfortable with them in the house. Besides, the library might be interested in preserving them. History of the town, you know?"

"Actually," I said, levering myself off the counter. My knees ached as I planted myself between Ethan and the staircase, blocking him from the path to Caroline's bedroom. "I'm going to hold on to them for a while longer."

"Really? Why?"

"Because I respect that this house belonged to someone else before we got to it," I said, holding my hand out for the journal. "And—I don't know—I feel connected to the Winchesters somehow. It might be interesting to see what life was like from the perspective of one of Black Bay's most prominent residents."

Ethan, somewhat reluctantly, handed over the journal. "I suppose that's admirable."

"Don't worry, Ethan. The library can have them when I'm done."

In the inside flap of the journal, Caroline had signed her

name in neat, loopy cursive. Beside that was a to/from date. This particular diary detailed Caroline's inner catalogue of thoughts from January of 1995.

"I know Patrick was the golden boy, but what about Caroline?" I asked Ethan. "What do you know about her?"

Ethan straightened out his blue collared shirt and sat down on an overturned cabinet that Bodhi had been using as a saw table. "She was precocious. Fifteen years old and only a year behind Patrick in school. She was as smart as a whip and headed for the Ivy Leagues."

"I noticed her bookshelf."

"Intimidating, wasn't she?"

"To say the least," I said, recalling Caroline's copy of *The Ethics of Ambiguity.* "I don't think I even knew who half of those authors were when I was fifteen. I was still reading young adult fiction."

"I think Christopher and Elizabeth had always expected Patrick to take over the family business," said Ethan. "And then Caroline declared that she would be the one to learn the tricks of the trade. Somehow, I don't think Patrick minded."

"What did her parents think of that?"

Ethan stroked his beard. "I think they were thankful to have two healthy, intelligent children who both had a passion for something productive. They were proud of Patrick and Caroline. A football star and an intellectual prodigy, both on their way to bigger and better things. How could a parent complain?"

"I certainly wouldn't."

The rumble of an engine outside disrupted our conversation. Raucous voices filled the air as Bodhi and his crew pulled up in the workman's truck we had borrowed from someone in town. They piled in through the front door, carrying takeout containers from the Sanctuary and other restaurants. Bodhi chatted boisterously with a few of the other men, a half-eaten hamburger cradled in one hand. As he took another bite, he noticed me and Ethan in the kitchen.

"What's going on?" he asked through a full mouth. He looked at my bandaged knees. "What happened to you?"

"She fell," Ethan answered, saving me from having to explain my nightmarish basement adventure. "Nothing major. Got her all patched up."

But that didn't stop Bodhi from leading me down the hallway, out of earshot of Ethan and the rest of the crew. I rested against the basement door, my mind wandering to the bottom of those stairs where my blood now decorated the concrete slab.

Bodhi forgot about his hamburger. It idled wistfully between his clenched fingers, dripping some kind of pepper sauce onto the hardwood floor.

"What happened?" Bodhi asked again. "Are you all right?"

"I fell, like Ethan said. I'm fine."

In actuality, the skin of my knees already felt stiff as it began the process of scabbing over, and if the dull ache was any indication, I'd wake up the next day with a colorful array of bruises.

"Where?" Bodhi demanded. "How?"

"Don't worry about it." The scent of the burger wafted up between us. My stomach growled. I hadn't eaten at all that day. "Did you happen to pick up lunch for me?"

A sheepish expression crossed Bodhi's face. "No. I'm sorry. Honestly, I got caught up with the guys."

"They seem like a good group."

"They are." He offered me the rest of his burger. "Want this?"

"Yes, but—"

"I'll eat the pickles."

We performed a familiar choreography, Bodhi dislodging

the pickles from the bun before trading the burger off to me. The sour taste of dill lingered. I crinkled my nose as I chewed. Bodhi almost smiled.

"Do you mind if I chip in today?" I asked him. "I need a distraction."

Bodhi hesitated. "I don't think that's the best idea."

"Bodhi, come on."

"Do you not remember slicing your thumb off? Or the hair incident?"

I fingered my shorn locks, cropped short around my chin. I wore it that length for a reason, ever since I'd found myself on the wrong end of a blowtorch. "That was years ago."

"Still."

"You act like I'm incompetent."

"I know you aren't incompetent," he countered. "I just don't want to see you get hurt. You should rest anyway."

"I want to work," I insisted. I wanted to knock down a wall or jimmy up tiles or even transport loads of garbage out to the dumpster. Anything was better than dwelling in the recesses of my own thoughts.

"Look at your knees, Bailey. Not today."

"Seriously? You can't tell me what to do."

Bodhi crossed his arms. "I wouldn't take that bet."

I shoved the burger into his chest, splattering his shirt with pepper sauce, and stormed off. In the kitchen, the construction crew still rowdily devoured their lunches. Someone had offered Ethan a chicken sandwich, which he munched heartily between anecdotes. They quieted as I passed, the conversation dying like a candle flame on a windy night. Had Bodhi confided in them? How much did they know?

"Bailey—" began Ethan, but I plowed through the workmen, kicked open the back door, and emerged onto the gray wooden deck outside.

I didn't pause to marvel at the blanket of clouds that encompassed the sky. It matched my mood, and I marched through the wilderness of the backyard without a specific location in mind. I only knew that I had to get away from Bodhi and the Winchester house. At the edge of the garden, as I plunged through the overgrown weeds, I ran straight into Milo.

"Ooph!"

"Whoa there." He held me by the shoulders to steady me. Today, he wore a blue-and-white striped nautical shirt. A captain's hat balanced jauntily on his head, as though he had planned on spending the day on a boat in the bay with everyone else. "Everything okay?"

I shook him off. "Why does everyone keep asking me that?"

"Maybe because you're making that face."

"What face?"

"With the crinkle."

I smacked a palm to my forehead in an attempt to hide the crinkle. "There's no crinkle. What are you doing here, Milo?"

"It's a small town, Bailey," Milo said. He tipped his hat, swept his unruly hair back, and trapped it again beneath his headwear. "And you're forgetting my indifference toward most of Black Bay's population. You, though. You, I like. I thought I'd ask what you were up to."

"Nothing, apparently."

"You're bleeding."

I looked down. Sure enough, the gauze around my knees was already discolored. Milo took me by the elbow, guiding me to the smooth surface of a nearby tree trunk.

"Sit," he said. It wasn't an order, but it didn't seem like I had much of an option to resist either. I sat. Milo knelt down and began to rearrange my bandages to cover more skin.

"Aren't you going to ask me what happened?"

"I figured if you wanted to tell me, you already would have."

"Milo, please pass that nugget of wisdom on to my husband."

Though my view mostly consisted of the top of Milo's head, I saw his cheeks plump up in a smile. "Not sure it would help. I was never much of a relationship guy."

"Why not?"

"You may not have noticed, but I'm a bit of a loner."

I had noticed. Milo wasn't exaggerating when he said he never went into town. The people of Black Bay didn't even know what he looked like. His Walden-esque existence warred with his handsome smile and amiable personality. To me, Milo looked and acted like a guy who would've been popular and adored in high school, especially in Black Bay.

"Did you have an argument with Bodhi or something?" he asked, helping me to my feet.

I gingerly tested my weight on each leg. "Of sorts."

"I don't mean to pry," Milo said. He extended an arm for me to balance on as I checked his handiwork. "But the two of you don't seem like you're entirely on the same page. Or am I reading that incorrectly?"

It became evident that Milo did not care to keep up with *Flipping Out*. If he did, he would be solidly convinced that Bodhi and I were ensconced in a blissful life of love and construction. There was a metaphor in there somewhere, one that I'd exploited regularly online, but Milo wasn't falling for it. I considered shutting him down. There was no point in confiding in a temporary someone. On the other hand, I boiled over with the hot turmoil of my mental state in the thick silence between me and Bodhi so often that maybe talking about it with someone else was exactly what I needed.

"Bodhi and I," I began. Separate. There was no "we" anymore. Or at least it didn't feel like there was. "—were perfect. Were. Past tense. Honestly, as soon as I met him, I felt at ease. It was like that at first. Easy." Milo lowered himself to sit on the tree stump as he listened. I paced back and forth, carving a pattern of footprints in the earth. "We went everywhere. We did everything. I don't have a lot of family, and neither does he. We bonded over that. We became each other's family. Did I ever tell you that we got married six months after we met each other?"

"No, you didn't," Milo said softly.

"I just knew," I declared. "I knew it was him. No doubt. It wasn't hard to believe in the concept of soulmates then. We got married in Nepal."

"Exotic."

"And then we got married again in the States because the ceremony in Nepal didn't officially count."

Milo laughed. "It sounds like the two of you had quite the adventure."

"We did," I said. I snapped a branch off of the nearest tree and swung it through the air like a director's baton. "We had a ton of adventures, one right after the next. We surfed big waves, white-water rafted, climbed mountains, explored ancient ruins. You said you wanted to go to Machu Picchu, right? I've been there."

"Wow. How was it?"

"Magical. Like everything else we did."

"Past tense?"

I nodded sadly. "Past tense."

"What happened?"

"I got pregnant."

Milo's eyebrows shifted upward in surprise. "Oh."

"It was unexpected," I blathered, circling around a tree Singing in the Rain style with the jagged stick as my umbrella. "We were young still. Or we felt young anyway. I was twenty-five. We had a decision to make."

"Did you—?"

"No," I replied sharply. The twig snapped. I'd been bending it at an extreme angle without realizing it. I threw the pieces to the ground. "We had a daughter."

Milo must've sensed that he was venturing into dangerous territory because his voice barely rose above a whisper as he asked, "What was her name?"

My throat tightened. I hadn't said it in so long. "It was Kali."

"Past tense?"

"Past tense."

I made the mistake of looking at Milo. His eyes had darkened with a sorrowful understanding. I looked away.

"It's ironic really," I said with a choked laugh. "I thought the name was pretty, but Bodhi warned me not to call her that. Kali was the Hindu goddess of destruction, and my God, was our Kali a destroyer herself."

Milo waited patiently for the other shoe to drop. I dropped it.

"She was three when she died."

There was a shine in Milo's eyes now, his lips pressed tightly together.

"It was an accident," I plowed on, determined to get through my story. "One that could've been prevented. Bodhi blames me. I blame Bodhi. Things are easier that way, you know? If there's someone to take the blame."

"Did you see someone? You know, did you talk to anyone?"

"We went to therapy together," I said. "It didn't help much. Bodhi wouldn't talk, not even to me. He internalized everything. That was when I knew things were going to change. He used to never shut up."

"That's why the two of you seem so distant."

"I don't remember the last time I had a genuine conversation with him."

"I'm so sorry."

"Me, too," I mumbled, wiping my eyes with the collar of my shirt. "Me, too."

IT WAS the soft melody of piano music that woke me from my slumber that night. I pinched myself hard enough to bruise the tender flesh of my inner arm just to make sure that I wasn't dreaming again. Nothing happened. All was at peace in the master bedroom. The French doors remained closed, the baby mobile was hidden away in the closet, and the light of the moon tickled the cozy carpet. Still, the music drew me out from under the bedsheets like an enchantress in the night.

I padded down the steps to the first floor. We had moved everything that we hadn't sold from the living room to the office near the rear of the house. I followed the gentle peal of piano notes down the hallway, lingering outside the closed door of the office to listen. Then I twisted the doorknob and peeked inside.

The music petered off as soon as I opened the door, yet another illustration of my woefully scant sanity. The piano waited beneath the moonlight of the window, its keys unmoving. Tired and sad, I wandered over to it. The music was so beautiful. I wished that it had continued to play. I rested my finger on the middle C key then pressed down. It was still out of tune. There was no possibility of this piano producing such a lovely song.

I sighed, running my fingers along the length of the keys. Near the bass end, something warm and wet met my wandering touch. I examined my fingers, squinting in the pale light of the moon to see what coated them.

It was blood.

A loud creaking noise caused me to whirl around. The grandfather clock teetered forward, balancing for a moment on its front edge before crashing to the floor with a boom. The glass pane shattered. At the same time, the piano bench slid out, sweeping my legs out from under me. I landed with a grunt, banging my head against a spare dining room chair. My vision swam as a folder of sheet music launched itself into the air. Pages swirled around me like a tornado, filling the room with crescendos and codas. I gripped the piano bench, desperate to hold on to something real. A small, shadowy figure stood in the open doorway of the office. Watching me.

I blacked out.

8

POST TRAUMA

"*B*ailey. Bailey!"

I woke to Bodhi furiously shaking my shoulders. His worried frown glided gradually into focus as though my eyes were two camera lenses that had to be adjusted manually. The office was a disaster. Broken glass from the toppled grandfather clock glittered on the floor. Torn sheet music blanketed every dusty surface. The piano lay tipped over, its strings exposed and ripped from the soundboard. The black and white keys were smashed in, and some of them had fallen off the instrument, as though someone had taken a baseball bat to them with a vengeance.

"Blood," I gasped, gripping Bodhi's arm in a feeble attempt to sit upright. "There was blood on the piano. Was anyone hurt?"

"Are you kidding me?"

It was then I realized that Bodhi had wrapped a T-shirt around my wrist, applying steady pressure. He pulled the T-shirt away briefly, just long enough for me to get a glimpse of a stretched, serrated gash that ran from my wrist to the inside of my elbow. It was shallow—I wouldn't need stitches

—but I had lost enough blood for my head to feel woozy and unstable. Bodhi quickly covered the wound again, securing the shirt so tightly around my arm that my fingers began to tingle.

"This is getting out of hand, Bailey," Bodhi said, shaking his head. "Look at this room! It's a wreck. It'll take us ages to clean all of this up."

"Hang on a minute," I said, trying to find my way around the English language again. "You think I did all of this?"

"Who else?"

"It wasn't me."

He tilted his head to look at me with a skeptical expression. "Just like you weren't the one who kept moving my keys to that crystal tray by the door? Just like you weren't the one to carry all the shovels down to the basement?"

"I'm not sleepwalking, Bodhi!"

"Baby, you probably aren't even aware that you're doing it."

I yanked my arm away from him, tucking it into my chest to keep the bloodstained shirt in place. "I'm not crazy."

His amber eyes softened. "I never said you were, but when I got down here, you were screaming your head off like some kind of lunatic. Then you passed out—just went completely limp out of nowhere—for no reason. Something's going on with you, Bailey. And this—" He choked up as he indicated my ruined wrist. "—did you try to hurt yourself?"

"No!" I insisted. "I told you. It wasn't me."

"Then who made this mess?"

I didn't have an answer for him. He already thought I was losing my mind, and telling him that I'd seen a strange figure in the doorway before passing out was surely to confirm his theory. My silence, unfortunately, didn't work to my advantage either.

"I want you to see someone," he declared. He took my

uninjured arm, swung it across his shoulders, and lifted me from the floor.

I leaned heavily on him as we picked our way through the minefield of demolished glass. "I don't need a psychiatrist, Bodhi."

He carried me into the nearby bathroom and set me down on the closed lid of the toilet. He washed his hands in the sink. "I don't want to make you do anything you don't want to do, but you can't honestly believe that this hasn't evolved into a full-blown problem. I've been ignoring it for a while, but ever since we arrived in Black Bay, something's changed."

"You've been ignoring *what* for a while?" I challenged as Bodhi disappeared into the kitchen. He came back with the first-aid kid, balanced it on the countertop, and popped it open.

"You're different now. Ever since—"

"Are we actually talking about this?" I interrupted. Bodhi wouldn't look at me. He busied himself with the first-aid gear, unwrapping the shirt from my arm to check if the bleeding had stopped yet. "Are we, Bodhi?"

"Ethan was telling me that the psychiatrist in town is really easy to talk to," he said as he cleaned my wrist and unwrapped a packet of butterfly closures.

"Why are you talking to Ethan Powell about my mental state?"

He pinched the edges of my skin together and secured it with a bandage. "You think I want to see you like this, Bailey? I know we've been distant with each other, but that doesn't mean watching you walk around like someone in a trance, hurting yourself, doesn't eat me alive. I care about you. I can't believe that I even have to say that."

"Sometimes, Bodhi, it doesn't feel like you care." As soon as I said it, I regretted it. Bodhi's carefully constructed mask fell for a fraction of a second, and I saw the hurt in his eyes. Hurriedly, I added, "And by the way, I have been talking to someone."

Bodhi paused in applying the butterfly stitches. "Really? Who?"

"Milo."

"Milo. Milo? As in the guy who sold us the house?"

"Yes, that Milo."

He didn't bother to disguise his scorn as he asked, "Is *he* a psychiatrist?"

"Is Ethan Powell?" I shot back.

Bodhi smacked the last bandage into place. "Real nice, Bailey. You won't talk to me, but you'll blab our entire life story to some random stranger in town. That's just great."

"You won't talk to *me*." I snatched a roll of gauze from him and began wrapping it around my arm on my own. "And he's not a stranger."

"What's that supposed to mean?"

"I mean he actually listens to me," I said, ripping off a piece of medical tape with my teeth and securing the gauze. "These days, I see Milo more often than I see you."

Bodhi went still. The first-aid kit fell off of the counter, spilling a box of Band-Aids across the checkered tile floor. "Are you—?"

"Am I what?" I demanded, confused by Bodhi's inexplicable paralysis.

His next words dropped from his mouth like a poison dart, piercing my soul and contaminating my very being. "With Milo, Bailey. Are you sleeping with Milo?"

I stared up at him. "I can't believe you just asked me that."

"I didn't hear a no."

I stood up, clutching the counter to prevent myself from falling over. I was still shaking from the night's events, but that didn't stop me from pushing past my husband and into the hallway. I climbed the stairs, gripping the banister to steady myself. At the top, I paused and looked over my shoulder. Bodhi watched me from the ground floor.

"You don't deserve the relief of hearing me say no. Good night, Bodhi."

Sleep refused to take me for the remainder of the night. I stayed awake, lounging on the balcony outside the master bedroom until the sun crept over the edge of the horizon, and read through the first of Caroline Winchester's journals.

Bailey and Bodhi: Flipping Out

ALL RIGHT, *flippers. I know it's been a while since I've updated this blog, so please forgive me. My inbox is loaded, which is why I haven't been able to accept any new mail, but I promise to go through all of your messages in the next few days! I'm sure the majority of you are wondering what kind of hilarity has occurred during our renovation of the Winchester house over the last couple of weeks, but before we get to that, I need to propose a question.*

Let's go into this with an open mind, shall we? You're going to need it. What I'm about to share with you is straight out of the Twilight Zone. You might think I'm crazy or you might think I'm making all of this up. For my sake, please try to consider the possibility of this being real. Is everyone ready? Here goes nothing.

I think the Winchester house is haunted.

Are you laughing yet? Rolling your eyes? Wondering if I'm pulling your leg? I don't blame you. In all honesty, I don't even know if I believe it myself, but there doesn't seem to be any other explanation for all of the weird crap that's been happening around me. Check out the attached pictures of the office. The room is demolished, and I was there when it happened. The twist? I didn't touch anything. And I swear I saw someone standing in the doorway. A girl, maybe.

This isn't the first eerie thing that's happened. Bodhi's keys keep disappearing. The piano plays itself, and not in that "on display at a department store" kind of way. I've seen things levitate in midair. And don't even get me started on the basement. Hands down, it's the creepiest room in the house. The back of my neck prickles just thinking about it. I swear there's something down there. Like an aura. Or a presence.

So I'm begging you, flippers. Hit me with your best conspiracy theories. Have any of you had a brush with the paranormal? If so, how did it all turn out? I'm open to any and all stories, advice, cleansing rituals, etc. Do I burn sage? Hold a séance? Please help!

Does anyone have a Ouija board?
Bailey

My cursor hovered over the "publish" button on the blog post. How many *Flipping Out* fans would I alienate with my plea for information? Would they think it was just a ploy to get more readers? My absence from the blog had already taken its toll, and I couldn't afford to lose many more followers. It took forever to build up an online presence, but losing it all could happen in a matter of minutes. Nevertheless, I needed answers. I clicked publish.

"Knock, knock."

I looked up from my seat on the kitchen counter, where I'd been munching on leftover bagels, cream cheese, and a bowl of red grapes. Milo hovered just outside the back door, which I'd propped open so that the cool breeze might gush through the musty house.

"Hey," I said. Instinctively, I smiled, but when the image of

85

Bodhi's face from the night before reared its ugly head, my expression faltered. Thankfully, Bodhi was away for the morning, buying materials in town. "Come in."

He stepped over the threshold. His cheeks were flushed, and he brought an inherent warmth into the kitchen, as though he collected sunshine like a solar panel and reflected it upon the others around him. I didn't care what Bodhi said. Spending time with Milo was refreshing, like taking a dip in a cool lake on a summer's eve. Even in the mysteriously sentient Winchester house, Milo managed to lighten the mood.

"How are you?" he asked, plucking a grape from the bowl and popping it into his mouth. He took my hand, stretching my arm out to examine the length bandage. "Did you get hurt again?"

"Unfortunately."

"Did you have a disagreement with a hacksaw or something?"

"Not quite." I chewed on my bagel, looking Milo over. "Milo, if I tell you something, will you promise not to automatically assume that I'm insane?"

He leaned against the kitchen counter, rolling the sleeves of his shirt past his elbows to rinse more grapes in a colander in the sink. "I don't make promises that I can't keep."

I rolled my eyes. "Fine then. Never mind."

"All right, I'll do my best," he relented, playfully tossing a grape at me. "What's up?"

I caught the tiny fruit, absentmindedly massaging it between the palms of my hands as I wondered how best to put my conundrum into words. "Do you believe in ghosts?"

"Whoa. That came out of left field. Why do you ask?"

"Some weird stuff has been happening to me here."

He tapped his hands on the side of the sink to shake off the excess water then tipped the colander of grapes into the bowl I was eating out of. "Well, I don't know about ghosts precisely, but I've always thought that energy was a real thing."

I popped the skin of a grape between my teeth, enjoying the sweet rush of fruit juice across my tongue. "What kind of energy?"

"You know. Vibes, auras, cosmic energy. Whatever you want to call it."

"What, like chi? Prana?"

"Why not?" he asked. He filled two water glasses and handed one to me. I nodded my thanks. "Don't you feel something when you first meet someone? Maybe it's just me. I can tell right away whether or not I'm going to like a person."

"I guess so."

"Not to mention, there are places where reality just feels a bit altered," Milo went on, sipping water between sentences. "Rooftops in the early morning. Empty parking lots. Laundromats at midnight. Your own bedroom at five a.m."

I looked sharply at him.

"Ring a bell?" he asked, shrugging his shoulders. "Energy."

I thought of the baby mobile dangling above my bed. "But can energy move things? We keep losing things in the house."

"I imagine energy manifests in different ways depending on the situation. Do you mind?" He lifted a bagel from the package. I nodded, and he began frosting it with cream cheese. "For instance, some people believe that poltergeist activity doesn't have anything to do with noisy ghosts at all. Things disappearing, objects levitating, electrical interference, unexplained noises—"

A shiver ran down the length of my spine, but I tried not to flinch as Milo casually called out everything wrong with the Winchester house.

"People think occurrences like that are actually psychic

manifestations due to stress or anxiety," he explained. "That type of energy comes from a living person who doesn't realize how or why they're channeling it."

Before I could fully digest this information, the steady hum of Bodhi's truck sounded in the front yard. I dropped my handful of grapes, hopped off the counter, and shoved Milo toward the back door. "You need to go."

His bagel dropped from his grasp, smearing cream cheese across the unfinished flooring. "All right, but why, may I ask, are you suddenly acting like I kicked your dog?"

"It's complicated," I said as I nudged him out of the kitchen.

"Was it something I said?"

"No. Bodhi's mad at me. It's just easier this way."

He hesitated in the doorway. "Is everything all right? Maybe I should stay."

I heard the key turn in the front door lock. "Please, Milo," I begged. "Just go."

I watched through the blinds of the window above the sink as Milo sprinted away through the garden, vanishing within the greenery just in time. Bodhi wandered into the kitchen, dumping his keys and a plastic grocery bag full of hardware next to the coffee maker. When he saw me, he paused. Looked at the bagel in my hand. The bagel on the floor.

"Hey," he said.

"Hey."

He nodded toward the second bagel. "Hungry?"

"Dropped the first one."

"Whatever." Bodhi cleared his throat and pointed over his shoulder. "Ethan's here."

Somewhere in the front yard, Ethan cursed as he hauled construction material out of the flatbed of Bodhi's truck. I resisted the urge to chuckle. "Okay."

He sighed and combed through his curls with his fingers. His hair was getting long. Usually, I cut it for him, teasing him for not having it done himself, but he always claimed that he had better ways to spend his time and money than in a barber shop.

"Is this how it's going to be, Bailey?"

He took a hesitant step across the kitchen, then another, until he was close enough for me to see the laugh lines around his mouth. When I didn't scurry off, he lifted one hand and brushed a strand of hair away from my face, the calloused tips of his fingers ghosting across my cheek.

"I'm sorry," he whispered.

"For what?"

There were so many things to be sorry for.

He rested his forehead against mine. "For the way I spoke to you last night. For accusing you. For being so wrapped up in this house."

Not everything, then.

"I love you," he murmured. "Don't you know that? It hurts me to see you this way. I can't stand it. I only suggested you see a psychiatrist because I really do think it might help you cope, Bailey. Just meet with her. Hear what she has to say."

I thought about what Milo said about poltergeist activity. Maybe the odd vibes in the Winchester house were my fault after all, amplified by the thoughts that haunted my dreams at night. Meeting with Black Bay's shrink would do me no harm, other than dulling my shiny badge of pride. Maybe, if therapy sessions became a regular thing, I could convince Bodhi to come along eventually.

Ethan cleared his throat, causing Bodhi and I to split apart like shrapnel, and came into the kitchen. "I apologize for eavesdropping, folks. Bailey, if you like, I can make a call to Doctor Marx and have her work you in this afternoon. She's a lovely woman. Easy to talk to. I spent a lot of time in her office after my father died. There's no shame in it."

I looked at Bodhi, who nodded encouragingly.

"All right, Ethan," I finally agreed. "Call up Doctor Marx."

DOCTOR MARX WAS A WELL-PRESERVED woman in her sixties who claimed to have postponed her retirement due to the fact that she was the one and only resource for mental health questions in the tiny town of Black Bay. She was tall and thin, wore a dress that I'd seen in the window of a Black Bay boutique and deemed too tight-fitting for my own figure, and sported impeccable winged eyeliner. In addition, she spoke with a tiny hint of a mid-Atlantic accent, as if she had watched a few too many Katharine Hepburn movies in her youth. As I took her through the last ten years of my life in exquisite detail—I figured if I was going to dive into therapy then I might as well commit—she listened carefully, didn't interrupt, and jotted notes on a clipboard. But the scratch of her ballpoint pen across the paper and the steady drip of her desktop Zen waterfall lulled me into a sleepy daze, and I fought to keep my eyes open as Doctor Marx finally said her piece.

"Now I don't want you to worry," she began, removing her glasses from her nose. I wondered if she really needed them or if she simply thought they tied together her ensemble. "But from the sound of it, you are experiencing some of the symptoms of post-traumatic stress disorder."

The Zen fountain bubbled.

"PTSD?" It wasn't the first time I'd considered it, but the concept was still daunting.

Doctor Marx nodded. "Hallucinations, night terrors, triggers. In fact, it sounds like you've been suffering for quite some time now. It likely began shortly after your daughter passed away. Do you feel you found closure after Kali's death?"

My stomach clenched. My voice shook. "Does any mother ever find closure after the death of her child?"

She reclined in her office chair, crossing one long leg over the other. "The world changes for them, no doubt. Are you familiar with the five stages of grief?"

"Denial, anger, bargaining, depression, and acceptance," I said, ticking them off on my fingers. "This isn't my first rodeo, Doctor Marx."

"Even so," she said. "Sometimes we get stuck in one of those stages, which prevents us from making it to acceptance."

"So I'm stuck in depression."

"It sounds to me as if you never found a healthy enough environment to recover in." Doctor Marx checked the notes on her clipboard. "No close family or friends due to the fact that you moved around so much. You only had your husband to lean on, but he was suffering from the same trauma that you were. Therefore, he was unable to help you. It's a common misconception that all marriages fail after the death of a child, but the couples that stay together talk with one another. They communicate. It's not a guessing game. And from what you've told me, all you and Bodhi do is guess around each other."

"So my marriage is failing?"

Doctor Marx shook her head. "Another conversation for another day, Bailey. Unfortunately, our time is up and I have another client waiting. For now, I want you to focus on yourself. Don't shut Bodhi out, but don't pester him to let you in either."

"In other words, do exactly what I've been trying to do."

Doctor Marx opened a desk drawer, extracted a prescription pad, and began scribbling. "There is no guaranteed cure when it comes to mental health. In the end, *you* have to decide to take the steps toward getting better. Meeting with me was a great first step."

She ripped off the topmost prescription and handed it to me.

"What's this for?" I asked, attempting to decipher her illegible handwriting.

"It's an antidepressant," she replied. "Low dosage. Take it once a day and see how it goes. It takes a little while to work its way into your system, so we'll check in with each other in a few weeks. Sound good?"

I nodded, folding the prescription in half and tucking it into the front pocket of my jeans. The local pharmacy was on my route home. I could fill the prescription there. Maybe a pill could push me through to that acceptance stage. Maybe the Winchester house would settle down long enough for us to finish the renovations without any more disruptions.

But a pill wouldn't bring back Kali.

9

TWO FOR ONE

*T*hat night, I lay in bed, propped against the headboard, reading Caroline Winchester's diary in the dim yellowish light of the lamp on the bedside table. I'd lost track of the time. The sun had set hours ago, and Bodhi's footsteps had long since faded from the hallway outside the master bedroom. A new object now sat on a shelf across from the closet: an orange prescription bottle filled with tiny capsules guaranteed to boost my serotonin levels. It glowed like a beacon just beyond my periphery, but as I became more and more immersed in Caroline's fifteen-year-old musings, the orange bottle melted away from my thoughts.

Caroline wrote in swirly, elegant cursive, weaving her personality seamlessly into the fibers of the thick paper. She wrote about everything, from book reports to the students and teachers at her high school to the family business. One page detailed just how "delectable" her brother's best friend looked during the most recent sailing competition in the bay, while the next contained a line-by-line literary analysis of a complicated Yeats poem. Still other pages boasted calculations of the Winchesters' various business deals. Were it not for the fact that her handwriting remained consistent, I would have assumed that the frisky teenager shared her journal with a college student and a forty-year-old business professional. I devoured her words and sketches, learning about Caroline's view of the world, her family, and the town of Black Bay. I was so engrossed by Caroline's day-by-day that the first flicker of the table lamp went unnoticed.

Then the room went dark.

As my eyes adjusted, I set aside Caroline's journal. I jostled the lightbulb in the lamp and toggled the switch on its base. It remained unlit. With a defeated sigh, I slid out of bed to find a replacement bulb, but just as I opened the door and reached the landing, the lamp brightened again.

Three short flashes. Three long flashes. Three short flashes.

The lamp paused then the sequence repeated itself.

Dot dot dot. Dash dash dash. Dot dot dot.

It was an SOS call.

In the hallway, someone—or something—sprinted past the master bedroom. I caught the movement out of the corner of my eye and whirled around. The hair on my arms rose. I was shivering. The temperature inside had dropped far too low for a warm summer night.

I stared at the wall in the hallway opposite my open door. Frozen in place. Waiting. Time went by the wayside. I stood in the same spot for a minute. For an hour. Finally, I gathered whatever courage I could muster, took a deep breath, and stepped forward to peek into the hallway.

It was empty.

And then a sound like a gunshot went off.

I shrieked, instinctively ducking down and covering my head with my hands, but there was no immediate danger in the hallway. However, behind the closed door of Caroline Winchester's childhood bedroom, a thunderous ruckus went on unhindered. Bodhi careened out of the guest room, clad in nothing but a pair of boxer shorts.

"What's wrong?" he demanded, racing down the hallway to pick me up from the floor. "Are you all right? What the hell is that noise?"

Without preamble, he reached for the door to Caroline's room.

"No!"

Too late. He threw the door wide, revealing the pandemonium inside.

Caroline's extensive library avalanched from the shelves. Books poured to the floor or flew through the air in an array of worn covers and torn pages, bouncing violently off of the walls and each other. Dust whirled through the room like gray fireworks as the canopy bed rattled and shuddered. The bench in the bay window tore clean from the walls with a cacophonous rip, leaving jagged plywood and ruined wallpaper in its place. Caroline's journals shot skyward, carving a savage path through the literary anthologies, calculus textbooks, and poetry collections.

Then, with no explanation, everything stopped.

The books rained to the floor. The bed came to rest at an uneven angle. The noise ceased. The journals settled to the topmost pile of rubble. Not a page turned. Not a breath was drawn.

When one of the journals flopped open, Bodhi grabbed my hand as though he expected the entire room to start heaving again. I looked at him.

"Do you believe me now?"

"There's got to be... an explanation..." he breathed, gasping for air in between phrases. "Magnetic pull. Or the house is on an incline. *Something.*"

"Sure, that makes sense."

I stepped toward the books, but Bodhi yanked me back. "Don't go in there!"

I shook him off. "Don't be ridiculous."

Tentatively, I walked into Caroline's room. I held my breath, carefully plotting each step so as to not tread on any of the wounded books. When I reached the pile of journals, I knelt down to examine the one that had fallen open, gathering its pages with a tender touch.

It was dated July of 1996. Roughly twenty years ago. Ethan's voice echoed in my head. The Winchesters' boat accident had occurred in the summer before Patrick's senior year at Black Bay High, which meant that this particular journal may have been the last one that Caroline Winchester had ever penned. I flipped the pages. Two-thirds of the way through, the entries stopped and gave way to blank paper.

"What is it?" asked Bodhi, still waiting in the doorway.

I collected a few other diaries and stacked them on top of the first. "More of Caroline's diaries. I've been reading through them. This is the last one she wrote before she died."

"A little morbid, don't you think?"

"You have your coping mechanisms. I have mine."

"Please, Bailey. Can we just get out of this room?"

I did as asked, joining Bodhi in the hallway again. As soon as I cleared the threshold, he slammed the door to Caroline's room shut.

"You know it's the whole house, right?" I told him as he escorted me back toward the master bedroom. "Or are you forgetting the office downstairs? You can't just close the door and pretend like none of this ever happened."

"We are hallucinating," Bodhi said determinedly. "This house is old. Maybe the fumes are finally getting to us."

"There are no fumes."

My hands were shaking. I thought of the shadow in the hallway, too humanoid to be a trick of the light. Something lived in the Winchester house, and it had grown tired of staying quiet. Had it always been there, lurking in the night? Or had mine and Bodhi's presence somehow woken it?

When we entered the master bedroom, Bodhi's arm tight around my waist, the first thing I noticed was that the orange prescription bottle had somehow moved from the shelf to the small wastebasket near the French doors. The second thing I noticed was the bedside table. A fresh glass of water and a vase of plumeria flowers stood beneath the lamp, which now illuminated the entire room as though the bulb had never faltered to begin with.

It wasn't until the shadows moved that I realized we weren't alone in the room.

A gust of cold wind engulfed us. It was as though someone had dumped a bucket of ice water over my head. The figure was a shadow itself, or perhaps its essence sucked up the light in order to power itself. It had been lingering on the dark side of the bed, but now it flashed across the room with a speed that was distinctly not human. The vase of plumerias tipped over, a victim of the shadow's haste, and shattered on the floor. Cold water gushed over my toes, soaking the hem of my pajama pants, but I hardly felt it. The French doors burst open so violently that the hinges gave way. As the doors fell, the glass windows smashed, and the umbral figure darted out of the room, disappearing into the black night.

I had never heard Bodhi pray before. Now he chanted unintelligibly under his breath, his eyes glazing over as he braced himself on either side of the doorway. I stood rooted to the same spot, unable to move. Unable to comprehend. Like a snapping rubber band, Bodhi suddenly came to. He took my hand, pulling me away from the master bedroom.

"Let's go."

"Where?"

"I don't care," he said as he took the stairs two at a time. "The inn. The truck. A cardboard box. Anywhere but this house. You were right, Bailey. There's something in here, and there's no way in hell I'm going to sit and twiddle my thumbs and wait for it to decide what to do with us like an idiot."

His car keys lay once again in the crystal tray. For once, he seemed happy to see them there, easy to pick up on our desperate escape through the front door and into the breezy night. Bodhi scanned the skies as he ushered me toward the white workman's truck, as if surveying the landscape for any hint of the rogue presence that did not adhere to the rules of reality. He opened the passenger door for me then circled around to the other side and climbed in. His hands shook as he fumbled the keys into the ignition. I could see the whites of his eyes. He revved the engine with an impetuously heavy foot, throwing the truck into reverse. I jerked against the seat as Bodhi wrenched the steering wheel. Then we were off, trundling down the winding road toward the center of town at a breakneck speed.

When we pulled into the parking lot of the local inn, a quaint bed and breakfast across from the Sanctuary, the windows were dark. A vacancy sign hung near the door.

"Stay here," Bodhi ordered, clambering out of the truck. I watched through the windshield as he approached the inn and tried the door. He hadn't even put pants on before evacuating the house. Even if someone was manning the front desk of the bed and breakfast, I doubted they would let Bodhi in looking like a naked vagrant with dirty feet. He knocked, peeking in through the window, but when no one answered the door, he slammed a fist against the vacancy sign and turned resolutely back to the truck.

"No one's answering," he said, clambering into the driver's seat once more. "What the hell did you bring those things for?"

I looked into the foot well to where Bodhi was pointing. Caroline's journals lay in a heap at my feet. I didn't even remember taking them from the house, but an odd sense of comfort washed over me at the sight of their leather covers.

"Never mind," said Bodhi. "Do what you like. But I guess we're sleeping in the truck tonight."

We did just that—the doors securely locked and the windows rolled all the way up—reclining the seats as far back as they would go. I drifted off, keeping Bodhi in my line of sight, our hands fastened together across the center console.

For the first time in months, I slept without nightmares.

A rapping on the driver's side window woke us up. Bodhi sprang into action. His core muscles clenched as he ripped himself from sleep in a panicked frenzy, but the fraughtful night was long over. The cab of the truck smoldered pink with the sunrise, and in the harmonious morning, as birds chirped and the residents of Black Bay began to stir, the details of the previous night slipped through the cracks.

Bodhi relaxed when he realized we were in no immediate danger then rolled down the truck window to greet our personal wake-up call.

"Oh, I've got to hear the story behind this," said Ethan, chuckling as he took in mine and Bodhi's attire. Or lack thereof. "You two drink a little too much booze last night?"

"Not even close," growled Bodhi.

Ethan stripped off his jean jacket and handed it to Bodhi through the window. "Wait here. I'll find you some pants. Then, if you don't mind, you can kindly fill me in on your evening."

A half hour later, our curious trio occupied a small table near the open window of the Sanctuary. Bodhi, dressed in

Ethan's jacket and a pair of borrowed sweatpants that were loose around his waist but too short for his long legs, nursed a cup of hot coffee as he explained to Ethan what had happened to us the previous night. I tried to ignore the wandering glances of the other customers in the cafe. Once again, we were the talk of the town. Word had traveled fast about the peculiar state we had been found in, but I suppose when you slept half-dressed in a truck outside the local bed and breakfast, people were bound to gossip. I kneaded a packet of artificial sweetener between my fingers to keep myself busy.

"A ghost," Ethan was saying, one eyebrow cocked in skepticism as he surveyed Bodhi over the lip of his coffee mug.

"Something," Bodhi confirmed. "A specter or poltergeist. I don't know, but it was definitely there. Ask Bailey. She's been seeing it for weeks."

"I haven't been seeing it," I said. I didn't appreciate Bodhi calling me out or Ethan's probing gaze. "I caught glimpses of it out of the corner of my eye, but weird stuff has been happening ever since we got to that house."

Ethan set his mug down and folded his hands on the tabletop. "Now I don't mean to be rude," he said. He kept his voice low, and his eyes shifted around the room as though to make sure no one else was listening in on our conversation. "But ghosts don't exist, darlin'."

I didn't blink, staring Ethan down. "You think I'm seeing things."

"I didn't say that," Ethan backtracked. "But let's face it, the two of you are under a lot of stress. Again, I mean no offense or harm, but maybe it's all starting to pile up. You did say you haven't been sleeping lately. Hallucinations may be a factor here."

"Bodhi sleeps fine," I pointed out. "And he saw it too."

But Bodhi stayed quiet, swirling his coffee around. It

swished over the edge of the cup, crept across the table, and stained the paper napkins near Ethan's folded hands.

"Bodhi?" Ethan asked. "Anything to add?"

"I haven't been sleeping much either," he muttered.

"You haven't?" I asked, surprised.

Bodhi shook his head. "I can't. I listen for you every night. The slightest sound wakes me up. Besides, the bed is cold."

"There you have it," Ethan answered, tipping his chair back so that it balanced on its hind legs. "The house isn't haunted, darlin'. The two of you just need a good night's rest."

"I know what I saw," I said sharply. "Right, Bodhi?"

There were purple circles beneath Bodhi's red-rimmed eyes, so dark that it looked like he had been punched multiple times. Was it just this morning that he looked so worn out, or had I missed the signs before now? Maybe I was so wrapped up in my own head not to notice Bodhi's constant exhaustion. Maybe I hadn't wanted to notice it. After all, problems were only problems if you acknowledged their existence.

"Maybe he's right, Bailey," he said, slumping in his chair. The coffee, which the Sanctuary continually boasted as the best wake-up recipe in the Pacific Northwest, hadn't done him much good. "Neither one of us has been at the top of our game lately."

I huffed in disbelief. "Bodhi, are you kidding me? Are you forgetting the avalanche of levitating books? Or the doors in the master bedroom being inexplicably forced off their hinges? The mess will still be there when we get back."

"I'm sure there's a scientific reason for all that," Ethan cut in. "You do know we get earthquakes here in Black Bay, correct?"

"See?" said Bodhi. He reached out to pat my hand in what

I assume he thought was a comforting manner. "That's probably what happened."

"Do you really believe that?"

He heaved a sigh, withdrawing to his side of the table again. "I don't know what to tell you, Bailey."

"You can tell me that you're being an idiot and trying to convince yourself that everything is all right." I threw the packet of artificial sweetener across the table at him. "As always."

Ethan's chair scratched against the tile floor as he pushed himself away from the table. "This sounds like a conversation between husband and wife. I'll see myself out."

As he crossed the cafe and joined a couple of men sitting at the countertop, I studied Bodhi. When he noticed my gaze, he spoke up.

"Bailey, come on," he said. "You have to admit it. An earthquake is way more likely than some random ghost haunting the house we're renovating."

"You weren't so convinced last night. What about that thing we saw in the master bedroom?"

He gave a half-hearted shrug. "Hallucinations brought on by lack of sleep. Like Ethan said."

I wasn't buying it. "So you think that we had some kind of joint hallucination?"

Bodhi pushed his coffee mug to the opposite side of the table and rested his forehead in his hands. "I don't know what to think anymore. I'm dead tired."

I pressed my lips together. There were so many things I wanted to say to Bodhi, but in that moment, all of the things that crossed my mind were bound to cause a fight.

Bodhi tilted his head to look at me. "I have an idea."

"What might that be?"

"Call Milo."

The suggestion threw me off. "Why?"

Bodhi perched his head on the palm of his hand. "He's owned that house for a while, and his dad owned it before him. If anything weird happened, he would know about it, wouldn't he?"

"Don't you think he would've told us about something like that before we bought the house?"

"Not necessarily. He was pretty desperate to sell it, remember? Maybe he already knew that something was going on in there."

The thought had never crossed my mind. Sure, Milo's insistence on selling the Winchester house had been a little out of the ordinary, but he seemed honest about his desire to move out of Black Bay. Then again, it had been nearly two months since we had officially signed the closing papers, and Milo hadn't mentioned anything more about relocating.

"I'll call him," I decided, taking out my cell phone.

"Good."

I dialed Milo's familiar number, never having entered his contact information in my cell, but instead of ringing, an automated voice message answered instead.

"*We're sorry,*" said the pleasant female tone. "*The number you have dialed has been disconnected or is no longer in service.*"

10

DEAD END

I hung up. Maybe I had remembered Milo's number wrong. I punched it in again.

"We're sorry. The number you have dialed—"

"He didn't answer?" Bodhi asked as I lowered the phone from my ear.

"Wrong number," I said. "That's weird. I could've sworn—"

Bodhi stretched over the back of his chair. Ethan's borrowed jacket swung open, revealing Bodhi's bare chest. He groaned then fastened the first few buttons. "I say we head back up to the house."

"You're not serious."

"Look, Bailey. Let's entertain the thought that the house is haunted for a moment." He sat up, swinging his legs around so that our knees kissed. "But it's daytime. So far, nothing bad has happened in the daytime."

"That's not true."

"It's not?"

"The day I skinned my knees. You weren't home."

"Why didn't you tell me?" he demanded.

"Oh, sure. 'Hey, babe. Just thought I'd let you know that I heard someone screaming in the basement, but when I got down there, I realized it was all in my head.'"

"You heard screaming?"

I nodded, staring down into the dregs of my coffee.

Bodhi stood up, tossing his used napkin into an empty mug. "Okay. Let's go. We're never going to figure this out if we cower in a coffee shop all day. We've already put a lot of time and effort into this house. I won't waste that over a few good scares."

There was no point in arguing. Bodhi had made his decision, and I knew from experience that talking him out of it wasn't an option. We left the Sanctuary, thanking Ethan on our way out, and got back in the pickup truck.

The ride up to the bluff was quiet and tense. Bodhi's knuckles were white on the steering wheel as we slowly ascended through the trees. I didn't dare to break the silence. There was a spell over the cab of the truck, an illusion of safety and normality, and if we allowed it to exist for long enough, maybe it would spread to the Winchester house.

It worked. When we trundled into the front yard, there was nothing inherently wrong with the house. There was no eerie vibe. No evidence of struggle. The front door was wide open, but we had left it that way in our rush to get out. All in all, other than the construction materials out front, the Winchester house looked just as it had when we first arrived in Black Bay: stately and serene.

"Here goes nothing," Bodhi said as he kicked open his door and hopped out of the truck.

We approached the front door warily, peering inside for any hint of discord. The entryway and living room were still, so we edged over the threshold. Once inside, Bodhi seemed to relax, his shoulder blades flattening against his back rather than hugging his ears.

"See?" he said, indicating the silent space around him. "Nothing. We should call the crew. It's not too late to get some work done today."

I wasn't so sure. I followed Bodhi into the kitchen, where everything was as it had been the night before, but the real test would be upstairs. If my past experience in the first floor office was any indication, Caroline's room would still be wrecked and the French doors would not have magically repaired themselves.

"We should check the bedrooms," I said.

"In a minute. I'm buzzing and anxious from all the caffeine."

He filled two water glasses at the kitchen sink and turned to offer one to me.

The glasses slipped from his grasp. Crashed to the floor.

Bodhi's eyes went wide, his pupils blown. He whispered:

"Someone's standing behind you."

The words had barely dropped from his lips before his amber eyes flooded with black. I screamed as he lunged toward me.

This was not Bodhi.

His hand covered my mouth as he forced me into the hallway. The length of his body heaved against mine. I felt every one of his muscles contract as he crushed me against the wall. His eyes weren't just black. There was nothing left. No iris. No whites. Just liquid pools of pure hell.

An inhuman sound escaped my throat as his face neared mine. Bodhi tilted his head, listening. The hand over my mouth loosened ever-so-slightly.

"Please," I whispered against his fingers. "Please let us go."

Bodhi stared vacantly back at me, but the creature inside him seemed to pause, considering my request. I drew a strained breath, waiting for the decision.

And then Bodhi whirled me around, wrapped an arm around my neck, and began to drag me down the hallway.

"No!" I choked out, wrestling against Bodhi's grasp. The crook of his elbow mashed against my windpipe. I cough spasmodically as we neared the door of the basement.

He threw me down the stairs.

A flash of light burst behind my eyelids as the back of my head hit something on the way down. My ankle caught the edge of the handrail and snapped. At the bottom of the steps, I lost the concept of reality.

My cheek rested against the cool concrete foundation. There should've been pain, but as my vision blurred in and out of focus, I could only register the sound of the basement door lock clicking into place.

Bodhi's footsteps thundered toward me. I squeezed my eyes shut, bracing myself for whatever came next.

"Bailey! Bailey!"

Gentle hands embraced my face. I looked up.

Bodhi's eyes were brown again. He was crying.

"I'm so sorry," he sobbed, his shoulders shaking uncontrollably. "Oh, God. I'm so sorry. That wasn't me, Bailey. I swear on my life."

My tongue felt heavy in my mouth. "I know."

He situated himself on the bottom step and lifted me to lie down in his lap. "The door's locked," he gasped. "From the outside. We can't get out."

"Your phone."

He fumbled in Ethan's jacket pocket and took out his cell phone. "Shit. Shit! There's no fucking service in this godforsaken pit."

Bodhi lifted the phone above his head in the hopes of finding a bar or two. Suddenly, it was smacked from his hand. It flew across the basement and shattered against the opposite wall.

Bodhi cradled my head in his arms, folding over me like a protective shell. "Leave us alone!" he yelled. A blood vessel burst in his eye. Somehow, the deluge of red around his iris was more terrifying than the black holes that had been there a few minutes ago.

My head throbbed, but my vision was clearing. If I had sustained a concussion, it was a mild one. I could see enough. I could see the basement come alive. Boxes upended themselves. Pool cues snapped and splintered. Spare boat sails ripped to shreds. The toolbox spat nails and screws like a loaded gun. An invisible child pedaled past on a pink bicycle with tasseled handlebars.

A baseball smashed through the one and only storm window, set at the very top of the basement wall. Through the opening, an object flew in from outside, navigating the turmoil until it landed at my feet.

It was Caroline Winchester's most recent journal, flipped open to the last page she had written.

As soon as my fingers touched the leather binding, the basement quieted. Objects paused to hover in midair, as though waiting on my reaction before deciding whether or not to resume the slaughter. I willed myself to focus on Caroline's polished penmanship.

AUGUST 16TH, 1996

WELL, so much for our weekly boat trip. In an unexpected twist of fate, Mom and Dad grounded us both. Patrick and his dumb football cronies stole the mascot head from Black Bay's rival school. It might have been funny if he'd managed to pull it off, but the principal caught him. I told him that he should have brought me along. I never would have gotten caught.

Anyway, he deserves to be grounded. I don't. All I did was point out to Mr. Powell that the sawmill would generate a lot more revenue if he stopped being a prick long enough to take Dad's management advice. Apparently, my tone was considered "rude." Give me a break.

I was actually looking forward to this week's outing too. Miss Watson scolded me for finishing the summer reading list for the upcoming seniors instead of the juniors. I told her I'd already read the juniors' list last summer. To make matters worse, Alex walked right by me in the lunchroom without a passing glance. So much for getting noticed for something other than my staggering wit this year.

The point is that it would have been nice to get my mind off of everything out on the water. Instead, while Mom and Dad get to gallivant about on their own, I have to spend my Friday night alone in the house with Patrick. He always orders anchovies on the pizza. It's disgusting. In fact, I might tie him down if he tries it tonight. Details to come.

"OH MY GOD," I breathed, reading over the words again.

Bodhi's gaze remained fixed on the levitating basement items. "What is it?"

"Caroline and Patrick Winchester were grounded on the night they died."

"So what? No offense, Bailey, but does it really matter right now?"

I propped myself up against the stairwell, balancing Caroline's journal on my knees. "Don't you get it? They never got on the boat, and if they never got on the boat, then they didn't die in a boating accident that night."

"What happened to them then?"

Before I could reply, the toolbox shot across the floor and bounced off the bottom of my foot. I howled in agony, dragging my broken ankle inward. The toolbox popped open, and a carpet knife lifted itself from the mess of hammers and wrenches. Bodhi tried to grab it out of the air, but it flashed toward me so quickly, I had no time to register the rough cut that it opened in the palm of my hand until after it already happened.

Something pressed into the wound like freezing cold fingers attempting to stanch the flow of welling blood. Then it began to write on the concrete, etching out two words in what could have been mistaken for dark red paint.

Bodhi swore beneath his breath. I took one look at the message before my head filled with rushing white noise. The world dissolved around me, but the words written in blood haunted the dark place behind my eyelids.

Help us.

PROLOGUE

*B*lood welled in the palm of my hand, staining the pale underside of my wrist dark red as though someone had poured a bottle of fine wine across a white tablecloth. As it dribbled to the cold concrete floor of the basement, time seemed to suspend itself. My husband, Bodhi, held me from behind—my back pressed to his firm chest, my throbbing head resting against his shoulder—and his fingers tightened around my midsection. Oh, to be held as though nothing else in the world mattered. It was a promise. Every touch, every kiss, was a silent pact to love and adore the person to whom it was given. People often forgot that. We handed out our affection freely, carelessly, finding easy comfort in interlaced fingers or the parting of lips or casual embraces. Then it crumbled. Love was not a rock at the edge of the sea, stoically weathering the storm. It was something to be nurtured, to be made and remade every day, but the work was often mistaken for tedium, and those who did not endure found themselves with a handful of dusty pebbles.

For Bodhi and I, it had taken a possessed house, a demonic spirit, and the locked basement door for us to realize how little we had tried. My body reflected our lack of effort. My knees were hardened and scabbed, the gash that ran from my wrist to my elbow oozed through the bandages, my ankle lay at an ominous angle, my head pounded with every inhale, and the new cut—the one that had just been opened with an animated carpet knife—pulsed in little red tides. Still, as the pain burned white hot, I found myself thinking that the entire house could go up in flames as long as Bodhi continued to hold me with the warmth I'd forgotten he was capable of giving.

But when something—a demon, a ghost—pressed its invisible frigid fingers to the laceration in my palm, it was hard to ignore its chilling impact. Words appeared on the concrete floor, written in the ink of my blood.

Help us.

"What the hell?" whispered Bodhi, his breath warming my ear.

It wrote the same words again, each letter fading as it ran out of bloody paint.

Help us.

My voice was thick and garbled. "Who are you?"

Bodhi's arms tightened around me. "Why does it matter?" he asked furiously. "Look at what it's done to you, Bailey."

A cardboard box zoomed across the room, bounced off the last step of the stairs, and settled against Bodhi's leg.

"What's in there?" he demanded of the empty basement. "A machete? Haven't you done enough already? Look at her—"

I squeezed Bodhi's knee as the box popped open. It did not reveal a machete or any other weapon of the basement's choice. Instead, it toppled over on its side and spilled out a slew of ancient first-aid supplies. A tube of antibacterial ointment came to rest against my bare foot. Then a supportive ankle brace landed in my lap.

"Thanks," I murmured. My head was still fuzzy. "But I don't think a brace will do me much good. It's broken."

"Stop talking to it," hissed Bodhi, taking the brace from my hands and chucking it across the room. It stopped in midair then changed direction and plunked Bodhi on the head. "Ow!"

"Who are you?" I mumbled again. The basement itself seemed to rumble, but no clear answer presented itself. "Can you write it down?"

An icy chill stole over me, and I tucked my ruined wrist behind my back.

"Not with my blood!" I ordered.

"Here," said Bodhi. He reached into the pocket of the denim jacket he was wearing and extracted a carpenter's pencil, which he threw to the floor unceremoniously. For a minute, the pencil lay still. Then something swept it up and scratched a message into the cement.

Help us.

"Oh, for the love of Pete," said Bodhi, exasperated. "Bailey, this is pointless."

"Do you want to stay locked down here forever?" I asked him, wincing as another shot of pain radiated through my skull. "At least I'm trying."

"To reason with a demon," he pointed out.

An embroidered purple throw pillow lifted itself from a pile of dusty linens and batted Bodhi around the ears.

"I don't think demons start pillow fights," I said.

"I don't care—"

"Shh."

The pencil scribbled across the cement again.

Bailey.

"That's me," I confirmed to the presence with a nod. "Can you tell me who you are?"

Bailey. Bailey. Bailey.

"That would be a no," said Bodhi.

I did my best to prop myself up in Bodhi's lap, hoping to convey a sense of confidence with my heightened posture, and announced, "I'll make you a deal."

Bodhi hugged me closer. "Bailey, don't you dare."

I ignored him. "If we agree to help you, whoever you are, then I want something in return."

The basement was motionless, as though whatever spirit occupied the space waited for my proposition.

"If we help you," I began tentatively. "Then you have to promise not to hurt us. No more of this haunted house nonsense. No more bodiless screaming or shattering windows. In fact, I want you to agree to protect us at all costs."

Bodhi scoffed. "Not likely."

"If you do that," I went on. "I promise to do whatever is in my power to help you. That's it. That's the deal. Take it or leave it."

For a long minute, the only sounds in the dank basement were my rushed inhales and exhales and Bodhi's labored breathing. We waited in the heavy silence. My chin dropped to my chest as the throbbing in my head worsened.

"Quickly, please," I murmured.

There was a click at the top of the steps. The basement door unlocked. It swung open, and a shaft of sunlight illuminated the dismal stairwell.

11

THE BEGINNING

There was no hospital in Black Bay, Washington. The tiny coastal town was home to several small family-owned businesses, including a walk-in clinic and a pharmacy, but none of them were equipped to treat my amalgamation of injuries. Bodhi drove us into the city, where a leery med student asked probing questions about the nature of my "fall" as he patched me up. Bodhi held my hand throughout the process, watching like a hawk as an orthopedic casted my ankle and provided me with a hard boot to fasten over the top of it so that I could walk without crutches. There was a pained look on Bodhi's face the entire time, despite the fact that he was not the one who had fallen victim to the whims of our house's ghost. My memory flashed back. Bodhi's eyes, black as night, bore into mine right before he shoved me down the basement stairs. It wasn't him. He had been taken over by whatever presence occupied our current residence, and in that respect, there was nothing to forgive him for. Nevertheless, I had a feeling that his involuntarily act of violence haunted him more than whatever being remained in the house.

The tension intensified when yet another doctor made a visit to our curtained-off corner of the emergency room, especially when he asked Bodhi to give us some privacy. I expected the questions he asked. Did I try to hurt myself? Was Bodhi responsible for any of my injuries, old or new? I stuck to my story. It made sense after all. Bodhi and I flipped houses for a living. We were often right in the thick of construction, renovation, and rebuilding. It was easy to craft an accidental scenario for each of my wounds. A rogue nail ripped the gash in my wrist. I bumped my head backing into an overhanging beam. I'd cut my hand with a carpet knife. That last one was half-true. Whatever I said was better than the truth. If I admitted that the real reason I was so banged up was because our most recent project was frequented by a bloodthirsty ghost, the medics were sure to send me off to the psych ward for an evaluation.

As we drove back to Black Bay, our borrowed pickup truck whizzing across the wet winding roads, Bodhi's hands clenched and unclenched on the steering wheel. His knuckles turned pink and white. A benign pop song played on the radio, crooning about a one-night stand that would surely morph into true love.

"What did they ask you?" Bodhi said at last.

"What do you think?"

He wrung the steering wheel like a washcloth. "That it was my fault."

"It wasn't your fault, Bode."

I reached across the center console of the car with my uninjured hand, taking care to move slowly to avoid jostling my mildly concussed head, and stroked Bodhi's arm. He released the wheel, taking my hand in his own and bringing it to his lips.

"Do you think there's a reason that *thing* targeted you instead of me?" he asked.

I pondered the question. It was true. Ever since we had moved into the Winchester house—a massive twenty-year-old home located on the outlook of an enormous bluff—I had heard voices that weren't real, seen humanoid shadows out of the corner of my eye, and watched objects levitate and destroy themselves without rhyme or reason, all while Bodhi remained convinced that the continued destruction was due to my unfortunate habit of sleepwalking.

"Maybe because I was more open to the possibility of it actually existing." I closed my eyes and rested my forehead against the cool glass of the truck's window. "I think, in the very back of my mind, I knew that I wasn't hallucinating or going crazy. I feel something in that house, Bodhi."

"All the more reason to get out."

I lifted my aching head from the window—the pain relievers were wearing off quickly—and switched off the radio. There was only so much Top 40 a girl could take, especially when recovering from a concussion. "What do you mean?"

Bodhi's gaze remained fixed on the slick pavement. "We're not staying."

"I promised—"

"To help the damn ghost. I heard."

"We can't go!"

He looked at me, his lips parted in disbelief. "Are you kidding me, Bailey? That thing tried to kill us. We're not sticking around to let it. We're packing up our stuff and getting out of town."

"And you think that will work?" I asked. "You think that thing's going to let us load up the truck and head on out?"

The two-lane road curved around a bend, and Bodhi leaned into the turn as he guided the truck at an uneven pace. "I've been thinking about that too. It wants you, right? But it also seems like it can't leave the house. You stay in the car. I'll get our things. Then we can go to Seattle or Portland or somewhere that is significantly less Stephen King."

"I think you're forgetting a couple of things."

"What?"

I tapped my fingers impatiently on the car door. "First of all, our not-so-friendly neighborhood ghost has the ability to possess you. Or have you forgotten?"

His lips pressed together in a tight line, but he remained silent.

"Secondly, we've already dumped a lot of money into the Winchester house," I went on. "We've barely begun renovations. We can't afford to pick up and leave now. Not unless you plan on us moving back in with my mother. Not that she wouldn't be happy to have us, so I suppose if you can handle the perennial smell of wet dog then—"

"Fine," Bodhi said. "I get it. But don't pretend like those are the only reasons you don't want to leave. You actually feel something for this ghost thing, don't you?"

It was my turn to stay quiet. Bodhi's guess was correct. There was some kind of connection between me and whatever resided in the Winchester house, but I wasn't going to admit that to him until I knew why.

"That's what I thought," he said with an air of finality.

"Look, it needs help," I insisted. "Maybe hurting me was the only way it could get my attention. It tried other things first, you know."

"Let's just take it slow." Bodhi turned the radio back on, tuning the channel to a classic rock station. "I don't trust that thing. Neither should you."

WHEN THE TREES cleared and the town of Black Bay glittered in its valley beneath the overlooking bluff, it was hard to believe that anything could go so wrong in such a charming place. By then, the sun had risen high in the sky, banishing most of the clouds that loomed in the mornings. August had just arrived, and the residents of Black Bay knew to make the most of the fine weather while they still had the chance. As we drove through the town square, it occurred to me how much had changed in the two months since we had started work on the Winchester house. Then, the locals regarded us with polite curiosity. Now, they waved at the truck as it passed by, familiar and comfortable with the new couple in the Winchester house.

I expected a sense of anxiety to set in as we crossed town and entered the trees again. The road wound back and forth here, snaking its way to the top of the bluff. Bodhi grew more and more agitated the closer we drew to the house, swearing with gusto every time he accidentally dropped a gear. I, on the other hand, felt inappropriately serene. Now that we had acknowledged the presence in the Winchester house, it was time to finally do something about it.

The house itself didn't present itself as some kind of haunted spectacle. It was as graceful and benevolent as ever, the sun beating down on its chipped blue paint as it rested like a particularly corpulent cat napping amongst the surrounding trees. From the outside, there was no evidence of the house's extra resident. White curtains floated languidly in the sea breeze that flowed through the open windows of the second story. The widow's walk was proud and stoic on the roof as though the house itself waited for our return. As Bodhi pulled the truck into the front yard and parked amongst the construction materials we had collected, the door of the house eased open on its own.

Bodhi's fingers lingered at the keys in the ignition. "Nope. No way."

I got out of the truck. "It was probably just the wind."

He had no choice but to follow me as I crossed the yard

and stepped into the foyer of the Winchester house. I waited in the hallway by the light switches. Was there a polite way to announce yourself to the ghost that had so recently attempted to kill you?

"Well?" prompted Bodhi. He waited on the doormat. "Anything?"

"So far, so good."

"I don't buy it."

"Just come in."

I yanked Bodhi across the threshold. Instinctively, his hands found my waist. I could see his chest rise and fall with every nervous breath he took. I could smell the lemon-coconut bar soap he used to wash his hair the night before mixed with the faint scent of sweat leftover from our panic that morning. It had been a long time since Bodhi and I stood so close to each other in such an honest way. I realized how bizarre my thought process was. I should have been worried about the ghost in the Winchester house. Instead, my focus wandered south. I shook my head to clear it, but a fresh pang at the base of my skull caused me to flinch.

Bodhi noticed, cradling my face between his palms. "Are you all right? Is it the house?"

"No, no. Just my head."

"Let's get you in bed."

He held me all the way up the stairs, guiding me toward the master bedroom where I had been staying, but when we opened the door, we were reminded that the ghost of the Winchester house had already had its way with this room. The French doors leading out to the balcony had literally been ripped out of place. The bedroom was exposed to the elements, and though the salty air from outside refreshed my warm skin, the dewy bedsheets were in no way fit to comfort me.

"Um, maybe you should stay in my room," suggested Bodhi.

"That's fine. Can you grab my computer though?"

He dashed into the master bedroom, seized my laptop and its charger from the bedside table, and dashed out again. I resisted the impulse to laugh as he tucked the laptop under his arm and led me down the hallway.

Bodhi's room was clean and tidy, untouched by the spirit that had wreaked havoc on other parts of the house. It smelled like him. There was no way to describe it. Every person had a scent, something that was uniquely theirs. Beneath his citrusy soap, Bodhi's reminded me of freshly cut grass and mint leaves and petrichor. He was of the earth, solid and grounded. Bodhi lowered me onto the full-sized bed, and I sank into the cool bliss of the cotton sheets.

"I'll make you some tea. Are you hungry?"

I shook my head.

"I'll bring you something to eat anyway. Just in case."

"Then what are we going to do?" I asked.

He fluffed the quilt and tucked the corners in beneath me. "*You* are going to rest," he said. "And I figured I would start by scrubbing the ominous bloody messages out of the basement floor."

"That's probably for the best."

"I thought so too."

He set my laptop down on the bed. I pulled it toward me to boot it up. "What if that thing is still down in the basement though?"

Bodhi swept his fingers through his dark curls, separating out the ringlets. "She's been quiet so far. If I have any problems, you'll be the first to know."

"She?"

"Just a guess. I brought these in for you as well."

He set a stack of leather-bound journals on the bed. In the

chaos of the morning, I had all but forgotten about them. Now I wondered if the identity of our mysterious presence was hidden somewhere amongst the pages.

Bodhi leaned over and kissed my forehead. "Take it easy. I'll be back in a few minutes."

My laptop chimed to life as he left. Immediately, I connected to the Internet and clicked through to our website. The familiar layout loaded, displaying a picture of me and Bodhi striking explorer poses atop the roof of the last house we had renovated. My inbox was full of messages from our devoted fans and followers. Some of them were interested in the flipping side of the blog, wondering about our progress on the Winchester house. Most of them, however, idolized mine and Bodhi's marriage, unable to read between the lines of the inane crap that I wrote. Online life was like that. You wrote what you knew your audience wanted to read. Everything else stayed in your head.

I scrolled down, skimming through my recent blog posts until I reached the dates from two months ago. In early June, we had just arrived in Black Bay, but it wasn't until we got to know some of the locals that we learned what had happened to its original family.

Bailey and Bodhi: Flipping Out

GOOD MORNING, *flippers, and what a glorious morning it is! The sun is shining, the birds are singing, and everyone in Black Bay is out sailing, swimming, or basking in the warmth. Today, Bodhi and the crew are tearing up the tile in the kitchen, which means that I'm free to fill you all in on the history of this enormous house. Hopefully, you all remember our new pal Ethan Powell, Black*

Bay's all-around handyman. Yesterday, he kindly answered my questions regarding the Winchester family. Be ready, flippers. It's a bittersweet story.

Let's recap. As you all know, this house has been vacant for twenty years. It was originally built by Christopher and Elizabeth Winchester, who moved to Black Bay when the town was on the brink of extinction due to a lack of successful businesses. Christopher rebooted the town's economy. I guess he was some kind of executive bigwig. Anyway, he consolidated what was left of Black Bay's assets and essentially saved the locals from having to move elsewhere. His wife, Elizabeth, was apparently a gem as well. She started book clubs, hosted charity events, and volunteered at any place that needed help.

The Winchesters had two children, Patrick and Caroline, who were adored by the town. Patrick was the quarterback of the high school football team, having made the varsity team as a freshman. He led the Black Bay Golden Eagles to victory for three out of four years. More on his senior year later. Caroline, who was two years younger than Patrick but only a year behind him in school, was some kind of intellectual prodigy. If you missed the pictures I posted of the books in her room, click here to check them out. This girl was a whole new breed of intelligence. She had plans to take over her father's business. At fifteen!

Back to Patrick's senior year. Here's why he didn't win the football championship for the high school that last year. He didn't have the opportunity to do so. Why not, you ask? Buckle up, flippers. This is where the story of the Winchester family gets utterly heartbreaking. On a Friday afternoon, the Winchesters took their sailboat out on the bay for their usual family outing. Miserably, they never made it back. The boat crashed against the rocks, right beneath the bluff where their giant house still sits. No one survived.

It's no wonder Black Bay so cherished the Winchesters. It's no wonder they were apprehensive to see Bodhi and I move in to a house that once belonged to such a highly-regarded family. The locals owe everything to the Winchesters, and in a way, so do we. We're going to do our best to preserve the underlying feeling of the Winchester house. It's the least we can do to keep their legacy alive.

KEEP YOUR CHINS UP, *flippers!*
    Bailey

I CLICKED out of the blog post, a lump growing in my throat. This was the story that all of the townspeople knew. The Winchesters had died in a sailing accident. However, the leather bound journals told a different story. I picked the first one up, looking at the inside of the cover. There, a hand with impeccable penmanship had written *Caroline Winchester, August 1st - August 31st, 1996.*

Caroline's journals had been left untouched in her bedroom. I'd found the entire collection stowed away in the storage area beneath the seat in the bay window. It had become a habit of mine to skim through them before I went to bed. Caroline's determination and spunk distracted me from my own troubles, easing me to sleep before I succumbed to the inevitable onslaught of nightmares.

The last journal, the one from August of 1996, held some-thing more than Caroline's usual diatribes. I flipped to the final entry, reading Caroline's sentences over and over again with a borderline obsessive fervor:

AUGUST 16TH, 1996

WELL, *so much for our weekly boat trip. In an unexpected twist of fate, Mom and Dad grounded us both. Patrick and his dumb foot-*

ball cronies stole the mascot head from Black Bay's rival school. It might have been funny if he'd managed to pull it off, but the principal caught him. I told him that he should have brought me along. I never would have gotten caught.

Anyway, he deserves to be grounded. I don't. All I did was point out to Mr. Powell that the sawmill would generate a lot more revenue if he stopped being a prick long enough to take Dad's management advice. Apparently, my tone was considered "rude." Give me a break.

I was actually looking forward to this week's outing too. Miss Watson scolded me for finishing the summer reading list for the upcoming seniors instead of the juniors. I told her I'd already read the juniors' list last summer. To make matters worse, Alex walked right by me in the lunchroom without a passing glance. So much for getting noticed for something other than my staggering wit this year.

The point is that it would have been nice to get my mind off of everything out on the water. Instead, while Mom and Dad get to gallivant about on their own, I have to spend my Friday night alone in the house with Patrick. He always orders anchovies on the pizza. It's disgusting. In fact, I might tie him down if he tries it tonight. Details to come.

CAROLINE'S ACCOUNT of that evening conflicted with the story that the town told. If she and Patrick were grounded that night, it meant they had never boarded their parents' sailboat. It meant that they never died in the accident that night. It meant that they spent their Friday evening safe and sound within the comfort of their big, empty house. But if that were true, where were the Winchester children now?

"All we have is leftover pizza from Lido's," Bodhi announced as he reappeared in the bedroom. He carried a mug of hot tea and a paper plate piled high with pizza. "I hope that's okay. If you want, I can run into town and pick up some soup."

"Pizza's fine. Any problems downstairs?"

"Not a whisper of our visitor. I even checked the basement. I think she's taking that deal of yours to heart."

I sipped from the mug. Bodhi had made some kind of turmeric and ginger tea. It tasted foul, but I knew from experience it would help with the inflammation in my body. I offered him Caroline's journal. "Bodhi, will you read this?"

He skimmed through the last entry. "This is what you were talking about earlier. Caroline and Patrick never got on the boat, right?"

"Not according to Caroline."

"So what does it mean?"

I folded a slice of pizza in half and took a bite. Grease dripped from the crust, pooling on the paper plate below. "Do you think they might still be alive?"

"The kids?"

"Yeah."

Bodhi scratched the back of his neck, thoughtful. "I'm not sure. I mean, that would make sense, wouldn't it? If they didn't die in a boat crash, then they should be alive. But if they are, then why does an entire town think they're both dead?"

I tapped Caroline's journal. "What if that's what the house is trying to tell us? The ghost or whatever is what led me to Caroline's diaries in the first place. What if Patrick and Caroline are still alive? Maybe they're in trouble, and we're meant to rescue them."

Bodhi's gaze softened as he rested a hand over mine. "Bailey, if they are still alive, you have to remember they're not kids anymore. They'd be able to take care of themselves."

"I'm not so sure."

"Maybe Caroline didn't write everything down,"

suggested Bodhi. He snuck a piece of sausage from my plate and popped it into his mouth. "You never know. Their parents could have changed their minds about grounding them. Maybe they ended up on the boat anyway."

"I guess that's a possibility."

"It's more likely than the Winchester children wandering around with amnesia for twenty years," Bodhi answered.

The pizza was less appetizing than I'd hoped. I set it down and dusted my hands off. "I just have a hunch that something else happened to them."

"A hunch?"

"I know it sounds strange," I said. "And I don't mean to scare you or anything, but I feel connected to this house somehow. It's nothing concrete. It's something intuitive."

"And you felt this as soon as we got here?"

"Maybe. I don't think I knew what it was at first."

He sprawled across the foot of the bed, carefully avoiding my broken ankle. "We'll figure it out. We have to now."

"What do you mean?"

He gave me a look before playfully squeezing the big toe of my uninjured foot. "You sold us out to a ghost, remember?"

A TRICK OF THE LIGHT

*F*or the first time in a number of years, Bodhi and I willingly slept in the same bed that night. For so long, we had had trouble sharing intimate space. It wasn't that we were repulsed by each other. Our marriage hadn't inexplicably crumbled due to lack of interest. It was that we had more in common with the Winchesters than expected. We, too, had experienced a run-in with death. Five years ago, we lost our three-year-old daughter. Kali's absence took its toll on our relationship. I couldn't look at Bodhi without seeing her dark curls. He couldn't look at me without seeing her hazel eyes. She had been all the best parts of us, and when she died, she had taken those parts to the afterlife with her. Bodhi and I had emptied ourselves out. We had nothing left to give to one another. The knowledge of that became unbearable in the hushed space between us, where our bodies no longer connected and the sheets remained cold and unforgiving. It was easier to avoid each other. It was easier to sleep apart. That way, when my nightmares came, only one of us suffered through them.

So when Bodhi returned from the bathroom, still damp

from his shower, it was with some hesitation that he slipped in under the quilt. We breathed together, side by side. I stared at the ceiling of the small room. The master bedroom had been massive, and even at night, it was illuminated, the moon smiling in through the windows of the French doors. Bodhi's room was smaller and darker. Snug and private. Maybe that was why I found the courage to sneak my fingers across the distance between us. To rest them lightly on his warm skin. Everything was easier in the dark.

His fingers intertwined with mine, rustling the bandages around my palm. We stayed like that for a while, clutching at each other. Then Bodhi turned on his side to face me. Before I lost my nerve, I shifted. Haltingly, I scooted closer to him, dipping my body to fit in the valley of his. His hand found my hip and then my waist before he draped his arm firmly around my midsection and hugged me toward him. His lips brushed against the back of my neck.

I tangled my legs in his, ignoring the plaster cast around my ankle. His heartbeat thumped unevenly against my spine. There, in the middle of the bed rather than on a designated side, I felt the familiar pull of unconsciousness and slipped comfortably into it as though greeting an old friend.

EVERYTHING WAS DARK. Icy. Hopeless. The crushing weight of water held me down. I struggled, flailing my arms to find the surface. My chest burned with the effort of holding my breath. I couldn't do it anymore. I inhaled. The bitter chill of freezing cold saltwater filled my lungs.

"Bailey! *Bailey!*"

I woke in a frenzy, drenched in sweat. Bodhi sat above me, his knees trapping my hips. He held my hands to the mattress, but as soon as he realized that I was awake, he let go. I gasped for breath, massaging my throat.

"It's all right," Bodhi said as he shifted his weight off of me. "You're all right, Bailey. It was just a dream."

"What happened?" I rasped.

He gently removed my hands from my throat, lifting my chin to check if I had done any damage to myself. "You were thrashing around like someone was trying to kill you."

"I was drowning."

He went still. Normally, I didn't share the details of my nightmares with him. "You were asleep," he reminded me. "You wouldn't stop kicking me. That's why I was holding you down."

"I'm sorry."

"Don't apologize. It's not your fault. Sit up."

I obeyed, letting Bodhi strip the damp T-shirt from my body. He replaced it with a fresh one of his own, carefully navigating my bandaged hand through the sleeves.

"Better?"

I nodded. The cool dry cotton soothed my flushed skin. Bodhi slipped off the bed.

"I'll get you a glass of ice water."

"No." I took his hand in mine and pulled him back to bed, kicking the quilt off of my feet in the process. If he went downstairs now, increasing the distance between us, there was a good chance we would never get back to how we had fallen asleep. "Stay. Please stay."

He curled up next to me, holding my hand. His voice was already thick with drowsiness. "Are you sure?"

"Yes. What time is it?"

Bodhi checked the nearby clock, its numbers casting a green glow across the bedside table. "Five o'clock. The sun won't be up for another couple of hours. You still have time to sleep."

"I'm sorry," I mumbled again, hugging a pillow to my chest.

I was already asleep when he replied, "I'm sorry, too."

I WOKE ALONE in Bodhi's bed, squinting in the bright light of the morning sun. Outside, deep voices shouted to one another. Some kind of hammering was happening on the roof. Bodhi had called the construction crew to resume renovation work on the Winchester house.

I got out of bed, maneuvered a pair of shorts on over my booted foot, and headed downstairs. I found Bodhi in the kitchen, sipping coffee as he fielded instructions to the crewmen through a walkie-talkie. Behind him, a skillet sizzled on the stovetop, and the sweet scent of real maple syrup filled the air.

"Hey there," he said with a smile when he saw me in the doorway. "I've been waiting on you."

"You have?"

"Yeah, I wanted to make sure you were okay before I went outside to help the guys," he said. He pointed to my bare feet. "Put your shoes on. The crew has been trekking through here all morning. I'm sure they dragged in a whole bunch of crap, and I don't want you to get a nail in your foot or something."

I raised my booted ankle. "Shouldn't be a problem with this foot," I said jokingly. Nevertheless, I slid my unguarded foot into one of the flip-flops at the bottom of the stairs.

"I made breakfast," he said, brandishing a frying pan full of eggs. "Would you like some?"

Before I knew it, I was reclining on a deck chair in the front yard, balancing a plate of blueberry pancakes and scrambled eggs on my lap, and watching Bodhi and the crew fix leaks in the roof. I mopped up a puddle of maple syrup. I'd forgotten how good of a cook Bodhi was. In the early stages of our relationship, he impressed me with everything from roast duck to chocolate soufflé, but just like everything else, he stopped cooking when Kali died. We relied on bakeries or cold donuts for breakfast nowadays, and it was a refreshing change to wake up to Bodhi's famous pancakes once more.

Caroline's journals kept me company that morning. I read through her older entries, trying to glean additional information about the Winchester children. One particular passage caught my eye.

JANUARY 12TH, 1995

FAR BE it from me to downplay the melancholia of a funeral, but can I just say how good Alex looks in a suit? For a guy who says he's most comfortable in a football jersey or boat shoes, he sure can pull off a three-piece. It was tailored too! He didn't swim around in it like most teenaged boys do. Mom has to practically drag Patrick to the tailor for his clothes. He says it's a waste of time. Sometimes I wonder how he and Alex ended up as best friends. Teaching me how to throw a football would clearly be a superior use of Alex's time. I already know how to throw a football of course—Patrick taught me—but for Alex, I would happily feign ignorance.

Anyway, other than Alex's irrefutable virility, today remains regrettably morose. I liked Mr. Powell Senior. He always answered my questions about running his own business, no matter how many times Dad told me to stop pestering him. Once, he even let me try smoking a cigar. It was disgusting and I may have forsaken a lung, but that's not the point. Dad would never have let me done something like that just for the experience. Mr. Powell Senior was a good guy. Why do the good guys always have to go so early?

Mr. Powell Junior keeps trying to get me to call him by his first name. Even today, when my mom made me offer him my condo-

lences, he said, "Call me Ethan, darlin'. Mr. Powell was my father."
And then he dissolved into a puddle of tears. I feel bad for him,
even if he does like Patrick better than me. He's supposed to run the
lumber mill all on his own now. Dad offered to help, of course. He's
been working wonders with the other businesses in town, but Mr.
Powell Junior adamantly refuses every time.

The wake is at our house since everyone in town wanted to
come and the only place big enough to hold everyone in town is
here. It's all still going on, and even though Patrick pilfered a bottle
of Mom's most expensive champagne, and I could be up on the
widow's walk with them watching Alex's priceless attempts to chug
said champagne without cringing, I just couldn't be with people
anymore. I've seen enough tear-streaked faces, enough black suits
and dresses. I stole a cigar from Dad's desk drawer to smoke in Mr.
Powell Senior's honor. I haven't brought myself to light it yet, but
keeping it in my mouth as I write seems just as good as puffing
away at it. Plus, you know, cancer. Anyway. To Mr. Powell Senior.
If I were wearing a hat, I'd tip it to you. May your afterlife be as
loving and as caring as your former one.

"GOOD MORNING, BAILEY!"

A shadow came over the journals, darkening the pages.
Ethan Powell himself had approached my chair from behind.
He was a stout, brawny man with a full head of luscious gray
hair and an ample beard to match. Today, he wore a polo
shirt with the name of his lumber mill embroidered across
the pocket, jeans that looked thin in the knees, and a pair of
steel-toed boots. His blue-gray eyes twinkled in the sunlight
as he smiled down at me. I smiled back. Ethan was the unof-
ficial mayor of Black Bay. The locals went to him for everything from simple advice on how to naturally remove a tick
from a dog's coat to heavier subjects such as possible unem-
ployment and coping with loss. Ethan covered it all, treating

everyone with warmth and respect. As such, I closed Caroline's diary, unsure if Ethan had seen what was written on the page or not. It wasn't my place to dredge up old memories.

"Hi, Ethan. How are you?"

One massive hand came up to shield his eyes from the sun. "I'm swell, thank you very much. Whatcha got there?"

I waved Caroline's journal. Ethan already knew about my discovery. The day I'd unearthed Caroline's journals from their hiding spot in her old bedroom, Ethan and I had discussed the possibility of donating them to the local library to further preserve Caroline's personality for the rest of Black Bay to appreciate. For some reason, I didn't like the idea of letting go of her journals just yet.

Ethan's beard bristled. "Still reading those, eh? Anything good?"

I debated whether or not to ask Ethan about his father. In the short time that I'd known him, he had never mentioned his family or that he had inherited the lumber mill from his father. I casually glanced at his left hand. No wedding band on his ring finger either. These days, that didn't mean much. The gold band on my own finger was enough proof of that. No matter how far Bodhi and I drifted apart, the ring remained as a reminder that we were going back on our promises to each other. Still, Black Bay was born out of tradition. It was inhabited by generations of families that had lived here for years. Ethan was a successful business owner, and he was the heart of the town, so why had he never married?

"Not really," I said, nonchalantly casting the journal aside. I decided against asking Ethan about his dad. There was nothing to be gained in reopening old wounds. Caroline provided enough information. Apparently, the former Mr. Powell was just as adored back then as Ethan was now. "She mostly complains about her brother and talks about her high school crush. Teenaged girl stuff, you know?"

Ethan chuckled, bracing his hands on his belt. "Afraid I don't."

"Take my word for it," I said. "It's all nail polish and pillow fights and the occasional rousing game of Truth or Dare."

"Sounds like fun." He tapped the cast on my foot. "Riddle me this, Bailey. How is it that it's been less than twenty-four hours since I've seen you last and you've somehow managed to go and break a foot between now and then?"

"It turns out the basement stairs are particularly tricky," I explained. Once again, it was a half-truth, but half-truths were easier to keep up with than a plethora of lies. "It's only fractured though."

Ethan shifted nervously from one boot to the other. "And, uh, what about your 'friend?'"

I feigned ignorance. "My friend?"

"Yesterday, you and Bodhi told me a ghost chased you out of the house, remember?"

I smacked my forehead as if suddenly recalling the conversation. "Right! Of course. No, I think your advice was on par for that one, Ethan. We just needed a good night's sleep."

"Really?" asked Ethan. "But you said—"

"I'm so glad you suggested I go see Dr. Marx," I interrupted. Dr. Marx was Black Bay's one and only psychiatrist, and while my ghastly nightmares were more than enough reason to pay her a visit, it wasn't until the Winchester house really spooked me that I went to see her. "She's clearing up a lot of stuff for me. It helps to talk it out, you know?"

Ethan knelt next to me so that I didn't have to squint into the sun to see him, leaning over the arm of my chair. "I absolutely agree. I'm glad you're on the road to recovery. It just seems a little rushed to me."

"Rushed?"

"Bailey, you were convinced that your house was haunted."

I moved away from Ethan. The paper plate of pancake crumbs tipped to the ground, and a rogue blueberry rolled through the dirt. "Ethan, I'm confused. Did you want me to continue thinking that ghosts exist? Should I call Mystery Inc.?"

"No, Scooby-Doo can rest easy," Ethan assured me. "I just wanted to make sure that you and Bodhi were all right. What about him? How's he doing?"

I looked up to where Bodhi crouched on the roof, grateful for the change of subject. Perhaps comparing the situation in the Winchester house to the ridiculousness of a children's cartoon had finally convinced Ethan to let it go. Bodhi and I decided that the best course of action would be to keep everyone else in Black Bay ignorant of our spiritual problem. After all, there was a fine line between small town charm and legitimate insanity.

"He'll be all right," I said. "I think we took a chomp out of something bigger than we're used to. This house is enormous, and we usually renovate much smaller properties. The stress is getting to him, but once we have a few more things in hand, it should all go back to normal. Besides, it's hot up here. Sometimes, the heat makes you see things."

Ethan picked my paper plate out of the dirt and crumpled it in one meaty hand. "I'm glad to hear that—"

A sudden clang drew our attention upward where a stack of tiles dominoed off the roof and shattered on the ground below. Bodhi had slipped, kicking the tiles out of place. He windmilled his arms, trying to regain his balance, but his feet slid out from under him and he landed hard on his back, skating toward the edge of the roof at a breakneck pace.

"No!" I gasped, upending the deck chair as I leapt to my

feet. My ankle threatened to buckle beneath me, and Ethan grabbed me around my waist to steady me.

Bodhi veered toward the side of the angled roof, flipping over on his stomach in an attempt to seize anything that might halt his rapid descent. No luck. Tiles ripped off in his hands, as did the gutter. I watched, my mouth stretched open in a yell of panic, as he plummeted off the edge of the roof.

But instead of hitting the ground with a brutal smack, Bodhi halted in midair, suspended ten feet above the dirt. He swung his legs down, getting his feet underneath him, before the unknown force released him. Then he landed on the ground in a catlike crouch, unharmed.

I limped over to Bodhi as fast as my plaster-covered ankle would allow, but Ethan got there first. His eyes were wide and anxious as he hauled Bodhi to his feet, dusting dirt off of Bodhi's white T-shirt.

"Did you see that?" Ethan exclaimed when I reached them. I took Bodhi by the hand, checking him over for injuries, but other than his pulse racing through the veins in his neck, he seemed completely fine.

"See what?" Bodhi asked. He glanced up at the roof, where the rest of the construction crew peered over the edge to determine if Bodhi was okay. He waved up at them. "That was lucky, wasn't it?"

"Lucky?" Ethan repeated incredulously. "Bodhi, something caught you before you hit the ground! Didn't you feel it?"

Bodhi caught my eye. There was something else going on in his mind. I could see that, but Ethan couldn't. I gave a nearly imperceptible shake of my head. We had to keep Ethan in the dark.

"It happened so fast," Bodhi answered, shaking his sweaty curls out of his eyes. "I didn't feel anything."

Ethan turned to me, his usually calm demeanor gone with

the wind. "Bailey, you had to have noticed that. He slowed down before he hit the ground!"

I laid a reassuring hand on Ethan's forearm. "Ethan, are you feeling all right? I didn't see anything like that at all."

"But— he—!" Ethan spluttered, gesturing from the roof to the ground.

Bodhi called up to one of the crewmen on the roof. "John!"

A burly black man, sporting a Seattle Mariners hat and wearing a T-shirt with a logo that matched the one on Ethan's polo, poked his head over the busted gutter. "Need something, Bode?"

"Can you take Mr. Powell inside to cool down?" Bodhi requested, patting Ethan on his broad back. "And get him a glass of water. I think he's dehydrated."

"Sure thing."

As John clambered down the ladder propped against the house, Ethan insisted, "I'm not dehydrated. I'm telling you. I know what I saw."

Bodhi clapped him on the shoulder. "You don't have to convince us, Ethan."

John hopped off the ladder. I played along with Bodhi's act, leading Ethan to where John stood. "Seriously, Ethan. This is what I was just talking about. The sun gets to you up here on the bluff."

"But—"

I handed Ethan off to John, who guided him through the front doors of the house. "Put some sunscreen on while you're at it," I called after them. As soon as they disappeared into the cool shadows of the living room, I turned back to Bodhi. "Okay, what the hell was that?"

"I lied," he said, glancing up to the roof to make sure none of the other construction workers were listening in on our conversation. "I felt something catch me. It gave me enough time to swing my feet down like that."

"Yeah, I saw it too."

"You did?"

"Technically, I didn't *see* anything," I clarified. "Nothing magically appeared to catch you. As soon as you slipped, I thought for sure we would have to make another trip to the hospital. And then you stopped. Stopped! Midair, Bodhi, as if you were flying. You said you felt something catch you?"

"Like two freezing cold hands took me by the arms."

Bodhi rubbed his shoulders as though the frigid touch still lingered on his skin. I longed to reach out for him, but he seemed distant, distracted by the thought of being held by something inhuman.

"Do you think it was our ghost?" I asked quietly.

"What else could have saved me like that?"

I sighed, chewing on the inside of my cheek in thought. "What do we do about Ethan?"

"Nothing," Bodhi replied. "We do nothing. Keep pretending the sun was getting to him. It was a trick of the light. One thing is for sure though."

"What's that?"

He looked down at me, the sun reflecting off of his golden irises. "The ghost is holding up her end of the deal to protect us no matter what."

"A shocking fact considering that she's spent the last two months trying to drive me insane," I said sardonically.

"My point is that she's trying," said Bodhi. "And if we don't want any trouble, we had better put some effort into holding up our end of the bargain. The last thing we need is for her to decide we aren't working hard enough. Is there anything we can do to jumpstart this investigation?"

I walked to the deck chair to collect Caroline's journal. "I imagine the first thing to do is figure out who our spirit actually belongs to."

"And how are we supposed to do that?"

I turned to Bodhi, reaching up to rest my hands on his toned shoulders. "You keep working on the house. Kindly try to avoid any potentially catastrophic scenarios. I'm going to dig into the history of the Winchester house."

He massaged my forearms with his warm, calloused hands. "How?"

"It's time to track down Milo."

13

RESEARCH TRIP

"*We're sorry. The number you have dialed has been disconnected or is no longer in service.*"

With an annoyed huff, I hung up the phone. The same automated message had been aggravating me since the previous morning, despite the fact that I was sure I had the number memorized.

Milo Holmes was the man who had sold us the Winchester house. He was young—far too young to own such a grandiose home—but he had a decent head on his shoulders and was easy to talk to. While Bodhi had immersed himself in tearing apart the Winchester house, I'd updated my blog and spent time with Milo. He had inherited the house from his father, who had bought it at an auction some time before. Other than those scant details, I wasn't familiar with the Winchester house's history. It seemed odd that it had remained vacant for so long. Sure, the fact that the original family had met an untimely ending wasn't exactly a selling point, but successful real estate sales were all about spinning the facts. Or hiding them entirely. Was I supposed to believe that not one person other than Milo's father had taken an interest in buying the Winchester house?

Milo's continued absence was starting to worry me. Usually if I called, he answered his phone on the first ring. I thought about the last time I had seen him. It had been at the house a few days ago. We were eating bagels and cream cheese together in the kitchen.

My stomach tightened as the rest of the memory came back to me. Bodhi arrived home, and I'd practically shoved Milo out the back door to prevent a bloodbath. For some ungodly reason, Bodhi had misconstrued the comfortable camaraderie between me and Milo as something entirely unforgivable. Maybe that was why Milo had distanced himself from me. A pang of resentment echoed through me. Milo's absence meant two things. First, I no longer had a comforting presence to confide in. Second, no one was available to fill in the blanks of the Winchester house's history except me.

It should have been an easy task. Property records were public and generally available online by county. Black Bay, I should not have been shocked to discover, didn't have a website dedicated solely to its local government. Instead, one measly subheading squished between "Visit Black Bay!" and "Things to do!" served as the only point of access to the town's online records, but when I clicked on it, I was immediately disappointed.

Online records are not available for this area. Please visit your local clerk's office to access public records.

"Oh, come on."

There was no other choice but to hobble into town to the library, since Black Bay didn't have a clerk's office, and ask for the hard copies of the property records. I sighed, resigning myself to what was sure to be a slow and tedious trip, and got to my feet.

. . .

AFTER ASSURING Bodhi that there was no need for him to abandon his work in order to drive me into town, I embarked down the footpath at the southeast corner of the house. I kept a leisurely pace, pausing every now and then to give my ankle a break. Though the walking boot helped me get around, I soon second-guessed my decision to refuse Bodhi's ride. By the time I made it into town, my foot was already swollen and throbbing. Thankfully, the library was nearby. With a wince, I made a beeline for it.

There was a line of children waiting to check out books from the sole desk in the library's lobby. I waited patiently behind them, favoring my good foot. One of them, a small brunette girl with black glasses that were far too big for her face, experimentally stepped on the firm toe of my walking boot.

"Does that hurt?" she squeaked, peering up at me from the stack of Beverly Cleary novels in her arms.

"I can't even feel it," I said, smiling down at her. I nodded toward the checkout desk. "It's your turn."

"Oh!"

The little girl's cuteness level faded when she realized she'd forgotten her library card. It took another ten minutes to track down her mother and get her squared away before I was able to approach the librarian myself.

Mrs. Poe was a compact woman in her late sixties. In all honesty, she reminded me quite a bit of an English bulldog, with her squat bowlegs, flat nose, and severe underbite. From my previous encounters with her, I knew that she defended the library books with the same savagery as a guard dog might. She sniffed from desk to desk, scolded children for giggling, and reprimanded adults for using the ancient PCs rather than reading. With any luck, her dedication extended to Black Bay's public records, and I could be in and out of the library within a few minutes.

"Hi," I said brightly to her over the desktop. "May I—?"

She held up her index finger to stop me from talking but said nothing, clicking through a file on her computer screen at a rapid pace. I waited, trying to keep my eyes from rolling toward the ceiling. My ankle was becoming more and more agitated, and if Mrs. Poe didn't address me soon, I was seriously considering taking a seat right there on her desk.

Thankfully, before I could throw a two-year-old-style tantrum, she looked up. "How may I help you, Mrs. Taylor?"

"I need to find the records for the Winchester house," I said hurriedly. "They aren't available online. Does the library have them?"

"Do you have the parcel number?"

"No…"

"It would be much easier with the parcel number."

"I don't have the parcel number," I declared. The boot around my foot felt uncomfortably tight. "Can't you look it up?"

Mrs. Poe glared at me over the frames of her horn-rimmed glasses. "One moment, please."

And then with a deliberate sluggishness, she returned to clicking through her computer. I rolled my eyes and bent down to adjust the Velcro straps around my boot. Behind me, the line to check out books grew longer. Parents spoke in hushed tones to one another, but in the quiet library, there was no mishearing the subject of their conversation. I tapped my fingers impatiently against my thigh, wishing Mrs. Poe would take her eternal dissatisfaction with the world out on someone else.

"The Winchester house, you said?"

"Yes, ma'am."

"The one on the bluff?"

There was only one Winchester house. "Yes, ma'am."

Mrs. Poe squinted at the screen. "According to this, Bailey and Bodhi Taylor currently own the Winchester house."

It took all of my willpower not to upend Mrs. Poe's desk. "Yes, Mrs. Poe. *I'm* Bailey Taylor. You already know this. I'm trying to figure out who owned the house before Milo Holmes."

"Who?"

"Milo Holmes, Mrs. Poe. H-O-L—"

"I can spell, thank you very much, Mrs. Taylor. There is no record of a Milo Holmes ever owning the Winchester house."

I sagged against the desk. "Are you sure?"

"I'm sure."

"Does the library have hard copies of public records available?" I pressed, unwilling to let Mrs. Poe off the hook so quickly.

Mrs. Poe removed her glasses, folded her hands together, and regarded me over the top of the monitor. "If my computer says that there is no record of Milo Holmes, then I'm afraid there is no record of Milo Holmes. Now if you don't mind, Mrs. Taylor, there's a line behind you."

A hook-nosed mother tried to shove past me, setting her child's picture books on Mrs. Poe's desk to check out, but I threw myself in front of her.

"Wait," I said, much to the chagrin of those waiting in line. "You wouldn't happen to have old copies of the *Black Bay Banner* somewhere, would you?"

Mrs. Poe fixed me with a withering stare. I stood my ground.

"Back left corner," called someone from the rear of the line. "Near the history section."

"Thank you!" I cried to whatever savior had come to my

rescue. I flashed Mrs. Poe my biggest smile, and her eye twitched as I limped away.

Past the biographies of previous presidents, I found an entire shelf dedicated to Black Bay's one and only newspaper. Each issue of the *Banner* had been laminated and carefully preserved, stacked one on top of the other in a neat bundle. I shuffled through the most recent ones, ignoring the headings. *New couple in town! Meet Bailey and Bodhi Taylor, house flipping extraordinaires!* Whoever had written the articles had even printed a photo of me and Bodhi from my blog in black and white to incorporate within the article. Apparently, news in Black Bay was so scarce that Bodhi and I warranted the front page.

The articles from the 1990s were less superficial. Back then, before the Winchesters had arrived, the residents of Black Bay were in over their heads. *More employees let go from Powell's Lumber Mill. Numbers in town dwindle as families move elsewhere. Local businesses continue to go belly up.*

Finally, I found what I was looking for. It was an issue from August of 1996. A photo of the Winchester family dominated the entire front page. In fact, the whole issue was dedicated to the Winchesters. One feature detailed Christopher's beneficial effect on the business community in Black Bay. Another praised his wife Elizabeth for all of her volunteer work, including raising funds to build a local animal shelter and creating an annual body-positive beauty pageant to inspire the young women in town. The third page boasted a picture of the Golden Eagles football team with Patrick at the center. I had seen the photo before in Lido's, the restaurant across town that Patrick and his fellow team members were known to frequent after games. Below, the accompanying article lauded Patrick as a hometown hero. I skipped over the quotes from his teammates, afraid to cry over a twenty-year-old event in a place so public as the library.

Caroline's article was short and sweet. The *Banner* had used a picture of her during one of her equestrian competitions. She bent low over her horse's mane as the pair leapt over a log fence, her porcelain features barely visible beneath the lip of her riding helmet. Of all the Winchesters, Caroline had been the most reserved. According to the article, she was a shy yet sharp young woman, but I knew from her journals that she tended to stockpile her scathing remarks, waiting for the opportune moment to unleash them. Those she did not use, she recorded in her daily diary entry. The vague air of the article almost offended me. I felt as though I knew Caroline better than whoever had written her piece for the *Banner*. Just as I made to flip back to the first page, a paragraph near the bottom of Caroline's article caught my eye.

EVERYONE KNEW *Caroline to be a persistent young woman. Previously, the Winchesters spent time on the Hawaiian island of Kauai, where Caroline fell in love with plumerias, the flowers used to make the traditional Hawaiian leis. Despite the fact that plumerias are not native to the Pacific Northwest, Caroline planted a plumeria tree in her own backyard. It is a tribute to her tenacity and brilliance that the plumeria tree still blooms. If you wish to honor Caroline at this weekend's memorial, please order plumeria flowers. The pink ones were her favorites.*

TWO MONTHS AGO, I discovered Caroline's plumeria tree on my own. The garden behind the Winchesters' house was still a wreck—Bodhi and I hadn't found the time to hack through the weeds or mow the jungly grass—but for some curious reason, the plumeria tree and its surrounding area remained immaculately pruned. On more than one occasion, I had found a vase of freshly trimmed plumeria flowers on my bedside table in the master bedroom. Another detail arrived at the front of my mind. Caroline often described her piano lessons in her journal, commiserating that her private instructor would not deign to teach her acid jazz. Once, on a rather bizarre night in the Winchester house, I heard the untuned piano in the office play itself. And like I'd told Bodhi before, the reason I'd found Caroline's journals at all was because her childhood bedroom had come alive, directing me toward the place she had hidden them.

My fingers tightened on the issue of the *Banner*. Could it be? Was the ghost of Caroline Winchester trapped in her family's old house?

I turned back to the first page of the paper, where the Winchesters' collective obituary did nothing to ease my angst.

CHRISTOPHER ALAN WINCHESTER *(48), Elizabeth Rosemary Winchester (45), Patrick Silas Winchester (17), and Caroline Alice Winchester (15) passed away on August 16th, 1996 in a tragic boat accident off the coast of Black Bay, Washington. The Winchesters were dedicated to improving quality of life in the local town through private business, volunteer work, and a collection of positive attitudes that influenced the entire community. Christopher Winchester is survived by his brother, Aaron Winchester of Brooklyn, NY...*

THE ISSUE of the *Banner* that had been printed prior to the Winchesters' memorial paper spoke of the accident in a more clinical tone.

CHRISTOPHER AND ELIZABETH WINCHESTER *were declared DOA*

at the scene of a fatal boat crash Friday evening. The Winches-
ters' well-known sailboat, Artemis, *left the marina around five*
in the afternoon but did not return that night. Sam Williams,
Black Bay resident and a former member of the U.S. Coast
Guard, happened upon the crash in the early hours of Saturday
morning.

"Not sure how it happened," he told the Banner. "The weather
was nice enough. I was out on the bay myself. The rocks around the
bluff are rough though. They should've known better than to try
and sail through there."

Authorities are still searching for the Winchester children, who
were reportedly aboard Artemis *when it ran aground.*

THE NAME SAM WILLIAMS struck a chord with me. I'd heard it before, in a conversation with Ethan a few weeks back.

"Who found them?" I'd asked.

"Retired member of the Coast Guard," Ethan had replied. "Sam Williams. He works in the lumber mill now."

I took pictures of the relevant articles and stacked the old papers on top of one another, haphazardly shoving them back onto the shelf. Mrs. Poe would probably kill me for leaving them in such a disorganized state, but I was in too much of a hurry to care. My ankle trembled as I dashed by the front desk, feeling Mrs. Poe's gaze boring into my back. Outside, I flagged down a passing car. The driver, a woman I recognized as the owner of a local boutique, slowed to a stop and rolled down her window.

"Yes, honey?"

"Any chance you're heading south?" I asked her. "I need a ride to Powell's Lumber Mill. I'd walk, but I don't think my ankle can take it."

She leaned over to push open the passenger door. "No problem. Oh, you poor thing!"

I boosted myself into the seat and closed the door. "Thank you so much. I really appreciate it."

If there was one thing I adored about the locals of Black Bay, excluding Mrs. Poe, it was their unwavering hospitality. The boutique owner, whose name I soon learned was Angela, chatted my ear off about the Winchester house for the five-minute drive across town. I asked her briefly what she knew about the family, but she was only fourteen when the Winchesters died. She'd gone to school with Caroline and Patrick, but didn't remember anything other than Patrick's prowess on the football field. When she idled at the curb in front of the mill, I hopped out gratefully. Angela was nice enough, but she sure talked a lot.

I had yet to visit Ethan's sawmill. I'd only seen it from a distance. It was hard to miss the towering cranes that hauled massive logs across the vast timber yard. Up close, it was even more daunting. Heavy machinery whirred through the extensive yard. Immense piles of logs rose above the dirt like the walls of a wooden fortress. The mill itself was an industrial warehouse, but a smaller building next door looked like some kind of office. I limped toward it, keeping my eyes peeled for potential falling lumber.

Inside, a sturdy man with flushed cheeks wearing a red flannel shirt and a hard hat sat behind a dusty desk, running through some kind of supply checklist. He glanced up as I stumbled in, and I hoped that he would be more accommodating than Mrs. Poe.

"What can I do for you, sweetheart?" he asked in a deep baritone.

"I'm looking for Sam Williams," I said. "Is he here today?"

"Oh, yeah. Sammy's out in the yard." He set down the checklist and reached for the phone. "You need to talk to him or something?"

"Yes sir."

He dialed a number and put the phone to his ear. "Hey, man. Send Sammy up front for me. There's a lovely young woman looking for him." He winked at me as he hung up. "Should be here in a few minutes," he told me. "Have a seat."

I sank into a plastic chair in the corner of the small office with a relieved sigh and ripped the Velcro straps off my walking boot, letting the blood flow back to my ankle. The man behind the desk studied my various bandages with a curious eye, but when he noticed I had caught him looking, he quickly smiled and returned to his work. Soon, the door to the office opened again, and a ridiculously lanky man bowed his head as he stepped through the frame. He swept off his own hard hat to reveal a shock of white blond hair and bright green eyes. He walked right past me, addressing the man in the hard hat instead.

"What's up, Marshall?"

Marshall nodded toward my plastic chair. Sam Williams turned to face me. From his great height, he asked, "Do I know you?"

"I thought everyone knew me," I said before realizing how pompous it sounded. Hurriedly, I strapped the walking boot into place and stood to shake Sam's hand. "I'm Bailey Taylor. My husband and I bought the Winchester house a couple months ago. Is there a place we can talk? I wanted to ask you a few questions, if you have a couple minutes to spare."

"What kind of questions?"

"I run a popular web blog," I said. It was the perfect excuse to dig for information. Everyone knew that *Flipping Out* covered more than just our renovation progress. "I wrote a few posts about the Winchesters, but my readers want to know more. Would you be willing to sit for a quick interview?"

Sam was a man who looked eternally tired. The skin of

his face drooped downward and his mouth angled toward the floor.

"Five minutes," I promised.

Perhaps Sam found it exhausting to fill the innumerable feet between his head and mine with words, because he simply nodded, held the door to the office open for me, and led me to a nearby picnic table in complete silence.

As we sat, I cleared my throat awkwardly. "I was just wondering if you wouldn't mind telling me about the Winchesters' boat crash."

Though his bushy eyebrows lifted in anticipation, he made a hand gesture that I took to mean I should continue.

"You found them that night, right? Christopher and Elizabeth."

His gentle voice barely rose above the noise of the machinery around us. "The next morning."

"And they crashed against the rocks?"

"Yes, ma'am. The front of the boat was ripped to bits."

"Just the front?"

"The back had taken damage too," explained Sam. He rested his elbow on the picnic table, picking at the faded red paint. "I'm not sure how they managed that if they hit the bluff head on."

"Did the Winchesters drown? Or—"

Sam's mouth contorted into a frown. "Mrs. Taylor, I don't mean to be rude, but do you think your readers really want to know about this?"

"Well, I—"

"Because what I saw that morning has haunted me every day for the past twenty years."

In my haste to obtain information, I'd forgotten to consider Sam's feelings. From what I gathered, the crash was dreadful, and if Christopher and Elizabeth were already dead by the time Sam arrived on the scene, I had to have stirred up a slew of bitter memories for him.

"I want to do this story justice," I said. "I'd like to do a series about the Winchesters. It helps to have as much information as possible."

His eyes were doleful, and he continued to strip paint from the picnic table as he resolutely filled me in. "I don't recall what the official cause of death was," he said. "But I imagine both Chris and Lizzie died from their injuries. They hit the bluff at full speed, Mrs. Taylor. There ain't no surviving a crash like that."

I hesitated to push Sam for further knowledge, but the thought of returning to the Winchester house without a head start on the identity of our ghost intimidated me more than risking insensitivity with Sam.

"I heard the weather was fine that day," I said. "No storms or rough waters. Why do you think the Winchesters crashed?"

Sam lifted his enormous shoulders. "The currents up that way are tough to navigate. That's why no one sails near the bluff."

"Then why would Christopher and Elizabeth go there?"

He rubbed his forehead between his forefinger and palm, smearing dirt or oil across his skin. "Mrs. Taylor, I don't have a straight answer for you. And I don't intend to speak poorly of Chris and Liz."

"Why would you speak poorly of them?"

Sam hesitated. He seemed to be choosing his next words carefully. "Everyone knew that the Winchesters loved a good party. They were inclusive too. If there was a shindig at their house, everyone was invited. They had all the best booze. Champagne, scotch, wine. It wasn't a secret that Chris and Lizzie let loose every once in a while. They were never sloppy, but they certainly enjoyed a good buzz."

"You think they were drunk when they crashed?"

"I don't know what I think anymore," replied Sam. He pushed himself up from the picnic table. "Honestly, I try *not* to think about it. But it seems unlikely Chris and Liz would risk sailing toward the rocks with their kids on board if they were both in a sober mindset."

"Speaking of the kids, what happened to them?" I insisted, clumsily getting to my feet and tripping over my boot in the process. "Patrick and Caroline?"

"Not a whisper of them on board," replied Sam. He offered me a hand to help me clamber over the bench.

"But their bodies were never found."

His low voice stuck in his throat. "Must've been thrown over the edge. Like I said, the currents up that way are strong. I suppose they got dragged farther out."

I debated whether or not to mention that I thought neither Patrick or Caroline had ever been on the boat to begin with. My time with Sam was wearing thin. He obviously wasn't comfortable with answering my questions. He drifted toward the lumber yard with every passing second, either eager to return to work or desperate to get away from me. I threw caution to the wind.

"But what if Patrick and Caroline never got on the boat?"

Sam paused and turned to look at me. "Mrs. Taylor. You were not a resident of Black Bay twenty years ago. If you want to raise questions about the nature of the Winchesters' accident, I highly suggest you speak to the police."

And with that, he lumbered off, replacing his hard hat on his head by way of goodbye. I sighed. Maybe coming to the lumber mill had been a bad idea. Once Sam spread the news of our impromptu interview, all of Black Bay would wonder why I was raising questions about the Winchesters. I'd have to publish more blog posts about them to keep up appearances. Not good for keeping our paranormal activity on the down low.

I looked up the road. The bluff was on the opposite side of town, and my ankle was in no mood to make the trip. I doubted the red-faced man in the office was willing to drive me back to the house, but if there was a chance to convince him to at least drop me off at the bottom of the footpath, it might be worth the awkward conversation. I turned toward the office.

And ran smack into Ethan Powell.

14

REUNION

*E*than grinned down at me. He still wore his Powell's Lumber Mill shirt, but here at his actual lumber mill, he didn't fit in as much as I'd expected him to. While the other employees' foreheads dripped with sweat, staining their white work polos, Ethan was cool and dry. As the owner of the mill, he evidently filled a supervisory role rather than joining in on the labor himself.

"Twice in one day," he announced, straightening the collar of his shirt. "If I didn't know better, I'd think you had a little crush on me, darlin'."

I fixed Ethan with a sardonic stare. He barked out a laugh.

"I'm just kidding, Bailey. I know an old dog like me don't have nothing on a young, impressive man like Bodhi."

"Oh, I don't know about that, Ethan." I patted one of his well-defined biceps. "I'm sure there's one or two women in town who would be impressed by your Popeye the Sailor Man build and—what is that? Do you actually have an anchor tattoo?"

Ethan yanked down the sleeve of his shirt to cover the ink. "I was twenty and stupid, darlin'. Make no mistake."

I pursed my lips, trying not to laugh.

"Anyway," he said. "What are you doing down here in my neck of the woods? Shouldn't you be resting that ankle of yours?"

Now that he'd mentioned it, my ankle reminded me that I had abused it all afternoon with an excruciating surge of discomfort. I wrinkled my nose, trying to camouflage the pain. "Bed rest gets boring very quickly. I wanted to see the mill. Bodhi keeps talking about it."

Ethan squinted dubiously at me. "Uh-huh. Is that why you upset Sammy like that? Boredom?"

"Crap." I sheepishly ducked my head. "You saw that?"

"I did indeed."

I picked up the walking boot, balancing like a graceless flamingo on my good foot. "I didn't mean to upset him—"

"Tell you what," interjected Ethan. He offered me a hand. "How about I drive you back to the house and you can fill me in on what you had to say to Sammy. Does that sound all right?"

Anything was better than limping the few miles across town and up the hill. I nodded, and Ethan hoisted my arm over his shoulder, letting me lean into him as he escorted me to his dark blue truck parked around the side of the office building. He opened the passenger door and lifted me inside.

"Thanks," I said, my face burning. I wasn't used to needing so much help.

"Don't mention it. You might want to look into a pair of crutches though. I don't think that boot's doing you much good."

He shut my door, rounded the truck to the driver's side, and hopped in. As he fired up the engine and backed out of the lumber yard, I surveyed the view toward the bay. The water picked up at the edge of the lumber yard, and with the sun on its way back toward the horizon, the bay and the mill glowed a peachy golden color.

"So?" prompted Ethan, peeking left and right before he pulled out onto Black Bay's one and only through road. "Why are you bothering my guys at work?"

"That was never my intention," I said. I rolled down the window to let the breeze play with my hair. "I wanted to know more about the Winchesters' boat crash."

"Why's that?"

Because the homicidal ghost in the Winchester house that probably belonged to Caroline Winchester wanted justice.

"For a few different reasons," I said instead. "I want to focus on the Winchesters for my blog, but there's also something about living in their old house, you know? I've been sidelined with all of these injuries. I can't help Bodhi much as of late. My mind wanders."

We rode past the library where Mrs. Poe was locking up the front doors.

"Bailey, the last thing I want to do is scold you for being curious," said Ethan, his gaze fixed on the road as he piloted through the pedestrians crossing the town square. "But you're digging into old wounds here. The Winchesters may have passed nearly twenty years ago, but the town remembers it as if it were yesterday."

"I know—"

"I'm not sure you do," he said in a tone that was firm but pleasant. "Everyone who lives here owes their livelihoods to the Winchesters, including Sammy. Can you imagine what it was like for all of us when we realized that the people who had made it possible to keep our homes ended up dead for no apparent reason?"

"I didn't think of that," I admitted, trying to ignore the tightening pressure of guilt in my chest.

"And that's not your fault," Ethan reassured me. He waved

to a young couple piloting a double-wide baby stroller through the crosswalk. "You didn't experience it firsthand. I can imagine it would be hard to understand the collective grief we went through."

"I guess that's what I'm trying to do though," I said. A small hand flung a milk bottle out of the baby stroller, and I grinned as the dad chased it across the road. "I just want a better understanding of the Winchesters themselves."

"You might do better to focus on their lives then, rather than their deaths," suggested Ethan.

"Where were you?" I asked suddenly, turning to him. "When you found out about the boat accident. Or is it callous of me to ask? You don't have to answer."

The family finally cleared the crosswalk and the truck continued on its way through town.

"No, it's all right," said Ethan. "Honestly? I was hungover."

I elbowed him playfully. "Tore up the town on Friday nights, did ya?"

"Not quite," grumbled Ethan. For the first time since I'd met him, his demeanor darkened. The dimming light in the cab of the truck bounced shadows off of his usually cheerful features. "I spend that whole night arguing with my fiancée."

"Your fiancée?"

"That confused look on your face is well-placed," he said, glancing my way. "We never married. High school sweethearts don't tend to stick, I'm afraid."

"So then that morning—"

"Was the worst morning of my life," finished Ethan. The truck bobbed up the road into the woods at the base of the bluff. "Lost my girl. Then, when I heard about the Winchesters, I had a nervous breakdown and crashed my truck."

His voice hitched in a way that had nothing to do with the bumpy dirt road beneath the truck's tires. He fell quiet.

"I'm sorry," I said. "That you had to go through all of that. It must've been really tough."

Ethan gave a mighty sniff. "You've no idea. That's why it's best to leave well enough alone. Not everyone wants to talk about it."

We fell silent. The trees swallowed the rumble of the truck's engine as we wound our way up the hill. I wondered what it would have been like to have lived in Black Bay all those years ago. To wake up one morning and realize that the best thing that had ever happened to the town had vanished without reason. It wasn't fair. That I knew from my own experience. Death was never fair. It took who it wanted, young or old, without regard or mercy for those left on earth. That was something I would never understand.

At long last, we arrived in the front yard of the Winchester house. Twilight beckoned, and the construction crew had gone home for the day. I hoped Bodhi was inside. I didn't have the courage to spend time alone with our avenging angel, if that's what she was.

"Need me to walk you to the door?" Ethan offered as the truck idled.

I gingerly stepped to the ground. "No, I think I'll be all right."

"Alrighty then. Take care of yourself, Bailey."

"You too, Ethan."

"And get off that foot," he called through the open window, pulling a wide turn to face the road again.

"I will."

As I crossed the yard, the rich scent of garlic and olive oil wafted from one of the open windows. Bodhi was cooking again. I smiled, picking up the pace as much as my booted ankle would allow. I couldn't remember the last time Bodhi made dinner for us.

"Bailey?"

My heart leapt as a lanky figure emerged from the shadows beyond the house. For a second, some instinctive impulse told me to bolt for the safety of the Winchesters' front door, but as the figure solidified into a familiar face, relief flooded through me.

"Milo!"

I rushed toward him, surprising myself by swinging my arms around his neck and pulling him into a hug. His thick hair fell forward, tickling my cheek.

"Oomph," he grunted, patting me tentatively on the back. "Hi."

I released him, and he automatically shucked his honey-colored hair back into place. "Sorry. Where have you been? I was worried about you."

"I had to take care of something out of town."

But Milo lacked something that evening. He was pale, a noticeable difference from his usual healthy tan, and the routine bounce that I'd come to expect with his every step was unmistakably absent.

"I tried to call you," I said, squinting in the moonlight for other signs of what might be ailing him. "Your phone's been disconnected."

"Really?" He reached into his pocket for his cell. "I haven't had any problems. Try again."

"All right, but I'm telling you, it won't work."

I dialed his number. Almost immediately, his phone lit up. He swiped across the screen to answer it.

"Hello?" he said with a mischievous grin. "This is Milo."

"You're annoying," I said into my own phone. The echo from his end of the line bounced back to me. We hung up. "Are you okay?"

"Never better. Why?"

"You just look a little... off."

He avoided my scrutinizing stare. "Must be coming down

with something. Did you need something? You said you'd called."

The sudden shift in his tone bewildered me. Milo and I had always been pleasant and relaxed around each other, but today he was stiffly professional.

"Yeah. Um…" I searched for the right words. "I had a weird thing happen down at the library today. They don't have any records for the house on file."

Milo made a sound like an irritated bumble bee. "Did you speak with Mrs. Poe?"

"Yes."

He shook his head. "That woman. I swear she's been working at that library longer than she's been alive. I'm not convinced she even knows how to use a computer, let alone search a database for specific information. Is there any particular reason you wanted the property records? I could probably answer your questions for you."

My ankle had begun to ache again, and I longed for Bodhi's cooking and the cozy interior of the Winchesters' kitchen, even if it was under construction at the present moment.

"I just wondered who owned the house before your father," I said.

Milo looked taken aback. "No one did."

"Ever?"

"Not that I know of."

"When did your father buy it?"

"I don't know. When I was a kid."

"So ten years ago? Fifteen?"

He rustled the sleeves of his windbreaker like an agitated bird fluffing its feathers. "I have no idea, Bailey."

"Shouldn't you?" I insisted.

"What do you want me to say?" he demanded. There was an abrupt animosity in his inflection, so acidic that I actually took a step away from him. "I told you when I sold you the house. I never wanted anything to do with it. My father didn't exactly give me a choice when he died. I wish he'd never owned the damn thing. Are you happy now?"

I held my hands up in a symbol of defeat. "Fine. You could've just told me that. I didn't need the Stanley Kowalski level outburst."

"You asked."

Milo glared angrily at me. The moon was slim, offering little light. With the uncomfortable effect of Milo's baffling conniption palpable in the air between us, I had no desire to spend another minute with him.

"I'm going inside," I announced.

But when I took a step toward the front door, Milo intercepted my path.

"Wait, Bailey."

"What?"

"I'm sorry," he said. He reached for my hands but I tucked them behind my back. "If you'll just let me explain—"

"You know, Milo. I'm already trying to patch things up with my husband. I don't need extra drama from someone who I thought was my friend."

"We *are* friends—"

"I'm going inside," I said again, this time more firmly. I sidestepped Milo. "You should go home. Get some sleep. Evidently, you need it."

I left him there in the front yard, feeling like an ass as I shut the door on his blanched, dejected face, but there was no excuse for his immature behavior. All I wanted was some additional information about the house. If Milo had baggage with his deceased father, that was between him and whatever therapist he employed. I wasn't a punching bag. Milo would have to take his impulsive aggression out on someone else.

In the kitchen, Bodhi sautéed fresh spinach in one skillet

and seared chicken in another. He had covered the majority of the room with clean white sheets, keeping the construction dust out of the food. The muscles in his shoulders flexed as he maneuvered the spinach around without any utensils, skillfully flicking his wrist to make the greens dance in the pan. Somewhere, he'd found one of Elizabeth Winchester's old aprons and had secured it around his waist with the lacy pink straps.

"Hey there," he said when he noticed me. "What was that all about outside?"

"Did you hear?"

"Just the headlines," Bodhi replied. He filled a glass with white wine and handed it to me. "Milo's back, huh?"

"Yeah, and in the pissiest of moods."

He returned to the stovetop. "Strange considering you and him are usually so buddy-buddy."

There was a hint of resentment in this observation. I set my wine glass down on the countertop. "You don't still think he and I are involved, do you?"

Bodhi's focus remained fixed on the cookware. "If you say you're not involved, then I believe you're not involved."

"We're not involved."

"Okay." The chicken sizzled as Bodhi poured wine into the frying pan. "Did you find anything out about the house? Or our lovely guest?"

"Not really. Although—"

At once, the frying pan violently upended itself, sending the scalding chicken skyward. Bodhi leapt away from the stovetop, rocketing into me and knocking my wine glass to the floor. As it shattered and the liquid seeped into the toes of my walking boot, the stove flared to life. Fire erupted from each of the four burners, scorching the spinach and burning the fallen chicken to a crisp. Thick, acrid smoke billowed upward, and the fire alarm overhead screamed a warning. Then, just as quickly, the stove shut off completely, bringing the spectacle to an abrupt end.

"That was rude," Bodhi shouted over the screeching alarm.

"And she didn't even let me finish." I glanced up at the ceiling, addressing our invisible entity. "Do you mind?"

The fire alarm shut off with an annoyed chirp.

"Thanks. Bodhi, open a window so we don't choke."

Bodhi propped open the back door and lifted the window above the sink. He used a dish towel to waft the smoke out into the garden. "Apparently, we're not eating tonight."

As if in response, a droplet of hot oil shot out of the pan of ruined spinach and landed on Bodhi's arm.

"Ow! Enough already!"

"As I was saying," I said, raising my voice. I was ill-suited to communicating with the dead. Everything was so much simpler when you had facial expressions to take visual cues from. "I did find a few articles on the Winchesters at the library. They didn't tell me anything that we didn't already know, but I think I have a guess as to who our house guest is."

"And?" Bodhi asked, coughing in the cloud of smoke.

I consulted the ceiling again. "Are you Caroline Winchester?"

All was silent. Bodhi continued to clear the air in the kitchen, but other than that, nothing moved. The frying pans didn't stir. The stovetop remained extinguished. Bodhi and I exchanged anxious glances.

"Really?" I said, throwing my hands up in frustration. "Now you're quiet? Look, I know we promised to help you, but it would be a whole lot easier if we knew *who* you were or *how* you ended up trapped here in the first place."

Bodhi watched open-mouthed as I paced back and forth

through the kitchen, having a conversation with myself. "This just keeps getting weirder and weirder."

"All I'm saying is that you can't throw a temper tantrum and then not bother to help us," I scolded the smoky kitchen. "We're not wizards. We don't magically know what you're thinking."

"Bailey, it's no use—"

Bodhi's voice cut off. His limbs stiffened, and he dropped the dish towel in a heap on the floor. Then, like something out of a horror flick, his brown eyes turned black.

"Don't you dare," I thundered. I took Bodhi by his shoulders and shook him. "You want to communicate with me, you're going to have to find a different way to do it. Do you hear me?"

Bodhi's head rolled back on his neck.

"I mean it!" I shouted, steadying Bodhi against the kitchen counter. "You want my help? It's not going to happen unless you let him go. No more of this possession crap! That was our deal."

But Bodhi's tongue lolled out, his lips opening and closing as if whatever was using his body couldn't quite figure out how to operate his vocal chords.

"Let him go," I demanded. "Let him go, or I am marching us both out of this house. You can't leave, right? You'll be left here to rot. I'll give you a grand total of three seconds, and then I'm out of here. Three, two, one—"

The door to the garden slammed shut. At the same time, Bodhi jerked back to consciousness, his eyes clearing to their regular brown. I sighed with relief as he sagged against me, his breathing ragged and uneven.

"Perhaps this may come as a shock," he said, his voice shaking. "But I would like to avoid similar experiences in the future."

I passed him the bottle of wine. He took a swift swig. "I

don't think she knows how to talk to us," I said. "She can't even use you to do it. We're going to have to figure something else out."

"Do you ever wonder what people might think if they knew we spoke so nonchalantly about my own demonic possession?"

"I don't think she's a demon."

Something rattled in the far corner of the room. Bodhi jumped, but it was only a teacup jiggling in its saucer.

"Was that there before?"

"I didn't have any tea today," responded Bodhi.

Carefully, I crossed the kitchen to examine the trembling china. As soon as I got close enough to touch the teacup, it stopped shaking. In the hallway, the analog clock—the battery of which had been dead for who knew how long—tick-tocked at a pace far quicker than seconds.

"Is that—?" began Bodhi, staring down the hallway.

"She wants us to follow her," I confirmed.

The hands on the clock began to spin in opposite directions.

Bodhi's face slackened. "This ought to be good."

Together, we inched down the hallway. The clock shook vigorously until it rocketed right off its nail on the wall and landed with a crash on the floor. Both the minute and the hour hands stopped spinning, pointing toward the basement door. Bodhi and I exchanged nervous glances.

"Maybe we should come up with a safe word," Bodhi said. There was no hint of amusement behind the suggestion, though I was tempted to laugh. "Something short and sweet. Like taco. Do you think she would go for that?"

The clock shot to the end of the hallway and ricocheted off the basement door.

"How do we know you won't lock us down there again?" I asked the empty corridor.

Something small and shiny flew out from beneath the door to the office, where Caroline's piano still waited for her to return to it. I knelt down to inspect the object. It was a key.

"I think we're making progress," I said to Bodhi.

"Speak for yourself," he muttered. "Easy for you to say when you're not the puppet master's plaything."

We tiptoed down the hall. The door to the basement swung open, and the fickle overhead light flickered on. I peered down the stairs. The landing was dark and foreboding. The hair on the back of my neck stood at attention.

The light blinked off and back on again.

"Well," I said, gripping the handrail tightly. "Here goes nothing."

15

THE SÉANCE

*B*odhi steadied me with a firm hand as we descended into the basement. The handrail was loose. It bounced against the wall if I put too much weight on it, so I let go and let Bodhi guide me downward. The door at the top of the stairs mercifully remained open, and the shaft of light from the hallway served as a reminder that the first floor of the house, though still hair-raising, offered some kind of retreat into normalcy. It was distinctly different from our last foray into the basement just a couple days ago. There wasn't much comfort in the thought, considering the entity that had savagely ambushed us then was the same one that encouraged us into the cellar now, but I hoped that she sensed our loyalty. Or, at least, my loyalty. Bodhi remained tense and rigid, ready to bolt up the stairs at the first sign of trouble.

"Relax," I murmured, squeezing his hand.

"I'll relax when we finally sell this damn house," he whispered back. "It feels like we've been here for an eternity already, and all we've done so far is demo the living room and kitchen area."

The steps creaked beneath our feet. We both paused, waiting for another direction from the invisible entity, but none was forthcoming. I inched forward.

"We knew this house was going to take us longer to renovate," I said.

"Yeah, but we didn't know we'd be playing Ghostbusters while we did it," he hissed. "And at least they were armed with proton packs."

"Something tells me our house guest wouldn't take kindly to being chased away with a proton pack."

We reached the bottom of the stairs. My eyes worked to adjust to the dingy moonlight filtering in from the shattered storm window. Bodhi took a flashlight from his pocket and shone it around the room. Everything looked the same as it had the last time we had visited. The Winchesters used the space as a storage area, a place to dump all of the junk that they didn't use on a daily basis. Cardboard boxes overflowing with odds and ends from different aspects of the Winchesters' lives balanced precariously on top of one another. Old, broken sailing equipment littered the concrete foundation. A child's pink bike lay on its side like a bird with a broken wing. In the far corner, a glass door marked the entryway to a once-luxurious wine cellar.

"Now what?" asked Bodhi.

The pink bike righted itself, settling on its training wheels. Bodhi and I jumped back as it trundled across the concrete, joyfully tooting the shiny bell that balanced on its handlebars. It rolled toward the back end of the room. As it steered itself through the towers of the Winchesters' leftover miscellany, Bodhi nudged me from behind.

"What?"

He indicated the tricky maze of rubbish before us. "I can only assume we're supposed to follow it."

"Then you go first!"

"Me? It likes you better!"

"I have a broken ankle! Besides, you're the man of the house."

"Okay, first of all, your ankle is only fractured. Second, that's sexist."

"What are we, twelve years old?" I shoved him in front, ignoring the smirk that played about his lips. "Just go."

With a groan, he stumbled forward. Somewhere beyond the stacked boxes, the bicycle gave a happy honk. "Oh, shut up," Bodhi ordered.

We plucked our way through the mess, trying not to disrupt any of the haphazardly stored items. I brushed by a small dog kennel, jumping when a rogue wire caught the sleeve of my shirt. Bodhi calmly detached me, and we met the pink bike near the door of the wine cellar.

"She wants wine?" Bodhi asked, cupping his hands to the glass to peek into the cellar. "Oh my God, this thing is still stocked."

"I don't think it's the wine cellar she's interested in."

"And you know that how?"

I pointed. The bicycle rolled back and forth, repeatedly bumping into a small wooden cabinet adjacent to the door of the wine cellar.

"Damn," sighed Bodhi. "I was hoping we could bond over a nice vintage red."

I knelt down, unlatched the door to the cabinet, and swung it wide. I wasn't sure what I had been expecting—after all, I'd never had the pleasure of interacting with the dead before—but a plethora of board games was not at the top of my list. The cabinet was chock full of them, from several collector's versions of Monopoly to Battleship to Clue. Everything was covered in a thick layer of dust and cobwebs. I pulled my shirt up over my nose, willing myself not to sneeze.

"I could use another clue here," I told the bicycle.

In the cabinet, a faded box rustled forward. I took hold of it, carefully maneuvering it out from underneath the mountain of other board games. Bodhi used the tail of his shirt to sweep the grime off the top. As the brand name printed on the cardboard became visible, we both moaned aloud. It was an original Ouija board.

"Seriously?" I asked, lifting the lid of the box. Inside, the shabby board smelled of must and mildew.

As if in apology, the locked door to the wine cellar sprang open. Without hesitation, Bodhi walked in to inspect the Winchesters' stash.

"All right," I said. "How should we do this?"

I shook the Ouija board out of its box. The pointer piece rocketed out and hit the floor, but before I could pick it up, it skidded away and settled in the only spot on the concrete floor that wasn't obscured by moldy cardboard boxes. Nearby, a plastic package tore open and spilled out a handful of ivory pillar candles.

"Candles. Really?"

"Maybe she needs the energy," suggested Bodhi, his voice echoing from the depths of the boundless cellar.

"Ask and you shall receive," I muttered. I set the Ouija board in the middle of the floor, placed the pointer on top, then arranged the pillar candles in a loose circle around the board. "I don't suppose you have a lighter?"

A packet of grill matches fell from a close shelf. At least our spirit was accommodating. I picked up the box, struck a match, and lit the candles one by one. They quivered inconsistently, as though our ghostly guest was in fact drawing strength from the flames. Bodhi emerged from the cellar, a bottle of scotch in one hand.

"I think this whiskey costs more than my life," he said, surveying my handiwork.

"So we're going to drink it?"

"The Winchesters certainly aren't coming back for it."
Bodhi peeled the wax off the mouth of the bottle, unscrewed
the cap, and sniffed the liquor. "Whoa, buddy."

There, in the haunted basement of the Winchester house,
I felt closer to Bodhi than I had in years. In the last few days,
something had shifted between us. Before, we were cold and
distant, walking on eggshells around each other to make sure
we never said or did anything that might set the other
person off. But the spirit of the Winchester house had made
us a team again. It had been a long time since I'd seen this
lighthearted, whimsical side of him, ready to respond to any
instance with a joke. I missed it, even if it was inspired by the
mystifying events that occurred inside the Winchester
house.

The candles nearly extinguished themselves. It seemed
the third party in the room was getting impatient.

"Let's get this over with," I said, taking Bodhi by the hand.
We sat cross-legged on the ground, and I picked up the
tattered instruction pamphlet for the Ouija board. I read the
directions out loud. "Place the board upon the laps of two
persons, lady and gentleman preferred, with the small table
upon the board."

Bodhi sipped from the scotch bottle, grimaced, and
offered the handle to me. "I'm not sure we need the instructions when we know the spirit we're trying to reach is
already in the room."

I pondered the bottle. "What the hell." I took a swig, shuddering as the potent liquid smoldered down my throat.

Bodhi scooched toward me until our knees touched,
settling the Ouija board on our laps. He picked up the
pointer and held the clear bubble up to his eyes before
placing it down on the board. "Here goes nothing, right?"

I consulted the instructions for good measure. "We're

supposed to assign one person to ask the questions. I guess that's me."

"Fine by me," said Bodhi. He took another sip of scotch. "Are we ready to do this?"

I nodded resolutely. Together, we bent over the board and placed our fingers on the pointer piece. The candles flared, the flames darting higher.

"Okay," I said, trying to keep my voice from shaking. "Um, let's start with something easy. Are you male or female?"

Almost immediately, an icy touch glazed over the back of my hands. I yanked my fingers away from the board with a yelp. Bodhi tilted backward, knocking one of the candles over.

"What?" he demanded. His fingers remained courageously on the pointer.

"You didn't feel that?" I asked, picking up the candle before it could light a box of linens on fire. "Something touched me."

"I didn't feel anything," Bodhi said. "I told you that she likes you better. Let's try again. And don't panic this time. You probably scared her."

"Oh, *I* scared *her*." Nevertheless, I adopted my previous position, my fingers trembling. "I promise not to overreact this time. Are you male or female?"

Once more, the glacial fingers covered mine. I squeezed my eyes shut, willing myself not to jerk away. The pointer moved across the board, hovering over the printed "no."

"I guess spirits don't adhere to gender roles," observed Bodhi with an inquisitive arch to his eyebrows.

"Or I didn't ask the correct question," I suggested. I tried again. "Are you a female?"

The invisible hands guided mine again, and the pointer crossed over to the "yes" side of the board.

"So you were right about that," I told Bodhi. He nodded

appreciatively. I chewed on my lip, wondering what to ask next. There was no good place to start. I wanted answers to so many questions. "Who are you?"

The board remained unmoving.

"Too much, too soon?" Bodhi murmured. "Maybe she doesn't want us to know who she is yet. Ask what she wants."

I took a deep breath. "Okay. What is it that you want from us? How are we supposed to help you?"

"Don't overwhelm her."

"Since when did you become a ghost whisperer?" I asked him fiercely.

The pointer piece drifted, and we stopped bickering to glance down at the board. The eye settled over a letter.

"J."

It moved again and paused. Then again, spelling out a single word.

"U-S-T-I-C-E."

"Justice," said Bodhi. "For what?"

"Or whom," I added. I spoke to the board again. "Did you live in Black Bay?"

The pointer moved to the "yes" before drifting back to a neutral position.

"Did someone in Black Bay hurt you?"

Yes.

Bodhi shifted closer to me, and our foreheads touched over the board. "Now we're getting somewhere."

"Who hurt you?" I asked.

The board was still.

"Okay then. How were you hurt?"

No answer.

I heaved a sigh. "Let's try something else. Did you know the Winchesters?"

Yes.

"Are you aware that this is their house?"

Yes.

"Did one of the Winchesters hurt you?"

No.

A bead of sweat rolled into my eye. I blinked, trying to clear it from my vision. I hadn't realized how hot the basement felt. Bodhi's skin was slick too, but my hands were still freezing cold. The candle flames flickered again.

"There's got to be a faster way to do this," Bodhi murmured, wiping his forehead on the sleeve of his shirt. "I feel like I'm sitting in a sauna."

I had plenty of questions, but there was no delicate way to ask them and the candles were burning low. Was there a time limit on how long you could use a Ouija board?

I dove into the deep end. "Are the Winchester children still alive?"

The pointer shifted. No.

My heart sank. There went my last shred of hope that the Winchester children had somehow escaped the tragedy that had befallen their parents. My throat tightened as I asked the next question. "Are you one of the Winchester children?"

There was a moment of stillness during which I thought the board wasn't going to answer. The spirit seemed to be thinking about how much information she wanted to afford us.

"We aren't going to hurt you," I said quietly. "We're trying to help. Tell us. Are you one of the Winchester children?"

After an agonizing pause, the frigid fingers guided my hands to the upper left hand corner of the board.

Yes.

"Caroline," I breathed. The candlelight flashed. A confirmation of sorts. "Did you give me your journals?"

Yes.

"Are there clues to who hurt you in the journals?"

A pause. Yes.

Suddenly, the candles extinguished themselves and the cold caress vanished from the tops of my hands. The basement plunged into darkness. A weight lifted from my shoulders, as though something heavy had been sitting there unnoticed.

"What just happened?" I asked Bodhi. In the gloom, only the whites of his eyes were visible.

"Maybe she burned herself out."

I felt his fingers leave the board. He fiddled with something, then the beam of his flashlight shone into my eyes. He swept the light around the room, but nothing stirred, not even the pink bicycle. Experimentally, I jiggled the pointer piece. Nothing happened.

"I guess you're right."

Bodhi held the flashlight between his teeth as he carefully packed up the Ouija board and put it back with the other games in the cabinet. "At least we found out one thing for sure. Our ghost is Caroline Winchester, and she has a bone to pick with someone in town."

I pushed myself up from the concrete, groaning as my knees stretched and popped. "But who would hurt the Winchester kids? Everyone in Black Bay loved them."

Bodhi linked my arm through his elbow, leading me to the stairs. "I guess we only got one side of the story. God, I'm exhausted. And starving. If Caroline really has retired for the night, do you think it's safe to turn the burners back on?"

Upstairs, the smoke had finally cleared out of the kitchen, but the stove and the floor were still covered in charred chicken, blackened spinach, and burned oil. Bodhi deposited me on a chair at the folding card table at which we had been eating most of our meals, poured me a new glass of wine, and got to work tidying the kitchen. I wanted to help, but between my day researching the Winchesters in town and the impromptu séance downstairs, all I could do was rest my forehead in my hands and focus on not falling asleep right there at the card table.

"What do we do now?" I asked as Bodhi threw the ruined chicken in the garbage can.

"Have you read Caroline's diaries?"

"Not all of them."

"I'd work through those first."

I massaged my temples with the tips of my fingers. "You know what this means, right? If we believe Caroline?"

"I'm not following."

"It means that the Winchesters didn't die accidentally," I explained. "Or at least the kids didn't. Don't you realize what she was implying?"

Bodhi froze as the realization hit him, the frying pan poised beneath the running water of the kitchen sink. "You think that someone murdered them."

Outside, a storm had rolled in while we were downstairs. The toiling skies opened up, and a torrential wave of rain enveloped the house. Thunder rumbled in the distance, and the roar of the water below was so loud that we could hear it clearly from the kitchen.

"Yeah," I said, gazing absentmindedly through the window above the sink, watching the world turn to gray. "I think someone murdered them. But you know what's worse?"

"There's worse?"

I looked at Bodhi. "According to Caroline, the murderer is alive and well."

Bailey and Bodhi: Flipping Out

Hello, flippers! It's a rainy morning here in Black Bay, but that won't stop us from making progress on this house. Before I talk about how knocking the wall down between the kitchen and the living room really opens the place up, I have to fill you in on my expert levels of clumsiness. Would you all believe that I fractured my ankle falling down the basement stairs? Bodhi drew architecture designs all over my cast, which makes the neon yellow plaster and the accompanying walking boot slightly less garish, but be warned! DIY is not always friendly.

Much to my chagrin, my ankle has made it more or less impossible for me to help Bodhi with the renovations. I've now resigned myself to cleaning up the rooms we haven't started work on yet. Believe it or not, we still haven't gotten rid of all the Winchesters' things. Normally, we would toss it all in the dumpster, but I feel like the Winchesters deserve better than that. As such, I've posted pictures of some of the cool things I've found in the last few weeks, so click here if you're interested in that.

I've also begun writing articles for a small side blog entirely dedicated to the Winchesters. I know this is a little off brand, but quite a few of you have expressed interest in the finest family of Black Bay. I've been talking to the locals about what life was like when the Winchesters were around. Let me know if you like the articles, and I'll do my best to fill you in on all things Winchester related.

Happy flipping!
  Bailey

In the morning, though the thunderstorm had passed, the clouds loitered above the bay. I set aside my laptop after publishing my blog post. It was starting to feel more like a diary than an update for our renovations. Maybe that was a side effect of reading Caroline's journals.

Bodhi slept soundly at my side. For a few minutes, I watched his back rise and fall with his breath as he lay on his stomach, a pillow propped beneath his chest. Delicately, I played with one of his dark curls, trying not to wake him. He stirred anyway. Once, it had been impossible to wake Bodhi with an atomic bomb. Now, he woke to the tiniest sound or slightest movement.

"What is it?" he slurred, rolling over. "What's wrong?"

"Shh. Nothing. Go back to sleep."

But the gray morning light had made its way in through the window. Bodhi pushed himself upright, rubbing his eyes with his fists. "I'm already up."

He turned to look at me. In the small bed, there wasn't much room to space out. We were only inches apart.

"Hi," he murmured, his eyes flickering sleepily toward my lips.

"Hi."

Torturously slow, Bodhi leaned in. My breath quickened as I met him halfway. We fit ourselves together, scarcely moving as our mouths met. We kissed sleepily. Bodhi touched my cheek as he pulled away, smiling gently.

"What are you up to today?" he asked.

I pushed his curls out of his eyes. "I thought I'd see if there was anything worth digging up in that mess of a basement."

"By yourself?"

"Yes. It shouldn't be a problem. But first, I was wondering if you'd be willing to do something with me."

"What's that?"

I hesitated, unsure of whether or not my request would upset him. "Will you come to the Winchesters' graves with me?"

Bodhi ducked his head, hiding his face behind a pillow, and mumbled, "I don't know about that."

"Look, I know that it's a sore subject," I said. "But now that we know Caroline is still around, I feel like I have to go. To pay my respects."

Bodhi's voice was muffled in the sheets. "I haven't been to a cemetery since—"

"I know."

He lay silently. I didn't know if he was pondering his decision or deciding on the best method of telling me no.

"You don't have to go," I said hurriedly. I slipped out from under the covers. "If you're not ready, then that's okay."

"Hey." Bodhi took me by the hand before I could escape from the small room and drew me closer to the bed. I stood between his knees, resting my hands on his broad shoulders. "I'll go."

"Are you sure?"

"No, but I'll go."

We were taking baby steps, but baby steps were better than not moving at all.

BEFORE WE LEFT, I went out into the garden and plucked a handful of flowers from the plumeria tree. Then, since my ankle had swelled to twice its normal size due to my exploits the day before, Bodhi drove us down the hill and into town. The cemetery was tucked behind Black Bay's small church. We parked on the curb and let ourselves into the short chain-link fence that bordered the yard. The headstones were small and modest, appropriately sized for the limited space behind the church. As we approached the first set of graves, Bodhi slipped his hand into mine.

"Henry and Maria Powell," Bodhi read off as he inspected a headstone. "Ethan's parents?"

I checked the dates. "Yup. His grandparents are here too. I guess the Powells have always lived in Black Bay."

"It's kind of sad though," said Bodhi. "He's the last one left."

We moved along, taking our time through the yard instead of searching specifically for the Winchesters. Even so, when we finally happened upon their headstones, there was no mistaking who they belonged to. Whoever had made arrangements for the Winchesters had ordered the largest markers available. An opulent concrete cross indicated their plot of land and Christopher's final resting place, beside which three slightly smaller crosses had been designated to Elizabeth, Patrick, and Caroline.

I knelt to place the bouquet of plumerias at the base of Caroline's cross. Beside me, Bodhi's hand shook as he reached out to trace the names carved into the stone.

"It's bizarre, isn't it?" he asked. "The kids aren't even really down there. The town had to bury empty boxes. What a mess."

"I don't think that would've made it any easier," I said, swallowing hard. In my experience, it was harder to watch a miniature casket lower into the dirt than an empty one.

"I never said that."

I stood up, slipping my hand into Bodhi's again, and leaned my head against his shoulder.

"You had another nightmare last night," he informed me. He stroked my hair, his calloused fingers catching in the short strands. "Did you know that?"

"No, I don't remember. Did I wake you?"

"Yes, but that's okay. Do you have plans to see Dr. Marx again?"

"Nothing definite," I answered. "The first time I met her, she said we'd schedule an appointment in a few weeks to check up on how I'm doing with the anti-depressants."

"Do you think—?"

Bodhi trailed off. When I glanced up at him, I noticed his focus had wandered. He stared up at the cloudy sky, watching a flock of birds chirp to each other as they flew in formation over the bell tower of the church.

"Do I think what?"

He looked down at me. "Do you think maybe we should go talk to her together?"

My heart swelled, flooding me with warmth, but I tapered off the flow of emotions, afraid to scare Bodhi off with any kind of exuberant reaction. "If you'd like to. Absolutely."

He kissed my forehead, hugging me closer. "I think I'd like to."

"Okay then."

We stood at the Winchesters' graves for a little while longer, even as a fine drizzle began to fill the air with a chilly mist. Then, when we were ready, we walked back to the truck.

16

FAMILY FUN

*U*nwilling to break the peaceful spell between us, Bodhi and I stopped at Black Bay's local coffee-house, the Sanctuary, for a late breakfast. As usual, the café bustled with activity, but we managed to squeeze into a cozy table by the foggy front windows. The Sanctuary's owner, a middle-aged woman named Ava, soon dropped by to greet us.

"Hello, you two!" she said brightly. "We haven't seen the pair of you order anything but coffee to-go since your first day in town. Did you find a place with better hotcakes or something?"

"Of course not," Bodhi assured her. I hid a smile. Though the Sanctuary's hotcakes were heavenly, they didn't hold a candle to Bodhi's blueberry batter. "We've just been busy. Got a lot to do up at the house."

"I imagine so," she said. "How's it coming?"

"Very slowly."

"You make sure to invite me up once it starts coming together. Hell, the whole town will want to see how you manage to spruce up that old house. You might have to throw a party!"

Bodhi caught my eye, and I knew we were thinking the same thing. I doubted Caroline would stand for the entire town of Black Bay visiting her house, especially if one of the locals was the reason she ended up dead in the first place.

"We'll see," I said politely.

"I can't wait." Ava took an order pad and a pen from the front pocket of her forest green apron. "Now what can I get started for the lovely couple?"

"Coffee. In a vat."

"And a blueberry muffin to share," added Bodhi. "I'm feeling a bit peckish."

"Coming up."

As Ava strolled away to place our orders, I looked around the cramped café. It was a Sunday, and the early morning churchgoers who'd already been to mass took up most of the tables in the middle of the restaurant. At the countertop, rowdy teenagers flung sugar packets at one another, dodging misfires and spilling orange juice. A baby fussed in the corner as his restless mother tried to soothe him with a pacifier. Bodhi and I sat quietly, people-watching in comfortable silence.

Soon, the door to the Sanctuary opened again. A gaggle of small girls danced in, accompanied by a few smiling chaperones. The girls wore flower crowns of daisies, marigolds, and baby's breath on their heads, which from the looks of the smushed petals, the elementary schoolers had weaved themselves. They skipped through the seated patrons, babbling brightly and handing out colorful flyers.

"Come to the summer festival," one particularly blonde rugrat sang as she passed by our table. She dropped a flyer between us and waved to Bodhi. "Hi mister. Funnel cakes and cotton candy and snow cones. Do you like cotton candy?"

"I sure do," replied Bodhi with a wink.

"Me too, but only if it's pink. You know I'm going to be dancing around the maypole this year."

"That's lovely, but it's August already."

"So?"

And with that silly declaration, the little girl bounced off. "Come to the summer festival, but you can only eat the blue cotton candy!"

"Excellent advertising strategy," Bodhi laughed as he watched her pirouette toward the other end of the café.

"Flawless," I agreed.

I picked up the flyer. The summer festival was set for a Saturday afternoon the following weekend, and it did indeed promise a whole host of sugary treats. But in addition to the maypole dance, live music performances, and a flag football tournament, the flyer also advertised something called "The Winchester Celebration" which supposedly began at six pm.

Ava dodged a wild seven-year-old, balancing two massive mugs and a small plate in her hands, which she set down on our table. "Two large coffees and a blueberry muffin."

"Ava, what's this?" I asked, pointing toward the curious words toward the bottom of the flyer.

She squinted at the lettering. "Oh, the Winchester Celebration. We do that at every summer festival since they passed away."

"What is it?" Bodhi asked. He tore the top of the muffin off and set it aside for me then munched on the bottom half.

"It's just a nice way for us to remember what the Winchesters did for Black Bay," explained Ava, licking her finger and flipping to a new page in her order pad. "We have a moment of silence. Usually, some people who were close to the Winchesters say a few words. Then they play Patrick's favorite song for everyone to dance to. And then there's a firework show in their honor. I think the festival committee has something extra special planned this year."

I pulled the muffin top apart with my fingers. "Why?"

"It's the twentieth anniversary of the Winchesters' deaths," Ava answered. "You two should come. The summer festival is always a blast. I promise the Winchester Celebration doesn't drag the mood down. Besides, I'll bet everyone will be glad to spend some time with the new owners of the house on the bluff. It'll give us a chance to get to know you better."

"Sounds fun," Bodhi said to my surprise. Usually, he wasn't so eager to jump into the local extravaganzas.

"Excellent," Ava said with a warm smile. "Now what can I get you for breakfast, my dears?"

Bodhi propped a menu up on the table so that it shielded him from view like a mini fort and peeked over the top. "What do you think, Bailey? The works?"

"Let's do it."

We ordered enough food to feed a family of four. As we tucked into the sky-high stacks of hotcakes and French toast, scrambled eggs, sausage links, bacon, and fresh fruit, I momentarily forgot that a long dead teenaged girl waited for us at home. It was difficult to concentrate on the supernatural when I hadn't seen the man who sat across from me in several years. Bodhi smiled and laughed throughout breakfast, his amber eyes sparkling with a lust for life that I thought might have gone extinct. It wasn't as vibrant as it used to be, but it was there nonetheless. It made me wonder what about Black Bay had the ability to encourage such a shift. For five years, ever since we lost Kali, Bodhi had been empty and sad. There was no way to reach him. His communication avenues had shut off, and we drifted like two lifeboats in the middle of the doldrums. But two months in a rainy little town smack in the middle of the Pacific Northwest and somehow Bodhi seemed to be on the mend. I allowed my imagination to run away with itself. Could we settle in Black Bay? I could see myself eating breakfast at the Sanctuary every Sunday morning, chatting with the locals and enjoying the weather. However, I couldn't see myself living at the Winchester house with a ghost for a roommate.

After breakfast, we reluctantly climbed into the truck for the ride up to the house. We rode with our fingers intertwined over the center console, Bodhi's thumb tracing patterns in the smooth skin of the back of my hand. It was nearly lunchtime, and by the time the truck lumbered into the front yard, Bodhi's construction crew had gotten started on today's work without him. Their work ethic astounded me. We paid them extra to work over the weekends, desperate to speed up the renovation process. Still, I admired them for being so prompt on a lazy Sunday morning. As we stepped out of the truck, the guys playfully teased Bodhi for his tardiness.

"Slackin' off," John said, shaking his head. "Shame on you."

Another guy clapped Bodhi on the shoulder. "Thanks for gracing us with your presence."

Bodhi raised his hands in defeat. "Okay, okay. I surrender. What's on the agenda, guys?"

"You tell us, Sleeping Beauty."

I grinned, kissed Bodhi on the cheek, and abandoned him to the devilish remarks of his crew. Inside, the house still smelled faintly of charred chicken and smoke from the night before. I warmed up a cup of leftover coffee, collected a handful of Caroline's journals, and carried my stash downstairs to the basement. It was strange that only a few days ago, the dusty storage area had felt so frightening. Now, it seemed relatively benign. Then again, we hadn't seen or heard from Caroline since her burnout with the Ouija board the night before. The absence of her chilling presence made the basement more bearable. In any case, I was glad to have the space to myself. It would make it easier to concentrate on the task at hand.

There was no simple way to tackle the number of boxes in the basement. The Winchesters had stored their entire lives down here, and when Bodhi and I first started clearing out the house, we moved even more of the Winchesters' possessions to the basement for safekeeping. With a sigh, I began sifting through the cardboard boxes. Though Caroline's journals were an eyeglass to the past, I wanted to know more about the Winchesters' personal lives. Who did they associate with the most? Who would want to murder Patrick and Caroline? Who had the ability to get close enough to the children to commit the murders in the first place?

After three hours of searching, countless run-ins with various spiders, one dead rat scare, and coaxing a small bat out through the busted storm window, I finally found a few things that might point me in the right direction. In a crushed box beneath a spare mattress, I'd found a collection of VHS tapes, labeled in faded permanent marker with titles like "Caroline's first step" and "Patrick's 16th birthday party" and "Labor Day sailing competition." Close by, there was another box full of photo albums. I carried my haul upstairs. There was an old VHS player in the first floor office. Hopefully, it still worked.

The office was a wreck, a victim of one of Caroline's recent outbursts. The grand piano lay on one ruined side, as did the demolished grandfather clock. I cautiously sidestepped broken glass and piano keys to reach the felt-covered desk. Gingerly, I tipped the VHS tapes out to rifle through them, eventually choosing one labeled "Summer Festival 1996." According to the rough timeline I'd worked out, the festival that year would have occurred shortly before the Winchesters met their premature end. The VHS player was attached to a bulky TV. I plugged both into the wall socket, and they slowly booted to life.

Though the video footage was grainy, there was no mistaking the fair-haired grinning boy who held the camera facing toward himself as anyone other than Patrick Winchester. I could feel his energy through the screen as I watched the sunshine halo around him. He flipped the camera around, aiming at a green stretch of grass that I recognized as the large park near the town square. The rest of the Winchesters came into focus. They wore matching orange t-shirts with football flags strapped around their waists. Christopher and Elizabeth waved happily at the camera as Patrick trained it on them. Caroline, on the other hand, plopped down in the grass and opened a book.

"And here comes Black Bay's most renowned wide receiver," announced Patrick, zooming in on a family of three walking toward the Winchesters. "The one, the only, Alexander the Great!"

The only information I had on Patrick's best friend Alex came from Caroline's diaries, but as the boy faked left around the camera then dodged right to knock a football out of Patrick's free hand, it became obvious why Caroline adored him so much. He was over six feet tall, tan, and wiry. With jet black hair, deep blue eyes, and dimples to frame his cheeky smile, Alex was the perfect opposite of Patrick's fair complexion. The friends bumped fists as their parents greeted one another, then Alex gently nudged the bottom of Caroline's tennis shoe.

"Hey, Caz," he said, spinning the football in the palm of his hand. "Wanna throw some warm-up passes?"

Caroline, like her brother, was blonde and pretty, with flushed pink cheeks and a mordant tilt to her lips. She rose to her feet, lithe and light, and I noted that she was nearly as tall as her father. However, the top of her head barely reached Alex's broad shoulders.

"Sure," she said, tossing aside her book.

"Hey!" Patrick protested from behind the camera. "I asked you if you wanted to warm up ten minutes ago, and you said no!"

Alex cheerfully punched Patrick's shoulder. "Don't act like you can compare your looks to mine, Winchester."

"Gross, that's my sister."

From off screen someone—Alex's mother perhaps—said, "Alexander, behave."

"Yeah, *Alexander.*"

Alex rolled his eyes. "Let's go, Caz."

He flicked the football to Caroline, who caught it effortlessly. As they jogged off, tossing the ball back and forth between them, the camera jostled as Patrick followed along behind them before the footage cut off entirely. The next scene was of the flag football game itself. I watched for a few minutes, grinning from ear to ear. Locals packed the sidelines, cheering every time Patrick made a pass to Alex. Patrick high-fived his dad after a particularly impressive play, kissed his mom on the cheek, then picked up Caroline and twirled her around. They were the superstars of Black Bay, but little did the Winchesters know that their time was running out.

I set aside the box of VHS tapes. As enjoyable as it was to see the family interacting with each other, it also hurt my heart. It wasn't fair. The Winchesters were kind and caring people, and they should have lived full, lovely lives. With such a positive influence on their community, they deserved that much. Instead, they were lost to the world, enshrined forever in static tapes and old photographs.

I pulled the box of photo albums toward me. The first few

were full of wedding, shower, and baby photos. I skipped over those. The Winchesters hadn't moved to Black Bay until the summer before Patrick's first year of high school, so I checked the dates in each album until I found a few closer to the Winchesters' deaths. The last album had 1995-1996 written on the inside cover. It was incomplete.

The Winchesters documented every family outing in photographs. Christopher and Elizabeth enjoyed a candlelit dinner at a restaurant in town. Patrick, Alex, and a few other boys from the football team dove from the docks and swam in the bright blue water of the bay. Caroline smiled alongside a friend, both dressed in riding boots and helmets, as they led two beautiful horses out of a stable. But there was one picture that I couldn't look away from.

All four of the Winchesters stood on the deck of a beautiful sailboat, waving happily at whoever was taking the photo. I stared at the photo, studying every aspect. The sailboat was well taken care of and bigger than any I'd seen in the marina. It was all white with a sky-blue stripe along the side, but the name painted in elegant script on the front of the seacraft was what really caught my attention. This was *Artemis*, the boat that Christopher and Elizabeth had ridden into the rocks on that fateful night in early August so many years ago.

I flipped to the next page in the photo album and found another picture of interest. In this one, Christopher Winchester shook hands with a stout bearded man out front of Powell's Lumber Mill. Beside them, a younger man smiled into the camera, his arm wrapped around a pretty brunette with brown eyes. I didn't recognize the man as Ethan at first. His hair was auburn instead of gray, and his warm grin looked completely different on a clean-shaven face. I studied the woman in his grasp. This must've been Ethan's fiancée.

They were an attractive pair. It was a shame they didn't end up working out.

Without warning, a book fell from a nearby shelf, landing on the desk in front of me with a loud bang. I jumped, startled by the abrupt noise, then leaned forward to get a better look. It was Black Bay's high school yearbook. I reached for it, but before my fingers grazed the cover, the pages began to flip on their own.

"Hi, Caroline," I murmured, watching the yearbook sort through itself. When the pages settled, I drew the yearbook toward me. "What am I looking at?"

It turned out that I didn't need Caroline's answer. The page was dedicated to some kind of spotlight on Alex. It boasted several pictures of him in his football gear, a clever interview by the yearbook staff, and the deserved superlative of "Best Smile." I traced the name on the back of his football jersey.

"Alexander Lido," I muttered under my breath. "Like the restaurant in town?"

Caroline made no effort to confirm or deny this.

I drew one of Caroline's journals toward me and flipped it open, searching for Alex's name. After all, Caroline had told us that her diary entries contained hints regarding who had harmed the Winchesters. Was Alex harboring some kind of grudge against the Winchesters? It seemed doubtful. Then again, the murderer had been hiding in plain sight for twenty years. Who better to fool an entire town into thinking him innocent than a charming, handsome, retired high school athlete? I paused to read one of Caroline's entries.

APRIL 26TH, 1996

. . .

I'M DYING. Okay, I'm not dying, but it sure feels like I am. My pulse is racing, my lungs feel tight, and my stomach keeps lurching as if I'm going to hurl. I always liked to think that if Alex ever reciprocated my feelings and actually asked me out, I would've been as smooth as Lauren Bacall in To Have and Have Nots. *You know how to whistle, don't you, Alex?*

Unfortunately, I did not tell Alex to just put his lips together and blow. Here's the great news: Alex asked me to junior prom. I can't believe I just wrote that. Alex asked me to junior prom. Wow. I'm not usually at a loss for words, but just... wow. Every girl in school would kill to walk into prom with Alex Lido, and for some unspeakable reason, he wants to go with me. However, here's the bad news. When he asked me, I spit on him.

Who asks a girl to prom right as she takes an enormous gulp of lemonade? He spent the rest of the lunch period with a stain on his shirt. In hindsight, he brought that upon himself. Seriously, you cannot present a woman with a dozen roses and not expect her mouth to drop open in shock.

The other kicker was Patrick's face. I guess Alex never told him that he wanted to ask me to prom. Patrick's angry. I understand why. It's his junior prom, and he wants to spend it with his best friend, not his kid sister. But as much as I love my brother, this is an opportunity that I can't pass up. What are the chances Alex and I win prom king and queen? I would look great in a tiara.

I CLOSED CAROLINE'S JOURNAL, my mind made up. I wanted to speak to Alex Lido. Both Caroline and Patrick knew and loved him, and if there was anyone who might know something about the Winchester kids' secret jaunts, it was their mutual best friend. I packed up the VHS tapes and the photo albums, storing them under the desk for safekeeping. Down the hall, the construction crew worked tirelessly to fix up the kitchen. Soon, it would be time to start tearing apart this room. We would have to donate or sell the rest of the Winchesters' things, a thought that weighed heavy on my heart.

In the kitchen, Bodhi and Ethan knelt on a rubber mat, their heads hidden from view as they inspected some kind of plumbing issue beneath the sink.

"Hey, Ethan," I said.

He poked his face out from underneath the counter. "Hi, darlin'. How are you?"

"I'm great. I'm glad you're here actually. Do you know who Alex Lido is?"

With a groan, Ethan pushed himself to his feet. "Of course. Everyone knows Alex. He helps his dad out with the restaurant nowadays."

I bowed my head in thanks. "You just answered my question before I even asked it. Do you think he'd be there now?"

"I imagine so. Why?"

"More blog stuff," I said vaguely. "I'm going to drop by."

Bodhi slid out from beneath the sink and tossed a set of keys toward me. "Take the truck. You really need to stay off that ankle."

So I left Ethan and Bodhi to their plumbing and rode into town for the second time that day. Lido's Restaurant was relatively slow by the time I got there. It was mid-afternoon, and there was a lull between lunch and dinner. Most of the tables were empty, save for the odd late lunch date. I walked in and waited awkwardly by the front door. A server soon approached me, taking a menu from the host's stand.

"Hi, there," she said. "Table for one?"

"Actually, I'm looking for Alex," I told her. "Is he around?"

"Sure. One minute."

She disappeared into the kitchen, and I took a seat at the bar. A large television broadcasted a replay of a Seattle

Mariners game. I watched absentmindedly for a minute or two before the door to the kitchen swung open again.

Alexander Lido looked much the same as he had twenty years ago, but now there were lines around his deep, sparkling eyes and his dark hair was now cropped close to his scalp. But his award-winning smile, highlighted by those dimples, was just as effective now as it had been then. He wore a black shirt, sculpted jeans, and a baseball cap. When he spotted me at the counter, he filled a glass from a beer tap and slid it across the bar. I caught it before it could topple off the end of the counter.

"Brewed that myself," he said, coming my way. He stretched his hand out, and I shook it. He had a firm, warm grasp that reminded me of Bodhi's. "I heard the new girl in town wanted to see me. Anything I can help you with in particular?"

"Yes, actually." I took a sip of beer. It was refreshingly light, with hints of grapefruit and citrus in the aftertaste. I looked at Alex's nice smile. "I was wondering if you could tell me about Patrick and Caroline Winchester."

In less than a second, Alex's grin faltered and fell.

17

LIDO'S

*I*mmediately, Alex busied himself with polishing glasses, buffing them so vigorously that one fell out of his hand and hit the floor.

"Sore subject?" I ventured. Another waiter stooped down to sweep up the broken glass.

"You could say that," muttered Alex, avoiding my gaze.

"You were Patrick's best friend."

His eyes snapped up to focus on mine. "How do you know that?"

I gestured toward the trophy case at the front of the restaurant. Inside, there was a picture of the Golden Eagles football team. Patrick and Alex were both front and center. "Doesn't everyone know that?"

"Yeah, but it's been a long time."

I passed my beer from one hand to the other and contemplated whether or not to ask for a basket of onion rings. "You knew the Winchesters well though."

"I did."

"How did you meet them?"

Alex turned his baseball cap around so that it faced backward then leaned on his elbows on the bar top. "Why does an out-of-towner like you have so much interest in a family that hasn't been around for twenty years?"

Alex's bottomless blue eyes were inches from my own. I suddenly understood that he was the type of man who knew that his mere presence had an effect on people. While he didn't appear to blatantly take advantage of that fact, he was aware that he could manipulate anyone just with his body language. I looked into my beer.

"I live in their house," I answered matter-of-factly. "I'm also writing a feature on the Winchesters for my blog. I wanted to make sure that I have an accurate representation of all of them, including Patrick and Caroline."

I expected Alex to retreat behind his invisible shield of emotions. Clearly, he wasn't fond of talking about his dead best friend. However, to my pleasant surprise, he sighed and answered my question.

"I met Patrick at football camp the summer before our freshman year," he explained. "We were the skinniest kids on the field and determined to prove that we could play better than the guys on the varsity team. I think we bonded over that. By the start of the school year, we were practically fused together."

"All I ever hear about Patrick is that he was a star on the football field." I swirled my glass around to even out the foam on top. "But what was he really like?"

"He was a total goof," said Alex, smiling as he sifted through his high school memories. "The teachers loved him because he somehow managed to disrupt class just enough to break up the monotony, but not so much that it was considered disrespectful."

"Class clown, eh?"

"Yes, but he was more than that." Now that the ball was rolling, Alex wanted to talk about his best friend. He spoke animatedly, and his eyes lit up with the memories of the past. "Pat was a great listener too. People always think teenagers are so wrapped up in their own problems, and admittedly, most of us were back then. Patrick was different though. He cared about other people. If it weren't for him, I don't think I would've made it through high school."

"Why not?"

Alex poured himself a shot of bourbon. "My parents went through a really rough divorce. They argued non-stop. Basically sued each other into the ground. We nearly closed the restaurant. I spent a lot of time hiding at Pat's house. His parents, Christopher and Elizabeth, were good people. I think they realized I needed a place to crash while my mom and dad worked their problems out. Do you want something to eat?"

My stomach rumbled. Despite this morning's extravagant brunch, my metabolism was in fine form. "That'd be great."

Alex snagged a passing waiter. "Hey, will you put in two orders for the catch of the day?"

"Sure thing, boss."

Alex thanked him and turned back to me. "Anyway, Patrick was much more than his football fame."

"Losing him must've been really difficult for you," I said softly.

He pivoted away, glancing up at the score of the baseball game that played on the television. His voice sounded thick when he answered. "Hardest thing I've ever had to deal with."

I gave him a minute to recover, quietly nursing my beer. He turned his cap back around so that the brim cast a shadow over his eyes, cleared his throat, and sipped his bourbon.

"What about Patrick's sister?" I asked. "Did you know Caroline well?"

"Of course I did," Alex replied, the twinkle returning to

his eyes. "She always tagged along with me and Patrick, much to Pat's chagrin. I didn't mind. I adored Caroline. Mind you, I couldn't always keep up with whatever she was talking about. She was much too smart for me."

"I heard you went to prom with her."

Once again, Alex fixed me with a penetrating stare. "Okay, now I'd really like to know where you're getting your information from. This is personal."

I considered telling Alex that I had found Caroline's journals in her old bedroom. He probably would have loved to read them, especially if he had such a soft spot for Caroline. But then I remembered why I was having this conversation with Alex to begin with. Someone in Black Bay had murdered Caroline, and advertising my possession of possible evidence was not a good move.

"Someone in town mentioned it," I said instead with a nonchalant shrug.

Alex's eyes narrowed. "They gave you the wrong information. I asked Caroline to go with me, yes, but she never actually made it."

I paused with my beer halfway to my lips. "Why not?"

"Because I had just turned eighteen and she was only fifteen," he explained. He poured another glass of bourbon for himself. "Her parents liked me and all, but I guess they thought that there was too much of an age gap. Plus, Patrick wasn't particularly pleased with me when I asked her to go with me."

The server delivered our lunches then, setting down two steaming plates of fresh fried cod, onion rings, and tartar sauce. Alex offered me a fork and knife wrapped tightly in a napkin.

"Thanks," I said. "So what happened with you and Patrick after that?"

"We fought," Alex admitted as he unwrapped his own

silverware. "We brawled right there in the hallway at school. It was the only thing we ever disagreed on. I think it was also the only time Pat ever got in trouble for something."

I squeezed an onion ring flat, dipped it in a ramekin of ketchup, and popped it into my mouth. "Did the two of you make up?"

"Partially," said Alex as he dumped his coleslaw on top of the fish. "But things felt different after that. Pat clammed up every time Caroline and I were in the same room together. The three of us couldn't hang out anymore the way we used to."

"Why was Patrick so upset over you wanting to date his sister?" I asked, discreetly studying Alex as we ate.

"I never knew," he replied with a wistful shrug. "I think it just surprised him. It surprised me, you know? I always liked Caroline, but I never thought of her that way until she changed."

"Puberty will do that."

Alex rolled his eyes. "Not like that. She used to be really shy around me when she was younger. I didn't really have the chance to get to know her. She became more talkative when she got older. Sometimes, if I was waiting on Pat, I'd talk to Caroline. She blew my mind most days. You should've heard her go on and on about the stuff she learned in her AP classes. I could barely keep up. Anyway, I guess Pat thought that the only reason I was at his house so often was because I wanted to see Caroline."

"Which was half-true," I guessed.

"I loved all of the Winchesters equally," Alex declared. "I never thought that would somehow be a bad thing. And then the night they died—"

He cut himself off abruptly, taking a bite of his meal to avoid continuing his sentence.

"What happened on the night they died?" I asked gently.

Alex lifted his cap nervously, running his hand over his buzzed hair. "I saw them. Before they got on their parents' boat. I was working here, and they stopped by to say hi."

"Both of them?"

"Yeah. It was a little weird. Good though. They were laughing together when they came in, and Pat sort of nudged Caroline toward me. They sat at the bar and drank Shirley Temples, watching me bus tables. It was the first time everything felt normal since the whole prom debacle."

"Did they tell you they were meeting their parents afterward?"

Alex shook his head. "Nah. Everyone knew the Winchesters went out on the bay every Friday if the weather was good. They even took me with them sometimes. Pat and Caroline said goodbye and headed out. For twenty years, I've wished that I asked them to stick around the restaurant that night."

I realized that I'd been shredding my paper napkin into bits as Alex spoke. Like everyone else in Black Bay, Alex was under the impression that Caroline and Patrick had died on their parents' boat. To make matters worse, he partially blamed himself for their deaths. I reached across the bar top to pat Alex's hand.

"It wasn't your fault," I told him quietly. "There was nothing you could've done to prevent that from happening."

"If I had just—"

"No," I said firmly. "Don't you dare blame yourself."

For a minute or two, we just sat like that, my hand over Alex's and the bar top between us. The commentary for the ballgame prattled on. At the front of the restaurant, the door opened to admit an elderly couple for an early dinner. The catch of the day went uneaten on our plates.

I sniffed, blinking to stop my eyes from watering, and

pushed away from the counter. "I should get going. Thanks for telling me about Patrick and Caroline."

Alex cleared his throat. "It was nice actually."

I pulled out my wallet. "What do I owe you?"

"Don't worry about it. On the house."

"All right. Thank you." I turned to leave, but the picture of Alex sitting alone at the bar, his own unfinished meal in front of him, caused me to pause. "Alex? If you like, my husband and I would love for you to come visit us at the house."

He nodded in appreciation, his stunning blue eyes remarkably solemn. "I might just do that."

As soon as I climbed into the driver's seat of the truck, closed the door, and shifted into first gear, I burst into tears. I'd gotten more than I had bargained for out of my conversation with Alex. He was closer to the Winchesters than anyone else I'd spoken to so far. If the reverent way he reminisced about Patrick and Caroline was any indication, Alex practically considered them family. It was terrible. All these years later, Alex suffered from the loss of his best friend. I thought about me and Bodhi. Would we ever heal? Or would we go our entire lives haunted by one fatal mistake?

The drive back to the house felt eons longer than usual. It wasn't good to be alone with my thoughts. They had drifted to a dark place, a place with brambles and vines that snaked around me and sucked me deep below the surface of reality. I rolled down the windows, hoping the breeze might help to clear my head. I tried to remember my conversation with Alex from an analytical standpoint. One thing stood out to me. Even though Patrick and Caroline had been grounded that day, they were out and about in town. If they didn't get on the Winchester family sailboat after they left Lido's restaurant, then where did they go?

Sunset beckoned on the bluff. Creeping rays of peachy light pierced through the front windshield as I pulled into the front yard. Bodhi and the crew lounged outside, eating pizza and drinking beer as they enjoyed the warm summer night. When Bodhi saw the truck, he hopped up from his comfortable seat on the ground and opened my door for me.

"The guys bought pizza," he said, kissing my cheek. "Would you like some?"

I rested my forehead against Bodhi's chest. He smelled like pine needles and musk. "I ate in town."

"Are you okay?"

"Yes. I think I'd just like to be alone. Is that okay?"

There was a worried tilt to his mouth, but he said, "Sure. Of course."

I waved to the rest of the crew and headed inside. I went straight to the office, where my research from earlier hid beneath the desk. I found the VHS tape I was looking for, popped it into the player, and sat down on the floor to watch it. As Patrick, Caroline, and Alex appeared on the television screen, I felt something cold press against my left side, as if someone with icy skin had sat down beside me.

"He loved you, you know," I murmured. On the screen, Alex spun Caroline around in a chaotic dance beneath a shower of colorful fireworks while Patrick looked on laughing. "He told me today. I hope you know that."

No one spoke back, but the frosty presence next to me grew chillier still.

"Where's Patrick?" I asked, the thought occurring to me at random. "You're dead but still here, right? So where has your brother gone? Did he pass over?"

There was no answer. Caroline was no longer the conversationalist she claimed to be when she was alive. Either that, or she didn't have the ability to conduct a conversation in her current state. I sighed, slumping against the ornate desk. On the TV, Patrick and Alex lifted Caroline onto their shoulders. But there was a fourth face on the small screen, reflecting from outside the office window.

I gasped, pushed myself to my feet, and whirled around. Milo's pale face looked into the office, his eyes wide and alarmed. As soon as he noticed me, he darted off, vanishing into the shadows of the overgrown garden in the backyard.

Heat burned in the pit of my stomach as I threw open the office door, sprinted down the hall, and burst out into the backyard. Breathing hard, I scanned the yard, but Milo was nowhere to be found. The wind whispered through the brambly branches of overgrown rose bushes and trip wire weeds. How had Milo gotten away so quickly? And why had he been spying on me in the first place? I heard footsteps behind me and whirled around.

Bodhi paused on the threshold between the kitchen and the wooden deck outside, looking me over. "Bailey, what are you doing out here? Is everything okay?"

"I just saw Milo looking in through the office window."

Bodhi tensed, and he rested a hand on the kitchen counter as though it might keep him from making a fist. Deadly calm, he asked, "You saw Milo doing what?"

"I was in the office, and he had his face pressed up against the window as if he was watching me," I explained, turning around to search the garden again. "He ran off when he realized I saw him."

"Wait here," Bodhi said as he stepped out on to the deck.

I took his arm. "Bodhi, don't."

His eyes roved the darkness, surveying each shadow for a glimpse of Milo. "Bailey, this isn't right. In fact, it's downright alarming. Milo specifically told us that he didn't care about what we did with the house. If he's suddenly changed his mind, he needs to speak to us in person, not spy on you through the windows. I'll be right back."

Bodhi stepped off the deck, disappearing into the garden. I watched nervously as he looked around. The plants rustled as he stepped through them, an easy indication of his path through the yard. His voice echoed back to the house.

"Milo! Come on out, man. We need to talk about this."

There was no answering call. The garden was quiet except for Bodhi's search. He emerged from the rose bushes, dusting pollen off of his shirt as he walked back to me.

"He's definitely gone now," said Bodhi. "Are you sure you saw him?"

"Without a doubt."

He led me into the kitchen, closed the back door, and double-checked the lock. "I thought he was strange right from the moment we met him. He practically gave us this house. I should've known he was shady."

"He wasn't always," I protested.

Together, we walked back to the office. The tape of Caroline, Patrick, and Alex still played on the television, but this time, they were not accompanied by Milo's sallow features. Bodhi watched the video briefly. I stared out of the window, wondering how Milo had managed to vanish with some ease.

"He looked ill," I noted. "He did yesterday too."

"If he's sick, it's not our responsibility to take care of him," replied Bodhi. He pressed the stop button on the tape player and ejected the VHS. "Where did you find these tapes?"

"Downstairs. I thought they might be a helpful addition to Caroline's diaries."

He flipped over the VHS to inspect the label. "I'm not so sure that watching these is the best idea."

"Why not?" I asked. "We need to find out what happened to Patrick and Caroline. We have footage of their lives in Black Bay."

"Yes, and I understand that this is important to you." Bodhi rifled through the other tapes in the box. "But I'm also afraid that this might hit us harder than it would someone else."

"Because of Kali?"

His shoulders tightened at the sound of her name, and though his back was turned toward me, I saw the tips of his ears redden. "Yes. Because of Kali."

I perched myself on the edge of the desk, but Bodhi adamantly continued his search through the box of tapes. At this point, I didn't think he was really reading the labels on the tapes. He simply did not want to look at me. I respected that decision, keeping my hands planted firmly on the desk rather than reaching out to him. Sure, we had made progress in the last several days with regard to the way we acted around each other, but I didn't want Bodhi to harden and cast me out again.

"Do you ever think maybe we ended up here because of Kali?"

The tendons in his hands rippled like tidal waves as he balled his fingers into fists.

"Not in a bad way," I went on, swinging my feet above the carpeted floor. "But maybe the universe knew that we needed something to push us to heal. Maybe we were meant to help Caroline in order to help ourselves."

He pushed the box of tapes under the desk then lifted himself up to sit beside me. "Like fate?"

"I suppose."

Bodhi sighed. "Can I be honest?"

"Of course."

"If that's true, I don't think I'm ready to think about it yet."

Our pinky fingers overlapped on the shiny wood surface.

"That's okay," I said softly. "You don't have to watch these videos, Bodhi. Or read Caroline's diaries. Or look at the photos. I don't mind doing it on my own. As it is, I already spoke to Alex."

"Who?"

"Alex, the boy in that video," I clarified, pointing to the television where the two-dimensional versions of the Winchesters so recently played with one another. "He was Patrick's best friend, and Caroline had a massive crush on him. At first, I thought he might have something to do with their deaths, but after talking to him, it sounds like he loved them most out of everyone in town."

"Do you think it's wise to ask so many questions about the Winchesters when their murderer might still be out there?" asked Bodhi.

"I told everyone I was working on something for my blog," I explained. "That should divert attention long enough for us to figure this out."

Bodhi nodded. He looked down at our hands then lifted his fingers to cover mine. "What about Milo?"

"What about him?"

"I know you like him, Bailey, but you have to admit that there's something about him that doesn't sit right." As an afterthought, he leaned across the desk to pull the curtain closed over the window. "What if he had something to do with all of this?"

Before I could answer, I noticed that something was missing from the desktop. "Did you move Caroline's journal?" I asked Bodhi.

He shook his head.

I scanned the floor, wondering if it had fallen in my haste to catch Milo outside, then hopped off the desk and knelt to check if it had somehow made its way into the box of VHS tapes. No luck. With a sinking feeling, I bolted out of the office. Bodhi followed along behind me as I chugged up the stairs as quickly as my ankle would allow me.

"Bailey, what's wrong?"

"Give me a minute."

I threw open the door of Caroline's old bedroom. Novels, textbooks, notes, and other evidence of Caroline's intellectual intelligence lay in a heap on the floor from the turbulent evening during which she had delivered her journals to me in the first place. I had only picked up a few, leaving the others on the top of the pile in the room. There were at least twenty of them, each one chock full of personal information about Caroline's life. But now the diaries were notably missing, absent from the assortment of literature in the small bedroom.

"Caroline's journals," I breathed. "They're all gone. Someone took them."

18

NOTHING TO SEE

The Winchester Family: Spotlight on Caroline

oday, I'd like to introduce you all to the wondrous fifteen-year-old intellectual equestrian that I have come to know as Caroline Winchester. The majority of Black Bay recalls Caroline as distant, curt, or shy, but if you speak to the right people, Caroline (or Caz as she was known to her close friends) was the subtle heart of the Winchester family. Though she often dwelled in the shadow of her football-loving brother, Caroline had more to offer the town than anyone could've anticipated.

Caroline followed in both her parents' footsteps. I found records of her father's business in her own handwriting. She'd calculated the rate of growth for the company over the next several years. The business jargon disorients me, but Caroline immersed herself in it. She had a better understanding of what it meant to make a profit than most men on Wall Street. She tweaked numbers and performed equations until she found the best way to get Black Bay back on its feet. In fact, I wonder if she ever brought those equa-

tions to her father. Did Christopher Winchester save the town, or did the locals owe their livelihoods to a clever teenager?

In addition, Caroline cared deeply for the community. She worked with her mother to improve morale and boost the overall quality of life in town. Together, Caroline and Elizabeth implemented free school lunch programs for underprivileged youth, created an equestrian center that rescued and rehabilitated horses, and ran a book club that focused on analyzing literature at a college reading level. Caroline's influence is still present in the community. To this day, the lunch program serves those less fortunate and the book club meets every week. The equestrian center has since morphed into an animal shelter with a ninety percent adoption rate each month.

So today, I want to remember Caroline Winchester for all of the positivity that she contributed to Black Bay. She poured everything she had into this town, and she should be recognized for that. Caroline may have been young, but she was not faint of heart.

UNTIL NEXT TIME,
  Bailey

THE NEXT MORNING, I helped Bodhi whip up a breakfast of chicken and biscuits, something we had never considered eating until we flipped a house in North Carolina and discovered such fried, buttery goodness. Unfortunately, between last night's theft and another nightmare, I was distracted, and I obliviously reached into the oven to retrieve the baking sheet of steaming biscuits without an oven mitt.

"Bailey!"

Bodhi caught my wrist, pulling me away from the heated surface just as the tip of my index finger touched the hot pan.

"Ow, ow, ow!"

Bodhi dragged me over to the sink and flipped on the faucet. As cool water soothed the small burn on my finger, he used a dish towel to take the baking sheet out of the oven.

"What were you thinking?" he asked, inspecting my finger. A tiny blister marred my skin. It could've been much worse.

"I wasn't," I grumbled. My finger throbbed, so I shoved it under the stream of water again. "I have a lot on my mind."

Bodhi pried the biscuits from the pan with a spatula. "Baby, we'll find the journals. I'm sure Caroline misplaced them or moved them."

"Why would she do that?" I asked as I turned off the faucet. I opened the old freezer, pushing aside a bottle of tequila that Bodhi had brought up from the cellar. In the very back, an ancient bag of frozen peas hid behind the ice box. I took it out to soothe my finger. "She gave me her journals to read. I swear, Bodhi. Someone stole them. Who else was in the house yesterday?"

"Everyone," he replied. "The entire crew was here yesterday, getting ready to demo the rest of the kitchen. Speaking of which, we're getting rid of these appliances today. We'll have to eat in town until the kitchen's finished."

I swiped a morsel of fried chicken. If this was our last home-cooked meal for a while, I wanted to savor it. "Do you think Milo took them?"

"I think that's more likely," Bodhi answered. "After all, he was the one peeking in our window last night. It supports my theory."

"Your theory isn't sound," I pointed out. "Milo can't be older than twenty-seven or twenty-eight. He would've been a kid when the Winchesters died. There's no way he had something to do with it."

Bodhi sandwiched a piece of fried chicken between two halves of a biscuit and offered it to me. "We don't know the whole story. What if Milo's dad had a grudge against the Winchesters?"

I accepted the sandwich, took a bite, and hummed contently. "The locals barely know Milo and his dad. Don't you think if they had problems with the Winchesters, the whole town would've heard about it?"

"Maybe," said Bodhi, preparing his own breakfast. "But let's not forget the fact that there are no records of Milo ever owning this house. If that's true, then how is it possible for us to legally own it?"

"Milo said it was a clerical error."

"Over Mrs. Poe's dead body."

"Oh, God. Don't even joke."

Bodhi chuckled through a mouthful of chicken. "I'm just saying. Everyone else in Black Bay is relatively transparent, but we don't even know where Milo lives."

I quietly munched on my breakfast, considering this information. Bodhi made a relevant point. The locals cherished the pleasant, familial feeling that came with living in Black Bay, but Milo had expressed his distaste for the town as soon as we met him. Stranger still, he claimed to live close by, but Black Bay was the only populated area for miles. Then there was the fact that he grew more and more idiosyncratic by the second. Milo knew intimate details about my personal life. Now, I wasn't entirely comfortable knowing that he was armed with those details.

"Today's your appointment with Doctor Marx, right?" asked Bodhi.

"Yes. It's at three."

He brushed crumbs from his hands as he finished his first sandwich. "Are you going to tell her that your nightmares are getting worse?"

My mouth felt dry. I swallowed hard. "How do you figure they're getting worse?"

Bodhi poured a glass of cold water and handed it to me. "I know you, Bailey. Your face tells me everything. Besides, you kicked and screamed all last night. No matter how many times I woke you up, you just went to sleep and started screaming again."

"Sorry," I mumbled.

Gently, he brushed my hair away from my face. "Why didn't you tell me?"

"I've never told you," I admitted, turning away from him. His hand fell limply to his side. "I couldn't. You didn't want to hear about it."

"I'm listening now."

To his credit, Bodhi waited out my silence, even when the atmosphere in the kitchen grew uncomfortably still. This was new for us. Talking. Or maybe it was the listening that was new. Either way, I felt apprehensive with Bodhi's golden eyes on me. Would he bolt as soon as I spoke about the content of my nightmares?

I tipped the rest of my chicken into the garbage can. "I can't," I said, backpedaling out of the room as quickly as possible. "I'm sorry, Bodhi. One day, I might be able to tell you the things I see at night, but for right now, it's too much."

I limped up the stairs before I had time to fully comprehend Bodhi's hurt expression. In the bedroom, I flopped on to the bed, hugging Bodhi's pillow. I had done him a favor. He just didn't know it yet.

My eyes fluttered shut. I heard the front door open as Bodhi greeted the construction crew. As they got to work, the whir of drills and the shuffle of heavy equipment across the unfinished floors lulled me to sleep.

LATER THAT DAY, I didn't have the heart to ask Bodhi if I could borrow his truck, so I walked into town for my appointment with Doctor Marx. I hadn't seen her since my first visit to her office. She'd diagnosed me with PTSD and prescribed anti-depressants to keep my horrors at bay. Caroline disapproved of the medication, and although I continued to take it, I was starting to side with the ghost of the Winchester house. So far, the small orange capsules had done nothing to ease my nightly dose of terror.

I arrived at her office ten minutes early, shivering in the chilly waiting room as the receptionist studied me over the top of the desk. I tried to ignore her. These were the times I disliked living in such a small town. Sometimes, gossip was the only source of entertainment, and my presence in the psychiatrist's office was sure to warrant a conversation or two. It was a relief when Doctor Marx opened her door to invite me inside. For one, it was considerably warmer in her office. And two, I enjoyed the comforting dribble of her desktop Zen waterfall a little too much.

"So, Bailey," said Doctor Marx, offering me a seat on the expensive leather sofa. "How have you been?"

"All right in some areas. Less so in others. I'm still having nightmares."

Doctor Marx flipped to a fresh page on her clipboard and began to scribble away. "Is that your biggest concern at the moment?"

I nodded, staring down at my hands. The gold band on my ring finger glinted beneath the fluorescent lights.

Doctor Marx noticed my gaze. "And what about Bodhi? The last time we talked, you mentioned that you thought your marriage was failing."

"No," I corrected. "You *implied* that my marriage was failing due to the fact that Bodhi and I never talk to one another which, by the way, we're working on."

"How's that coming?"

I remembered that morning's conversation. "Slowly."

Doctor Marx leaned back in her chair and crossed her legs. "Why don't you tell me about your dreams, Bailey. Did you have a nightmare last night?"

"Yes."

"Do you remember any of it?"

"I remember most of my nightmares," I told her. "It's the same thing every night. I dream that I'm drowning, or that Bodhi's drowning, or that—"

My throat closed up. Doctor Marx raised an eyebrow, jotting a note down on her clipboard.

"Or that your daughter is drowning?" she asked.

I nodded again, unable to craft a verbal confirmation.

"Is that how Kali passed away?"

I folded over, covering my face with my hands. White noise roared in my ears. The image of that night was burned into my brain. I had spent five years trying to force it down, but it haunted me still. There was no way to escape the truth of what happened.

"I left her for a minute." My voice came in rough bursts as I attempted to control the fountain of regret welling up inside me. "One minute. To get her a fresh towel from the laundry room."

There was no more I could say. Doctor Marx got the gist of it. As I dissolved into hysterics, she simply scooted a box of tissues across the coffee table between us. Patiently, she waited out my waves of grief as, for the first time, I allowed the full weight of my shirked responsibility to fall on my shoulders.

"The paramedics say she probably tried to get out on her own, slipped, and hit her head," I sobbed, covering my eyes with my hands.

When I finally began to relax, hiccupping for breath, Doctor Marx asked, "Where was Bodhi?"

"He was out." I sniffed, reached for a tissue, and wiped my

nose. "When we had Kali, we tried to settle down for a while. That wasn't his thing. He constantly wanted to be on the move. To make up for it, he occupied himself with other things."

"What kind of things? Drugs?"

I shook my head. "No, Bodhi was never into substance abuse. He preferred to seek out natural adrenaline rushes. He raced street cars, went sky-diving, and played paintball. One time, I found out that he'd been bare-knuckle boxing in some kind of underground ring. We fought a lot then. All I wanted was him to come home safe, and I couldn't help but think he was going to get himself killed."

"Do you think Bodhi resented Kali?"

Kali had come out of the blue. That was certain. Her conception ended our extensive traveling plans. We landed in Los Angeles of all places, holing up in an expensive shoebox of an apartment in order to get our act together before Kali made her official appearance. But while I was happy to give up a trip to the pyramids in order to care for our newborn daughter, Bodhi often wished that Kali would age faster so that we could bring her with us on new adventures.

"Resentment may be too strong a word," I said. "I don't think Bodhi understood what it meant to be a father until Kali died. That was when he woke up. It was only after she was gone that he really appreciated what Kali meant to him."

"And what about you?" asked Doctor Marx. "These dreams of yours seem to indicate that you've never forgiven yourself for what happened to Kali."

"Would you?"

"This isn't about me."

I crossed my arms. The leather sofa felt clammy beneath me as I avoided eye contact with Doctor Marx.

"Bailey," she said quietly. "Think about it this way. Kali

would not want to see you suffer like this. You loved her for her entire life, even if it was cut tragically short. Learning to let go of your guilt does not mean you're letting go of your child."

"It was my fault," I said, staring at a spot on the floor. "You're talking about parents that had a child die due to something that was beyond their control, but this was my fault. I left her in that bathtub. I took my eyes off of her. She died because of me."

Doctor Marx set her clipboard on her desk and took off her glasses. "Bailey, listen to me. You did not intend to do anything wrong. Your actions were loving actions. You are not a doctor, and no matter what, you cannot keep your child in a bubble to protect her from harm. Accidents happen, and it just so happens that a tragic one happened in your household. Blaming yourself only creates the illusion that control over situations like that is possible."

I took a deep breath, trying to process Doctor Marx's advice. No matter what she said, it seemed unlikely that I could ever forgive myself for leaving Kali alone that night.

"I want you to try something when you go bed tonight," Doctor Marx said. "Clear your mind. Let your thoughts come and go as they please, but try to focus on achieving a sense of calm."

I laughed humorlessly. "Doctor Marx, I haven't been truly calm in a very long time."

"Which is exactly why we're going to practice together now."

For the remainder of the hour, Doctor Marx taught me a myriad of breathing exercises to help me relax at night. Then she guided me through a meditation routine. By the time she excused me from her office, I was lightheaded, woozy, and ready for my second nap of the day.

"Same time next week?" she asked, opening a file cabinet to put away her notes for our session.

"Sure."

"See you then."

I glanced at the names printed on the tabs of the files as I gathered my things and walked to the door. Most of them, I didn't recognize, but one in particular reminded me that I wasn't alone in my quest for help. Ethan Powell had once needed Doctor Marx too, after the death of his father. With some luck and a bit of effort, maybe I could achieve some semblance of his self-satisfaction.

I TOOK my time on my way home, wiping the evidence of tear tracks from my cheeks. The fresh scent of tree sap helped clear my mind as I trekked up the southeast footpath to the house. It was a hot day, and the afternoon sun permeated the thick branches of the trees to warm the back of my neck. I stopped to sit on a large boulder, propping my ankle up against the rock to catch my breath. Nearby, a stream gurgled, and my parched throat wished that I'd brought a water bottle on my trip into town. The hot air shimmered around me, a sure sign of dehydration.

A twig snapped. I spun around, searching the trees for the source of the noise. No one emerged, but I had the eerie sense that someone was watching me. Uneasy, I heaved myself off the boulder and resumed my walk to the top of the bluff. My ankle ached with every step. I glanced over my shoulder.

There. Behind a particularly wide fir tree. A shadow lingered.

"Hello?" I called. "Who's there?"

No one answered. I squinted in the hazy sunlight. There was definitely a person standing just beyond the border of the dirt path. I could see the outline of the tall figure. They stood hauntingly still, as if whoever it was didn't feel the need to draw breath.

Despite the sun overhead and the sweat on my forehead, a chill swept over me. I turned my back on the figure and picked up my pace, stumbling over the uneven terrain.

At once, something slithered across the leaves behind me.

I broke into a disjointed run, landing heavily on my good foot to avoid damaging my ankle any further, but my footsteps weren't the only ones on the path. Ahead, I caught a glimpse of the Winchester house through the leaves of the trees. Some of the guys were hauling the vintage refrigerator out to the truck. If I could get close enough, whoever was following me would have to give up the chase or risk being pounded by twenty burly construction workers.

Just as the thought crossed my mind and I put on an additional burst of speed, someone tackled me from behind. My breath whooshed out of my lungs as I went crashing to the ground, tucking my head in and somersaulting over my shoulder to avoid injuring myself further.

"Help!" I yelled, struggling against the weight that pinned me to the ground. Covered in dirt and leaves, I managed to flip over to face my attacker.

It was Milo.

"I need to talk to you," he gasped. He looked even more terrible than the last time I had seen him, almost as if he was wasting away. His cheeks were hollow and gaunt, and his usually luscious hair was limp and damp with sweat.

"Milo, get off!"

"I need to talk to you," he said again.

I bucked my hips, dislodging Milo just long enough to squirm out from under him, but he seized the plaster cast around my ankle and pulled me back. I yelled in pain, kicking out at Milo with my good foot.

"I need to talk to you."

Something was wrong with him. His eyes had glazed over, and he apparently couldn't say anything else. I decided to try a different tactic. I stopped struggling, drawing my legs into my chest. Milo sat cross-legged in the dirt. He stared directly at me, but his vacant eyes did not seem to accept his surroundings.

"So talk," I ordered. I glanced at the house again. Bodhi was up there somewhere. If I could fish my cell phone out of my pocket without Milo noticing, maybe I could get Bodhi to call the paramedics. Milo clearly needed help.

He sat with his mouth wide as though he were screaming internally. Then, with no warning whatsoever, he reached up to wrap his fingers around his own neck and squeezed.

"No!"

I shot forward, ignoring the pain in my ankle to seize Milo's wrists and attempt to pull them away from his throat. But Milo was a strong, wiry guy, and no matter how much I wrenched at his hands, he continued to strangle himself.

"Help!" I cried again. I slapped Milo's reddening face, hoping to snap him out of his delirium, but his knuckles turned white as he exerted even more pressure. "Milo, stop!"

"Bailey?"

Bodhi's faint call echoed through the trees.

"Here!" I yelled, still fighting Milo. "Come quickly! Something's wrong with Milo!"

The trees parted, and several pairs of boots thundered down the dirt path. I breathed a sigh of relief as Bodhi, Ethan, and two other construction workers appeared in my line of sight. Bodhi knelt beside me and picked a leaf out of my messy hair.

"Bailey, what happened to you?"

"It's not me. It's Milo!"

"Where is he?"

"What do you mean? He's right—"

But when I looked again, Milo had vanished from beneath my fingertips. It was only me, kneeling on the path, crying and covered in dirt.

"He was there," I said, glancing left and right to make sure Milo hadn't run off into the shadows again. "I swear—"

Bodhi lifted me from the ground, carrying me past Ethan and the other workers. "Let's get you inside."

"We'll check around," Ethan said in a gruff tone. "Just in case."

"Thanks, Ethan," Bodhi said.

I buried my face in Bodhi's shoulder as he toted me to the house, but the darkness behind my eyelids wasn't enough to block out the image of Milo's reddening face as he tried to kill himself.

19

HANGING OUT

*C*lear blue. I floated in the bay, my arms stretched out wide to welcome whatever eternity lay in wait. There were no clouds in sight. Everything was bright and endless. Sunshine sparkled on the surface of the water, warming my skin. I breathed a sigh of relief. If only I could feel this sort of inner peace at every moment of my life.

The scene shifted. Something pulled at my waist, tugging me beneath the surface of the water before I could take another breath. The sky rippled as I went under willingly. There was no sense in putting up a fuss. It would be over in a few minutes. I let myself sink, watching the sky roam farther and farther away.

Then I looked down into a bathtub. Kali stared back, her light hazel eyes identical to mine. Dark curls bloomed around her pink cheeks in the water. She reached out. Little fingers. Little hands. Asking for me. Her tiny mouth opened, and she coughed, releasing a baby-sized air bubble. It rose to the surface and popped. I stared back, unmoving. My arms wouldn't reach for her.

Kali's brown eyes morphed into blue ones. Suddenly, the

body in the bath was Caroline. The white subway tiles of the Winchesters' first floor bathroom made her tan, freckled nose look pale. Hands encircled her throat. Not my hands. They held her down. She thrashed, splashing water over the lip of the tub. Her face turned blue.

I woke screaming. I felt it tear out of my throat. Felt the ringing in my ears. A ripping sound resonated through the room. I'd literally torn the sheets from the mattress. Beside me, Bodhi rocketed up, groping around in the night like a panicked blind man. He found my hands, clenched in the sheets, and pried my fingers apart.

"Bailey. Bailey! Stop. *Stop screaming!*"

With a jolt, my mouth snapped shut. I hadn't even realized that my vocal cords were still working on overdrive. I drew in a raspy breath. My throat burned with the effort. Bodhi cradled my face between his warm hands.

"Hey. Look at me. Look."

I found his warm brown eyes with my own.

"You're okay," he promised. He swept my sweaty hair away from my forehead, where it lay plastered to my scalp. "Everything's okay."

"She's dead."

"Who?"

"Kali. Caroline. Everyone."

In the light of the moon, Bodhi's jawline rippled, his teeth grinding together at my declaration. "Not everyone. You and I are alive."

I pushed Bodhi's fingers away from my face. I needed air. Space. He understood, backing out of my personal area. I kicked the heavy quilt off my legs.

"Can you open the window?" I asked.

Bodhi crossed the room to draw the curtains back and lift

the frame. The window was just large enough to let a draft inside. I inhaled the salty scent of the air.

"That was bad, Bailey," Bodhi said, sitting on the edge of the bed. "That's the worst I've ever seen you. What did you and Doctor Marx talk about yesterday?"

I wiped my forehead with the hem of my shirt. "It's not because we talked. I think Caroline had something to do with it."

"You think Caroline is messing with your dreams? Can she do that?"

"I felt her there," I said. Exhaustion overwhelmed me. All I wanted to do was go back to sleep, but the horrors of the past waited in unconsciousness. "It's hard to explain. It was like when we were in the basement with her. You feel something. You *know* you're not alone, but there's no rational proof to back you up."

Bodhi curled up at the foot of the bed like an oversized cat. "Do you think she's trying to tell you something?"

I hugged my legs into my chest and rested my chin on my knees. "If she is, she's not doing a very good job."

"I'm starting to think that this lack of sleep is causing you more trouble than anything else," said Bodhi, propping his head up on his elbow. "You start hallucinating after three days of insomnia. I looked it up."

"You think that's why I saw Milo on Monday night."

He bit his lip, as if hesitant to continue the conversation. "Bailey, he wasn't in the woods. Ethan and the crew combed every inch of land around the house. There was no sign of Milo. If he was in such bad shape, I doubt he would've made it so far."

"So then he wasn't in the backyard either."

"I don't think so."

Even with Bodhi's level head, I found it hard to believe that I'd imagined both events. They were so vivid, just like

Caroline's presence in my nightmares. "It doesn't make any sense," I told Bodhi. "Why would I be seeing things?"

"Stress, lack of sleep, change in medication," Bodhi listed. "Bailey, I want you to take it easy for the next couple days. Caroline's investigation can wait. You're no good to her like this anyway."

I silently agreed, but Caroline was far from patient. It had been three days since the two of us sat together on the office floor, watching the Winchesters' home videos. She hadn't contacted me since then, but a feeling of urgency coursed through my veins, as though my heart pumped blood at a faster rate to encourage me along. I needed to slow down enough to gather my thoughts. I needed more information to figure everything out. But why did Caroline's unexpected appearance in my usual nightmares make it feel like time was running out?

Bailey and Bodhi: Flipping Out

SUMMER IS WINDING DOWN, *flippers, and we are finally making serious headway on the Winchester house. The kitchen and living room are stripped bare. The bay windows are gone, replaced by the biggest sliding doors we could order. I've reorganized the entire first floor so that we can tackle the rest of the rooms, which by the way was no easy feat with a fractured ankle. There's good news on that front too. I've finally conquered my stubbornness. Temporarily, at least. Black Bay's family doctor warned me that if I didn't give my bones a break (no pun intended) that they would never heal. As such, I've stayed off my feet as much as possible, and what do you know? My ankle has stopped throbbing every time I put weight on it.*

This weekend is Black Bay's infamous summer festival. Apparently, the entire town pitches in to prepare for it, including a lot of the guys that Bodhi and I employ to renovate the house. We gave them Friday and Saturday off, because who are we to tamper with tradition? In the meantime, Bodhi and I are working alone. It's just like the old days before we could afford to pay anyone else to help us. You may think I'm crazy, but there's something romantic about sweating the days away, getting down and dirty with just your husband. Wow. That sounded racier than I intended it to be. Then again, it's been a wild couple of days!

Anyway, we can't wait to kick it off with the locals tomorrow afternoon. I'll be sure to take plenty of pictures. I want you all to experience the full force of Black Bay's small town charm. Hell, I might even take a few videos. Apparently, the flag football tournament can get pretty rowdy!

STAY TUNED,
  Bailey

THE SUMMER FESTIVAL was all the locals could talk about. The park lawn had been mowed in anticipation of the flag football tournament, lemonade stands and food trucks appeared in the streets, and a small stage had been erected for whatever performances were being featured that year. It was the first community event that Bodhi and I really wanted to go to. Before we moved to Black Bay, we had never lived long enough in one place to get to know the people in our neighborhood. Here, every person we ran into encouraged us to go to the festival. For once, Bodhi and I were excited to spend some time out and about with each other.

"It's the best event of the year," Ethan promised to me one day as I watched Bodhi install new wood flooring in the living room. A couple guys helped lay down the planks, and they nodded in agreement with Ethan's words. "Everything's local. Great beer, good music, and excellent company. The two of you can't hole up in this house forever. It will do you some good to get outside and socialize."

So we planned to take Saturday easy. Blissfully, my sleeping habits had improved over the last few nights without rhyme or reason. According to Bodhi, I still tossed and turned, but ever since I'd focused more of my attention on rearranging the Winchesters' personal items rather than combing through them for clues, my nightmares were less vivid. I expected Caroline to disapprove of my relaxation techniques, but she had been inactive ever since I'd seen her in my dreams. On some level, I felt guilty. My promise to help Caroline pass over was wearing thin, but I justified it by telling myself that as soon as I fully recovered, I would jump back into the mystery surrounding her and Patrick's deaths.

With our kitchen out of service, it was up to Bodhi or me to pick up breakfast in town. I stopped by the Sanctuary on Friday morning, ordering blueberry muffins and two cups of coffee to go. As I waited at the counter for Ava to pour the coffee, a woman sitting in the far corner of the cafe caught my eye. She absentmindedly stirred honey into a cup of tea as she read through a battered copy of *Pride and Prejudice*. Her round face and layered brown hair was familiar to me, though I was certain I'd never run into her in town before.

When Ava returned, passing the paper bag of muffins across the countertop, I asked, "Hey, Ava. Who's that woman in the corner?"

She glanced over. "Oh, that's Jane Lacroix. She teaches English at the high school."

"Would I know her from anywhere else?"

I handed over a ten-dollar bill. The cash register pinged

as Ava answered. "I'm not sure. I don't suppose you're a part of the book club. Jane runs it these days."

I shook my head. "No, that's not it."

"Sorry, sweetie. I'm at a loss then."

"Don't worry about it," I said, smiling. "Thanks for the coffee."

"Any time."

I turned to leave, my gaze lingering on the woman. She turned a page, immersed in her novel, and the sun glinted off of her whiskey-colored eyes. I could've sworn I'd seen her somewhere before. My curiosity got the best of me. I walked over to her.

"Excuse me?"

The woman looked up with a polite curiosity, but when she saw who had interrupted her reading, she smiled in recognition. "I know you."

"You do?" I asked, taken aback. "I was just trying to figure out why you looked familiar to me."

Delicately, she closed her book and set it aside. "Oh, we've never actually met, but I'm an avid fan of your blog."

"You're kidding!"

Her answering laugh pealed like bell tones in the cafe. "Not at all. Actually, I followed your adventures long before you ever landed in Black Bay. Can you imagine how surprised I was when you showed up in our little town? I'm Jane, by the way."

"Bailey," I said, balancing the coffee and muffins against my chest to shake her hand. "I still can't remember how I know you."

"I'm not sure—oh!" She snapped her fingers as if she'd just remembered something. "Ethan has been helping out at your house, hasn't he? He and I go way back."

The comment jogged my memory. I had seen this woman before, but not in person. There was a picture of her in the

Winchesters' photo albums, the one with Ethan and his father. No wonder it took me a while to recognize her. That photo had been taken twenty years ago.

"You were Ethan's fiancée, weren't you?"

She sipped from her teacup, though I guessed it had gone cold by now. "That was a long time ago."

There was no iciness in her tone, but I sensed that I had broached a topic of conversation not often acknowledged. "I'm sorry," I said. "I didn't mean to pry. Ethan's mentioned you. That's all."

"Ah, if it's Ethan who's mentioned me, I doubt you have a positive impression of my personality."

"Pardon?"

Jane pulled her novel toward her, opening it to the first page. "It is a truth universally acknowledged that a single man in possession of a good fortune must be in want of a wife," she read off. She tapped the page with her index finger and looked up at me. "At one time, the locals might've described Ethan as a young, modern version of Mr. Darcy. He was proud and aloof, and I sure fancied myself his Elizabeth. Unfortunately, our story didn't end happily ever after."

"Would it be intrusive of me to ask why?"

She waved a hand dismissively. "The whole town knows the story anyway. Ethan went through a rough patch after his father died. You would never know it now, but for a while, all he did was drink and gamble. I broke it off when I realized he'd emptied his bank account playing roulette." She shook her head, chuckling lightly. "Boy, did the town hate me after that. No one could believe I broke Ethan Powell's heart."

"Wow," I said. "I never would've guessed Ethan had that kind of trouble when he was younger. He seems so put together now."

"He finally got help," Jane explained. "It did him a world of good. All of a sudden, he was the town's golden boy again.

He stopped drinking and wasting his money. Got the guys at the lumber mill back on their feet after Chris Winchester died. It was like he was an entirely different person."

"But the two of you never got back together?"

"Oh, I tried to get him back," she said, pushing her cold tea across the table. "I sent him a letter, telling him to come find me when he was ready, but he never took me up on it."

"That seems like a shame."

Jane sighed heavily, tracing the printed face of Mr. Darcy on the cover of her book. "I only have myself to blame. Ethan and I dated on and off since high school. Everyone expected us to end up together, but I blew it. I left him when he needed me most. I wouldn't forgive me either."

Jane's regret struck a chord with me. Her relationship went south and she bailed out, unwilling to take on the challenge of making it work. When Bodhi and I lost Kali, I had considered the same option, but where would I be now if the two of us had decided to divorce then? The last five years had been full of remorse and empty promises, but if I were alone, would I have ended up with the same misgivings as Jane?

"Ethan never married though," I pointed out. The wedding band on her finger had not escaped my notice. "You did."

She wiggled her ring finger. "Yes, it all worked out in the end. But you know how it is. Sometimes, you can't help but wonder what could have been."

I nodded in agreement. "I'll leave you to your book. It was nice to meet you. If you like, stop by the house. I've never met one of my followers in real life before. It would be fun to show you how we get things done."

"I would love that," said Jane. "Have a good day, Bailey."

"And you."

. . .

BACK AT THE HOUSE, Bodhi stood on a ladder, inspecting the giant wooden beams that stretched across the ceiling of the living room for wear and tear. With any luck, we wouldn't have to replace them, but Washington was infamous for termite damage. As I set the coffee and pastries on the card table—now the only surface free of construction dust—Bodhi glanced down.

"Took you long enough," he said. "Was there a line?"

I unwrapped a muffin and took a bite. "No, I ran into Ethan's ex-fiancée."

"How was that?"

"Enlightening."

"Really? What did she—"

The ladder clanged, and Bodhi's voice cut off, replaced with a horrifying gagging sound. When I spun around, he dangled just below the support beam, as though an invisible hangman's noose was strung around his neck. Bodhi kicked his feet wildly, eyes bulging out of his skull as he groped for the rope around his neck that wasn't there. I sprang into action, limping across the living room to pick up the fallen ladder. I grunted as I lifted it and propped it against the beam. Then I grabbed Bodhi's sneakered feet and placed them firmly on the rungs of the ladder. As soon as his weight settled, the force released him, and he practically fell down the ladder and into my arms.

We sank to the floor together. Bodhi massaged his throat, drawing in short gasps of air. His eyes watered, bloodshot, and his face was bright red from the pressure.

"Patrick," Bodhi declared hoarsely. "I saw Patrick."

My pulse thundered through my veins, pounding in my head. "What?"

"He was there," Bodhi went on, pointing upward weakly. "Next to me. Already dead. Bloody, too. Like someone beat him with a baseball bat before stringing him up."

The image made my stomach lurch, and I felt that one bite of blueberry muffin rise in the back of my throat. I tried to think rationally. "Let me get this straight. Three days after I dream that Caroline drowned in a bathtub, just like Kali, you suddenly see Patrick being hung up in his own house."

Bodhi squeezed his eyes shut as if trying to banish the thought from his mind. He lay still on the newly installed wood flooring, his hands still resting on his throat. I brushed his curls back, wondering what would've happened to Bodhi if I hadn't been around to put the ladder back up.

"Bodhi."

"Hmm?"

"I don't think this is a coincidence."

He opened one eye to study me. "Meaning?"

"At first, I thought I dreamt of Caroline in the bath because that's how Kali died. Now I think she's been trying to tell us how she and Patrick were killed."

Bodhi propped himself up on his elbows. He looked like hell thawed out, but at least he was no longer in immediate danger. "Bailey, what are the odds that Caroline died the exact same way as Kali?"

"In Caroline's case, I don't think it was an accident."

Bodhi looked nauseous at the implication, a pale green tint coloring his features. "It does have a perverse romance to it, doesn't it? Christopher and Elizabeth drown at sea. Their kids suffocate to death in different ways. Whoever did this was sick in the head, Bailey."

"No doubt, but knowing how the Winchester children died doesn't help us figure out who in town wanted to kill them."

Bodhi sighed and looked up at the support beams. "Caroline?" he called. "I know you're there. We could really use a hint that doesn't involve bodily harm, if you don't mind."

Upstairs, several doors slammed in quick succession.

Caroline was listening in. Carefully, I helped Bodhi to his feet. He swayed, leaning heavily on me. I steadied him against the wall.

"You okay?"

"Head rush," he said. "I'm fine. Let's go."

Together, we climbed the stairs. In the hallway, the door to each bedroom and bathroom was closed except for one. Caroline's bedroom lured us toward it, but we hesitated in the landing. I had yet to find the time to pick the books up from the floor. They lay abandoned, spines cracked and pages torn, as though waiting for someone to light a match and set them ablaze. I frowned at the continued absence of her journals. We hadn't found them in the house, and I strongly suspected that someone had confiscated them from the premises.

A small paperback fell from the broken bookshelf, joining its brethren on the floor. Bodhi jumped, bracing himself against the door frame in anticipation of a bigger event, but nothing else moved. I stepped through the wreckage and knelt to pick up the book.

"What is it?" asked Bodhi from the hallway.

I held up the paperback to show him the mournful painted face on the front cover.

"*Ethan Frome.*"

20

RECONNAISSANCE

*B*odhi and I sat at the card table in the empty living room, nursing our cold cups of coffee. I skimmed through the pages of *Ethan Frome*, wondering if Caroline had left another hint between the front and back covers. The margins were full of notes, and I recognized the cramped handwriting as Caroline's own, but there were no clues as to why she led us to the book.

"Why don't we just ask Ethan if he knows anything?" Bodhi suggested. A faint red line had appeared around his neck, as though the noose that had strung him from the ceiling earlier had really been there.

"Obviously, he knows something," I countered, flipping to the last few pages. I'd filled Bodhi in on my interesting conversation with Jane Lacroix that morning. "Otherwise, why would Caroline have given us his name? God, this book is depressing."

"Why, what happens?"

"It's about this guy who pines over his sick wife's cousin," I summarized. I remembered reading the short novel in high school, but the ending was what stuck in my mind. "He has no money to run away with her, and he feels bad for wanting to leave his wife, so they decide to make a suicide pact. Neither one of them actually dies though. Ethan walks with a limp, the cousin becomes paralyzed, and both of them ironically end up in the care of Ethan's wife to live the rest of their miserable lives together."

"Cheery."

I tossed the book across the card table. It slid off the edge and landed on the floor with a light thump. "We can't just roast Ethan for information. Talking about the Winchesters upsets him. Besides, we don't know if he's on our side or not."

"Ethan?" said Bodhi incredulously. "Are you kidding? You were the one who told me how devastated he was after the Winchesters died. Now you think he was in on it?"

"All I know is that a murderer has been on the loose in Black Bay for almost twenty years." Reluctantly, I picked the book off the floor and studied the cover. "And Ethan already knows about Caroline."

Bodhi rubbed the welts on his neck. "He hasn't mentioned anything about it since that day I fell off the roof."

"Maybe he didn't buy our explanation."

"This is silly," said Bodhi. "If we can't ask Ethan what he knows, how the hell are we supposed to figure out what Caroline meant by giving us that book?"

The muffins were stale now. I swallowed a chewy morsel before discarding the rest in a garbage bag full of construction waste. "I have an idea, but you're not going to like it."

He threw me a skeptical glance. "Okay. Hit me with it."

"Ethan's fiancée told me that he had drinking and gambling problems after his father died," I explained. "He eventually sought help. As you and I already know, he used to visit Doctor Marx on a regular basis. I saw his file in her office during my last appointment. What if we were able to get our hands on it?"

Bodhi narrowed his eyes. "You want to break into a psychologist's office and steal confidential medical records?"

"Yes."

"And you think that's easier and safer than casually asking Ethan if there's anything he'd like to tell us?"

Ethan Frome fixed me with an accusing stare from his two-dimensional home on the cover of the paperback. I turned the novel over so that he faced the table instead.

"Listen," I said to Bodhi. "Doctor Marx and her secretary both take their lunch hour at the same time. We could sneak in, have a look at Ethan's file, and get out of there before Doctor Marx even orders a drink."

"You're forgetting something. How are we supposed to get in without a key?"

I rolled my eyes. "Please. This is Black Bay. Who here ever locks their doors?"

"We could go to prison for something like this."

"Oh, come on." I nudged Bodhi's leg beneath the table. "Like you've never been arrested before."

He jabbed the table with his index finger to emphasize his following point. "Getting booked for trespassing because you were peacefully protesting and practicing civil disobedience is entirely different from accessing medical records that don't pertain to your own self."

"Whatever you say, Ghandi."

"Bailey, I'm serious."

"So am I," I declared. I gestured to the red marks around his neck. "Look at your neck, Bodhi. Look at my ankle. Or my arm. Or my knees. How long before Caroline loses her patience entirely and kills one of us?"

"Don't say that."

"It's a possibility," I insisted. "She's proved time and time again that she has no problem with injuring us, even if we are trying to help her. Do you want to figure this out or do you want to become the next ghost that haunts the Winchester house?"

Bodhi toyed with a rip in the plastic covering of the card table. I stayed quiet, waiting out his response. I'd already made up my mind. With or without Bodhi, I was going to Doctor Marx's office, but it would be a lot easier if I had someone to act as a lookout.

"I know that look," Bodhi said, regarding me from across the table.

"What look?" I asked innocently.

"That smirk on your face," he clarified. "That's the same face you make every time you've decided to do something outrageous. Like jump off a cliff in Santorini."

"Admit it," I said, grinning. "That was the most fun you've ever had. Besides, I only did it to impress you. You were the one with an adrenaline addiction. Whatever happened to that?"

"I grew up."

"Hardly. Come on," I wheedled. "It's nearly noon. We could be there and back in less than an hour, potentially armed with new information about the Winchesters. What say you?"

Bodhi considered the mischievous look on my face, one eyebrow raised. Then he threw up his hands in defeat. "Aye," he said wearily.

"Aye!" I cried in triumph, rising from my seat at the table. "Wow. We haven't done that bit in a while. Feels good, doesn't it?"

Bodhi rolled his eyes and got to his feet. "Come on, you nutcase. Let's get this over with."

· · ·

BODHI DROVE US INTO TOWN. The locals waved as we passed by, recognizing our familiar white truck. We pulled into the crowded parking lot of the fresh market across the street from Doctor Marx's office. Bodhi piloted the truck into a free space behind a long, blue dumpster, craning his neck to get a better look at our target.

"This is foolproof," he muttered, shrinking in the driver's seat as people around us loaded up their groceries. "No one's going to see us at all."

"Shh." I watched the door to Doctor Marx's office. It was five minutes until noon. "As soon as Doctor Marx leaves, we'll go in. That way, we have plenty of time to read through Ethan's file."

"Bailey, no one's going to believe that we're just here for groceries," he snapped. He glanced out the side window, where a mother strapped twin boys into the booster seats of her minivan. She waved cheerily to Bodhi, who gave a tight-lipped smile as he waved back.

"Would you rather stay in the car?"

"No!"

"Then stop complaining."

I kept my eyes trained on the door, occasionally checking the clock radio. Sure enough, right at twelve, the office door swung open. Doctor Marx and her secretary emerged from the small building, strolled down the street, and disappeared around the corner. I turned to Bodhi.

"Here we go."

As soon as we stepped out of the truck, I linked my arm through Bodhi's. "Smile," I told him. The worried lines between his eyebrows were no good for our cover. "Pretend we're out for a stroll."

His lips tilted upward ever-so-slightly.

"Convincing," I said.

Together, we crossed the road. Traffic was light. Most of

Black Bay was still at work, with the exception of a few stay-at-home moms shopping for back-to-school items with their kids. Bodhi and I edged around Doctor Marx's office, ignoring the glass-paneled door with the practice's name printed in white font. There was an emergency exit around the back side of the building, which gave us a better opportunity to keep our mission covert. I tugged on the handle, and the door swung forward easily.

"I told you," I said to Bodhi with a hint of satisfaction.

"Just get inside."

The office was empty and dark. Without Doctor Marx's soothing presence and the annoying fluorescent lights overhead, it felt like an entirely different place. Even the Zen waterfall was still and quiet. Behind Doctor Marx's desk, the filing cabinet waited like a soldier at attention. I rolled Doctor Marx's office chair out of the way and tried to pull the top drawer of the filing cabinet open. It stubbornly protested.

"That's that," said Bodhi. "Can we go now?"

I shot him a look. "You have no faith in me."

I upended a decorative can of pens sitting on Doctor Marx's desk. Sure enough, there was a paper clip at the bottom. With a dramatic flourish for Bodhi's benefit, I shoved it into the filing cabinet lock. After a few seconds of maneuvering the paper clip around, the drawer sprang open with a gratifying click. I took a bow then rifled through the files, looking for Ethan's name.

"Watch the front door," I told Bodhi.

He obeyed, heading out to the waiting room and perching on the arm of one of the uncomfortable chairs to peek out of the vertical blinds on the front windows. Meanwhile, I searched the files as rapidly as possible. Ethan's name hadn't appeared as quickly as I'd liked, even though I could've sworn I'd seen his file in the top drawer. I growled in frustration and checked the next drawer down. No luck. On a whim, I knelt down and yanked open the bottom drawer. I was rewarded with the sight of Ethan's file, stuffed haphazardly at the very back, and extracted the manila folder.

It was thinner than I expected. The other patient files boasted pages upon pages of Doctor Marx's notes, copies of prescriptions, and official insurance documents. Ethan's folder felt light. I sat down at Doctor Marx's desk to leaf through it. The doctor's notes were organized by date, starting with the most recent, so I took one from the bottom of the pile. It was dated January fifth of 1996. From Caroline's journals, I knew that Ethan's father had died roughly a year before. Had he waited that long to seek help?

DATE OF EXAM: 1/5/1996
   Patient Name: Powell, Ethan

ETHAN PRESENTS with a history of a manic mood type. His associated symptoms include decreased need for sleep and repeated hypomanic episodes. He reports feeling "off" since the death of his father in January of last year, increases in compulsive and addictive behavior, and lapses in memory. His disturbances began or have been occurring for six months. Ethan reports feeling strained over his position at the local lumber mill. He was unable to keep the business afloat on his own. He feels that he has let his father and grandfather down by relinquishing ownership of the family business to another party. Ethan reports mixed melancholia and rage at being demoted to a shift supervisor. Current stressors include work environment, pressure to please his significant other, and economic anxiety despite the monetary benefits of his recent business sale.

· · ·

I FLIPPED THE NOTE OVER, hoping there was more information about the lumber mill on the back, but Doctor Marx's concise reports moved on to a suggested treatment plan instead. Nowadays, Ethan owned and managed Powell's Lumber Mill, but from the hints in Ethan's file, it hadn't always been that way. Apparently, Christopher Winchester finally managed to convince Ethan to give up the family business, but at what price? Ethan was blatantly displeased with the route his professional life had taken. According to more of Doctor Marx's progress reports, he took that frustration out through less than productive methods.

DATE OF EXAM: *3/7/1996*
    Patient Name: Powell, Ethan

ETHAN REPORTS his mood is much improved but cannot recall what made him feel so angry last week. In comparison to his morose attitude during our last session, he is hyperverbal, speaking rapidly, and gesticulating as he talks. Ethan's version of his recent social interactions are at odds with eyewitness facts. He claims to have reconciled with his previous fiancée in a recent public meeting. However, witnesses report that the couple argued and the meeting ended when Ethan's fiancée abruptly stormed out. In addition, Ethan claims to have come to terms with his new position at the lumber mill, but records indicate that he has not been present at work for the past two weeks.

DATE OF EXAM: *4/15/1996*
    Patient Name: Powell, Ethan

. . .

Ethan blatantly exhibits signs and symptoms of worsening alcohol addiction and compulsive gambling. He reports fatigue and depression and hints that he has engaged in self-harming activities. Ethan appears increasingly paler and skinnier with each of our visits, and he often has dark circles under his eyes. In addition, a distinct smell of vodka enters the room when he does, but he vehemently avoids any questions, no matter how subtly delivered, that have to do with his possible addictions.

My brow crinkled as I read through Doctor Marx's notes. The Ethan Powell I knew was always jovial, kind, and helpful. It was hard to believe that he was once so volatile, unreliable, and inconsistent. Did his father's death really provoke such mania in him? And if so, what happened to inspire Ethan to change his ways?

In the waiting room, the vertical blinds rattled noisily. Bodhi retreated from the window and poked his head into the office.

"Bailey!" he hissed. "Incoming. Doctor Marx's secretary is on her way back."

"What?" I checked my watch. "It's only been fifteen minutes!"

"She probably forgot something. Let's go."

I shook off Bodhi's grip as he tried to steer me toward the back exit. "One more minute. I think we're on to something here."

Bodhi glanced out to the waiting room, his eyes popping with alarm. "Are you insane? Put Ethan's file back and let's get out of here."

"In a second."

I scanned Ethan's most recent progress report, reading through it as fast as humanly possible. If the scant file was

any indication, Ethan hadn't returned to talk out his problems with Doctor Marx since the date of his last visit.

DATE OF EXAM: 9/23/1996
  Patient Name: Powell, Ethan

*ETHAN CONTINUES TO IMPROVE. He reports greater control over
impulsive thoughts and increased ability to think rationally. He
appears healthy, calm, and collective today, speaking evenly
without excessive fidgeting. He continues to frankly address the
matter of his addictions and credits the town's recent tragedy as the
motivation he needed to better himself. Ethan claims that this event
caused him to "wake up" and realize that he had been squandering
his potential. He has taken an active role in helping the locals
recover from the tragedy, and those who interact with Ethan on a
daily basis report that he plays a crucial part in Black Bay's read-
justment efforts.*

AT THE BOTTOM of the page, Doctor Marx had listed a
number of weekly dates. Next to each one, she had scribbled
"session canceled and rescheduled by patient." A blue sticky
note was stuck to the back of the progress report, display one
last brief detail concerning Ethan Powell.

*10/29/1996: Ethan visited the office without an appointment
today. He was in good spirits, thanked me for all I had done for
him, and announced that he no longer required our weekly sessions.
Though I encouraged him to schedule a checkup with me in six
months, he politely declined. I wish him all the best.*

. . .

THE BELL over the front entrance chimed as Doctor Marx's secretary let herself in.

"Bailey!" Bodhi pleaded in a low whisper, propping the back door open with his foot and gesturing through it.

I hastily shoved Doctor Marx's notes into the manila folder and wedged it back into its place in the bottom drawer of the filing cabinet, but when I kicked the drawer shut, it echoed with a metallic clang through the office. I winced.

"Hello?" called the secretary. The click of her heels stalled in the waiting room, as though she had stopped moving to listen for other irregular noises.

"Let's go," mouthed Bodhi silently.

I tiptoed toward the back door, praying that apprehension rooted Doctor Marx's secretary to her spot in the waiting room. But when I heard the tap of her heels across the floor again, growing more audible as she neared the door to the office, I dove for the exit, dragging Bodhi along behind me. We sprinted around the corner of the building before the door had even swung shut. My walking boot skidded across a patch of loose gravel in the parking lot. Bodhi caught me under my armpits before I fell, but with the squeak of the back door's hinges, I knew we didn't have enough time to make it across the street to the supermarket before the secretary caught sight of us. Hunched over, I tugged Bodhi into the landscaping that bordered the building, pressing him flat against the uncomfortable bed of redwood mulch.

Through the leaves of the dense bushes, we watched as the secretary's black pumps crossed the blacktop toward our hiding space. She paused on the other side of the shrubbery that concealed us, pivoting to check her surroundings. Bodhi's breath hiccupped. I clapped a hand over his mouth and put a finger to my lips. His chest rose and fell like a vibrating drumhead beneath me, but he stayed quiet. After the longest minute of my life, the secretary sighed, turned, and went back inside.

Air whooshed out of my lungs in relief. I'd been holding my breath without realizing it. I rested my head against Bodhi's chest, trying to mellow out. He moved my hand from his lips.

"That was close."

"You're telling me," I murmured.

"You were right though," he said, shifting underneath me.

"About what?"

Bodhi pushed himself to his elbows so that he could look at me. "This was a fun adrenaline rush. But do you know what would make it even better?"

"What's that?" I asked, confused.

He waggled his eyebrows suggestively.

"Oh my gosh." I smacked his shoulder lightly, shoving myself up from the ground so that we were no longer pressed together. "Bodhi!"

He laughed and got to his feet. "I'm only saying!"

I brushed mulch off of Bodhi's back, trying to keep the grin off my face. This was a reconnaissance mission after all, and we couldn't afford to get caught for goofing off now. As we darted across the street to the supermarket parking lot and jumped in the truck, the mood grew serious again.

"So?" Bodhi prompted as the ignition turned over and the truck roared to life. "What did you find out?"

I squinted as a cloud shifted, spraying sunshine through the windshield. "That Ethan wasn't always the guy we know today. He had a lot of problems after his dad died. Alcohol, gambling, arguing with his fiancée."

Bodhi steered the truck out of the parking lot. "That doesn't really explain why he would want to hurt Patrick and Caroline."

"Maybe not," I agreed. "But one of the reasons his health

deteriorated so quickly was because the lumber mill was failing under his ownership and Chris Winchester bought it out from under him."

"So he might've had a grudge against the Winchesters," Bodhi speculated. "That doesn't mean he killed their kids."

"I just find it all too convenient that a month after the Winchesters died, Ethan's suddenly back on his feet and feeling better than ever," I said, recalling the date on the last progress report. "People don't learn to cope with mental illness in a month, Bodhi. Something doesn't add up."

As we trundled along the main road, I spotted a familiar figure walking along the sidewalk. It was Jane, holding a plastic bag with the name of the local used bookstore printed on its side. At the sight of her, my conversation with Ethan from several days ago echoed in my mind. He claimed to have been with Jane on the night the Winchesters died. If there was anyone who could confirm or deny that, it was Jane herself.

"Bodhi, slow down," I requested, rolling down my window. The truck braked, and I waved to the woman on the sidewalk. "Hey, Jane!"

Jane glanced up. When she saw who was in the truck, she waved merrily and crossed the grass to lean in through the window. "Long time, no see," she joked.

"Want a ride?" I offered.

"Do I!" Jane opened the door behind me and hopped into the truck. "Whew! Thank goodness for the pair of you. This summer must be breaking all kind of heat records." She slid to the center of the bench seat, resting her elbows on the console between me and Bodhi. "You must be Bodhi," she said, offering her hand as Bodhi pulled away from the curb. "I'm Jane Lacroix. Bailey and I met this morning."

Bodhi shook hands over his shoulder without looking

away from the road. "So she told me. I hear you're a fan of the blog. Where can we drop you off?"

"At the high school, please," said Jane. "Can you believe summer's nearly over? I spent the whole week reorganizing my classroom."

"I'm almost glad," I said. "Bodhi and I can't wait for the cooler weather. It's hell renovating a house in this heat."

"I can't imagine!"

We drove past the park, where volunteers were putting the final touches on the venue for the summer festival the following afternoon. One man lined the flag football field with fresh white paint. A woman with a pig snout printed on her black apron manned a mammoth barbeque smoker. On the modest stage, two volunteers worked in tandem to raise a colorful banner advertising the twentieth Winchester Celebration.

In the backseat, Jane clicked her tongue. "I can't believe it's been twenty years already. Sometimes, it feels like the Winchesters just died yesterday."

Bodhi and I exchanged loaded looks.

"Have you read my recent blog posts?" I ventured carefully.

"Of course I have," replied Jane. "I love that you've done a few pieces on the Winchesters. God, it's nice to think about them again. I joined the book club because of Liz, you know. She was something else."

"I'd like to continue writing about them," I said, hoping that my tone felt light and casual. Bodhi's hands tensed on the steering wheel as though anticipating my next sentence. "With the anniversary approaching, I want to do something that commemorates their influence on Black Bay. A tribute of sorts."

"That would be lovely."

"I thought so too." I pivoted in my seat to look Jane in the eye. "Here's the thing, Jane. I want to gather as much information as possible before I publish anything. That way I don't flub the whole thing. You wouldn't happen to remember anything about that day, would you?"

Jane's perfectly plucked eyebrows scrunched together. "I remember that day vividly, but I'm afraid none of my recollections pertain to the Winchesters themselves."

"Oh?" I said, feigning ignorance. "What happened?"

"Ethan invited himself over for an early dinner," she said, rolling her eyes. "I'd broken off our engagement months before, but he spent a good long time begging me to take him back before the Winchesters died. Anyway, he promised that he'd finally stopped drinking, but he turned up at my apartment smelling like the floor of a distillery."

"That's no good," said Bodhi sympathetically.

"It sure wasn't," agreed Jane. "Ethan stormed out, and I cried myself to sleep nice and early. I didn't even hear about the Winchesters until the next morning, right after I got a call from the police telling me that Ethan had run his truck into a telephone pole late that night."

"Ethan left?" I asked. "He wasn't with you that night?"

"We didn't even make it to the appetizers," Jane recalled wistfully. "Total waste. I threw out an entire platter of stuffed grape leaves. I didn't have the heart to eat them myself."

Bodhi reached across the console to hold my hand. The gesture was casual enough—Jane had no reason to suspect anything of it—but Bodhi's cold fingers and racing pulse said everything that we were currently unable to voice out loud.

FEAR OF WATER

$\mathcal{A}$s soon as we dropped Jane off at the high school, waving as she disappeared with her bag full of books through the front doors, Bodhi stepped on the gas pedal. The truck growled as we pulled a rough U-turn and barreled toward the bluff.

"Ethan told you he was with her all night?" Bodhi asked, his eyes fixed to the road in front of him. The speed limit through most of Black Bay was twenty-five miles per hour. I grabbed the handhold above the door as we roared past startled pedestrians.

"That's what he said," I confirmed.

"Let's not get ahead of ourselves," said Bodhi, but his words didn't match his actions as he cut off a Jeep in the main roundabout and sped off. "It was a difficult night for all of Black Bay. Maybe Ethan just doesn't remember it correctly."

"Or he needed a cover story," I suggested instead. "Face it, Bodhi. Ethan had a motive. He wanted to get back at the Winchesters for taking over his business. And now we've just discovered that he lied about his alibi. Do you really still think that he's innocent?"

A traffic light ahead turned yellow. Bodhi floored it, and the truck shot through the intersection just as the opposing light flickered green. "Don't you think the police would've opened a murder investigation if there was any evidence that Ethan was up to no good?"

"Not if the entire incident looked like an accident," I pointed out. "You said it yourself. The whole town thinks the family died in a boat crash, including Patrick and Caroline."

"We're missing something," said Bodhi. We finally cleared the shopping district, and Bodhi sped up even more as we passed through Black Bay's one and only neighborhood. "I don't know what, but we sure as hell don't have all the puzzle pieces, Bailey."

Ahead, the space between the trees marked where pavement gave way to packed dirt and the road swiveled upward to the Winchester house. As we plunged into the shadows of the forest that blanketed the side of the bluff, the truck's tires drifted over the dirt. The tail end cut loose, and Bodhi wrenched the steering wheel to correct our path.

"Baby, slow down," I warned, bracing my hands on the dashboard.

He eased off the gas ever-so-slightly, but we still careened up the hill at a hazardous pace. "What do we do now?" he asked. "Do we go to the police with this?"

"It's not the police I want to talk to."

Bodhi threw a sharp look at me. "You want to ask Caroline first, don't you?"

I watched the trees whiz by, blurring together in a haze of dark greens and shadowy browns. "She is the one who convinced us to look into this whole mess."

"To be honest, I would've been perfectly happy living in blissful ignorance," grumbled Bodhi. "What I wouldn't give

251

to believe all four of the Winchesters really did die in a tragic boat accident."

The sunlight filtering in through the trees vanished, darkening the path in front of us. I glanced skyward. Roiling black clouds were moving in over the town. It felt like an omen. Would the storm dissipate by the following afternoon, or would the Winchester celebration be ironically rained out?

"That's why we're doing this, isn't it?" I asked Bodhi. "Because the Winchesters deserve to be at peace?"

"I thought we were doing it because a homicidal teenaged ghost threatened to kill us if we didn't," Bodhi bit back.

"Fair point."

The truck surged over a steep incline. As we crested the small hill, a bolt of lightning flashed across the sky. I looked up, watching as the energy boomeranged through the clouds. When I glanced back down at the front windshield, a truly terrible sight waited for me to notice it. Milo stood in the middle of the road, coated in blood.

"Bodhi, stop!"

With an incoherent yell, Bodhi slammed both feet on the brake pedal. The truck's tires locked up, but our ballistic momentum propelled us across the merciless dirt road. Bodhi's arm flew out, slamming me against the passenger seat, and he yanked the steering wheel to the left. The entire truck turned sideways, slowing us further, but Milo was still in harm's way. He stood stock-still in the middle of the road, blood pouring from a gash in his head. The vacant expression of his startling blue eyes was the last thing I saw before we careened into him.

With a horrible thump, Milo bounced off the passenger side window. I screamed, sobbing at the bloody imprint his face left on the glass. Finally, the truck skidded to a halt, and I threw open the door to leap out of the truck. Milo lay in the space between two spruce trees, his legs bent at an unnatural angle. I raced over, throwing myself to the ground.

"Milo! *Milo!*"

Bodhi slammed the door of the truck closed with unnecessary force. "Christ! What was he doing in the middle of the road? We all could've died!"

I bent over Milo. He was unconscious, and I didn't want to move him in case the impact had somehow affected his spine. Behind me, Bodhi dialed 911.

"Hello? We've just hit someone. Yes, with a car!" His voice pitched and cracked as he paced back and forth, glancing down at Milo's unmoving body. "Halfway up the road to the bluff. Please come quickly. No, he's not responsive. Bailey, is he breathing?"

I leaned over Milo, furiously wiping my eyes to clear my clouded vision. Milo's chest was still. I moved closer, reaching out to press my fingers gingerly to his throat in order to find a pulse, but as soon as I made contact with his blood-soaked skin, Milo inhaled sharply. I yelped, scrambling away from him. His hand shot toward me at an impossible pace and wrapped around my wrist so tightly that my fingers throbbed. Milo dragged me downward, bringing my face within an inch of the horror of his own.

"We're running out of time," he whispered, the words bubbling as though his airway was restricted. "Tomorrow."

"What's tomorrow?" I asked, heaving for breath as I tried to ignore the coating of blood on Milo's long blond eyelashes. "Milo, stay with me."

Milo's eyes rolled back as his head lolled on his neck.

"He's going to pass out," Bodhi said. Whether the information was for me or for the emergency dispatchers on the phone, I didn't know. Regardless, Bodhi's prediction was completely incorrect.

Milo's head snapped upright. He ripped himself out of my

grasp, stumbling to his feet, and stabilized himself against a tree. A smudged bloody handprint marred the bark.

"What the hell are you doing, man?" Bodhi shouted as Milo staggered through the trees.

He looked back at us, a crazed embodiment of hell itself.

"Tomorrow," he rasped.

And then he was gone, swallowed by the darkness of the woods. The heavens opened up, and fat raindrops fell from above, soaking us to the skin within seconds as we stood in shocked silence beside the dented truck.

I WATCHED from beneath the overhang of the Winchester house as Bodhi spoke to Black Bay's fire department team. They arrived on the scene shortly after Milo ran off, searched the surrounding woods for hours, and found neither hide nor hair of him. No footprints. No trail of blood. No indication at all that we had met Milo on our way back up to the house. Even the blood on the side of the truck had been washed away by the rain.

The thunderstorm had fully unleashed its wrath. Rain poured off of the roof in buckets, turning the front yard into a mudslide. It hammered on the top of Bodhi's big yellow umbrella as the wind threatened to yank the small bit of coverage right out of Bodhi's capable hands. The words exchanged between Bodhi and the fire captain were lost in the rolling thunder, but even from a distance, I could see that the captain was frustrated and confused. I didn't blame the guy. His squad had braved the narrow, slippery road, the top of the truck trimming the overhanging branches off of the trees, for what appeared to be a false alarm.

The conversation wrapped up, and Bodhi nodded his thanks to the fire captain as the thick man stepped up into the truck. As they drove off, tires squelching through the mud, Bodhi jogged over to me. Beneath the overhang, he shook the excess rain off the umbrella. It hadn't done him much good. The wind blew the rain sideways, drenching him from the shoulders down.

"Well?" I prompted as Bodhi shucked off his sopping shirt. It landed with a wet plop on the wood decking.

"I'm pretty sure the captain thinks we're pulling his leg," reported Bodhi. He shook out his damp curls like an overexcited dog. His hair had grown well past his chin now. In Black Bay's clean-cut community, Bodhi's casual nature boy look stood out like a sore thumb.

"Meanwhile, Milo's out there somewhere." I squinted into the woods, but the heavy rain shrouded the view beyond the front yard in a gray curtain. "Hurt and bleeding."

"What did he mean anyway?" asked Bodhi. He picked up his shirt and wrung it out. "We're running out of time. To do what? What's happening tomorrow?"

I draped a dry bath towel across Bodhi's shoulders. "The summer festival is the only thing I can think of, but why would Milo care about that? He's made it perfectly obvious that he doesn't care for the local color."

Bodhi tugged me forward, nuzzling my shoulder. The soft, terry towel felt cool and comforting against my cheek as I linked my hands around the small of Bodhi's back. We stood like that on the deck, a moment of peace tucked safely away from the turbulent weather.

"Let's go inside," I murmured. Bodhi nodded and pushed the front door open for us, but as soon as we stepped over the threshold, it became obvious that Milo wasn't the only distraught soul on the bluff that day.

Conversation and song blared in the first floor hallway, as though one of us had left the television on at full volume, but the old 90s era TV in the office didn't have the power to fill every corner of the massive house with sound. Something—

or someone—amplified the audio, and the melodious peal of Caroline's laughter reverberated so loudly it felt as though the house itself was alive and emoting.

"*Alex!*" cried Caroline's voice, followed by an immediate giggle.

"*Shh. You'll wake someone.*"

Bodhi and I looked at each other. At the same time, we broke into a run toward the office where the television was. The front door banged shut behind us, although I didn't know if it was an effect of the wind or Caroline's temper. We skidded across the floor into the office and watched the action on the television screen with mounting confusion.

It was footage from one of the Winchesters' home videos that I hadn't seen yet, but instead of playing straight through, the tape rewound itself over and over to show the same ten seconds of film. On the screen, Alexander Lido twirled Caroline around a candlelit glen in the dark woods while Alanis Morissette crooned from a small, battery-powered boom box. He wore a tuxedo jacket over a black T-shirt and jeans with a red rose pinned to the pocket. Caroline danced about in a flowing white nightgown, a matching corsage around her wrist. Above them, stars twinkled in the cloudless night sky. The moon shone down, highlighting the couple's smiles as Alex pulled Caroline close and kissed her. Then the tape rewound again.

"Alex!" Caroline laughed as Alex dipped her dangerously low to the ground, his strong arms firm around her waist to prevent her nightgown from sweeping through the dirt.

"Shh," he said, the joy of their taboo nighttime caper evident in the upward tilt of his lips. "You'll wake someone."

They twirled. They kissed. The tape rewound again.

Bodhi crossed the office, stepping over the fallen grandfather clock, and pushed the eject button on the VHS player. Nothing happened. The footage played on. He tried the volume control next, but Caroline's giggles intensified instead.

"What does she want?" he asked me, studying the screen.

My heart cracked a little more with every additional viewing of Alex and Caroline's dance. "Something she can't have probably."

The footage lagged, distorting Alex and Caroline's voices. They whirled in slow motion, Caroline's nightgown rippling around her legs like wispy clouds. The tape rewound and played again, this time even slower.

"I already talked to Alex, Caroline," I shouted over the twenty-year-old warped dialogue. "He doesn't know anything else."

The tape rewound.

"Alex!" called Caroline.

Again.

"Alex!"

Bodhi covered his ears. With every repetition, Caroline's altered voice sounded more and more like a morbid call from beyond the grave. The video froze, focused on Alex's laughing face, and white noise drowned out even the thunderous downpour outside.

"Just a guess," Bodhi yelled over the deafening hiss of the TV. "But I think she wants us to talk to Alex again."

As soon as he finished his sentence, the television went black. The abrupt absence of static was a welcome respite, and I let out a relieved sigh.

"I'll drive down to Lido's," I told Bodhi. "You stay here."

"What? Why?"

"Because if Milo comes back, at least someone will be around to take care of him," I said. I left the office, pausing just long enough to fetch my raincoat from the small closet beneath the stairs. Bodhi followed me out.

"Then you stay here," he suggested. "The road is too

muddy. You'll spin out. Not to mention how terrible visibility is right now. I'll go talk to Alex."

I swung the raincoat over my still damp shoulders and freed my hair from the collar. "I can drive a truck, Bodhi. Besides, I've already met Alex. He's more likely to talk to me."

Bodhi tracked me to the front door as I picked up the truck's keys from the card table. "What are you supposed to ask him, Bailey? 'Hey, Alex. I was just wondering. Do you happen to know if Ethan Powell murdered your high school girlfriend?'"

"Yeah, that's exactly how I'm going to phrase it," I said sarcastically, pulling my hood over my head. "Maybe Milo's message shook me up, but it feels like Caroline's getting more and more desperate. We need answers. Soon."

I yanked open the front door and stepped out onto the deck, but Bodhi pulled me backward. "Bodhi, let me—"

He silenced me with a kiss, tilting my chin up with the tips of his fingers. Heat rose in my belly as his other hand roamed beneath the raincoat and found my bare skin. Then he pulled away, panting, and cradled my face between his palms.

"Be careful," he murmured quietly.

"I will," I promised. "If I'm not back in an hour, come find me."

And without looking back, I plunged into the deluge.

THE ROAD into town promised more than just a muddy ride. The truck slipped and slid through the trees as I guided it downward. Muck splattered the windows, smeared by force of the rain, and by the time I reached the bottom of the bluff, the muscles between my shoulder blades ached from the effort of keeping the truck upright. When I finally took to the asphalt, steering toward Lido's restaurant, I watched the truck kick sludge from its tires in the rearview mirror in relief.

I drove as fast as I dared in such tricky conditions. This was the worst storm I'd seen since we moved to Black Bay, and it took its toll on the town. Locals sprinted for cover as heavy branches fell from the trees. Near the supermarket, a trash can tipped over and rolled down the street, spewing garbage into the gutters. In the park, one corner of the Winchester celebration banner had come unpinned. It flapped mercilessly in the brutal wind.

Half the town had sought refuge at Lido's. The parking lot was full, so I left the truck on the curb and powered through the weather to reach the entrance. The bell chimed overhead but went unheard. It was barely five o'clock, and the restaurant already bustled with conversation, music, sports commentary from the televisions, and the raging storm outside. I bypassed the host's stand, ignoring the curious looks from the crowd waiting to be seated, and craned my neck to see over the heads of those sitting at the bar. At the end near the register, Alex towered over the patrons, expertly mixing cocktails and pouring beer. I made a beeline for him.

"Alex!" I called over the hum of the restaurant. He made no indication that he'd heard me, carrying on a boisterous discourse over the fate of the Mariners with a young couple sitting at the bar. I waved furiously, trying to get his attention. "Alex!"

He looked up. "Bailey! Glad to see you've weathered the storm. What can I get you?"

I shook my head, squishing myself between two occupied bar stools. The customers on either side of me scooched over to give me a wide berth, avoiding the drip of water from my raincoat. "I don't want a drink. Can I talk to you? In private?"

Alex glanced around the busy bar. "I'm a little occupied at the moment."

"Please," I persisted. Beside me, a man nursing a glass of whiskey eyed me appreciatively despite my wet rat appearance. "It's about Caroline."

Alex's gaze snapped to mine. I rearranged my expression to look as earnest as possible, hoping to convince him to speak with me.

"Two minutes," I promised, holding up a peace sign.

He ducked under the end of the bar, jerking his head toward a back door. I shouldered past a group of thirty-somethings, all wearing Black Bay community center base-ball jerseys, and met Alex at the rear of the hectic restaurant. He held the door open for me, and I dodged through it, emerging onto an empty patio. Clear plastic drop panels sheltered the space from the rain, but the noise of the storm was so clamorous that no Lido's customers decorated the tables here. On a sunny day, with its unobstructed view of the marina and the bay beyond, the patio would've been a perfect place for a lazy meal.

Alex pulled out a chair for me, but I shook my head. I was too anxious to sit down.

"What's this about?" he asked, concern wrinkling the lines on his forehead.

I paced back and forth beside the outdoor minibar, seriously considering swiping a bottle of rum for courage. "I need to ask you something about Caroline, but first, you have to promise to keep this conversation between us."

Alex's dark eyebrows furrowed. "This isn't for your blog, is it?"

"That depends," I said. My hands trembled and I clenched my fingers to stop them from shaking. "What answer will encourage you to tell me the truth?"

"When it comes to Caroline, I don't have anything to lie about."

"A video I found at the house would imply differently," I said.

Alex froze, his deep blue eyes hardening beneath his ball cap.

"The one of the two of you dancing?"

"I know the video," he whispered, glancing furtively toward the door that led back to the main section of the restaurant. "But you don't understand."

"Did she know she was being taped?"

"Yes!" he insisted. "It was her idea. She said it was for posterity, since we never got to go to a real prom. She hid it underneath the window seat in her bedroom, but her parents found it when they were spraying the house for bugs."

"When?"

"What?"

"*When* did her parents find the tape?"

"I don't know. Early August maybe?"

"So shortly after Christopher and Elizabeth Winchester figured out that you were dating their underage daughter against their will, the entire family mysteriously ends up dead?"

Alex's face fell, and he looked at me with such an expression of grief that anyone else watching our conversation from the windows of the restaurant might have thought I'd just told him that I shot his dog.

"I would never do *anything* to hurt any of the Winchesters," said Alex. "My home life was absolute garbage, Bailey. They were my second family."

The tremble in his voice alone convinced me once and for all that Alex was innocent. It was something else that Caroline had wanted me to ask Alex, something that I suspected more and more would lead us to the truth about what really happened twenty years ago.

"What about Ethan Powell?"

Alex sniffed, adjusting the brim of his hat so that it concealed the shine in his blue eyes. "What about him?"

"You told me Patrick and Caroline came to visit you before they got on their parents' boat that night," I reminded him. "After they left, do you remember seeing Ethan at all? Did he come into the restaurant?"

"Ethan used to come to the restaurant every Friday night with his dad," said Alex. "After he died, Ethan stopped coming."

"So you didn't see him."

Alex shook his head. "No, I—" He cut himself off abruptly, his lips parted in sudden remembrance. "Actually, now that you mention it, I did see Ethan that night. He took his fishing boat out."

"On the bay?"

"North. Toward the rocks." He pointed out the patio windows, where I could just make out the black silhouette of the bluff at the topmost part of the bay.

Blood rushed to my head, pounding in my ears. This was the missing piece of the puzzle that Bodhi had been talking about. "When?"

Alex shrugged. "Patrick and Caroline were here at the time. We were goofing off. Around six o'clock maybe? It was still light out."

"Did you seem him come back to the marina?"

"No," said Alex. "But I was working. I could've missed him."

I swallowed hard. "I have to go."

Alex caught the wet sleeve of my raincoat before I could take another step. "Bailey, what's going on? Why do you want to know about Ethan?"

I tried to break free of his grasp, but he held on tight. "Please," I said to him. "If you care about Caroline and Patrick at all, you'll let me go and stay quiet about this entire conversation."

Invoking the names of the Winchester children did the trick. Alex let go of my raincoat, even though he looked as though he had a hundred questions to ask me.

"Promise me one thing," he said.

I checked my watch. My hour was wearing thin. If I didn't get back to the house soon, Bodhi would come looking for me. "What is it?"

Alex took me by the shoulders, his expression serious. "Fill me in on whatever's going on as soon as you can."

I stared into his eyes. They were the same color as the bay on a bitter evening like this, a tempestuous deep blue, sullied equally by determination to know the truth and despair for the girl he had lost twenty years ago.

"I promise."

UNTO THE BREACH

*B*odhi and I spent the majority of the tumultuous night awake, hunched over what little research we had of what might have gone wrong with the Winchesters' afternoon jaunt. We spread out across the new floorboards in the living room, laying out pictures of *Artemis*, Ethan, his father, and the Winchester family themselves. I printed out the pictures I'd taken of the relevant articles from the *Black Bay Banner*. On the side of a cardboard box from the basement, we bullet-pointed what we knew about the chain of events that day, writing hastily with a fat, black permanent marker.

"Here's what I figure so far," I said, leaning back on my knees to read what I'd jotted down on the side of the box. I'd taken the walking boot off. It was coated in mud from my trip into town. "Ethan goes to Jane's house early, right? Let's estimate that around four o'clock. According to this article, the Winchesters took *Artemis* out at five."

"And we already know that Patrick and Caroline weren't on it," supplied Bodhi, chewing on the marker cap. "They were at Lido's with Alex."

"Alex sees Ethan take his fishing boat toward the bluff around six," I went on. "But he doesn't know that Christopher and Elizabeth had already left the marina. When Patrick and Caroline left Lido's, he figured they were joining their parents at the dock."

"But Alex never sees Ethan bring his boat back to the bay." Bodhi studied the scribbles on the box. "Then, according to Jane, Ethan crashes his truck in the middle of the night."

"Which contradicts what Ethan said about the accident occurring in the morning, after he heard the news about the Winchesters."

"Right," Bodhi agreed. "So we have this entire chunk of time during which Patrick, Caroline, and Ethan were all simultaneously missing."

"Don't forget the visions," I reminded him. The support beam overhead loomed in my periphery, as if to remind me how easily Bodhi could've died that very morning.

Bodhi inadvertently rubbed the red marks around his throat. "Which we can assume are courtesy of Caroline. If we're to take that at face value, it means that Patrick and Caroline both died here at the house."

"That would make sense considering Caroline's ghost can't seem to leave the premises," I agreed. "I'm working off clichés here, but spirits usually haunt wherever they died, right?"

"Sure." Bodhi scratched his chin, deep in thought. "The question is, did Ethan take his boat out with the intention of sabotaging the Winchesters' trip?"

I snapped my fingers, recalling the conversation I'd had with Sam Williams. "Sam told me that *Artemis* took damage in the back as well as the front. Any boat involved in a collision like that would definitely need repairs."

"Which would certainly explain why Ethan never brought

his fishing boat back to the marina," Bodhi pointed out. "It would've automatically raised questions."

"But we're still at a loss when it comes to how Ethan ran into Patrick and Caroline."

Bodhi tapped the marker impatiently against the wood floor. "If he was trying to get rid of the entire family, he would've panicked when he realized the kids weren't aboard *Artemis*. Maybe he looped around and met them at the house?"

I massaged my temples with the tips of my fingers. "My head hurts."

Bodhi passed me the bottle of tequila that he had pilfered from the Winchesters' stash. I sipped straight from it. The smooth warmth of the alcohol soothed my jittery nerves and cleared my mind.

"We need a plan," declared Bodhi. I handed him the bottle. He swigged the contents and wiped his mouth. "We need something to confirm Ethan's involvement, because all we've got right now is a scattered timeline and a couple of hunches."

"I have an idea."

"Shoot."

I stretched my legs out in front of me, stifling a moan as my muscles unclenched. "Tomorrow's the summer festival, right?"

Bodhi checked his watch. "Today, actually."

"Whatever. We already know Ethan's going to be there."

"I'm with you so far."

"So what if one of us went to the festival to keep an eye on Ethan while the other breaks into Ethan's house to look for clues?"

"We wouldn't even have to break in," Bodhi said matter-of-factly. He lay on his stomach on the floor, kicking aside a few photos by accident, and perched his chin in his palms. "Ethan keeps a key under the mat."

"How do you know that?"

He inched toward me, flipped over on his side, and rested his head on my thigh. "Because he invited the crew for lunch one day," he said, his eyes drifting shut.

Absentmindedly, I combed my fingers through Bodhi's thick hair. "That's bold. If he's hiding something, I doubt he'd be so nonchalant about having visitors over."

"Unless whatever he's hiding isn't in the house," he mumbled drowsily.

"Still. You go to the festival and track Ethan down. I'll go to his house."

Bodhi's eyes flew open. "Why do I have to be the one to distract Ethan?"

"Because you know him better than I do," I said. "And you're a better liar. All you have to do is keep him busy for an hour or two."

He tapped my nose with his index finger. "I resent that liar comment."

"Bodhi."

"Fine. Later it is. Right now, however, I highly suggest we get some rest."

He stood up then reached down to help me to my feet. Together, we abandoned the mess of photos and notes in the living room and went up to Bodhi's bedroom. I fell into the sheets, exhausted and uneasy. Bodhi pulled me close.

"Bailey?"

"Hmm."

"What happens if we actually do find something that incriminates Ethan?" he asked, his voice soft and uncertain. "Do we go to the police?"

I was quiet, thinking about it.

"No," I finally said. "We go to Caroline."

. . .

IN THE MORNING, the storm had burned itself out, leaving nothing in its wake but a cloudless cerulean sky and a mess of tangled debris in the front yard and in the garden behind the Winchester house. Earlier, Bodhi and I ate leftover pancakes on the back porch, soaking up the sun and trying to ignore the anxiety that built between us in anticipation of that day's event. Ava from the Sanctuary called my cell phone to inform us that the summer festival kickoff had been pushed from noon to two o'clock in order to allow more time for the volunteers to clean up the storm damage in the park. Bodhi groaned at the news.

"It figures," he commiserated. "I wanted to get this over with as quickly as possible. My stomach's been turning since last night."

For the remainder of the morning, Bodhi and I reviewed our strategy. We would head down to the festival together to find Ethan. I would fake some kind of mysterious illness and excuse myself, leaving Bodhi to entertain Ethan. Then I would sneak off to Ethan's house, have a look around, and be back at the festival within the hour.

"This feels too easy," Bodhi said as we boxed up the photographs strewn across the living room floor. We both decided it wouldn't be a good idea to leave our notes out in the open for anyone to see.

"Don't jinx it," I scolded him.

Unlike Bodhi, I was glad for the extra time to prepare. The hours melted away too quickly for me. Before I knew it, it was time to put away the last of the old pictures and head down to the festival. We decided to walk. It was too nice of a day to spend any time at all inside a car, and my ankle finally felt like it was on the mend. Bodhi chattered like an excited bird as we strolled hand in hand down the path. If I didn't know better, I'd have thought that we were just another couple excited for the fresh food, football games, and fireworks. In an alternate universe, an eight-year-old Kali gallivanted along beside us and pleaded for ice cream, but in this universe, I pondered possible problems with our plan instead.

Black Bay was in its element. Beneath the affectionate sun, the park whirled with activity. The main street had been closed off to make room for food trucks, fruit stands, and small booths advertising fun crafts, handmade jewelry, and face painting. Children giggled underfoot, twirling ribbons and spinning pinwheels. Dogs gamboled from frisbee to frisbee, chased after squirrels, and trailed behind messy kids in the hopes of finding a free snack. The flag football tournament kicked off with an immediate touchdown from a lithe teenaged girl whose slender legs blurred as she ducked beneath the arm of a brawny boy and barreled into the end zone. Near the stage, speakers pumped cheesy singles by mainstream artists from the last several decades. Everyone from five to sixty found something to sing along to. The Winchester Celebration banner had been re-pinned, slightly worse for wear after the storm but devoted to the cause nonetheless.

Bodhi stopped at a food truck advertising baozi, peered at the menu, and then stepped into line. "Want something?"

"Uh, I'm not sure I'm in the mood to eat," I said. As it was, my stomach leapt into my throat every time I spotted a man with a build similar to Ethan's.

Bodhi fished a few dollars out of his back pocket. "We might as well enjoy ourselves, Bailey. After all, this is Black Bay's premiere event."

So we snacked on baozi and sipped fresh hibiscus tea from a stand nearby, and as we watched Ava direct an uproarious game of Simon Says, I almost forgot what we had come to the summer festival to do. However, I abruptly remembered when a looming presence approached me from behind.

"There they are!" boomed Ethan. He stepped between Bodhi and I, tugging me into a side hug. I swallowed down my disgust lest my lunch reappear at Ethan's touch.

"Ethan!" Bodhi performed some kind of complicated handshake with Ethan before clapping him on the back, his pleased grin never faltering. I marveled at Bodhi's abilities to stay cool and collected in the presence of a man we suspected to be a sociopathic murderer.

"I see you've already found the food trucks," Ethan said, nodding toward the unfinished half of my snack.

"Would you like the rest?" I offered, trying to take a leaf out of Bodhi's book. "It's delicious, but I'm afraid I'm not feeling very well."

Ethan accepted the morsel. "That's a damn shame. What's wrong?"

"Stomachache," I answered truthfully.

Bodhi took my hand, squeezing my fingers to comfort me. "Bailey's been a little under the weather these past few days, but she was determined to see the festival."

Ethan swept a hand out to indicate the hubbub around us. "I don't blame you, Bailey! Look at all of this. Come with me. You don't know entertainment until you've seen Black Bay's comedy troupe attempt improv."

He waved us in front of him, but I stood my ground. "Actually, I don't think that baozi really agreed with me. You two go ahead."

Bodhi, ever the accomplished actor, frowned, and worry lines appeared on his forehead. "You sure, baby? I can take you home."

"No, no," I insisted, trying to ignore Ethan's persistent gaze in my periphery. "I'll be fine. Go on, and have fun."

"All right." Bodhi kissed me. His lips lingered near my ear as though he wanted to say something, but he drew away again without speaking. "Ready, Ethan?"

"As ever. Feel better, Bailey."

"Thanks, Ethan."

They vanished amongst the busy crowd. I watched them go, keeping an eye on Bodhi's strong back and long hair for as long as I could. Then, dodging a wandering toddler, I squeezed past the last two food trucks at the end of the street, glanced over my shoulder, and dipped down a side street.

Bodhi had given me directions to Ethan's house. He lived on the south side of Black Bay, opposite the quaint collection of houses to the north. There, a series of winding canals led to the bay. The landscape was swampier, and the air felt moist and sticky. Ethan owned a private plot of land tucked away from the rest of the town. The dirt road was muddy and viscous from the storm, so I kept to the grassy shoulder. It had taken me a good hour to wash the mud out of my walking boot from the night before.

I paused in the driveway, bewildered, when Ethan's house came into view. I didn't know what I'd been expecting. An obvious bachelor pad, maybe, or a rundown shack. Instead, I found a pretty yellow cottage with white shutters, pruned bushes, and blooming primroses in flower pots on the window sills. A hand-laid stonework path led to the porch, where a swinging bench rocked languidly in the light wind. In front of the red door, a welcome mat proclaimed, "Ask not for whom the dog barks. It barks for thee."

Sure enough, when I picked up the mat to find Ethan's spare key and turned it in the door, a series of high-pitched ruffs met my ear. I opened the door cautiously and blew out a sigh of relief when Ethan's portly dachshund flipped over to offer me her belly instead of attacking my ankles. I knelt to give her a quick rub, looking around the inside of Ethan's house.

A woman had lived here once. The house sported a feminine touch, from the printed couch to the lace curtains to the lilac tablecloth in the breakfast nook. It was small and cozy but smelled distinctly of cigar smoke and men's aftershave. As I set Ethan's key on a coffee table by the television, the dachshund curled up with a rope toy in a plushy bed beneath a window.

"Okay, Ethan," I muttered. "Let's see what you're hiding behind that teddy bear personality of yours."

I swept the living room from top to bottom, lifting rugs, inspecting drawers for false bottoms, and upending sofa cushions to check beneath them. The dachshund—whose name was Winnie according to the elegant cursive printed on the side of her water bowl—watched in confusion as I raided Ethan's cupboards in the kitchen, but there were no clues amongst the dishware as to whether or not Ethan secretly harbored homicidal tendencies. I did, however, discover that the cabinet under the kitchen sink was chock full of bourbon. I inspected the bottles with a frown. According to Doctor Marx's files, Ethan had been sober for several years, but the open wax seals and half-empty bottles said otherwise. Still, Ethan's drinking habits weren't proof that he had murdered all four of the Winchesters twenty years ago.

I hesitated before checking the bedroom. There was something invasive about entering someone else's sleeping space without permission. A lump rose in my throat as I peered in through the open door, but like the rest of Ethan's house, the bedroom was clean and snug. The bed was made, the floor was clear, and a pile of freshly folded collared shirts from Powell's Lumber Mill sat atop the dresser waiting to be put away. I looked under the bed, rifled through the dresser drawers, thoroughly searched the closet, and inspected the adjoining bathroom to come up empty-handed. With an annoyed groan, I pushed my sweaty hair away from my face. If Ethan had hidden something, he'd done it damn well.

For good measure, I ventured out onto the back porch. I considered the floorboards beneath my feet. Would Ethan go as far as to conceal his secrets beneath the house itself? I checked the time. I'd already been absent from the festival for forty-five minutes. Hopefully, Bodhi was keeping Ethan busy. My cell had limited service out here in the boonies. If Ethan threw Bodhi a curveball, I wouldn't hear about it until I got back into town. I needed to expedite my search.

I surveyed Ethan's backyard. The immediate area was perfectly maintained. Trimmed, lush grass flattened out like a green carpet across the yard, but the landscape grew wild near the edge of the canal. Trees soared overhead, darkening the ground below, their lower branches tangling up with overgrown shrubbery, reaching vines, and towering rose bushes, but nothing of interest caught my eye. I stepped off the porch to circle around the side of the house. The space beneath the porch was blocked off by wood panels, making it impossible to search without leaving evidence of my presence behind. I combed through the contents of Ethan's small shed. It was full of power tools and hardware, but that was only to be expected in Ethan's line of work. Frustrated, I planted my hands on my hips and examined the yard one last time, wondering if there was something I might have missed.

Nothing. I turned back to the porch—one last sweep of the inside of the house wouldn't hurt—but sunshine reflected into my eyes off of something within the tangle of weeds near the water. I crossed the impeccable lawn then used the hem of my shirt to pull the thorny rose bushes out of the way. The sunlight fought to filter through the trees, and I squinted into the gloom. Finally, I saw it. A dilapidated boathouse sat near the edge of the canal, its weathered walls the same color as the trees around it. Vines and weeds inched up the sides, a natural camouflage. Were it not for the one window glinting in the feeble sun despite a layer of mold and grime, I never would've seen the building at all.

I clambered through the overgrown weeds, tripping every time a particularly grabby vine got caught in the Velcro straps of the walking boot. At the door to the boathouse, I stood on my toes, wiped the muck from the window, and peered inside. In the murk, I could just make out the shadow of a boat.

A rusty padlock secured the decrepit door. I braced my feet against the boathouse and gave it a good wrench, hoping to tear it from the decaying wood. No such luck. I needed something to help me break in.

In Ethan's shed, I found a flashlight and a handy carpenter's axe that felt nice and easy in my grip. I trekked back through the weeds to the boathouse, wound up, and aimed for the padlock. I was rewarded with the satisfying sound of the rusty latch separating from the wood. I struck again. This time, the entire padlock tore free. With a grunt, I jerked the door open, fighting against the corroded hinges.

I shone the flashlight inside. A large fishing boat sat in dry dock, suspended above the greenish water of the canal. It looked as old as the boathouse itself. The paint was peeling and it was covered in foul-smelling mildew. I circled around, carefully navigating the uneven floor, but as the flashlight swept across the bow of the boat, I inhaled sharply.

The front right side bore a hefty dent. It wasn't enough to put the boat out of commission, but it was significant all the same. But the real kicker was the long scratch of blue paint that accompanied the dent. It didn't match the white of Ethan's boat. In fact, it was the same color as the blue stripe on the Winchesters' sailboat. As I examined the damage, the baozi from earlier turned in my stomach. If this wasn't confirmation of Ethan's involvement, I didn't know what was. I took a picture of the dent with my phone.

Tentatively, I stepped one foot into the boat, wanting to search the inside. It rocked precariously as the rusted winches that held the boat creaked under the extra weight. When it settled, I swung my other leg inside, lifting my walking boot high to clear the edge. The boat was empty—there was no tackle or gear on board—so I pulled open the door to the cabin and flashed the light around.

The first thing that caught my eye was the pile of Caroline's journals, tossed carelessly into the corner of the cabin. A bottle of lighter fluid stood nearby as though Ethan had planned to burn them. I swallowed hard, examining the rest of the cabin.

A glimpse of something white lying beneath a storage bench caught my eye. I tugged the object into full view with the toe of my good foot, leaning down for a better look.

My stomach surged. I burst out of the cabin just in time to heave over the side of the boat. Leaning heavily against the warped fiberglass, I drew in ragged, wet breaths, shaking from head to toe and coated in a clammy layer of cold sweat. When my stomach settled, I steeled myself and went back in the cabin for a second look at the object.

It was a length of white nautical rope, tied in a noose, and encrusted with the unmistakable reddish brown color of dried blood.

In my imagination, Patrick Winchester dangled from the ceiling in the living room.

I slammed the cabin door shut and vaulted over the edge of the boat, landing heavily on my uninjured foot. Outside, I kicked the ruined padlock beneath the shrubbery. From the state of the boathouse, I doubted Ethan would ever notice that it had been broken into. Then I returned the carpenter's axe to the shed, locked up Ethan's house, and hid the key under the mat again.

On the road, I steadily jogged toward town, ignoring the ache in my ankle. When the summer festival came into view, I skirted around the edge, cutting through parking lots and backyards to avoid being seen. My phone chimed. Without slowing, I took it out of my pocket to find a message from Bodhi.

Lost Ethan. Get out now if you haven't already. Find anything?

I texted back hurriedly. *Ethan guilty. Meet me at the house ASAP.*

By the time I made it up the path to the house, I was sweating heavily and out of breath. I limped across the front yard and threw open the door to the house.

"Caroline?" I called out. "I know what happened. What do you want me to do now?"

The house was silent. The only sound was my uneven breathing.

"Caroline, come on!"

"Caroline isn't here," said a deep voice.

I whirled around to find Ethan stepping out of the hallway and into the living room. He held up one of the pictures from the Winchesters' photo album. It was the one of him and his father, standing with Christopher and Jane in front of Powell's Lumber Mill.

"It's such a shame, Bailey," Ethan said calmly, caressing the photo with tender care. "I quite liked you."

My heart pounded as he glanced up at me and smiled. There was no warmth in his eyes. They remained cold and gray, like the unforgiving waves that crashed against the rocks below.

"But now I'm afraid I have to kill you."

WHITE LIGHT

I always wondered if that moment right before you died was real. Everyone knew the moment. It was written about in famous works of literature, sung about in heart-wrenching songs, and the classic tragedies of film wouldn't be complete without the hero's life flashing before their eyes just prior to succumbing to the inevitable. Sure, the notion was romantic, but realistically, if you had the chance to save your own skin, why would you waste time reminiscing on the past when you could be fighting to ensure the future?

I stood in the foyer of the massive house, mere feet from the mountain of a man who, I'd discovered mere minutes prior, was a homicidal sociopath.

"It's such a shame, Bailey," he said. Calm. Collected. Nonchalant. "I quite liked you."

He held a photograph of himself between his fingertips. He was no longer the man printed on the twenty-year-old faded picture. He was someone else entirely. I calculated every one of his movements. The brush of his fingers across the surface of the photo. The steady rise and fall of his chest.

The subtle rasp of one boot inching across the newly laid wooden floor. The triumphant shine in his blue-gray eyes.

"But now I'm afraid I have to kill you."

I didn't wait for Ethan Powell to lunge toward me. I didn't pause in the doorway and beg for mercy. I didn't cry or sob or attempt to reason with a man who had long since lost track of his humanity. Instead, in the precious seconds between his declaration and its attempted execution, I considered my options.

Time was relative. Arbitrary. A construct conceived to establish some semblance of control over our lives for us simple mortals. Sometimes, time betrayed you. Others, it worked to your advantage. In that moment, the hands on the clock slowed to an impossible rate, and my mind chased innumerable escape routes in search of the one with the highest survival percentage.

I'd seen enough slasher movies and yelled advice at enough girls through the television screen to know that haggling with a killer, or running upstairs, or hiding in closets or under beds never ended well for whoever was being chased. But this house was different. This house was haunted. And the phantom inside it had good reason to protect me against Ethan Powell. If I could only get her to react.

Behind Ethan, a long corridor led to the basement door. The room below was a cold spot. Our house guest was more active there than anywhere else. But dodging around Ethan to reach it risked immediate capture. Option number one was a no-go.

On the card table beside me, the keys to my husband's truck glimmered in the sunshine that poured through the open door to my rear. The truck itself was parked in the lawn fifty feet away. Usually, I could cross that distance in seconds. Today, a fractured ankle wrapped in a plaster cast and a walking boot decreased my odds. I needed a distraction.

To my left, a red toolbox lay open. Nail gun. Pliers. Drill bits. A hammer. I made up my mind. My time was up. Ethan tensed, readying himself for the chase.

I seized the hammer from the toolbox and flung it with all of my might across the short distance between me and Ethan. Without bothering to see where it had landed, I took the keys from the card table, spun on my heel, and dashed outside. Pain pulsed through my ankle with every frenzied heartbeat. I ignored it. There was no point in tending to an injury when your entire life was on the line.

Twenty-five feet to the truck. I limped on. Ethan's boots scuffed across the rotted wood decking of the front porch. I didn't look back. Ten feet.

I practically slammed into the side of the white workman's truck, yanked the driver's door open, and vaulted into the seat. My feet didn't reach the pedals. I fumbled with the seat adjustments as I shoved the keys into the ignition. Then I caught sight of the rearview mirror. Ethan leaned casually over the deck railing, watching me with an amused expression.

The truck wouldn't start. No matter how much I jiggled the key. No matter the number of whispered pleas from my lips. The engine whined. Dead. Outside, a light chuckle floated across the yard, permeating the cab of the truck.

"I took out the battery," Ethan called.

Panic threatened to overwhelm me, rising like a tidal wave rushing toward the shore. I fought it down. "Think, Bailey," I muttered, my forehead pressed to the steering wheel. "Think."

Across the yard, a footpath led down the steep incline of the bluff and into the town below. It was at least a ten-minute walk to civilization, but it was my only chance at making it through this. I bailed out of the truck, but as I sprinted toward the footpath, hoping to make it to the cover of the trees before my ankle gave out completely, Ethan stepped down from the porch. For a man of his size, he loped with an impossible grace to cut off my escape route as easily as a lion cornering its prey. Breathing hard, I skidded to a stop. I cursed the fractured ankle. I couldn't outrun him. Time to move on to another strategy: mind games.

"Did you meet Caroline?" I huffed, steadily backing away from Ethan as he stalked toward me.

I was rewarded by his look of skeptical bewilderment. "I thought you had it all figured out, Bailey," Ethan answered. "Or did I overestimate your sleuthing abilities? I killed Caroline. Twenty years ago."

I shook my head. "Not that Caroline."

He looked over his shoulder at the house. "Oh, you mean *your* Caroline. The ghost you tried to convince me didn't exist."

"She'll come for you," I told him, standing my ground. "Justice. That's what she wants. She told me."

Ethan smiled serenely. "Would you like to know a secret, Bailey?"

"Not particularly."

"I already knew about Caroline," Ethan said anyway, rolling his eyes. "Like it wasn't obvious. People told stories about this house. Real estate agents tried to sell it only for their clients to see horrifying visions during the grand tour. For nearly twenty years, none of the locals would go near it. They claimed it had creepy vibes. But I used to come up to the house every year, just to make sure everything was nice and taken care of. Caroline was never subtle, even when she was alive. So enlighten me, Bailey. If Caroline is so determined to enact her revenge, why hasn't she done it yet?" He spread his arms wide, spinning on the spot. "Come on, Caroline. Do your worst. Smite me down."

The yard and the house were quiet. Motionless. Even the usual breeze was absent. The leaves of the trees didn't rustle. The grass didn't ripple underfoot.

Ethan surveyed me with a satisfied smirk. "Looks like you're out of luck. I guess you can never really rely on the consistency of fifteen-year-old girls, no matter if they're dead or alive."

"What did you do to Bodhi?" I demanded, trying to keep my tone steady.

"Your pathetic husband?" Ethan picked dirt from under his fingernails. "I killed him."

My head rushed. A dull roar rose in my ears. The line between the trees and the sky bleared into a muddied portrait.

And then Ethan laughed.

"Oh, darlin'," he said, chortling. "You should've seen your face just now. Good Lord. I didn't kill your dolt of a spouse. Although don't get me wrong, I thought it was hilarious that you were under the impression he could distract me long enough to get away with your little scheme."

I spoke in a low, rough voice. "Where is he?"

"Taking a nap," Ethan replied simply. "But let's not stray from the subject. Where did you jet off to after your fake little food poisoning episode? My house?"

He circled around, his laser-sharp gaze never straying from me as he prowled in a steady loop. I shuffled along the same route, keeping an even distance between us.

"Didn't find anything, did you?" Ethan asked, but it didn't sound like a question. "You wouldn't have. My house is completely clean."

"Your boathouse isn't," I hissed.

He halted his hunt, glaring at me across the damp grass. "You found my boathouse."

If only I hadn't. The memory would plague me forever. The pieces of the mystery falling into place. A murder weapon covered in blood. A sadistic crime hidden in plain sight.

"Tell *me* something, Ethan." I balled my hands into fists, nausea and rage rising within me. "When you realized I had found Caroline's journals, did you panic? Did you feel short of breath? Did your heart get stuck in your throat? If you have one anymore, that is." The strain grew palpable between us, as if a frayed rope bound me to Ethan, stretched to its limits, waiting for one of us to snap. "Did you know then?" I went on. "That the game was up? That you would finally face the consequences of murdering Black Bay's most beloved family?"

He stared at me, deadly calm. "No, my dear. Because who would believe the silly, mentally unstable woman who's only lived in Black Bay for a few months over the man whose family built this town from the ground up?"

"The *Winchesters* saved Black Bay," I corrected him. "Not you. And the one reason you possess even a sliver of respect from the locals is because they don't know that it was *you* that ran Christopher and Elizabeth's sailboat into the rocks that night."

"That's not all I did," Ethan replied with a feral grin.

"I know," I confirmed. "You drowned Caroline in her own bath, didn't you? And hung Patrick from the rafters. There's one thing I can't work out though."

"What might that be?"

It was bizarrely conversational now. I had to take advantage of it. If I made it out of this alive, I was going to do it with as much information as possible.

"Patrick and Caroline were in town when you murdered

their parents," I said. "How'd you end up killing them in their own house without raising suspicion?"

Ethan took a step toward me. My eyes flickered to his boots, measuring the interval between us. When the time came to bolt, I needed enough of a head start to make it worth it.

"I'm so glad you asked, Bailey," he answered. "See, Patrick and Caroline were grounded that night. Not many people knew that, but I did. I overhead Chris and Liz talking about it right before I ran them aground. So I dropped my boat off and drove back into town. I checked the house first, but they weren't there. They'd snuck out, as teenagers are apt to do." He shook his head in disbelief. "Listen to your parents, kids."

"What did you do with them?" I demanded.

"I found Patrick and Caroline around the block from Lido's," Ethan explained. "Told them I'd seen their parents heading back into the marina early. Boy, did they panic. I offered them a ride. God, they were so stupid. It was so easy to convince them to hop into the truck. I drove them up to the house before anyone realized they'd been gone."

Ethan crossed the yard to the bed of Bodhi's truck where he rifled through the hardware tools for a moment before finding a machete. He hefted it, testing the weight in his hand. I thought of the footpath behind me. If I made a run for it, what were my chances of reaching town before Ethan caught up with me?

"It went well enough," he continued, swinging the blade experimentally. "I suffocated them both. There was something poetic about all four of the Winchesters dying without a breath to spare, choking in panic. Originally, I wanted to drown them all, but Patrick ruined that. Caroline was small. Easy to hold down in a bathtub. She didn't have a chance in hell, but Patrick just had to try and defend her."

"You're sick," I declared, swallowing the bile that had risen in the back of my throat at Ethan's blasé recollection.

Ethan appeared not to have heard me. "He got in a few good punches before I hit him over the head with a golf club and strung him up in the living room. Watched the light go out of his eyes. God, what a beautiful moment it was to realize that I was finally free of all four of the Winchesters."

I took a step backward. The footpath beckoned. "You killed the very people that saved your family's business."

"They didn't *save* anything," growled Ethan, advancing toward me. "Every one of the Winchesters deserved to die. Taking over the town. Showboating and strutting about like they owned the damn place. For God's sake, they put so much pressure and stress on my father that he had a damn heart attack and died."

"So everything you told me about them was a lie," I said. I had to keep him talking. Divert his attention. "All that stuff about how wonderful they were, how loved Patrick was, how intelligent Caroline must've been. Talking about how you owe everything to them, as does the rest of Black Bay. It was all a crock."

"They thought themselves superior to us," Ethan snarled. "Buying up my family's pride and joy. Black Bay belongs to the Powells, Bailey. We ran this town before the Winchesters, and we'll run it long after you and your nonconformist husband are gone."

"That might be difficult without any other Powells to take over the family business," I pointed out.

For the first time, Ethan dropped his facade of bravado. "You bitch," he spat. "I'm done talking. Start running."

He didn't have to suggest it twice. I whirled around, aiming for the footpath, but he quickly intercepted my route.

"Boo," he whispered. And he swung the machete.

The blade whistled through the air, but it didn't come

close enough to pose a real threat. Ethan got a thrill out of trying to frighten his target. I skidded to a stop and changed direction, cutting around the corner of the house. If I could make enough headway, I might be able to lose Ethan in the confusion and shadows of the woods. There was no way I could outrun him—my ankle was proof enough of that—but there was a slim chance that I could outsmart him. I plunged into the foliage. Behind me, I heard Ethan tearing through the trees. I was small enough to duck under and around the maze of plants, but he barreled through them instead.

"Bailey, I can tell you from experience that this kind of thing is always less hassle if we skip the whole chase scene bit," he called casually after me as though we could sit down and negotiate the terms of my murder.

I huffed, making a quick left and sliding under a fallen tree trunk. Ethan was close on my heels. Even if I kept out of his line of sight, he could hear the sound of my feet shuffling across the leaves and branches on the ground.

"Bailey," he called in a singsong voice. The machete made swift work of the wilderness behind me.

I scrambled up an embankment. He was boxing me in. I realized that when I tried to cut around him and he swiftly herded me uphill again. I spotted the backyard of the Winchester house through the leaves. Ethan was steadily pushing me up the bluff. There was no way down that wouldn't lead me right into his arms. I needed a better tactic. I glanced upward, toward the steep angle of the rock, and got an idea.

I hefted myself on to a ledge. Ethan grunted as he tried to follow but lost his footing. I caught my breath on the outcrop as Ethan looked for another way up. When he found a lower rock to hoist himself over, I resumed my climb. A protruding branch caught on my T-shirt. I ripped free, tearing a hole in the fabric. My ankle trembled beneath my weight as I put on another burst of speed. I could only keep this up for so long. I looked skyward again. Somewhere up above, years of erosion had carved a tiny alcove out of the stone. It was the perfect hiding place: small, secluded, and nearly impossible to find if you didn't already know where it was. If I could just reach the grotto, I would be able to defend the modest space from Ethan long enough for someone to come looking for me. To my rear, Ethan tore down a thorny rose bush with his bare hands. His breath now came in short gasps. He was built for strength rather than stamina, a flaw in his build that I was determined to use to my advantage.

I made a flying leap across a gap in the terrain, catching myself on the opposite ledge by the tips of my fingers and scrambling to the top. Below, Ethan looked around in confusion. I'd finally thrown him off my trail. Taking advantage of my head start, I darted across the smooth, flat stone. The hideaway was up ahead, completely invisible from this side of the rock. I tiptoed around the narrow edge, flattening myself to the stone wall and keeping my gaze level. If I looked down, the distance to the ground would surely overwhelm me.

Finally, the rock opened up and revealed the little grotto. I slid into it with a relieved sob, shrinking into one corner of the shadowy cave. I closed my eyes and tried to control my breathing. My hiding place was no good if Ethan heard me blubbering like a five-year-old. With trembling hands, I pulled my cell phone from the back pocket of my shorts and dialed Bodhi's number.

It went straight to voicemail. Bodhi's phone was either off or the battery had died. Or worse, Ethan made sure Bodhi wasn't able to answer it.

"Damn it," I whispered. I dialed 911 instead.

"911. What's your emergency?"

"I'm being stalked," I reported in the softest voice I could manage. "There's a man chasing me through the woods."

"Okay, ma'am. Please stay calm. What is your location?"

"I'm hiding up in the rocks above the Winchester house—"

A violent blow to the back of my head knocked the phone out of my hand. My vision doubled, and a heavy boot crushed the cell to pieces before kicking the remains over the edge of the rock. Ethan dragged me upward by my hair.

"Didn't I tell you this would be easier without the chase scene?" Ethan rumbled, tipping my head back to show me a long, bloody scrape on his forearm. "Look what you've done. Got a nice scratch climbing up here. How'd you find this little hidey hole anyway?"

Ethan's girth made the intimate space claustrophobic. He had to crouch to reach me, his back flush against the rock above. I tucked my knees into my chest and kicked out with all of my might. My feet bounced off the hard muscles of Ethan's stomach. He grunted, the wind knocked out of him, but grabbed my ankles and hauled me flat against the stone. I struggled as he straddled my hips and pressed his thumbs to my windpipe.

I pushed at his hands. It was no use. There was no escaping out from under Ethan's full weight. In a last-ditch attempt, I clawed at his face, digging my nails into his skin. He yelled, lifted my head, and slammed it into the stone. Dazed, my hands fell limply to my sides. Blackness beckoned at the edges of my vision. Ethan's scratched, bleeding face loomed above me. His hands found my neck again. He leaned into it.

I convulsed. White light popped and fizzled in my line of sight.

This was it. This was the end.

Sorry, Bodhi. Sorry, Caroline. Sorry, Kali.

I did my best.

And then the pressure around my throat was gone. Through an agonizing haze of disorientation, I watched as a pair of tan hands ripped Ethan off of me. They did not hesitate. They did not consider the aftermath of their actions. With a ferocious power that seemed more godlike than human, they heaved Ethan over the edge of the rock face. Ethan's resulting yell cut off with an abrupt thump. He'd landed somewhere below, dead or injured.

I looked up at my rescuer. He looked at the trees beneath the outcrop, his back to me. Blond hair rustled in the breeze as his shoulders rose and fell with the intensity of his breath.

"Milo?" I asked hoarsely.

The person turned around. My eyes widened. I had hit my head too hard. I was surely seeing things.

Patrick Winchester stood before me, seventeen years old and the picture of perfect health.

THE DEAD BOY

*P*atrick stretched a hand toward me. I stared at it, unable to comprehend how it was possible for Patrick to exist in such a capacity. Caroline's presence was simpler to wrap my head around. She stayed mostly invisible, appearing every once in a while as a glimmer in the shadows, but Patrick was corporeal. Solid. Of flesh and blood.

Or so it appeared.

When it became apparent that I did not possess the mental faculty to allow Patrick to help me to my feet, he knelt and scooped me up from the rock. As he looped my arm over his shoulder, I gawked at his angled cheekbones, golden baby scruff, and boyishly arched eyebrows. This was the young man who had once been the heart and soul of Black Bay. The locals thought he'd been lost, yet here he stood, perfectly preserved at the height of his high school success.

"I'm sorry I lied to you," Patrick said as he guided me across the narrow ledge that linked the mouth of the grotto to the safer side of the cliff face. "I didn't have much of a choice."

I stuttered, the words getting lost in my stupefaction. "M-Milo."

Patrick arched an eyebrow. "I regret to inform you that Milo Holmes never existed," he admitted. His grip was soft, his breath was warm, and a pulse beat in the blue veins of his neck. For a dead boy, he looked more alive than ever. "You already figured that out. Or you guessed, at least. I knew when you asked me about the property records that I'd have to come clean sometime soon."

"But how—?"

"Did you not recognize me?" He shrugged and gently lowered me off the edge of the flat stone outcrop until my toes reached the softer ground below. "To be honest, I've been doing this sort of thing for almost two decades, and I still don't understand the science behind it."

Patrick leapt down from the outcrop, landing in a crouch beside me. As he rose to his full height, I studied his features. Now that I thought about it, his honey-colored hair, bright sky-blue eyes, and the mischievous tilt of his lips did seem familiar.

"You look like him," I noted.

"I am him," Patrick replied. "If I'd had the opportunity to age, I would've ended up looking something like Milo did to you."

He beckoned me to follow him through the mess of trees and plants. Ethan's pernicious effect did not go unnoticed. A path of destruction led us downward, the landscape cut to smithereens by Ethan's machete.

"How did the townspeople never realize who you were?" I asked Patrick, stumbling over a lifted root. He caught me mid-trip. I nodded my thanks.

"No one in town ever saw me, remember?"

"But they knew about you."

Patrick skated down an embankment then paused at the

bottom to catch me. "It's easy to plant stories when you're dead, Bailey."

I slid into his outstretched arms. Respectfully, he set me on my feet.

"Wait here," Patrick said. "I need to check something."

He vanished through the trees, twigs and leaves rustling beneath his deck shoes. Nervously, I scanned the area around me, but the forest was pleasant and benevolent. The trees whispered secrets, a stream bubbled happily out of sight, and a family of finches danced by, chirping merrily to one another. There was no sign of Ethan or any other danger.

I touched the back of my head, wincing when my fingers found the tender lump from where Ethan had slammed me into the rock. This was the second time in a matter of weeks that I'd ended up with some kind of head injury. If I wasn't careful, the trauma would add up.

Patrick returned from his short exploration, ducking low to avoid disturbing a small nest on an overhanging branch. "It's as I thought," he reported. "Ethan's gone."

"Gone?" I repeated. "What do you mean he's gone? He fell off a cliff!"

With a light touch to my forearm, he encouraged me to continue down the hill. "If you recall, I told you I fell from the exact same ledge once. There's another overhang below it. Ethan might've broken a few bones, but he definitely survived it."

In my haste to depart from the forest, I lost my footing on a patch of fallen leaves. The walking boot slid out from beneath me, and I landed with a thud before Patrick could intercept my fall. Pain laced through my tailbone and the back of my head. I groaned, cradling the sore spot.

Patrick lifted me helpfully. "Bailey, please relax. I'd hate to see you get hurt even more. Ethan's in no state to attack us anytime soon. We have a little downtime."

"How do you know?"

"Believe me, I know. You'll be safe at my house for a few days at least."

I took his word for it. After all, he was a ghost. Or something superhuman. Maybe omniscience came with the territory. I had more pressing things to worry about, like if Bodhi had survived his outing to the summer festival with Ethan.

The trees thinned out, and the wild garden of the Winchester house welcomed us back to relative safety. I lengthened my stride, cutting through the back door of the house and the unfinished living room to the front yard. Patrick followed me to Bodhi's truck. I popped the hood.

"What are you doing?" he asked, peering at the truck's inner mechanics.

To my relief, Ethan hadn't actually removed the car battery. He had just disconnected it. I reached in, reconnected the cable clamps, and slammed the hood shut.

"I need to go find Bodhi," I told Patrick, climbing into the driver's seat.

He leaned against the open window. "Do you think it's wise to drive in your condition?"

I fired up the engine. The truck roared to life. "I don't have a choice. I'll be back as soon as possible. Stay here."

Patrick retreated, giving the truck a wide berth so that I could pull out of the front yard unhindered. "I don't have a choice either," he called to me.

I waved through the window and steered the truck down the dirt road and into town.

THE SUMMER FESTIVAL was still in full swing, which meant Main Street was closed off to accommodate the number of food trucks, craft booths, and other entertainment for the locals of Black Bay. I parked the truck near the orange barricades that blocked the start of the festival and hopped out. The sun crossed low over the horizon, sending its blinding beams directly into my eyes. I shielded my face with the palm of my hand, stepped between the barricades, and scanned the area for any sign of Bodhi.

"Bailey?"

I swiveled around. Ava, the kind, middle-aged woman who owned the local coffeehouse, peered worriedly at me. For a moment, I wondered why. Then I remembered that my trek through the woods with Ethan probably left me looking a little worse for wear.

Ava took me by the hands. "My goodness, what happened to you?"

I fished a leaf out of my hair and flicked it to the ground. "Oh, you know. Summer festival shenanigans. I picked the wrong dog to play Frisbee with."

"But your head! That bruise!"

Self-conscious, I covered the lump at the base of my skull with my hand. "It looks worse than it is. I'll be fine. Have you seen Bodhi?"

Ava's pretty gray eyes widened anxiously. "Isn't he with you?"

"We lost track of each other."

Ava brushed dirt from the front of my torn T-shirt. "I saw him with Ethan about an hour ago. They were playing with the Tibetan singing bowls."

Of course. Bodhi played to his strengths. He loved those bowls, and it would've been effortless for him to distract Ethan by coaxing dulcet tones from the brassy rims.

"Where was that?" I asked Ava.

She pointed to the far corner of the park. Past the flag football tournament, a row of booths advertised specialty items. The one nearest the stage boasted an impressive meditation display, from Baoding balls to challenging puzzles to the singing bowls that Bodhi so adored.

"Thanks," I told Ava.

"Sure, honey. You should really get that bump looked at."

"I will," I called over my shoulder as I trotted away from her.

Ava wasn't the only Black Bay resident concerned with my haggard appearance. Children pointed out my sweaty, dirty face to their parents, who politely piloted their mini-me's in the opposite direction. I dodged a rogue flag football player and approached the meditation booth. Bodhi was long gone, but the ethereal woman who manned the merchandise was as good a source as any.

"Excuse me?"

The woman looked me up and down, expertly spinning a pair of Baoding balls in the palm of her hand. "Oh, darling," she said. "Your energy is all bad."

"Don't I know it," I replied darkly. "Have you seen my husband? He's about six feet tall with golden-brown eyes, an olive complexion, and long dark curls."

"Ah, yes. The handsome Nepali man."

"That's him," I said, nodding. In a town like Black Bay, Bodhi's ambiguous ethnicity was always a good icebreaker.

The woman heaved a dramatic sigh. "Shame he's taken. He was so very charming."

"Uh-huh. He was here though, right?"

"Yes, with that behemoth of a man that your townsfolk seem so enraptured by. They went that way." Her long fingers danced in the direction of the platform stage. "Bring him by again when you find him, won't you?"

"I'll try."

I circled around the meditation booth. On stage, the owner of the local bookstore was auctioning off rare texts to a small, subdued audience. I slipped around the back, where the metal support system beneath the platform was hidden by lengths of black tarp. I glanced around. I was alone. No one else bothered with the back end of the entertainment.

My heart pounded as I lifted the tarp and peered under the stage. The black fabric prevented the sun from illuminating the space underneath. I squinted, forcing my eyes to adjust. Several feet to the left, a large shadow lay unmoving. I shimmied over to it.

"Bodhi," I whispered, turning him over. "Baby, wake up."

He groaned, and I exhaled a sigh of relief. A purple bruise decorated his temple. Ethan had hit him. Hard.

"What happened?" Bodhi asked, blearily opening his eyes.

I tugged him into my lap, inspecting the discoloration on the side of his head. "Ethan gave you the slip and came after me."

"Where are we?"

"Under the stage at the summer festival."

He groaned again, rolling over to sit up.

"Easy," I told him, shielding his head with my hand to prevent him from bumping it on the cross rails of the stage's support system. "Everything's okay for now, but we need to get to the house. There are some things we have to talk about. All of us."

"Who's all of us?"

"You, me, Patrick, and Caroline. Do you think you can walk?"

Bodhi gently probed his injury with the pads of his fingers. "Yeah. Hang on a minute. Did you say Patrick?"

I peeked out from under the tarp, checking that the coast was clear, then scurried out from under the stage. Bodhi followed, and I pulled him to his feet. "Yup. Patrick is Milo. Milo is Patrick. This way."

I led Bodhi around the back side of the merchandise

booths, where we were less likely to run into curious locals, but Bodhi held me back.

"What?"

"We can't go back to the house."

"Why not?"

"Ethan."

Before I could fill Bodhi in on Ethan's current state, microphone feedback interrupted the balmy summer evening. I winced as the shrill tone found my eardrums. On stage, the book auction had ended, and a tall, handsome man wearing a black flat-brimmed hat and a dazzling smile had taken the mic. Bodhi and I watched from our secluded spot behind the merchandise booths.

"Ahem. Hi, folks," he said, giving a friendly, awkward wave to the gathering crowd. "As you probably already know, I'm Alexander Lido. I own Lido's Restaurant across the way."

A cheer erupted from the growing assembly, and Alex grinned. Lido's was the most popular establishment in Black Bay, and it had been for quite some time.

"Anyway," Alex went on. "You know why we're all here." He gestured to a large banner that hung on the stage curtains behind him. "Welcome to the twentieth annual Winchester Celebration!"

The crowd hooted and hollered, and someone even fired off an air horn. Alex gestured for silence, smiling widely.

"All right, all right," he said. "So our schedule is a little cramped this year because of today's late start, but we've still got time for the fun stuff, including the fireworks show over the bay. But first, get your competitive spirit on because we're doing an egg toss, water balloon fights, and my personal favorite—" He pointed across the lawn to a black pickup truck with gold accents. "Whoever can throw a football through the open window of that truck from twenty yards gets to take the truck home with them."

Another roar of applause rose from the crowd.

"Don't worry though," Alex went on. He tipped his hat to the crowd. "For those of you with less than stellar aim, we're giving you the chance to win one of these amazing hats. They have the vintage Black Bay Golden Eagles football team logo on the front from 1996 and Patrick's jersey number on the back."

Alex rotated his hat around to showcase the number twenty-two embroidered in bright gold thread.

"We're also selling these hats to raise funds for this year's Patrick Silas Winchester Memorial Scholar Athlete Scholarship," Alex said. He pointed to a booth near the opposite end of the stage, draped in Black Bay High School's signature black and gold, where the hats were stacked high on the table. "As you know, this award is presented to one outstanding senior student at the end of the school year in honor of Patrick's lasting athletic influence on Black Bay High."

Alex cleared his throat as the crowd chattered, nervously adjusting the mic cord to prevent it from tangling around his ankle. He pulled the brim of his hat low over his eyes. When he spoke again, the tremble in his tone echoed through the park. "Before we get the festivities under way, I'd like to say a few words about the Winchesters. Chris, Liz, Patrick, and Caroline were four of the best people I've ever met."

My heart grew heavy. I knew firsthand that Alex missed the Winchesters more than any of the other residents of Black Bay.

"They were practically my second family," Alex continued, pacing back and forth across the stage. "Chris and Liz welcomed me with open arms, Patrick was like a brother to me, and my day wasn't complete if Caroline didn't direct some kind of smart aleck remark my way."

Everyone chuckled. Caroline's sardonic personality and tailored wit was remembered fondly.

"Were it not for the Winchesters, I firmly believe I would've missed out on a lot of important life lessons," Alex said. He sniffed lightly, wiping his nose with the back of his free hand. "They taught me love, respect, and the value of family, and for that I am eternally indebted to all four of them. I know that growing up in Black Bay would've been an entirely different experience without them."

A general murmur of agreement filtered through the crowd. Nearly everyone who'd attended the summer festival now listened intently to Alex's speech. He wasn't the only one who had been so positively affected by the Winchesters. The locals gave him their full attention, reminiscing on the Winchesters' influence as one united community.

"So," Alex went on. He took off his hat and held it to his heart. "Everyone please join me for a moment of silence in memory of Christopher, Elizabeth, Patrick, and Caroline Winchester."

The park grew quiet. Hats were respectfully removed, heads bowed, and a collective sense of honor lingered in the air. Even the children were calm and hushed, sensing the change in the atmosphere as the setting sun bathed the park in peachy pink light. My eyes watered, and I blotted the unexpected tears from my cheeks with the collar of my frayed shirt.

"Thank you," said Alex as the crowd began to stir again. "Let the games begin!"

The throng dispersed, dividing to the different areas of the park to start the first round of friendly competition. Bodhi had sank to the ground at some point during Alex's speech. I nudged him to his feet.

"We should go," I murmured.

"But Ethan—"

"Patrick said we're safe at the house," I reassured Bodhi. "At least for a little while."

We leaned heavily on each other as we lumbered through the less populated areas of the park. My head swam with the effort of keeping myself and Bodhi upright, and when we finally reached Bodhi's truck, I folded over the steering wheel and lightly rested my sweaty forehead on the horn. In the passenger seat, Bodhi mumbled something incoherently.

"What?" I asked.

"Snowcones," he clarified. "We deserve snowcones."

"Sure, baby. We'll get some later."

I put the truck in drive and hit the gas, jerkily accelerating to leave the summer festival and the Winchester celebration and the Black Bay locals in the rear view.

An hour or so later, I lounged in a deck chair on the widow's walk of the Winchester house. From this height, the view of the bay was stunning. Fairy lights twinkled in the marina as the moon reflected off the surface of the rippling water. Beside me, Bodhi, slumped in his own chair, was holding a sandwich bag full of ice to the side of his head. He stared across the walk to where Patrick—whose blond locks danced in the breeze—leaned over the railing. I tapped Bodhi's shin with the toe of my good foot.

"Stop staring," I whispered.

"I can't help it," Bodhi answered, his gaze unwavering.

"You know, the sound carries up here," Patrick said without turning around. "It's because of the wind."

"Sorry," said Bodhi.

Patrick pivoted on the heel of his deck shoes to face us. "Don't mention it. I know the situation is a little weird."

"Beyond," Bodhi corrected, adjusting his ice pack. "Um,

Patrick? Not to be rude, but what exactly is it that you want from us?"

Patrick sat down, dangling his legs through the gaps in the railing of the widow's walk. "Today, Black Bay celebrated the twentieth annual Winchester celebration, right?"

"Right."

He looked over his shoulder at me. "They're a week early. The official anniversary isn't until next Saturday."

"What does that have to do with anything?" Bodhi asked. The sandwich bag full of melting ice dripped steadily, dampening his T-shirt, but the conversation at hand demanded his full attention.

Patrick peered wistfully out at the water. "Do you remember what I told you a few days ago, Bailey? In the woods?"

I wasn't likely to forget it. The run-in with Patrick, who then appeared as Milo, was frighteningly violent. He'd been covered in blood—something I had not yet been able to persuade him to explain—and we had literally, albeit accidentally, hit him with the truck.

"You told me that time was running out," I recalled.

Patrick nodded solemnly. "Caroline and I have been fading for twenty years. I'm not sure how to explain what it feels like, but as you've probably already guessed, we don't have the ability to move on to whatever's next. Lately, it's gotten worse. I feel this pull to stay near the house, almost like I'm tethered to it, and at the same time, I feel less and less *human*."

"Probably because you're dead," Bodhi interjected. I smacked his arm.

Patrick, thankfully, didn't seem to take offense. "I came to terms with that a long time ago, Bodhi, but what I can't accept is being stuck here forever to live out some kind of half-life. That I won't do."

300

I perched my casted foot on the edge of Bodhi's chair, sighing as the elevation soothed the steady ache. "And you think you're running out of time to move on."

"Yes," he confirmed. "Again, I can't explain it, but I *know* that if Caroline and I don't figure out how to pass over before next Saturday, we'll be trapped here without another chance."

Bodhi rubbed his head, grimacing as he tested the bruise on his temple. "What are we supposed to do about it? Turn Ethan in to the cops?"

Patrick shook his head. "That won't help. It's not enough."

"Why not?" Bodhi asked. "We have enough proof. The damage to Ethan's boat alone is enough to bring him down."

"The process of bringing Ethan to justice would take too long," Patrick said. His shirt billowed in the pleasant wind. "Way more than a week."

"So we need another way to free you and Caroline," I confirmed. "Do you have any ideas?"

Patrick kicked his feet in the open air below him as if he wanted to hop off the widow's walk and learn how to fly. "I do, but I have a feeling you're not going to like it."

I laid a reassuring hand on Patrick's shoulder, marveling at how real and warm he felt under my touch. "Patrick, we'll do whatever we can to help you and Caroline move on."

He swallowed hard. "I'm not so sure of that."

"Why?" Bodhi asked, his tone tinged with suspicion. "What is it that you need from us?"

Patrick looked at us, pursing his lips as if anticipating our reactions. Then he held up three fingers and ticked off his conditions. "One, I need you to bring me the weapon that Ethan used to kill me. Two, I need you to find whatever's left of mine and Caroline's bodies. And three, I need you to lure Ethan Powell back to this house. What happens then will be up to me and Caroline."

Bodhi and I sat in stunned silence, staring at Patrick openmouthed. The first firework of the evening burst into the sky with a deafening boom, and a shower of pink and gold sparks rained down on the bay. The three of us looked up, losing ourselves in the colorful explosions. The night was young, but the day was old, and Bodhi and I were much too exhausted to even begin to ponder Patrick's requests until the morning.

MISSING PERSON

Bailey and Bodhi: Flipping Out

*T*he day has come, flippers! I've finally lost my mind. Remember when I told you all that the Winchester house was haunted? I was right. It is. Both Patrick and Caroline are still kicking. Figuratively, of course. And you know Milo, the friendly Black Bay local who sold us the house? He doesn't actually exist. It was Patrick all along! Anyway, we have less than one week to help Patrick and Caroline dig up their own bones and take revenge on the guy who murdered them. Sounds like fun, right? Don't worry. When we find the bodies, I'll take pictures—

I DELETED THE ENTIRE PARAGRAPH, slammed the laptop shut, and cast the computer aside. This was ridiculous. How was I supposed to keep up my happy-go-lucky blog when Patrick's requests weighed so heavily on my mind and a sociopathic killer was on the loose in Black Bay? Not to mention, Bodhi and I needed to keep up appearances in town. That meant continuing construction on the Winchester house as if nothing was wrong, but what if one of the guys from the construction crew spotted Patrick hanging out on the widow's walk?

Bodhi slept beside me, snoring lightly. I didn't understand how he did it. I'd been awake all night, staring at the ceiling and wondering how the hell we were going to riddle ourselves out of this one. Figuring out who killed the Winchesters was one thing. Locating dead bodies was a whole different ball game. The good thing was that I already had a head start on Patrick's first request. The nautical rope that Ethan had used to hang Patrick from the rafters in the living room was in Ethan's boathouse. The challenge remained in returning to Ethan's house without knowing whether he was there or not. I wasn't about to charge into the lion's den empty-handed.

Patrick's second request posed an even bigger challenge. The entire town of Black Bay understood Patrick and Caroline to be lost at sea. As such, their graves in the cemetery behind the local church were most likely empty. The problem was that, for some reason, Patrick couldn't just *tell* us what Ethan had done with the bodies and with no one else in town aware that the Winchesters were murdered, we had zero resources to further our investigation.

I kicked the quilt off my legs, stood up, and stretched. Bodhi lay unmoving. It was the first time in a while I'd seen him sleep so soundly. These days, if I so much as flipped over, it stirred him from slumber. I knelt by his side of the bed to study him. The bruise on his head looked worse than yesterday, and I'd kept an eye on him all night to make sure he made it to morning. His breath was nearly imperceptible, but he breathed all the same. Relieved, I pulled the quilt over his shoulders and left the room as quietly as possible. Bodhi needed his sleep. Otherwise, we had no chance of pulling off our operation.

In the kitchen, Patrick sat on the floor of the living room, gazing out of the massive sliding glass doors that we'd recently installed. He wore black workout shorts, a gold sweat-wicking shirt, matching sneakers, and one of the flat brim Golden Eagles hats that Alex had advertised yesterday. If I didn't know better, I would have thought that he was on his way to football practice. He glanced my way as I padded down the stairs.

"I like what you've done with the place," Patrick said. "Though I'll admit it was easier to watch the sunrise when there was furniture in the room."

When we first bought the Winchester house, we had no idea how long it would take us to renovate. It was meant to be an easy project—the house was in great shape, and our original intention was to simply update the interior—but the presence of a restless spirit had set our schedule way back. The living room, kitchen, and dining area were nearly done. We'd knocked down the walls between the three rooms to open up the area, repainted, refinished the floors, replaced the cabinets and counters in the kitchen, and nixed the bay windows to make room for the industrial-sized glass doors. All that was left was to install the new appliances.

"It's not our job to furnish it. Whoever buys it from us will take care of that," I told Patrick. I unlocked the first set of doors and slid them open. This entire side of the house had an unhindered view of the water, stained pink and purple as the sun rose opposite the sea. I sat next to Patrick, stretching my legs out in front of me. My ankle itched beneath the neon yellow cast, but I tried to ignore the persistent irritation. "Where did you get that hat?"

Patrick grinned, flipping the cap off his head and twirling

it on one finger. "It's nice, isn't it? Alex always had great taste."

I snatched it out of his grasp to inspect it. Sure enough, it was tangible, not something dreamt up or created by a bored ghost. I could wear it myself if I wanted to. I gave it back to Patrick, who pushed his messy blond hair away from his face and put the hat on with the brim facing rearward.

"I don't get it," I said, analyzing his lifelike appearance. "How is it that you look like you could run a marathon and Caroline is nothing more than a passing thought?"

A clatter from across the room caused me to jump. The toolbox had upended itself, spilling a jumble of hardware across the floor. Patrick watched as a package of nails popped open and spewed its contents in a metallic arc.

"I think Caroline would like me to keep that to myself for now," he said.

"Of course." I sighed and scooted forward to let my feet hang over the decaying wood of the outside deck. "Would you like to know what we want to do with the rest of the house?"

"That would be nice."

I launched into our plans, happy to talk about something that kept my mind off the insanity at hand. "First of all, we're going to get rid of this entire deck and replace it with water-proof flooring. It'll look like wood, but it won't rot like it. We want to extend the deck over there—" I pointed across the way, where the edge of the house's yard dropped off. "—so you can stand safely over the water."

I went on, describing in detail what Bodhi and I envisioned for the rest of the house. I lost myself in the conversation, gesturing animatedly and drawing pictures in the air in an attempt to illustrate to Patrick what we had in mind. I talked about how much potential the house had and how lucky a family would be to live here once we finished all of the renovations. Patrick listened quietly, but it wasn't until I noticed the faint smile on his lips that I interrupted my own ramblings.

"—which would make the master bedroom look even bigger than it actually is. Why are you staring at me like that?"

Patrick's slight smile morphed into a full-on grin. "You remind me of my mom."

"Really?" I felt heat rise in my cheeks. According to history, Elizabeth Winchester was a goddess. The compliment was evident in Patrick's tone of voice.

"Yeah," he said, leaning back on his palms. "She was passionate about this house too. She said it was a love project. We moved a few times before we found Black Bay, but I think Mom really wanted to stay here."

"That's another thing she and I have in common."

"What's that?"

I blew air through my lips like a horse, wondering how best to phrase it. "When we were younger, Bodhi and I loved to travel. It was like an addiction. Flipping houses was a good way to keep up with that while making enough money to support ourselves."

"And now?"

"I'm tired," I admitted. I hugged my legs into my chest and rested my chin on my knees. "I want a home base. I'd love for it to be Black Bay."

Patrick extended his long legs and reached out to touch the toes of his sneakers. "Your supernatural roommates are ruining that plan, huh?"

I chuckled humorlessly. "Honestly, I could probably put up with you and Caroline. It's Ethan's existence that worries me most."

Patrick folded further, his wing-like shoulder blades

outlined by the fabric of his shirt. "So my plan benefits everyone then."

My gaze drifted away from Patrick's athletic agility, and I watched a flock of squawking seagulls fly by instead. Yes, I wanted Ethan to finally pay for what he had done to the Winchesters, but I grew apprehensive thinking about Patrick's requests. It would be far easier to do things the legal way: present the police with the evidence of Ethan's murders and let the officials take care of the rest. But apparently that plan wouldn't help Caroline and Patrick move on to whatever came after death.

Footsteps pounded down the stairs. Patrick and I turned to see Bodhi coming into the living room, his cell phone in hand. When he spotted us, side-by-side in the door frame, he paused, taken aback.

"I don't think I'll ever get used to this," he said.

"Good morning to you too," Patrick quipped.

Bodhi walked over to us, popped Patrick's hat off with a quick jab to the underside of the brim, and caught it midair. Then he placed it on his own head and nudged me with his foot. "I hate to break up the breakfast bonding, but we have to go into town, Bailey."

"Why? Is something wrong?"

Bodhi wiggled his cell phone. "One of my guys just called me. The town is on high alert. Ethan Powell is officially missing."

WE DROVE into town to meet Bodhi's contact at the Sanctuary, the local coffeehouse that Ava owned. When we arrived, there was a distraught tone to the usual Sunday morning bustle. The locals chatted to one another in low, distressed voices, sporting worried brows and concerned looks. Bodhi spotted his workman at a table in the corner and waved.

"I'll be right back," Bodhi murmured, kissing me on the cheek. "Talk to Ava. See what you can find out. We need as much information as possible."

As he navigated through the busy cafe, I squeezed between two chairs and made for the counter. There were no stools available, so I aimed for an empty space to lean against. A warm hand found my forearm.

"Bailey."

Alex Lido sat at the counter. He too wore Patrick's memorial hat. He stood up from his seat to give me an affectionate hug. I practically disappeared in it. Alex was so tall that the top of my head barely reached his chest.

"Here," he said, scootching me toward his recently vacated stool. "Have my seat."

I boosted myself on to the bar stool, grateful to lift the heavy walking boot to the footrest beneath the counter. Alex flagged Ava down, and she gathered the ingredients for my usual cappuccino without asking what I wanted. When she slid the steaming mug across the counter, I nodded my thanks and took a sip. The espresso scalded my tongue.

Ava set a poppyseed bagel piled high with deli meat, veggies, and cream cheese in front of Alex. "Eat something," she ordered. "You're no good to us if you're starving."

"What's going on?" I asked Alex as Ava left to tend to another customer and the murmur of conversation crescendoed around us.

"Haven't you heard?" Alex took a big bite of his breakfast. "No one's seen Ethan since yesterday. We're worried something might've happened to him."

I feigned consternation. "But Ethan was fine when we saw him at the summer festival yesterday."

Alex shook his head, wiping cream cheese from the corner of his mouth. "Something's up. Ethan loves the summer festival. He hosts the water balloon fight at the

Winchester Celebration every year, and he usually helps us set off the fireworks. There's no way he would miss that unless something was wrong."

I quietly drank my cappuccino. Across the cafe, Bodhi was deep in conversation with a few of the guys from the construction crew. He was always better than I was at moving a discussion in the direction that he wanted.

"Hang on a minute," Alex said. He set down his breakfast sandwich and inspected me with narrowed eyes. "You asked me about Ethan that night at Lido's during the storm."

I stirred the foam into my coffee. "Yes, I did."

"If I recall, you also promised to fill me in on the situation."

I chewed on the inside of my cheek. Though the other cafe customers were wrapped up in their own musings about what might have happened to Ethan Powell, I couldn't tell Alex the truth without the risk of unwanted ears overhearing it.

"Not here," I told him in a low voice. "Not now."

Alex pushed his half-eaten bagel across the counter and rested on his elbows so that he was on the same level as me. "Bailey, do you know something about Ethan?"

Bodhi saved me from answering. He came up from behind, clapping Alex on the back. "Hey, man. How's it going?"

"As good as it's going to get," Alex answered as he and Bodhi shook hands. As far as I knew, they'd only met in passing, but everyone in Black Bay was friendly enough. Alex eyed the bruise on Bodhi's temple. "Ouch. How'd you manage that one?"

"Rogue two-by-four," Bodhi replied vaguely. "Are you coming with?"

"Where?"

Bodhi reached past me to steal a sip of my coffee. "A

group of us are heading to Ethan's house to check if he's home or not."

My eyes widened at this information, and I pinched Bodhi's arm. He ignored me, waiting for Alex's reply.

"Yeah, I'd like to go," said Alex. "Now?"

"In a minute or so." Bodhi pointed to the door of the Sanctuary. Just outside, a few locals waited for others to join them. "We're heading over in a bit."

Alex wrapped the remainder of his breakfast sandwich in a napkin to eat on the go and left a ten dollar bill on the counter. "Sounds solid. You coming, Bailey?"

I stared at Bodhi for direction. He shook his head a fraction of an inch to either side.

"Yeah, actually," I said to Bodhi's discontent. "I'll come."

"Good." Alex paused by my stool before heading for the exit. "Because our conversation is far from over."

With a roguish wink, he took a bite of his bagel and turned away. As he maneuvered through the other café patrons, Bodhi fixed me with a look of disapproval.

"What?"

"I think you should go home," he said. "It's safer."

I finished off my coffee and left the dregs at the bottom of the cup. "Nowhere in Black Bay is safe until we find out where Ethan is. Besides, I need to get back into Ethan's boathouse."

Bodhi shifted from one foot to the other, glancing nervously at the growing group that waited outside the Sanctuary. "Today?"

"It's a good a time as ever."

"And what if Ethan's actually there?" Bodhi asked. "Then what?"

"I can assume he won't be pleased to see either one of us," I said, hopping down from the bar stool. Another waiting customer took my place. "But Ethan won't dare to lay a hand on us in front of a bunch of locals. Everyone's in the dark about the Winchesters, remember?"

Bodhi guided me through the crowded tables with a light hand at the small of my back. "I guess. What did Alex mean anyway? About your conversation not being over?"

I kept my voice quiet. "He's figured out I know more about Ethan than I'm letting on. We might have to clue him in soon."

"Are you crazy?" Bodhi hissed. "There's no way we're telling him that we're best friends with Pat—"

"Shh."

I pushed through the door of the Sanctuary to meet up with the group of locals outside. Alex counted heads. There were about eight or nine of us who wanted to make sure that Ethan was all right. Or at least pretended to.

"We got everyone?" Alex asked. "Let's head out."

WE WERE ROBBED of the opportunity to discuss strategy when Alex suggested a few of the construction guys carpool with us. I sat squished between Alex and Bodhi in the cab of the truck while everyone else rode in the bed. We trundled through the marshy woods around Ethan's home in silence, listening to the guys in the back pitch ideas on Ethan's whereabouts.

"Maybe he had a few too many to drink."

"Ethan's been sober for years, man."

"I'm sure he just got sick or something."

If Alex wanted to talk about Ethan, he wasn't comfortable addressing the topic in front of Bodhi. Bodhi steered gently across a muddy pothole, trying not to jostle the guys. Around the bend, a pretty yellow cottage came into view. Ethan's blue truck sat in the dirt driveway, a white magnet advertising Powell's Lumber Mill stuck to the side. Bodhi pulled in behind it. Another carload of locals parked beside us, and everyone got out to stretch.

"I suppose we should knock first," Alex suggested, bounding up to the porch. "Just in case."

Bodhi and I lingered near the cars as the rest of our impromptu search party joined Alex on the porch. With every rap of Alex's knuckles against Ethan's front door, my ribs tightened a little bit more around my lungs. No one answered, so Alex picked the key up from under the mat and let himself him. Ethan's dachshund didn't bother to greet him. She dashed down the porch steps and immediately relieved herself in the front yard as if no one had come home to let her out in a while. Alex checked the house then emerged on the porch again.

"Ethan's not here," he declared. "Everyone split up. Check the surrounding area."

"We'll check the backyard," I volunteered before anyone else could claim the area. If Bodhi and I were the only ones back there, it would be much easier to reach the boathouse without anyone else noticing.

Alex nodded. "All right. Bailey and Bodhi have the back-yard. John and I will take the north side…"

As Alex delegated, Bodhi pulled me around to the side yard, surveying the landscape for any signs of Ethan's return. "How are we going to do this?" he whispered. His fingers found mine and squeezed tightly when we arrived in Ethan's backyard. "I mean, how are we supposed to walk out of here with a murder weapon, for Pete's sake?"

"I'll shove it under my shirt or something," I replied, shuddering at the thought. I led Bodhi to a small opening in the overgrown brush that bordered the edge of the canal in Ethan's backyard. "The boathouse is through here. You stand watch. I'll make it quick."

"Wait!" Bodhi pulled me away from the wild plants. "We

need a signal, a way for me to alert you if someone comes this way."

"Can you still do that bird whistle?"

"Yes."

"There you go."

I punched through the underbrush before Bodhi could change his mind, treading carefully. The landscape had been overlooked for so long that it proposed more of a challenge than the Winchesters' jungly garden. A vine adhered to the Velcro straps of my walking boot and trapped my foot. I wrenched the boot upward, tearing the weed from the ground. Up ahead, I could see the roof of the crumbling boathouse. Like the rest of the yard, Ethan had abandoned it to Mother Nature. The paint peeled, the wood rotted, and the entire structure was blanketed in a layer of moss and mold. The thick trees shaded the area from the sun. Even on the brightest day, the boathouse seemed to exist in a phantom zone of gloom.

Finally, I reached the door. The padlock was gone. I'd torn it free with a carpenter's axe on my last visit, leaving a fresh jagged gash in the deteriorating wood. The hinges of the door were rusted over, but one good tug forced the door open. I stepped backward, my heart pounding as I stared into the dismal interior of the boathouse. Half of me expected Ethan to emerge from the murk in a fit of revenge, but the boathouse was just as eerily quiet as it had been the last time.

I readied myself, taking deep breaths to settle my rollicky nerves. This was not the time for a weak stomach. It was in and out. Thirty seconds. That was all the time I needed to grab what Patrick had asked for. I hurtled into the gloom. When my eyes adjusted to the darkness, my jaw dropped.

Ethan's boat was gone.

Which meant so was the murder weapon.

PROGRESS REPORT

*C*ome Monday morning, Bodhi and I had no choice but to continue renovation work on the Winchester house. Calling a respite for no reason would draw more attention to us than we needed. It was best to pretend like everything was as it should be, so Bodhi and the rest of the crew started ripping up the rotting deck wood in the back-yard early that morning.

I sat on the balcony off the master bedroom, keeping an eye on the activity below. Bodhi's shoulders tensed as he tore another board up and threw it into a pile of debris. He rested his hands on his knees, breathing hard. It had only been two days since his head injury. I knew it still ached, even if the purplish bruising had faded to a less intense shade. But Bodhi was Bodhi. If there was work to be done, he would do it without complaint. So I supervised from above, making sure that Bodhi paused every once in a while to sit down or grab a drink of water, and wondered where on earth Ethan could've hidden his boat.

It was a hell of a setback. Here I was thinking at least one of Patrick's requests would be easy to fulfill. Ethan had kept souvenirs of the Winchester murders: his wrecked boat, Caroline's personal journals, and the nautical rope that Ethan had used to hang Patrick. Now all of those things were gone. When did Ethan have the time to get rid of them? Was it before or after he cornered me in the rocks of the overhead bluff? And more importantly, how was I supposed to locate those items in the five days left before the anniversary of Patrick and Caroline's deaths?

That was yet another burden to juggle. Before, when he had been Milo, Patrick steered clear of the house. Now that his window to move on was closing, he spent more and more time with me and Bodhi. Caroline was active as well, often contributing to the conversation by slamming doors or levitating silverware. It wasn't too much of a problem for us—at this point, we were used to her supernatural antics—but hiding Patrick and Caroline's existence from the construction crew was already proving to be quite the challenge. Just before they'd started work, one of the guys, John, came out of the first floor bathroom to hear me scolding Patrick in the hallway above for being careless about his appearance. He'd called up the stairs, and I shoved Patrick through the doors of the master bedroom before he was seen. Nevertheless, it was a close call, and I didn't care to repeat the experience.

As if babysitting two long dead teenagers wasn't enough, I still needed to work on my blog. It had been far too long since I'd posted something for *Flipping Out*, and my followers were getting antsy. The problem was that I was having trouble writing anything about the renovation progress when my mind was so addled with other thoughts. For so long, *Flipping Out* acted as a coping mechanism for me. It allowed me to live through my own imagination in a world where Bodhi and I were happily ensconced in our house flipping business. There, no ghosts begged for my attention. No murderers threatened my sanity. At one time the blog had been my safety net, but now even the wondrous world of my online life wasn't enough to distract me from my current woes.

I scrolled through my old posts, trying to find some inspiration in them. Here was the record of mine and Bodhi's last four and a half years together, the time between the death of our daughter and now. I marveled at how bubbly my earlier posts sounded. At the time, I was heartbroken. In fact, I was broken in general. Kali was gone, Bodhi felt gone, and I had no idea where my life was headed. Yet here were the photos of our first ever flipping project. Granted, I didn't take half as many selfies back then, but there were still pictures of me smiling up at Bodhi as he laid new roofing on a suburban home in Colorado. I'd been so good at faking my happiness, but maybe that was the problem. Shoving my grief below the surface and pretending to smile hadn't done anything to make me feel better or aid my relationship with Bodhi. It wasn't until the Winchester children made us confront our problems that Bodhi began to feel less like a stranger to me.

There had to be something I could do to satisfy *Flipping Out*'s followers without compromising my freshly discovered emotional integrity. I opened the page to create a new post, staring at the blank text box. Finally, I began to type.

Dear Flippers,

It's Bailey here. Today I present to you something a little different from my usual blog: a confession. But before we get to that, I feel the need to fill you in on a few things that have happened over the past couple of days. First off, I lost my cell phone. As in, it fell off the cliff face and into the water. I suppose that's one of the hazards of living so close to the edge of the world.

Eventually, something goes over. The good news is that without my phone, I feel strangely free of modern technology. The bad news is that I lost all of the progress pictures of the Winchester house that I had yet to post on the blog. Sorry about that. I promise to make up for it. Second, you may be wondering how the Black Bay summer festival went. I have to report that it did not go as expected and (because I lost my phone) I was unable to take pictures of the festivities for you. Once again, my deepest apologies.

Okay, Bailey, get to the point.

You may be wondering what exactly it is I have to confess. Here it is: I'm not happy. Hard to believe, right? Especially since this blog is full of pleasant anecdotes and cheerful content? It's true. I'm not happy, and I haven't been for as long as Flipping Out has existed. Again, I apologize. I crafted a story to tell you. Social media is like that. You show your followers only the good parts of your life, and you hide the rest for your own private contemplation. My story is what you've read so far. Bodhi and I travel the States in search of our next great adventure as the inseparable house-flipping duo. What you don't know is everything that happened to lead up to Flipping Out's conception. The following information is hard for me to share with you, and it may be hard for some of you to read. Nevertheless, I feel like the time has come to finally be honest with you all. I think it will help me to move on. Here it goes.

Roughly five years ago, right before we decided to flip houses for profit, Bodhi and I lost our daughter. Her name was Kali. She was three years old at the time, and she was the light of my life. Honestly, before Kali, I wasn't particularly fond of children, and I certainly did not plan on having any myself. Bodhi was of the same mindset. As all of you know, we traveled extensively before we started our own business, and children aren't conducive to such a nomadic lifestyle. Nevertheless, things happen, and we found ourselves with a baby that we didn't know what to do with.

I know what you're thinking. It sounds like Bodhi and I resented our daughter. I'll admit, I had no idea how Kali was going to affect us. I was scared to death when I found out I was pregnant. A slew of anxieties hid behind every corner. Could I raise a child to be adventurous yet cautious? Sensitive yet strong? Hardworking yet laid back? And more to the point, could I seamlessly weave a child into the intricate tapestry that was me and Bodhi? I spent nine months reading every parenting book on the shelf, but each page terrified me more than the last. Kali's appearance was nigh, and I felt no better prepared than when those two pink lines popped up on my at-home pregnancy test.

Fast forward to the day Kali was born. She had a full head of hair, and my God, was she the most beautiful thing I'd ever seen. It was like something inside me clicked into place. Maybe it was maternal instinct. Maybe it was love at first sight. Whatever the feeling, I knew that I belonged wholly to the little girl in my arms, and no amount of wanderlust would make me wish she didn't exist. Don't get me wrong; I was panicking internally. I truly did not know if I was capable of keeping that tiny nugget safe, but when her baby fingers wrapped around my own for the first time, I knew that I would go down trying.

Go down, I did. I'm crying writing this, but I need to get it out. Kali died on my watch. Sure, there were extenuating circumstances, but it boils down to one quick moment of poor judgement on my part. For five years, I have blamed myself for that. Most likely, I won't dash that feeling anytime soon, but I'm trying. God, I'm trying.

You may be asking yourself why I'm telling all of this to you now. Why bog down all of this quality positive house flipping content with such a melancholy secret from what feels like a past life? Here's why. It wasn't right. It wasn't right fooling you all into thinking that mine and Bodhi's life together was perfect. It wasn't right pretending that we existed in perfect harmony and that our biggest concern was a sinkhole beneath a house in Fort Lauderdale. It wasn't right taking photos of Bodhi while he worked and posting them to Flipping Out when I specifically knew that the reason he put in such an insane amount of effort was to stop himself from thinking of Kali. It wasn't right, and it wasn't fair. For that, I owe all of you and my husband the deepest and sincerest of apologies. I'm sorry. Plain and simple.

So! Where do we go from here? Truthfully, I don't know. I love this blog. I love documenting the work we do. To me, every project is an accomplishment, and Flipping Out is a real life record of how far we've come since we first decided to make this our career. Even so, something's gotta give, flippers. I'm not sure what, but be on the lookout for some changes. Don't worry. I know how obsessed you all are with the Winchester house. Believe me, I am too. I'll continue to post updates as much as possible.

I'll wrap this up with a thank you to all of you. Without our followers, Flipping Out would be just another URL in the vast and endless space we call the Internet. I cannot even begin to tell you how much I love and cherish your support. Please stick with me. We'll leap over these upcoming hurdles together.

ALL MY BEST,
   Bailey

I WIPED my wet cheeks with the hem of my T-shirt. The cursor lingered over the Publish button on the web page, but I couldn't bring myself to click it just yet. There was a disadvantage to sharing something like this on the Internet. For everyone to see. It was equal to releasing a part of yourself for the rest of the world to have access to, and that was not an action I considered lightly. For all I knew, publishing such a post would send *Flipping Out* to a premature death. My followers didn't tune in for a cry fest. They did it to learn about flipping houses and to live vicariously through me and Bodhi. Would a post like this put followers off? Was it stupid to publish something in direct opposition of the blog's usual tone?

"You should publish it," a voice said behind me.

I jumped, overturning the cup of fresh orange juice beside my chair. As the liquid stained the old decking, I turned around to face Patrick. "Seriously, you have got to stop doing that."

He leaned against the ruined door frame of the master bedroom and flashed me his signature quarterback smile. "Sorry about that. Sometimes I forget."

I glanced down at the men hard at work below. "They can't see you from down there, can they?"

He stood on his tiptoes to peer toward the ground. "I'll stay here, just in case. You should publish it."

I skimmed through the personal letter with a frown. "I'm not sure."

"I think you'll be surprised by how many people will appreciate your honesty and love you for your flaws anyway," Patrick said.

"What are you, my shrink?" But something in Patrick's tone lent me the courage to click the Publish button. With a dramatic *whoosh*, the page refreshed itself, and the letter was available for all to read.

"There it goes."

"You won't regret it," Patrick assured me.

I scooted my patio chair away from the edge of the balcony so that I could speak with Patrick without the workers noticing. As I settled in again, he handed me a fresh glass of chilled orange juice.

I stared at it. "How'd you do that?"

"Perks of the job."

"Har har." I rotated the glass. It was the one Patrick had pilfered from Lido's Restaurant when he had still been alive.

The Lido's logo was printed across the glass in frosty lettering. A sudden realization hit me. "It was you."

"Pardon?"

I looked up at Patrick, squinting in the sunlight to see him properly. "It was you. I told Milo that drinking ice water helps calm me down. That same night, there was a Lido's glass on the bedside table. I always thought it was Caroline because of the plumerias, but it was you, wasn't it?"

Patrick sank, sitting on the floor beside my patio chair and resting his elbows on his knees. "Yeah, that was me."

"And the night Caroline destroyed her bedroom? That shadow in the master bedroom?"

"That was me too."

I gestured to the jagged hole in the side of the house where a pair of exquisite French doors had recently been ripped from place in a supernatural attempt to flee my notice. Ever since, we kept the opening covered with black tarp unless we wanted to sit on the balcony. "This is *your* fault?" I demanded, flapping the tarp dramatically. "*You* tore a hole in the house?"

Patrick bowed his head sheepishly. "Sorry. I didn't mean to. I just—remember how I said you remind me of my mom?"

"Yes."

He fiddled with his fingers, picking at a hangnail on his thumb. "My mom was amazing. She did so much for this town. She did so much for me and Caroline. I don't think I knew how well she was raising us until she was gone." He paused, his eyes shining as he looked across the water. "I miss her. I miss my dad too, of course, but my mom had this warmth to her. She could put anyone at ease. If I was ever upset, she always knew exactly what to do or say to make me feel better. Honestly, it wasn't until I met Alex that I realized most kids don't have that."

Patrick sniffed. He avoided my gaze and tried to pull a loose nail from the aged wood of the upper deck. My heart swelled. I'd forgotten that Patrick was seventeen. At that age, you thought you were invincible, a year away from the illusion of independence. At the same time, you needed someone to pave the road for you.

"Anyway," Patrick continued. "My mom had depression. She handled it rather well. It's why she did so much work in the town. She said that holding herself accountable for that kind of stuff helped her get up in the morning when she didn't want to." Having pried the nail from the wood, he rubbed the rust from the metal. "Every once in a while, she had a bad day. She wouldn't get up or eat breakfast. She would just lie in bed in this room all day long with the curtains shut. There was nothing we could do to make her feel better. We all just rode out the bad days with each other."

Patrick dug the tip of the nail into the tip of his index finger. It punctured the skin, and a droplet of blood welled to the surface. Instinctively, I set down my orange juice to confiscate the nail from his grasp.

"Don't do that," I said gently, rolling the nail across the deck beyond his reach.

"It's fine," Patrick replied as he held up his finger. He wiped the blood away. Underneath, there was no sign of the puncture wound. "See?"

"It's the concept though," I rebutted.

He smiled softly. "*That's* why I left you things and tried to help you. The warmth that my mom had? You have it as well. When I figured out you were sad too, I wanted you to know that someone was there with you. Not to talk or argue or try to help. Just someone to be there."

If a teenaged boy had to haunt my house, I was glad it was Patrick Winchester. Like he said himself, his mother had raised him well. If Kali had made it to seventeen, I would've hoped she turned out as kind and caring as Patrick.

I smoothed Patrick's hair back. It felt natural. Intuitive. All this talk about mothering was having an effect on me. "Your mother loves you, Pat. Even now."

He rested his forehead on his knees. I rubbed his back in comforting circles.

"And I know you didn't murder the French doors on purpose," I added, trying to lighten the mood. "Unlike Caroline, you don't seem to obtain pleasure from wreaking havoc. At least you've never possessed either one of us."

My change of subject had the opposite effect than I'd hoped. Patrick's jaw clenched. "She's not supposed to do that."

A cloud shifted, and the sun beat down on the balcony, warming my skin. My foot was sweating underneath the cast. Ugh.

"I'd have to agree," I told Patrick. "But is that because they make you sign some kind of morality clause when you become a ghost? Or is there another reason?"

Patrick covered his eyes to look up at me. "Yesterday, you asked me why I look human while Caroline can't so much as blink."

"And you told me that Caroline didn't want me to know the answer to that question."

"She doesn't."

"What do *you* want to tell me?"

Patrick blew out a breath. "I think you need to know. The more you know, the better prepared you are to take on this fiasco."

I swung my feet off the patio chair to face Patrick head on. "I'm listening."

He stretched out his legs and leaned back on his palms, tipping his face up to the sun and closing his eyes. "Let me preface this information by telling you that I'm not exactly up to date with every aspect of afterlife mechanics. Caroline and I figured this crap out the hard way. There's no manual or guide book."

"Fair enough. Continue."

"When we first realized we were stuck here, Caroline soon discovered that we could leech energy from living humans," Patrick explained. "It helped us feel somewhat alive again and to maintain a quasi-physical presence. However, it also had an effect on the people that we fed off of."

The resulting look of horror on my face must've been more conspicuous that I imagined because Patrick sat up to pat my hand.

"No one died," he assured me hurriedly. "It drained them. They would get sick, and it would take them a few days to recover. For a while, everyone thought some kind of bug was going around town. Because of that, I stopped doing it. I couldn't stand watching people suffer because I wanted to feel something again. Caroline, on the other hand, made an unfortunate habit out of it."

"What happened then?" I asked, unsure if I wanted the answer.

"You already know," Patrick replied. "We found out that what you took had to be given back eventually. That's why Caroline faded so much faster than me. She couldn't help herself. Anytime she had access to a human, she stole from them. Her highs started getting shorter and shorter, and before we knew it, she was no more than a shadow."

"That's why you looked ill," I realized, thinking back to the weeks prior. I remembered Milo's gaunt appearance and testy temperament. "You disappeared for a while, and when you came back, you looked like you had the flu."

Patrick nodded. "I knew I had to look as human as possible for when you and Bodhi arrived here, so I found a hiker in the woods. It lasted long enough to get you to trust me, but if I was going to keep up the ruse, I needed someone else to suck energy from. I wasn't willing to do that, especially not to you or Bodhi."

"And what about that time you tried to strangle yourself?" I asked. The memory was still fresh in my mind. "Or when you were bleeding out?"

"I was getting desperate," Patrick admitted. "At that point, I was running out of steam. Both times, I was trying to show you how I was killed. Ethan hit me over the head before he hung me. That's why I was bleeding so badly."

"Right," I said, swallowing a surge of nausea. "I knew that."

We were quiet for a moment, listening to the bustle of the construction work on the ground below. Bodhi's voice floated up to the balcony as he asked someone for a bottle of water. Another thought occurred to me.

"Patrick?"

"Yes?"

"If you need to absorb energy from a living person in order to look alive, who did you suck dry this time around?"

Patrick's blue irises crystallized, hardening as he looked me in the eye.

"Ethan Powell."

TALK OF THE TOWN

*T*hat evening, I returned from town with an amalgamation of items from the prepared foods section of the local market. The kitchen at the Winchester house was finished at last, but Bodhi and I were far too exhausted to make use of it. The few guys that hadn't been working on the deck outside installed the new appliances. The stainless steel refrigerator, dishwasher, and oven really tied our industrial theme together. The color contrasts between the exposed brick accent wall, the new cabinets, and the appliances were fresh and clean. As I lifted the bags of groceries onto the polished countertops, I let out a satisfied sigh. The kitchen looked great, as did the living and dining areas. It was always such a rush to see my original design sketches come to life.

The construction crew had gone home. Bodhi was outside. He sat cross-legged on a completed portion of the deck facing the water. His hands rested lightly on his knees. From the even flow of his breath, I could tell that he was meditating. The breeze blew his hair around in a spasmodic dance though he remained serene and motionless. It used to be something he did every day, but Bodhi's ability to sit still had waned in the last few years. I watched from the glass doors. Meditation was never something I could get the hang of, no matter how often Bodhi asked me to practice with him. For some reason, clearing my mind was a challenge I'd yet to overcome. Even Doctor Marx had suggested something similar in one of my sessions with her, but no matter what I did, thoughts raced through my brain at top speed without any regard to my personal emotions. I couldn't bring myself to interrupt Bodhi, even to tell him that dinner was available. He deserved time to himself, so I turned away from the glass door.

"I read your letter today," he said suddenly, the light wind carrying his voice across the deck and into the house.

I would never understand how he did that. I hadn't made a noise, yet Bodhi somehow sensed me watching him. "You did?"

He took a deep breath and looked over his shoulder. "Mm-hmm."

"I didn't think you read Flipping Out anymore," I said, lingering in the space between the deck and the living room.

"You left your laptop on the balcony earlier," Bodhi replied. He stretched his arms overhead, the muscles in his back and shoulders standing at attention. "The page was still up."

"Sorry."

"No, don't apologize." He rose from the deck in one continuous motion. He always had a fluidity to him after meditating, something that I had forgotten about until just now. He met me in the door frame, taking my hands in his. "I'm proud of you for writing that."

My bottom lip trembled. "You are?"

Bodhi smiled and threaded his arms around my waist. "So proud. But I need to say something too."

I tugged on one of his long curls and watched it spring back into place. "What's that?"

He hugged me tightly to him, making sure to catch my eye. "It wasn't all your fault. What happened to Kali. I was responsible too. I don't think I ever apologized to you for the way I acted while Kali was alive."

My fingers twisted nervously in the fabric of Bodhi's T-shirt. This wasn't something we usually talked about. "No, you didn't."

"I'm sorry," he said firmly. "I was a jerk. For some reason, I thought having Kali meant I couldn't have other things that I wanted. I loved her though." Bodhi's voice cracked, and he crumbled. "I promise I loved her, Bailey. I never wanted that to happen."

"I know," I whispered as he folded into me. "I know, baby."

The setting sun bathed us in its pleasant glow. I closed my eyes, tilting my head so that it rested in the crook of Bodhi's neck. His skin was warm and soft, and his pulse beat out a steady rhythm. I pressed onto my toes and kissed his battered temple. The swelling had gone down, but the yellowing bruise looked uglier than ever.

Bodhi took my fingers and kissed them one by one. "I love you."

Something released inside me. As if there'd been a padlock on the door to my heart. It popped open and everything gushed out, flooding me from head to toe with a rush of heat and happiness and confusion.

"I love you, Bodhi."

He squeezed me so firmly that my feet left the ground when we kissed. I half-laughed, half-cried into it as relief surged through me. We had a long way to go—there was no doubt about that—but in that moment, I was purely myself and Bodhi was purely Bodhi for the first time in five years. I laughed, laughed, laughed. What a feeling to be myself again.

Bodhi set me down again with a grin. "Get anything good for dinner?"

I walked into the kitchen, dumping the bags on the counter. "Deli meat, olives, a fresh baguette, pasta salad, actual salad. A bunch of stuff. What would you like?"

"Mm. Pasta salad to start."

I popped open the container and handed Bodhi a plastic fork. We leaned on the new granite countertops, taking turns as we ate from the same box. Fifteen minutes later, all of the containers lay open like a buffet, and we took bites from whichever item we pleased. I sat on the counter, kicking my bare feet out like a little kid, while Bodhi did a hilarious impression of one of the guys from his construction crew. We roared with laughter, and when the sun set and the kitchen darkened, we hardly noticed.

"In all seriousness," Bodhi said, chuckling as he popped a martini olive into his mouth. "What exactly is our plan for the next few days?"

The mood sobered immediately. In the freshly remodeled kitchen, I'd almost forgotten that we were staying in the infamous Winchester house and that a greater task lay in wait.

"According to Patrick, we have until Saturday night to find a way for them to cross over," I answered. My appetite abandoned me. I threw a half-eaten piece of prosciutto back into the deli tray.

"Five days."

"Yup. And so far, we have no idea where Ethan's hidden his boat, that rope, or the bodies."

Bodhi frowned as he kneaded a piece of crusty bread between his fingers. "If we're trying to rescue the kids, we don't need to worry about the boat for now. That's more for the police, and I'm sure they'll find it eventually."

"Maybe they would," I agreed. "If they were even looking for it."

"Solid point." He dunked the bread into a cup of olive oil and took a bite. "But let's focus on getting what we need to help Caroline and Patrick. The rope and their bodies. Piece of cake."

"Ugh, don't say cake and bodies so close together."

Bodhi rolled his eyes and stuffed the rest of his baguette between my lips to silence me. "We need more information about Ethan. I'd say we should check his house again, but I keep thinking he's going to show up out of the blue and pretend like nothing's wrong. That would not exactly work well in our favor."

"Actually—" I countered, mumbling around the food. "Patrick let slip that he drained Ethan's energy before he pushed him over the edge of that cliff."

Bodhi's eyes widened in alarm. "He did what?"

"Long story. Anyway, it apparently takes humans at least three full days to recover from a draining like that. They've clocked it before."

"How very reassuring," Bodhi deadpanned.

I ticked off the days on my fingers. "Patrick drained Ethan on Saturday night, which means he needed yesterday, today, and tomorrow to recover."

"So we should expect Ethan to come looking for revenge sometime on Wednesday?" Bodhi confirmed.

I lifted my shoulders. "What are the chances he decides that it's not worth the trouble and moves on to some other no-name town?"

"That would be good for us," said Bodhi. "Not so great for Caroline and Patrick."

"Oh. Right."

Bodhi cleaned up, closing the containers and storing them in the massive, pristine, and vastly empty refrigerator to eat at a later date. "So Patrick has no idea what Ethan might've done with the bodies?"

I shook my head, hopping off the counter to help Bodhi. "Nope. He doesn't remember, and neither does Caroline. I guess there's a blank period between life and afterlife."

"That's unfortunate. Ethan could've done anything with the bodies. Burned them, buried them, thrown them in the ocean."

"We're talking Ethan Powell here, Bodhi," I reminded him. "We have to consider what we know. He's the most well-liked man in town. That's how he's managed to go so long without being discovered."

Bodhi's brow crinkled as he lost himself in thought. "He also owns a lumber mill with plenty of machinery that would aid in destroying a body."

"Yeah, but how much of a mess would that have been?" My nose wrinkled at the gory imagery in my head. "Ethan wouldn't have risked something like that. Besides, Ethan killed Patrick and Caroline in this house. I doubt he would've towed two bodies through town for everyone to see. No, he must've buried them close."

"Or he threw them over the bluff," Bodhi suggested. "That would've been easiest, right? Everyone would've assumed they died along with their parents."

"Two things." I held up one finger. "First, Patrick sustained injuries that obviously weren't from a boat crash." I held up a second finger. "Second, if Ethan had thrown them over, their bodies would've most likely been stuck in the rocks, not washed out to sea. The police would've found them."

Bodhi considered this as he framed me against the countertop, his hands on either side of my waist. "Can I just point out how attractive you are when you're playing detective?"

I tickled his side. His abdomen contracted as he laughed. "We're not playing, Bodhi. Don't forget that."

He drew away, apologetic. "I know. I'm sorry. It's just nice to be with you again."

I linked my fingers through the belt loops on his shorts and tugged him toward me. "Hey. We are with each other. And getting closer every day."

Bodhi rested his forehead against mine. "I guess it's crazy to worry about our relationship when a homicidal murderer has just added us to his hit list."

"It's not crazy," I told him. "It's human. We'll work on both."

His fingers found the tension in my neck, and he massaged the muscle there. "Okay. We still need to figure out a plan though."

I rolled my shoulders beneath Bodhi's touch, pondering our limited options. "What's on the agenda tomorrow? Do we have time to go into town?"

"We're installing the rest of the deck tomorrow," Bodhi answered as he focused on releasing the strain from my body. "And then I figured you and I could sit down and map out our plans for the remainder of the first floor."

"Let's put a short hold on the plans." I lazily closed my eyes. "I'm thinking we should find someone who was close to Ethan. Maybe we could trick them into giving us a hint about the bodies."

"Who would we ask though?"

"Who did Ethan have a really good relationship with?"

Bodhi scoffed. "Everyone."

"Then it should be easy to dig up some information. We'll start at the Sanctuary."

The pads of his fingers dug into the base of my skull, smoothing the tendons there. An involuntary moan escaped from my lips. Bodhi chuckled, and he flipped me around to find better access to my shoulders. His breath tickled the hair at the nape of my neck.

"Want to go upstairs?" I murmured, bracing myself against the countertop.

His calloused palms traveled south and dipped under the hem of my shirt.

"Oh, do I."

I SLEPT SO SOUNDLY that night that by the time I woke up on Tuesday morning, I felt more refreshed and awake that I had in years. Bodhi was already up, and even though I woke up alone in bed, I didn't feel lonely. The echo of cookware clinking together and the savory scent of crisp bacon found its way up the stairs as Bodhi made breakfast. I smiled and snuggled into the warm sheets, not quite ready to get up. My laptop lay on the bedside table, so I pulled it over and booted it up.

As the webpage for *Flipping Out* loaded, I tried not to let my anxiety get the best of me. I needed to check how my followers had reacted to my personal letter. The page buffered at an agonizingly slow rate. The temporary Wi-Fi that we had set up at the Winchester house wasn't exactly top notch. Finally, *Flipping Out*'s welcome screen greeted me.

And my inbox had maxed out at over five hundred new messages.

I clicked on the first one, steeling myself for constructive criticism, but as I read the short email, my mouth dropped open in surprise.

DEAR BAILEY. First of all, I am so sorry for your loss. Even if it was five years ago, I know how hard it can be to push through losing

someone you loved. I enjoyed Flipping Out from the very begin-
ning, and that won't change. Stay strong. Karen.

THE NEXT SEVERAL messages expressed similar sentiments. Most of them were concise. Others contained big blocks of text recounting life stories that mirrored my own. All of them made me want to cry.

DEAR BAILEY. THANK YOU! I have never read such an honest blog post before, and I just wanted to say how grateful I am that you finally opened up to us. I, too, have lost a child. Your blog was a major part in helping me cope with the heartbreak. We are here to love and support you. Love, Emily.

DEAR BAILEY. My wife was the one who introduced me to your blog, and I'm more addicted to it than I care to admit. You and Bodhi are our role models. We're often told that our relationship won't work out because of how young we are, but knowing that you and Bodhi have fought through such a tragedy inspires us more than anything. We are so sad for your loss, but we hope that you continue to confide in your followers. Much love, Dylan.

DEAR BAILEY. You are the strongest woman I know. I admire you so much. Never apologize for doing the things you thought you needed to do in order to stay sane and healthy. Keep up the phenomenal work. Sincerely, Sandy.

I SPENT SO LONG COMBING through the influx of well-wishes that Bodhi actually came up to the bedroom to check on me.

He had a plate of eggs and bacon and a glass of orange juice in hand as he inched the door open with his hip.

"Bailey? Are you okay?"

I sniffed and blotted my eyes with the corner of the bed sheet. I gestured to the open laptop. "They read my letter."

Bodhi set the plate of food on the comforter and rested his chin on my shoulder to read through the visible replies. "Baby, these are great! Why are you crying?"

I laughed, the sound getting stuck in the back of my throat. "Because they're great!"

"People love you, Bailey," Bodhi said. He brushed his lips across the skin of my shoulder. "I can't believe you ever thought they might think otherwise. Now eat your breakfast. We've got work to do."

IN THE LULL after the morning breakfast rush, the Sanctuary was rather docile. A group of students who attended the nearby state college studied in one corner, hunched over a communal organic chemistry textbook. A cute elderly couple lounged in a pair of leather armchairs by one of the large windows, reading each other passages from their respective sections of the newspaper. The counter space was clear except for two young boys sitting at either end—each about ten or twelve years of age—swatting a poppy seed bagel across the bar top between them. The dark-haired boy nearest us, who looked vaguely familiar for some reason, rocketed the bagel toward his friend. The fairer boy attempted a block but missed, and the bagel shot off the end of the counter and onto the floor, sending poppy seeds flying in every direction.

"Score!" cried the dark-haired boy, pumping his fist. He cupped his hands to his mouth to create a makeshift megaphone. "It's Anthony Lido with the game-winning gooooooooal!"

Ava emerged from the Sanctuary's kitchen and reached across the counter to smack the dark-haired boy lightly across the head. "Anthony, you make another mess in my café and I'll ground you both until Christmas."

"Ms. Miller, you can't ground me. I'm not even your son." Ava fixed him with an intimidating stare. The boy raised his hands in defeat. "Okay, fine. You can ground me. Just don't tell my dad, or I'll have to mop the floor at the restaurant for the next month."

The blond boy hopped off his stool to fetch the mistreated bagel. "No one likes the poppy seed bagels, Mom."

"And yet I don't make them for the two of you to play bagel hockey, Max."

"I like the poppy seed ones," I piped in.

Max's shoulders dropped as he stared at me like I'd set fire to his baseball card collection. "Way to pick sides, lady."

Ava knocked her son over the head with a broom and dustpan then thrust both objects into his small chest. Across the room, Anthony sniggered. "Clean up your mess. And be polite. Anthony?"

Anthony straightened, assuming perfect posture. "Yes, ma'am?" he replied in an innocent tone.

"Your forehand needs work." As Max finished sweeping the poppy seeds into the dustpan, Ava walked over to the Sanctuary's door and held it open. "Get to school, boys. You're late already."

"But I haven't had breakfast," Max protested, swinging a backpack across his shoulders as Anthony bounced off his stool.

"Eat your bagel next time," Ava replied. Max paused at the door, frowning, and Ava leaned down to give him a kiss on the cheek.

Anthony pranced by, tightening the straps on his own backpack as he stood on his tiptoes to reach up toward Ava. "Do I get a kiss too, Ms. Miller?"

Ava relented, planting one on Anthony's roguish cheek too. As the boys trotted off, Ava shook her head. "Stay out of trouble!"

Bodhi and I took seats at the counter, still chuckling at the boys' antics. The countertop was speckled with crumbs and remnants of their game.

"Sorry about that," Ava said, brushing the seeds to the floor with her hand. "They're a bit of a handful sometimes."

"No worries," Bodhi replied.

"Was that Alex Lido's son?" I asked Ava.

Ava nodded as she emptied the espresso filter of the cappuccino machine and poured fresh grounds into it. "He's a character, just like his dad. Cappuccino, Bailey?"

"Yes, ma'am."

"Bodhi? Tea?"

"Green, please. With honey."

"Coming up." Ava bustled around, scooping loose leaves into a small teapot to steep. As she filled it with hot water, she asked, "How's it going up at the Winchester house?"

"It's coming along," Bodhi answered. He nudged me discreetly. "Although it's a little difficult to concentrate when one of the guys is missing."

The cappuccino machine gurgled as Ava tended to it without looking. "Oh, Ethan," she said sadly. "You haven't heard from him at all?"

We both shook our heads. I kept my gaze on the countertop, crushing a wayward poppy seed beneath my nail. Bodhi was a great actor. The despondent hunch of his shoulders and his unhappy frown almost convinced me that he really was worried about Ethan. I, on the other hand, had trouble creating an iota of fake sympathy for a man who murdered an entire family and got away with it.

"Why would we?" Bodhi asked. "I doubt we would be his first point of contact, right?"

Ava combined the cream and espresso in a fresh mug and set it down in front of me. "Oh, I just figured since he was heading up to your place the last time he was seen—"

I choked on my first sip, and coffee splashed over the lip of my mug. Bodhi silently handed me a napkin. I wiped hot milk from my nose. "What do you mean? Who saw Ethan last?"

"Pam Lopez, I think." Ava poured a cup of steaming tea for Bodhi, who stirred in a spoonful of local honey. "They ran into each other on his way up. Weren't you sick that day, Bailey? He said Bodhi asked him to check on you. Right, Bodhi?"

It was Bodhi's turn to cough into his drink. "Uh. Right. Ahem. Sounds like he didn't make it up the bluff though."

"You think?" Ava rested her elbows on the counter.

"He certainly wasn't at the house," I supplied firmly before I could lose my nerve. "I spent most of my afternoon in the bathroom. I would've heard if Ethan stopped by."

Ava made a face. "Shame. I think we were all holding on to a shred of hope that Ethan might be somewhere in your area."

"Nope."

"Not a sign—"

The door to the Sanctuary opened again, and I looked over my shoulder to see a svelte older woman wearing a sophisticated, plum-colored pant suit enter the café. She had secured her hair—a perfect shade of auburn only available to those with enough cash to visit an out-of-town salon—in a neat bun near the top of her head and painted her nails to match her outfit.

"Doctor Marx!" I waved, grateful for the distraction.

"Morning, Bailey." Doctor Marx strolled over, her heels clicking across the tile floor, and lit upon the stool beside me, hanging her designer handbag over the back of it. "Ava, may I have an Americano please?"

"You got it."

As Ava drifted away, Doctor Marx reached over me to offer her hand to Bodhi. "Hello there. You must be Bailey's husband. I've heard all about you."

Bodhi shook Doctor Marx's hand. "Not all bad, I hope."

Doctor Marx smiled slyly. "Doctor-patient confidentiality, Mr. Taylor."

I whacked Bodhi lightly across his shoulder. "It's not all bad."

"Good," he said, sipping his tea. "Actually, Doctor Marx, what's your availability like as of late? Bailey and I were thinking about attending a session together."

Ava returned with Doctor Marx's order. Doctor Marx blew delicately across the surface of her coffee and sighed. "I'm afraid we're a little swamped this week. Someone broke into the office last week and tampered with the patient files."

Bodhi and I exchanged panicked looks. His fingers trembled on the handle of his teacup as he bounced his leg up and down anxiously. I rested a hand on his knee to stop him.

"Who would've done something like that?" I asked, disguising my jitters behind the lip of my coffee mug.

Doctor Marx even shrugged in a way that seemed inherently posh. "No idea. And it's not like we have cameras here to catch things like that. The crime in Black Bay is practically non-existent."

Bodhi hawked into his teacup. I rubbed his back. "You all right, babe? Got something in your throat?"

"Mm-hmm."

"Anyway," Doctor Marx continued as she nursed her

Americano. "Lots of paperwork. Lots of trouble. We're a bit behind schedule. I can pencil you in for next week?"

"That sounds great," I told her. I swigged the remainder of my coffee, trying not to wince as the hot liquid coursed down my throat. "We better get going. Got a lot to do today! Right, Bodhi?"

Bodhi, who'd been rendered momentarily speechless, found his voice again. "Right. The guys will never let me hear the end of it if I'm late again."

"Call me later to schedule a session," said Doctor Marx.

"We will," I promised. I set a five dollar bill on the counter and waved to Ava as she washed dishes in the kitchen. "Have a nice day!"

"You too!"

And then I grabbed Bodhi's hand and ushered him out of the Sanctuary. We hurried down the street without direction.

"Oh my God," said Bodhi.

"Don't panic," I ordered.

"Don't panic?" he repeated incredulously. "Bailey, you do realize that if they find out we were the ones who tampered with those files, we could go to jail, right?"

"They won't find out."

"We didn't even wear gloves! Oh, and don't get me started on Ethan. Pam Lopez. Damn Pam Lopez! Spreading it around town that Ethan was on his way to see you."

I pinned Bodhi's hands to his sides before his gesticulating could get any wilder. "Calm down. I have an idea."

"Does it involve fleeing the crime scene?" Bodhi muttered darkly.

"On the contrary," I replied, steering Bodhi past the fountain in the town square. "It involves employing a co-conspirator."

28

BONDING

*W*hen we arrived at Lido's restaurant, we stood on the curb for a solid minute as I tried to decide whether or not it was a good idea to go inside. Thankfully, there weren't many people around to watch us deliberate. It was too early in the morning for any kind of lunch rush. The neon open sign mocked us. It seemed to grow brighter the longer we waited.

"What are we doing here?" Bodhi asked, one arm around my shoulders.

"Like I said, we need an ally."

"And you think golden boy Alex Lido is the best person to recruit?" Bodhi looked at me like I was crazy. "He's one of most high-profile town members."

"He was also Patrick's best friend and completely in love with Caroline," I reminded him. "He already knows Ethan was up to something that night. Besides, I promised to fill him in."

Bodhi's arm dropped from my shoulder as he stared at me in disbelief. "You did what?"

"You don't think he deserves that much?"

"I think if we tell *anyone* that Patrick and Caroline's ghosts asked us to round up a murderer so that they can enact their revenge, we'll be committed to a psych ward faster than you can say Doctor Marx's full name," Bodhi bit back.

A young woman crossed the street, cooing as she pushed a baby stroller. I hushed Bodhi as she passed by, and she eyed us nervously.

"Nice day, isn't it?" I said to her with what I hoped was a convincing smile.

"Sure is," she replied, but she gave us a wide berth as she continued on her walk.

Bodhi dropped his head into his hands. "This is all going to hell."

"And so are we if we don't find a way to help Patrick and Caroline." I yanked open the door to Lido's. "Get in here, Bodhi, and activate that undeniable charisma of yours."

A bell chimed over the door. The restaurant was empty. I could see all the way to the back of the long room, where the pretty patio opened up to the bay. One random employee wiped table tops down with a wet rag. Bodhi looked green as he joined me at Lido's host stand, where we waited patiently for someone to notice us.

"On second thought, let me do the talking," I muttered to him under my breath. Doctor Marx's revelation had caused Bodhi to pitch his confident deception skills right out the window. I shook my head. Sure, the undead didn't bother him, but the thought of spending any time at all in a jail cell chilled him to the core.

At last, the pretty hostess emerged from the kitchen with a look of confusion on her face. She checked her watch. "You guys here for brunch or something? We don't serve pancakes."

"Actually, we were wondering if Alex was around," I told her.

She deflated with visible relief at not having to work before expected. "Oh, sure." She pushed through the swinging doors to the kitchen. "Alex! Bailey's here to see you."

Bodhi shifted his weight, the length of his arm pressed against my mine. He was sweating, but not because the summer day was so hot. It was a cold, clammy sweat. He was that nervous about involving anyone else in our paranormal shenanigans.

Alex pushed through the swinging door with a thud, ducking his head to avoid bumping into the low frame. When he straightened to his full height, he looked slightly surprised by our presence. "Bailey. Bodhi. I figured you guys would be working hard on the Winchester house by this time."

"We are usually," I replied. "Do you have a minute?"

He gestured to the vacant restaurant. "I'm swimming in time. What can I do for you?"

I pointed to the patio. "Can we sit?"

Alex arched a wary eyebrow before ducking under the bar top to join us on the other side. "I have to sit down for this, do I?"

"Trust me," Bodhi grumbled. "It's better that way."

We followed him out to the patio where the three of us took seats at one of the freshly cleaned tables. Alex patted his employee on the back. "Thanks, Ryan. Can you bring us three waters?" As Ryan scurried off, Alex tilted back in his plastic chair and kicked his feet up on the adjacent table. "Does this have to do with the last time Bailey and I talked out here?"

I looked out across the water. The bay was calm. Sunshine glinted off the ripples like little stars that dared to grace the light of day. Boats floated languidly at the docks of the marina. A seagull cawed, passing by overhead. I longed for the day Bodhi and I could sit at Lido's and enjoy the weather, but Bodhi jolted me quickly out of my daydream with an elbow to my side.

"We need your help," I told Alex.

"With what?"

I looked at Bodhi, who nodded in encouragement. "We have a problem with the Winchester house."

"Uh-huh. What kind of problem?"

"An infestation of sorts," Bodhi cut in.

"What, like bugs?"

"No, not bugs," I said, rolling my eyes at Bodhi. "It's more that someone's still living there."

Alex opened his mouth to reply, but Ryan returned with our waters. Alex waited until he set the glasses down on the table and went back inside. "Did you find squatters?" he asked us, tapping a straw on the table to rid it off its paper wrapper. "I don't understand. Why didn't you just call the police? What am I supposed to do?"

"It's not squatters," said Bodhi.

"Then what is it?"

I looked Alex over, wondering if he could handle what we were about to tell him. There was no point in beating around the bush. Alex was the only person we could remotely begin to trust with this information, and considering how lost we were on our own, we desperately needed his help. I inhaled heavily.

"It's Patrick and Caroline."

Alex stared at me. Then his eyes shifted to Bodhi as if asking for a clue. He looked back at me. "Are you messing with me?"

"No, we—"

"Because if you are, you should know how cruel it is of

you to do something like this," Alex interrupted, his inflection sharpening. "Especially so soon after the Winchester Celebration."

Bodhi held up his hand to stop Alex. "Calm down. We're not trying to mess with you at all."

"Then what is this?"

"A call for help," I answered. Droplets of condensation rolled down my water glass. I traced them with the tips of my finger, avoiding Alex's gaze. "Here's the thing, Alex. If we tell you what's really happening up at the Winchester house, you have to promise to keep an open mind."

Alex took his feet off the table and rubbed his temples as if he was suddenly hit with a tension headache. "I'm not sure I'm following along, so I'm going to have to ask again. Does this have anything to do with what you were talking about the night of the storm, Bailey?"

"Do you remember what we spoke about?"

"Yeah, you asked me about the night Patrick and Caroline died."

I glanced at the door of the restaurant to make sure no one else was listening in and lowered my voice. "I also asked you if you'd seen Ethan Powell."

"Right. And I told you that he took his boat out."

"What if I told you the reason you didn't see Ethan come back into the marina was because he was the one who ran the Winchesters into the rocks?"

There was a beat of silence between the three of us during which Alex's eyes ping-ponged from me to Bodhi and back again. Then, calmly, he replied, "I would ask if you had any proof."

"We did," Bodhi answered. He licked his lips, as if his mouth had gone dry in anticipation of filling Alex in, and took a long draw from his water glass. "We found the boat Ethan used to do it, among other things. Unfortunately, once Ethan realized we'd figured him out, he relocated all of it."

Alex crushed the straw's paper wrapper in his fist. "So let me get this straight. You came here to tell me that you think Ethan Powell caused the Winchesters' deaths, that you *had* evidence but you don't now, and that for some inexplicable reason, you need my help?"

"There's more actually," I said.

"This ought to be good."

"Like I said, something is still living in the Winchester house," I told Alex, trying to see past his angry expression. "Someone, more accurately. Two someones. Patrick and Caroline never got on the boat that night, Alex. Ethan killed them in their own home. And now they're haunting the Winchester house."

Alex burst out laughing, his shoulders shaking as he chuckled from deep in his belly. He wiped his watering eyes with the collar of his shirt. "Oh, man," he said with a sigh. "You two really had me going there. You guys always do something like this to the locals? Is this for that blog of yours?"

"We're not kidding," I insisted. In some sense, I should've known that Alex wouldn't take us seriously at first. After all, Bodhi and I didn't believe something supernatural was going on at the Winchester house until Caroline wrecked several rooms. Even so, time was of the essence, and the more we wasted trying to convince Alex of the Winchesters' continued existence, the less we had to save Patrick and Caroline from eternal purgatory. "Caroline reached out to us almost as soon as we arrived. Patrick, too."

Alex's humor subsided as he realized we weren't pulling his leg. "Whatever stunt you're trying to pull—"

"We already told you," Bodhi interjected. "It's not a stunt."

The door to the patio swung open again and Bodhi shut

his mouth as Ryan stepped out again. "Hey boss? We need you in the kitchen. Something's wrong with the fryer."

"What's wrong with it?"

"It's not frying."

"Go figure." As Ryan went back inside, Alex stood up and pushed his chair in. "I'd say it's been a pleasure, but I would be lying. Could the two of you do me a favor? The next time you come to my restaurant, would you mind actually ordering some food?"

I rose to my feet, kicking over the plastic furniture in my haste to delay Alex. "Come up to the house when you close the restaurant," I pleaded with him, my fingers closing around his wrist. "And we'll prove it to you. I swear, Alex."

He looked down at my grip. "What makes you think that even if you were telling the truth that I'd want to go and have a conversation with my dead best friends from high school?"

"Because they need our help," I replied softly. "Please."

Alex lingered in the doorway. Then he gently removed my hand from his arm. "I'll think about it. You can see yourselves out."

He held the patio door open for us. Reluctantly, Bodhi and I let him guide us through it. As Alex disappeared into the kitchen, we made our way to the front of the restaurant with the acrid scent of burning oil in our nostrils. When we emerged in the sunlight outside and turned toward the high street to make our way back up to the bluff, Bodhi slipped his hand into mine.

"So," he said, kissing the back of my hand. "Now what?"

I sighed, gazing wistfully over my shoulder at Lido's Restaurant. "Now we wait. See if he shows up."

THERE WAS nothing more to do with the rest of our day other than work on the house. When we arrived home with several boxes of donuts as an apology to the rest of the construction crew for ducking out that morning, the guys had already started renovating the rest of the backyard's decking. After a bear claw and some teasing, I convinced Bodhi to let me get in on the labor. It had been too long since I'd contributed physically to the Winchester house—my multitude of injuries had set me back on that one—but I couldn't sit around the entire day and let my thoughts fester. It was better to distract myself with hard work.

After a few hours of securing the new decking, the back of my neck and the tips of my ears were starting to crisp from the effects of the summer sun. Sweat dripped down my back, soaking my T-shirt, and the cast around my ankle made it feel like I'd stepped into a shin-high puddle of hot mud. I straightened, groaning as my knees protested, and wiped my forehead.

"Anyone need a bottle of water?" I asked the guys around me. "Or an extra donut?"

A few hands went up, so I wiped my one dirty sneaker on the tarp we were using as a welcome mat and stepped into the kitchen. I washed my hands and grabbed another donut, holding it between my teeth as I plucked cold water bottles from the fridge. When I shut the refrigerator door though, the face behind it made me jump and the bottles careened from my arms.

"Patrick!" I put a hand to my heart, which was working overtime. "God, you nearly gave me a heart attack."

"What are you doing?" he asked, leaning against the fridge.

I checked that the guys outside were concentrating on the decking rather than my conversation with a dead boy. "Fixing the deck. What does it look like?"

"Shouldn't you be working on a plan to get us out of here?" Patrick demanded. There were the slightest shadows under his eyes, as if he'd missed a couple hours of sleep. It looked like Ethan's involuntary energy donation was starting to wear off.

"I am."

"Really?" he snapped. "Because to me it looks like you're more concerned with the content for your blog."

In the hallway, a door slammed of its own accord, but I didn't know if it was Caroline's doing or a result of the frustration that boiled off of Patrick.

"Watch your tone, Pat," I warned, keeping my voice low and even. "I know you're worried about running out of time, but Bodhi and I are doing our best."

"And what have you done today that constitutes doing your best?"

I knelt to pick up some of the fallen water bottles. "We went to see Alex."

Patrick receded into the relative shadow of the hallway. "You what?"

"We need help," I told him. "The locals are getting suspicious. Someone saw Ethan come up this way the day he disappeared, and the town psychiatrist knows someone broke into her office. I thought having someone like Alex, someone that everyone trusts, to dispel rumors about us would help. Not to mention, he knew you and Caroline personally. Without Ethan around, we need another resource. How else are we supposed to find your bodies?"

"What did you tell him?"

"That you're still around," I answered, stacking the water bottles under one arm. "He didn't believe us. I wouldn't either to be honest, but there's a chance he could turn up tonight, so be prepared for that."

When I looked up, Patrick was staring at the floor, lost in thought. He looked like a seventeen-year-old boy in need of a reassuring word from his mother, but I was the best he had.

"Patrick, if Alex does visit, just remember that Bodhi and I will be there for you," I said to him. "You won't be alone."

He took a step backward, his physical image fading as he retreated down the hallway. "It's not me I'm worried about," he said. "It's Caroline."

And then he was gone. I swallowed. Maybe inviting Alex to the house had been a mistake. Would Caroline go off the deep end if she saw him? I banished the thought, turning on my heel to go back outside, and brandished the water bottles.

"Who's dehydrated? Catch."

After tossing bottles to the guys that needed them, I picked up where I'd left off with my section of the decking, ignoring the squelch of the plaster cast against my skin. Blissfully, it wasn't long before the heat and the work scrubbed away the worry manifesting about what might happen later that night.

WHEN THE DAY was done and the crew was gone and we had finished dinner, Bodhi and I moved the Winchesters' old chairs from the widow's walk to the backyard in order to enjoy the newly completed deck. The sun was long gone. We had worked extra hours to finish up, and the moon hovered over the garden like a glowing orb. Bodhi and I shared a chair. He sipped wine from a plastic cup and played with my hair.

"I could get used to this," he murmured.

I snuggled into him. Near the edge of the bluff, the blooms on Caroline's plumeria tree waltzed in the wind, sending waves of their sweet scent wafting in our direction.

"Me too," I said.

His fingers combed through my hair. "No Alex though."

I sighed, closing my eyes. "It's only nine-thirty. Lido's probably hasn't closed yet."

"They close at nine on weekdays."

"Damn it."

I heard footsteps behind us and craned my neck to see Patrick hovering in the doorway. He juggled a football anxiously between his hands.

"Mind if I come out?" he asked shyly.

"Not at all," I answered.

Patrick walked the length of the deck, peering over the far end to look down at the rocks. He cradled the football to his chest as if afraid it might leap over the edge.

"What do you think?" Bodhi asked. He adjusted me a little so that he could sit up straight on the deck chair.

"It's nice," Patrick answered.

Bodhi got up, walked toward the opposite end of the deck, and opened his hands toward Patrick. "Here. Throw me the ball."

Patrick looked down at the tattered football in his grasp. "Really?"

"Yeah. Unless you don't want to."

"No, I want to."

I stretched my legs out along the chair. Patrick drew circles with his right arm, warming up muscles and ligaments that no longer served him much of a purpose. Then he found the laces of the football with his fingers, wound up, and tossed the ball across the deck in a perfect, spiraling arc. It was like watching art in motion. Bodhi caught the ball and returned it, but it wobbled through the air uncertainly. Despite its shaky path, Patrick caught it with one hand.

I watched as the ball traveled back and forth, entranced by its crescent-like path across the starlit sky. Bodhi's throws improved with each pass, and he started challenging Patrick by aiming outside of the younger boy's reach. But Patrick snapped up the ball at every turn, darting all over the deck and grinning every time he made a particularly impressive catch.

"Be careful," I called as Patrick reached backward over the railing to snag the football with the tips of his fingers. Then I realized there was no point in warning a dead boy to watch his step. It's not like anything could happen to him.

Bodhi squinted in the moonlight in order to catch Patrick's return pass, but the football bounced off his hands and rolled into the garden. Bodhi bounded off the deck, pushing aside overgrown bushes in search of the ball. When he returned, he hurled the ball back at Patrick with a wide grin on his face. I couldn't remember the last time I'd seen him look so carefree. Was this what it would've been like? In an alternate timeline, did Bodhi kick a soccer ball back and forth with Kali? Or go to her dance recitals? Or teach her how to meditate?

We were all missing something. Patrick, Caroline, Bodhi, and I. Opportunity. Patrick and Caroline missed growing up. They missed celebrating good SAT scores and college acceptance letters. They missed learning how to do their own laundry and cooking grilled cheese with an iron in a dorm room. Bodhi and I had experienced all of that—to some degree at least—but we missed the chance to raise our kid the way we wanted to. With the same hope and happiness and adventure in her heart that I saw now on Patrick's face.

"Okay, okay," Bodhi huffed, holding up his hands in defense before Patrick could throw the ball again. He stretched his arm over his head with a groan. "I think I'm done. My shoulder's going to be all kinds of sore in the morning."

"Geezer," Patrick joked, spinning the football in the palm of his hand.

"Hey!" Bodhi smacked the football out of Patrick's grasp

and sat down on the edge of my chair as the younger boy chased after it.

When Patrick returned, he leaned against the new deck railing. Frowning, he stared down at the old ball. "He's not coming, is he?"

"Who?" I asked, forgetting for a moment.

"Alex."

But just as Patrick said his name, a knock echoed through the open sliding glass doors that led to the combined entryway and living room.

29

ALLIED FORCES

The three of us looked at one another. The knock sounded again. Someone was definitely at the front door. Patrick's eyes widened. He dropped the football, pacing back and forth across the deck.

"Um, how do we do this?" Bodhi asked.

I peered over my shoulder into the house. Through the small window pane set in the door, I could see the outline of Alex's strong, shaded chin. He bounced nervously on the balls of his toes. "I'll answer the door. Patrick, you wait here. Where's Caroline, do you think?"

"Hiding, I hope," Patrick muttered.

I shushed him and pushed myself out of the deck chair to walk into the living room. At the front door, I looked behind me. Bodhi was visible, waiting for me to invite Alex inside. Patrick was hidden beyond the frame of the sliding glass doors, but I could picture his anxious frown. I opened the door.

Alex stood with his hands tucked deep in the front pockets of his jeans, his shoulders hunched up to his ears as if it was the dead of winter rather than the middle of summer.

"Hi," I said. "I'm glad you decided to stop by."

Alex lingered in the doorway. "I haven't been here in twenty years."

"That's okay." I stepped aside to make room for him in the entryway, but he remained on the threshold. I linked one of my arms through his and pulled him inside. "Come on. You'll be fine."

He gazed around the new living room. "It looks different."

"That's kind of the point of house flipping," I reminded him as I led him to one of the aluminum folding chairs that accompanied the card table we ate off of. They were the only pieces of furniture in the living room. "Here, sit. Bodhi?"

Bodhi stepped in from outside. "Hey, Alex. Doing okay so far?"

"So far."

Bodhi wandered into the kitchen. "Would you like a glass of water? Or something stronger?"

"Water's fine, please."

Bodhi brought over three water bottles and placed them on the card table. We sat down next to Alex. I glanced out to the deck, but Patrick was nowhere in sight. Had he lost his nerve?

"Well?" Alex prompted, popping the cap off his water bottle and draining half of it in one gulp. "What am I doing here?"

"Are you sure you're ready for this?" I asked Alex.

"Ready for what exactly?"

Bodhi and I looked at each other. There was no preparing Alex for what he was about to see. Instead, I prepared myself for Alex's potential reaction.

"Patrick," I called to the backyard. "Why don't you come in now?"

For a moment, no one moved. Alex's breathing quickened. I could hear the strain of his inhales, the rapid burst of his exhales. Outside, the wind tickled the overgrown garden and the moon shone down on the decking. At last, Patrick's blond hair edged out from behind the frame of the sliding glass door. He peeked into the living room.

"Alex?"

Alex shot out of his chair faster than a bullet from a gun, backing up against the far wall of the living room as Patrick tiptoed into full view. His chest heaved as he stared at the younger boy, unable to wrap his head around the situation.

"Pat?"

"It's me."

Slowly, Alex peeled himself away from the wall. He took a tiny step forward. Patrick inched into the living room. Bodhi and I watched with bated breath as they neared each other. When they met in the middle of the floor, I half-expected for the world to implode. Patrick stared at Alex. Alex stared at Patrick. And then Patrick said:

"Man, you got lines now."

Alex looked stunned. Patrick punched him in the shoulder in a fruitless attempt to lighten the mood, but all it did was confuse Alex even more. His hand rose. He placed it on Patrick's shoulder. He stood still for a moment. Then Alex tugged Patrick into a tight hug.

"I can't believe this," Alex said, releasing Patrick and stepping back to look at him up and down. "You haven't aged a day! This is insane!"

Patrick struck a goofy pose. "Perk of being undead."

Alex let out an incredulous sigh, shaking his head. He held his hand out to shake Patrick's. "Do you remember?"

"Of course."

They performed a complicated handshake, complete with high fives and some variation of jazz fingers. Alex was eighteen again, playing with his best friend. I could envision them in the end zone during a high school football game, doing a touchdown celebration dance together.

"I'm not hallucinating, right?" Alex asked me and Bodhi as he grasped Patrick's forearm. "He's really here?"

"He's really here," I confirmed.

"What about Caroline?"

It was a good question. Caroline had been uncharacteristically quiet for the past few days. I assumed it was because she was running out of energy as the anniversary of her death approached, but I also thought that Alex's visit would lure her out of dormancy. On the other hand, maybe it was a good thing that Caroline was lying low. Alex wore a wide smile. He was ecstatic to see his old friend again, but the reality of the situation hadn't sunk in yet. If Caroline made an appearance—knocking things about in that reckless way of hers—it might prevent Alex from helping us.

"She's around," I told Alex. "But she's not like Patrick. She can't appear like he does."

Alex looked disappointed. "Oh. Why are they here at all?"

"Hey, man," Patrick interrupted. "Don't talk about me like I'm *not* here."

Alex patted Patrick on the shoulder. "Sorry, bud."

"Take it away, Pat," Bodhi said.

Patrick steeled himself, adjusting his T-shirt as if it were a nervous tic of his. "Honestly, Alex, I don't want to relive the events of that day again, so here's the long and short of it. Ethan killed us. All of us. He ran Mom and Dad into the rocks, then he circled back to finish off me and Caroline."

"How?" Alex asked, his devastation evident in the downward turn of his mouth. "Why?"

"Believe me," Patrick replied. "You don't want to know. It was bad. As for why, I guess Ethan blamed his troubles on us. He thought that my father caused the heart attack that killed his father."

"That's absolutely ridiculous," said Alex.

Patrick shrugged. "I agree, but that's what it was. After we were gone, Ethan had every opportunity to regain his status in town. It turned out well for him. I honestly thought we were never going to get a chance to find peace. Luckily, Bailey and Bodhi have changed that."

Alex glanced at us. "Are you guys some kind of ghost hunters or something?"

Bodhi and I laughed.

"No," Bodhi answered. "Caroline terrorized Bailey when we first got here. It took us a while to figure out she wasn't actually trying to kill us."

"And you need our help," Alex said to Patrick.

"That would be correct."

"With what exactly?"

Patrick fiddled with the buttons on the front of his shirt. He seemed unable to voice his needs out loud to Alex the way he had with us a few days ago. I took over for him.

"This Saturday is the official anniversary of the Winchesters' deaths," I told Alex. "Patrick and Caroline need to cross over to the next life, or whatever it is, before then. Otherwise, they have to stay here forever."

"Okay," Alex said slowly. "So what are we supposed to do?"

"In order to move on, Ethan has to pay for what he did," I explained. I squeezed Bodhi's hands. This is where things got a little dicey. "Patrick needs us to locate a few things."

Alex shifted from one foot to the other, eyeing Patrick uncertainly. "What kind of things?"

"The murder weapon he used to kill me," Patrick answered.

"And their bodies," Bodhi added.

Suddenly, the glass doors flew shut, shaking in their frames. Without the breeze, the air should've grown quickly humid. Instead, a chill settled over the living room. Goose bumps rose on my arms, making the fine hairs there stand straight up. The coffee maker in the kitchen gurgled to life.

"*That's* Caroline," I said to Alex, who had frozen in horror. Looking over my shoulder into the kitchen, I added, "Caroline, please don't break anything. We just bought that coffee maker."

She replied by sending the metal carafe crashing to the kitchen floor.

"Her listening skills need work," Bodhi said to Alex. An apple levitated from the kitchen counter, zoomed across the room, and hit Bodhi in the back of the head. "Ow!"

Alex was rooted in place, watching the action unfold.

Patrick nudged him. "Say hi," he suggested.

Alex's mouth dropped open. "Uh," he said. "Hi, Caroline?"

The temperature in the room shifted again, this time warming us as though we were sitting next to a cozy bonfire outdoors. It was something Caroline had never done before —I didn't know she was capable of it—but there was a distinct change in the overall mood. I was overcome with a feeling of pleasure, and judging from the goofy smile on Bodhi's face, I wasn't the only one affected.

"She missed you," Patrick said to Alex.

Alex smiled, looking toward the ceiling as if hoping to locate some sort of physical manifestation of Caroline. "Missed you too, Caz. I really wish you were still around."

Another swell of warmth undulated through us. Caroline hadn't been this happy or satisfied in all the time we had been at the Winchester house.

"However," Alex continued. "If your intention is to distract me from what these three just told me, it isn't working." He turned to me and Bodhi. "Did you say that we have to find their *bodies?*"

Thankfully, Patrick intercepted the question. "Caroline

and I were never buried properly. That's one of the reasons we haven't been able to pass over. Our bodies need to be dug up and reburied respectfully."

The thought made me shiver. By now, Patrick and Caroline were most likely no more than a collection of bones, depending on what Ethan did with them.

"But we don't know where they are," Bodhi added. "And Patrick can't remember."

"So how am I supposed to find them?" Alex asked, perplexed.

"You know this town better than we do," I said. "You know Ethan better than we do. You can dig for information without being noticed. The town is already suspicious of me and Bodhi."

"Which is another reason we need you." Bodhi scooted his chair closer to mine to rest his hand on top of my knee. "For the next few days, we need to go unnoticed, but that's not going to happen if the locals start thinking we cooked Ethan for dinner. You can distract them. Lead the conversation away from Ethan. Away from this house. They trust you."

Alex sat down in the aluminum chair again, running his fingers over his short buzz cut. He seemed rather calm compared to when Patrick first appeared. In fact, Alex was receiving the news with a lot more finesse than Bodhi and I combined.

"That's easy," he said to us. "The town is just worried about Ethan. No one really thinks that you two had anything to do with it. It's all speculation."

As Alex drained his first water bottle, Bodhi offered him his own drink. "We need them to speculate about something other than us."

"Got it. What about Ethan? I'm assuming you know what actually happened to him."

Patrick, Bodhi, and I exchanged glances, wondering how

much information was too much when it came to the subject of Ethan.

"Kind of," I told Alex. "But if he's coming back, it's going to be soon. If he does return, we need you on our side."

Alex's face hardened into a frown. "He killed my four favorite people. I'm definitely not on his side."

"Can you convince him that you are though?" Bodhi asked. "He's already going to be looking for ways to get back at me and Bailey. If he realizes that you know about the Winchesters, who knows what he'll do."

Alex clenched his fists. "He won't figure it out. What's the plan? What's our end goal? You said we had until Saturday, right? What happens between now and then?"

"We're trying to figure that out," I answered. "Patrick? Care to comment?"

Patrick drew the fourth and last chair out from under the card table and plopped down. Alex stared at him, still in awe of his best friend's appearance.

"Here's what I want," said Patrick. He drew invisible instructions on the surface of the card table with the tip of his finger. "First, rebury the bodies. Give us a funeral. Caroline and I need that. Second, find the murder weapon. I need it for when we finally confront Ethan. Third, Caroline and I need energy. A lot of it."

"I thought you said that had major disadvantages," I reminded Patrick. "How are you going to do that?"

"Draining humans has disadvantages," clarified Patrick. "We can charge off of other things. Weather, fire, electricity."

"Shall we just plug you into the car battery?" Bodhi suggested sarcastically.

"That might actually work," Patrick replied. "But we need humans to conduct that energy. That's where you guys come in."

A nervous jolt rocked my stomach. Ethan had been gone

for nearly three days recovering from Patrick's influence. I wasn't sure if Bodhi and I were healthy enough to act as human energy outlets. "Is it safe?"

"Totally," said Patrick.

"So assuming we accomplish all of this in the next four days," Alex cut in. "What exactly is going to happen to Ethan?"

Calmly, Patrick looked Alex in the eye.

"I'm going to kill him."

Bailey and Bodhi: Flipping Out

GOOD MORNING, *all! First off, I wanted to thank everyone for your outpouring of support. I have to admit that it took a lot of courage for me to write that letter, and I certainly wasn't expecting such an enormous amount of positive feedback. I was also touched by your own stories. Many of you expressed that Flipping Out has helped you all through some tough points in your lives. I'm so glad to hear this, and I'm so glad that we're on the same page now. It will make us stronger going forward.*

Anyway, back to the Winchester house! I have posted updated pictures of the deck for you. Click here to check them out. The backyard is gorgeous. The view off the edge of the deck is breathtaking. Please ignore the weeds in the background. I have to admit we haven't managed to trim the garden yet. With any luck, we'll tackle that jungle today. With the kitchen, dining area, and living room finished, we're moving on to the rest of the first floor. Thankfully, the hardest part is over. No more tearing down walls or hardcore renovation. We're keeping the floor plan the same for the back half of the house and just updating whatever needs updating.

As for Bodhi and I, we're working through some personal

things. This entire week is going to be one big ball of stress for reasons that I would prefer to keep to myself for now. There's a big event on Saturday that everything is riding on. If it goes well, it could mean a huge change for not only me and Bodhi but everyone in Black Bay. However, if it goes poorly... I don't even want to think about it.

KEEP YOU POSTED!
  Bailey

NO MATTER how I tried to occupy my mind on Wednesday, nothing worked to expel the strain and pressure I felt. According to Patrick, Ethan should have fully recovered by now. I was awake the entire night. I kept expecting Ethan to show up and attempt to finish what he started, but morning arrived calm and untouched. Bodhi and I got to work with the crew, preparing the rest of the rooms on the first floor so that we could repaint and install new flooring. For an hour or two, I primed the walls of the massive hall that the Winchesters had used for their extravagant parties, but the fumes were giving me a headache and the filter mask was making it hard to breathe. After wheezing through it for a while longer, I left the last wall for the crew to finish and went outside in search of fresh air. In the backyard, as I gazed out at the overgrown garden, I was overcome with sudden determination. I dug out the Winchesters' old lawnmower and got to work.

Despite the challenge of taming the garden, I couldn't stop thinking about Patrick's declaration from the night before. It had unsettled all of us. Alex looked the most alarmed. I don't think he expected to hear those words pop out of his dead seventeen-year-old best friend. In hindsight, I think I already knew what Patrick's plan was from the very start. It made sense. Ethan killed Patrick, so Patrick had to kill Ethan to balance it all out. That was the reason Patrick needed the murder weapon too. There was a greater chance of success if Patrick mimicked Ethan's homicide. To me, it didn't make any sense. To find peace, Patrick and Caroline had to create more violence?

It didn't matter. We had already promised to help Patrick and Caroline however possible. Not to mention, it wasn't like Ethan didn't deserve it. Even so, I hoped Bodhi and I didn't have to stick around for the reckoning. Of course, with our time running out, it was looking more and more like we were going to fail our mission anyway. What would we do if Saturday came and went? What if Ethan never showed? Without him, Patrick and Caroline would never move on. Would they blame their eternal misery on me and Bodhi?

Though Bodhi disguised his stress better than I did, there was no doubt that he too was feeling the effects of last night's meeting. He barked curt instructions at the construction crew all day long. The guys took it in stride. At this point, they knew Bodhi well enough to understand that he didn't mean it personally. To make up for his behavior, Bodhi let the crew go home early. We finished the day's work alone, pruning and painting in silence. I made little headway on the garden. The rest of it would have to wait until I found a hedge trimmer.

In the evening, we arranged a meeting with Alex at the Sanctuary. Apparently, he had taken his assignment to heart. He left Lido's Restaurant in the capable hands of his wife for the day and took the opportunity to refresh his knowledge of the Winchester boat crash and everything that followed. He wanted to update us on what he'd found out, and we needed a place to talk where Patrick and Caroline wouldn't over-hear. Just in case.

At first, the Sanctuary felt like a bad idea. Who plotted revenge murder in a busy café? But when Bodhi and I arrived, I remembered how loud Ava's place was in the evenings. We snagged a small table in the corner of the room to wait for Alex. It was set slightly away from everyone else, so it afforded us some privacy. The chatter morphed into a dull hum. It was impossible to eavesdrop on anyone when the conversations overlapped and all of the language sounded foreign.

The bell over the door jangled, just noticeable over the buzz of the cafe. As Alex ducked under the doorway and looked around for us, I waved a hand to get his attention. He waved back, flagged down Ava for a drink, then wove through the crowded tables to join us.

"Here's what I found out," he said without preamble, shaking off his light jacket and hanging it on the back of the empty chair at our table. The chair legs screeched against the floor as he drew it out and sat down. "I went to the church today and spoke with the pastor. He's been there forever. I'm surprised he hasn't met God yet. Anyway, I went to Pat and Caroline's graves and got him talking. They're definitely empty, and no one's touched the Winchesters' graves since they were buried."

"Hang on," Bodhi said, casually draping an arm across my shoulders and pulling me closer. "You thought Ethan would've dared to bury Pat and Caroline in their own graves?"

Alex shrugged. "Hidden in plain sight, right? It didn't hurt to check. Anyway, here's the next thing I found out. Pat's dad had one brother. He was the one who took care of everything when the Winchesters died. He was a good guy. I met him a couple times. He left most of Christopher's money to the town so that we could continue to rebuild. Anyway, I called him up and pretended to be a reporter for the Black Bay Banner. Apparently, he considered moving into the Winchester house to help out Black Bay for a while."

"So did he?" I asked.

Alex shook his head. "Nope. He had the house inspected and found out that the concrete foundation in the basement was soft, as though it had taken water damage, but that house was practically brand new. There was no way that foundation would have deteriorated so quickly."

This information jogged my memory. "Caroline was always more active in the basement," I said. "Like it was easier for her to manipulate things down there. And there's that patch of concrete that's lighter than the rest, as though it was laid down later."

"So what?" Bodhi stirred a packet of sugar into his cup of decaf. "Ethan kills the kids, buries them beneath the house, and pours fresh cement all in one night? Kind of a stretch, isn't it?"

"It's possible," Alex said. His leg jiggled up and down beneath the table. "Who knows what you can accomplish on a rush of adrenaline like that."

"And it's our only lead," I added.

"Maybe," said Bodhi. "But I'm going to need more proof before we go jackhammering the basement floor."

The doorbell jingled again. We ignored it at first—everyone hung out at the Sanctuary in the evenings—but when the customers by the door cheered merrily for whoever entered, Alex, Bodhi, and I looked up for the source of the commotion.

Ethan Powell had returned, healthy and happy.

THE RETURN

*T*he fact that Ethan had the audacity to waltz into the Sanctuary and wave and bow and accept the cafe's cheers at his safe return bothered me more than anything else. My blood boiled, and my face burned at the sight of him. His kind smile looked sick to me now, and it was downright disturbing that a murderer had hid behind it for so many years. Ethan had convinced the entire town of Black Bay that he was its savior. I blanched each time someone clapped Ethan on the back, or shook his hand, or told him how glad they were that he was all right. Even Ava came out from behind the counter to give Ethan a big, welcoming hug. If the locals knew the truth, Ethan wouldn't last another day. Couldn't we all just team up and get rid of him?

Ethan waved his big hands, asking the crowd to settle down. "All right," he said gruffly. "I'm glad to be back too. What does a man have to do for a coffee around here?"

Ava scurried back to her place behind the counter to oblige. As she bustled around, the rest of the crowd mumbled to one another. Finally, someone asked, "What happened,

Ethan? Where have you been since the festival? Are you all right?"

"Good question," Bodhi muttered to me under his breath.

"I'm just fine!" Ethan boomed as he accepted a steaming mug from Ava. He sat down with a few locals at a table by the door. "Had to take care of a little family emergency out of town."

"What family emergency?" Alex whispered to us. "His parents died years ago, and as far as I know, Ethan doesn't have any other family."

"*We* already know he wasn't taking care of family," I whispered back. "Let him ramble. Maybe he'll dig himself a nice little hole. Then all we would have to do is push him in."

"Oh no. Is everyone okay?" another random local asked.

Ethan waved one massive hand in dismissal of this question. "Everyone's fine! It gave me a scare, that's all. You know me! Otherwise, I would've never left the summer festival so early! How were the fireworks without me, kiddos?"

The café dissolved into conversation again, filling Ethan in on the happenings of the last few days. It was so surreal. The last time I'd seen Ethan, he was trying to choke me to death on the edge of the bluff. Now he appeared no more threatening that an overstuffed teddy bear, tickling babies and wiping frothed milk from his beard. No wonder he had gone so long without being discovered. His benevolent mask was well-crafted.

Bodhi unfurled my clenched fingers. "Are you okay, Bailey?"

"No," I snarled, unable to rip my eyes away from Ethan's innocent act. "I want him to bite it. I hate him."

"Easy," Bodhi warned. He turned my chin so that I would look at him. "Believe me, I want to see Ethan go down too, but we have to bide our time. Think of Caroline and Patrick."

"He's looking this way," Alex cut in.

My gaze snapped back to Ethan. Sure enough, he was staring straight at us. At first, I stayed frozen, locked in a staring contest with him. Then I smiled and waved as if I had been just as worried about Ethan as the rest of the town. If my reaction put him off, Ethan didn't show it. He returned a smile of his own, lifting his coffee mug in mock salute. Then he got up from his table and headed our way. My stomach plummeted.

"What now?" Bodhi asked in a strained voice.

Alex bumped my knee under the table. "Follow my lead and don't say anything stupid."

"No promises," I muttered back.

Alex stood up before Ethan reached the table, shaking the other man's hand with gusto. "Ethan! Welcome back. We were worried about you, sir."

"It's good to be back, Alex," said Ethan. He spread his arms wide as he approached our table as if welcoming us to his turf. "There they are! Nasty bruise you got there, Bodhi. How'd that happen? Did you have another accident at the house?"

Bodhi glared at him, his lips pressed together in a thin, tight line. "Yup. Accident. That's it."

"I keep telling you to be careful," Ethan replied with a wink. He found an unoccupied chair, turned it around, and straddled it. His attention shifted to me. "Great to see you, Bailey. How've you been?"

Were if not for the fact that Ethan's giant face had been looming over mine just a few days ago as he attempted to kill me, I never would've taken him for a murderer. Even now, he spoke calmly and kindly. It was like Dr. Jekyll and Mr. Hyde. Did Ethan have two personalities? Or did he just hide his true intentions that well?

To make matters more interesting, Ethan didn't look as though he'd spent the last three days recovering from having his life source sucked out of him by a ghost. However, his left arm was secured in a sling, and the skin on his forearm was scabbed over. In addition, four long scratches marred his cheek from where I'd dug my nails into his face. It was satisfying to know he hadn't escaped our scuffle on the rocks completely unscathed.

"I'm great," I told him, flashing him the biggest smile I could muster. "Better than ever actually."

"Glad to hear it," Ethan said. "How's that ankle?"

"It itches," I answered truthfully as I brandished the walking boot in his direction, burying the desire to kick Ethan squarely between the legs. "What happened to your arm?"

Ethan tucked his injury closer to his chest. "Ah, you know kids. My nephew left his skateboard out. I tripped over it."

"Aren't you an only child?" Alex asked.

"Yeah, this is my cousin's kid," Ethan corrected without hesitation. "We were close cousins, so I'm basically the kid's uncle."

Bodhi made a scoffing sound but then quickly covered it by faking a coughing fit. Ethan thumped him on the back.

"You all right, Bodhi?" he asked as Bodhi sputtered into his coffee. "Don't sip too fast now."

"I'm fine," Bodhi said.

Ethan took a long gulp from his mug, sighed, and wiped his beard with one of my napkins. "I feel like I've missed so much. How's the house coming along? I'd love to come up and see it."

"It looks great," Alex chipped in, saving me and Bodhi from having to make such casual conversation. "I was really impressed. I can't wait until it's finished."

"When did you have time to make it up there, Alex?" Ethan asked. "Aren't you a bit busy with the restaurant?"

Alex shrugged, reclining in his chair. "It's slow during the day. I got time."

"Uh-huh. I'm just a bit surprised. You never went up to the Winchester house before. I thought you said it gave you the heebie-jeebies."

Alex never broke eye contact with Ethan. "I guess all this talk of Patrick and Caroline made me nostalgic. And you know what?"

Ethan rested his good elbow on the small round table, far too close to me for comfort. "What's that?"

"I think it really helped me out," Alex said earnestly. "I was never able to visit that house before. Every single time I looked up at that bluff, I was reminded of everything I lost. A set of parents that cared about me more than my own, my best friend, and—"

"Your future wife," Ethan finished.

Alex looked taken aback. "What do you mean?"

"Oh, come on, Alex," Ethan said with a chuckle. "Everyone in town knows you would've eventually married Caroline. Talk about a power couple. I remember when there was a line out the door waiting for you, Alex, and the only girl you ever wanted was Caroline."

Alex turned a darker shade of red the longer Ethan spoke. The nervous jiggling of his leg had stopped, but his hands had formed fists so tight that his skin was stretched white over his knuckles.

"Of course, your current wife is no slouch either," Ethan added as an afterthought.

Alex now looked as though his head might pop clean off his body, but Ethan rambled on, either unaware of Alex's discomfort or intentionally poking the bear with a stick. I assumed it was the latter.

"She's an out-of-towner, right?" Ethan asked, as if he

didn't already know. Everyone in Black Bay knew about everyone else. "Did you tell her about Caroline?"

"There was nothing to tell."

"Could have fooled me," Ethan replied with a wink. Across the cafe, someone called Ethan's name. He looked over his shoulder, waved, and then stood up from our table. "I have to make the rounds. Enjoy your evening."

Alex was too occupied with his own thoughts to respond. So much for following his lead.

"We intend to," I told Ethan smugly.

He tipped his hat to us and with a grin that left his eyes empty and cold, he said to me and Bodhi, "Sleep tight."

And then he was gone, moving to sit with a few older gentleman that I knew worked at his lumber mill. They welcomed him into their circle rowdily, budging up to make room for his enormous form.

"I want to kill him," Alex said. With Ethan gone, his face had faded from crimson to pink, but he still looked ready to explode. "Did you hear what he said? About Caroline? About my *wife*? Like the only reason I married her was because I couldn't have Caroline. What utter bull—"

Bodhi bumped Alex's shoulder. "Ignore him. He just said that stuff to get you riled up."

"It worked."

"Don't let him know that," I said. "Besides, sleep tight? What was that all about?"

Bodhi placed his hand over mine, stopping my fingers from shredding a paper napkin to tiny pieces. "He's just trying to psych us out. Don't think about it."

It was unrealistic advice. Until Saturday, the only thing I could think about was Ethan Powell. The real questions was if Ethan had a plan for us. He couldn't allow us to exist with the information we possessed. At the same time, we had no definitive proof of Ethan's crimes considering he had hidden all the evidence.

"Let's go home," I said to Bodhi, standing up. I couldn't stand being in the same room as Ethan. "We'll regroup tomorrow. Alex?"

"Hmm."

"You should go too. Don't torture yourself."

But Alex's gaze was trained on Ethan's back. "No, I'm going to stay a while longer. Keep an eye out, you know?"

"Suit yourself," said Bodhi. He clapped Alex on the back. "Have a good night. Stay safe."

"You two, as well."

We left a few bucks with Alex to pay for our coffee and left the Sanctuary, making a point to say a quick goodbye to Ethan. It was good for the rest of the town to see us on good terms with each other. The more normal things appeared, the easier it would be for us to continue our quasi investigation unhindered.

We drove back to the Winchester house in silence. The woods seemed darker than usual. There was no hint of the moon or the stars. It felt appropriate. Darkness loomed literally and figuratively. Our job was to shine a light into the black.

The house's exterior lights welcomed us back as we pulled into the front yard. Warmth enveloped me, much like the feeling that Caroline had spread through the room the night before, and I realized that it was the foreign concept of comfort. The sight of the Winchester house soothed my anxieties. For the first time in who knew how many years, I felt like I was coming home.

If I wasn't mistaken, Bodhi felt it too. His posture changed as soon as we approached the front door, no longer stiff and tense. His shoulders released and his gait grew languid. He was relaxed at the Winchester house despite the fact that we were currently sharing the space with two dead teenagers.

"Hello?" Bodhi called as we stepped into the entryway and kicked off our shoes. "We're back!"

Patrick trotted down the staircase as though he had been waiting for us to return in his old childhood bedroom. "What did Alex say?"

"We have a lead," I told him. "But that's not the biggest piece of news for the day."

"What is?" Patrick asked warily.

"Ethan's back," Bodhi said. Plain and simple.

For some reason, I expected Patrick to react like a scared teenager. In my mind, that's how it should have happened. He was young, even if he had died twenty years ago, and it wasn't fair for someone who hadn't even made it to the legal voting age to think about things like murder. But Patrick continued to throw me off balance.

"Good," he said. Resolution solidified in his inflection. "Right on time. How's he look?"

"Annoyingly healthy," I reported.

"Look, we need you to watch the house tonight, Patrick," Bodhi said. "I don't know what Ethan's planning, but he's got to have something up his sleeve. The house's old alarm system doesn't work, so we need you to act as our personal attack dog. Can you do that?"

"Woof, woof."

"Atta boy."

Patrick sat down on the floor near the glass doors, looking out at the black night. The porch light's illuminated the garden, but beyond the wild tangles of roses and vines, there was only darkness. Caroline's plumeria blooms were tiny pink fireflies in the gloom, and the bluff's dropoff was entirely invisible. I suppressed a shudder, thinking of how much the backyard reminded me of the inevitable void. It was the one thing about the Winchester house that filled me with anxiety. That and the potential bodies buried in the basement.

Bodhi and I showered together. I tried to convince myself that the reason we did it was for fun. Or for old time's sake. There was a time when we were younger that we had trouble paying our water bill. Then showering together had been romantic and adventurous. Tonight, I knew we did it because we were scared to be alone. At least I was. I wouldn't feel safe until Ethan Powell no longer had any kind of access to us. But with Bodhi there beside me, it was easier to pretend we could lock the doors of the Winchester house and go to bed like a normal couple.

Instead, Bodhi locked every door in the house including the one that led to our bedroom. Then he propped a chair against the inside before climbing into bed beside me. He even found an old aluminum baseball bat left over from Patrick's time in Little League in the basement. This he kept by our bedside table.

"Where exactly is the line between prepared and paranoid?" I asked him. I meant it teasingly, but the question came out in a more serious tone of voice than I intended.

"I don't know," he said, curling up around me and pulling me close. "But I'm not taking any chances."

I snuggled into him beneath the blanket. "Did you ever expect any of this to happen?"

Bodhi snorted. "What? Befriending ghosts? Hunting down killers? No, I can safely say becoming a ghost whisperer was never on my to-do list."

"Yeah, but do you think it was fate?"

He was quiet for a minute. "I don't believe in fate."

"But you believe in karma and destiny."

"It's different though."

I rolled over so that I was facing him. "How so?"

Bodhi propped his head up on his elbow. Though we were inches away from each other, his head seemed to be in another dimension. "Think about it this way. Say you had a decision to make. Two choices are offered to you. The first one is the easy choice. It's a shortcut to your destination, but it also comes with negative ramifications. The second one is less appealing. You know that it's technically the right choice, but there are challenges to overcome before you reach your desired destination."

"I'd choose the second."

Bodhi held up a finger to indicate he wasn't finished. "That's not the lesson. This is. Fate teaches you that it's okay to choose the first path. If we believe that our future is predetermined, it means that taking the easy way out won't affect the overall outcome. You convince yourself that you are not responsible for your choices or the consequences that accompany them. Karma, on the other hand, teaches you that all things arise from the mind. Practice wellness. Practice progress. Everything that you do and say is your own responsibility. You are not controlled by fate. Your future depends on what you do now. So when the time comes to choose between the easy path and the right path, the stronger meditative mind is more likely to choose the right path."

"And what about destiny?"

"Our destiny is frequently met in the very paths we take to avoid it."

"Buddha?"

"Jean de La Fontaine. French poet."

I pondered this quietly for a minute before another thought crossed my mind. "Fine, then riddle me this. If fate doesn't exist, how did we end up in this house? Say we decided to go to Nevada or New Mexico instead? Then what?"

"Then we would be renovating a home in Nevada or New Mexico without having to worry about ghosts or murderers," Bodhi said. "What a dream."

"But that would've been the easy path," I pointed out. "Not the right one."

Bodhi smoothed the crinkle that appeared in my forehead whenever I was thinking too hard. "What's in your head, babe?"

"Say we had chosen another place to go," I said, avoiding Bodhi's gaze. "Sure, we wouldn't be dealing with ghosts or homicide, but we would still be sleeping in separate bedrooms."

He looked at me for a very long time. So long that I wondered if by mentioning that simple fact, I had pushed him away again. Then he said:

"You, my love, make a very good point." He drew me closer, framing my face with his hands as he kissed me softly. "Remind me to thank Patrick and Caroline tomorrow."

"For what?"

Bodhi nuzzled his nose against mine. "For bringing you back to me."

"We have a long way to go, Bodhi."

"I know that," he said. "But it's a start."

"It's a start," I agreed. We lapsed into silence, breathing each other's air. I looped my arm around Bodhi's waist. "By the way, you're wasted on carpentry."

"Oh, really? What makes you say that?"

"Because you clearly missed your calling as a monk or a yoga teacher."

Bodhi chuckled and playfully nudged me beneath the blanket. "Hush, you. Go to sleep."

THE SOUND of something shattering downstairs jolted me

from slumber. I shot upright, tapping Bodhi on the chest to wake him up, but he was already awake and alert. He shushed me as he climbed out of bed and pressed his ear to the door.

"I don't hear anything," he whispered. "It was probably just Caroline."

"Caroline hasn't broken anything in days," I reminded him.

He took the baseball bat from where it rested against the bedside table. "Stay here. I'll go check it out."

I scrambled out from under the covers. "Fat chance. That's how every terrible horror movie starts."

"Baby, I don't know if you've noticed, but we're already living in a horror movie."

I grabbed a flashlight. "Whatever. I'm coming with you."

In the landing, all was quiet. Shadows drew strange patterns on the creaky floorboards as we inched toward the stairs.

"Patrick?" Bodhi whispered. "Caroline?"

No one answered. That was disconcerting. I didn't expect Caroline to reply. She was notoriously anti-social in her afterlife. Patrick, in comparison, almost always appeared when we asked. Not to mention, he had promised to watch over the house for the night. Where was he now?

"Turn off the flashlight," Bodhi murmured.

"Why?"

"So if someone's here, they won't know we're awake."

"In that case, we should turn on every light in the house," I muttered darkly, switching the flashlight off. "Do you think the Winchesters owned any guns?"

"I think they were more into sailing than hunting."

"Pity."

We crept down the stairs and tiptoed into the living room. Patrick no longer sat by the glass doors—a disturbing sign—but nothing out of the ordinary caught my attention at first. The back of my neck prickled in anticipation as I scanned the room.

"There," I whispered, pointing. "The front window's broken."

The shards of glass on the new flooring reflected the porch light from outside. A cement block lay amongst the wreckage. Someone had thrown it through the window, leaving a jagged flaw in the house's security. Bodhi raised the baseball bat as he snuck forward to inspect the damage.

"Should I call the police?" I asked.

"Wait. It could just be a couple of kids making trouble."

I gathered to courage to join Bodhi in the living room. "If it is, it's still vandalism."

He lowered the bat with a sigh. "Whoever it was, they're gone now."

But I was rooted in place, staring at the spot near the sliding doors where Patrick had so recently lounged. "I'm not so sure about that."

"Why?"

I pointed. Bodhi turned. He saw what I saw.

"Run," he whispered.

I ran.

Because Ethan Powell was waiting for us on the new decking of the back porch. Because he had been watching us calmly through the glass the entire time we had been downstairs. Because at his side, he held a length of white nautical rope, tied in the shape of a hangman's noose.

31

UNINVITED

*M*y feet carried me without consulting my brain. I careened down the first-floor hallway with Bodhi on my heels, heading for the basement. Behind us, Ethan pounded on the sliding glass door. The resulting booms shook the house. Each one hit me like an electric shock. I skidded across the floor, sliding into the basement door.

"Go, go, go," Bodhi urged as I coaxed the tricky door open.

A resounding smash rattled my bones. It sounded like Ethan had broken one of the glass doors in the living room. I gritted my teeth. "If Patrick doesn't kill him, I will. Those doors were expensive."

"That'll be the least of our worries if Ethan finds us," Bodhi said.

As if on cue, Ethan's voice echoed down the hallway and through the basement door. "Bailey! Bodhi! Come on out, you two. We can settle this like adults."

Bodhi locked the door, but we both knew the old door wouldn't hold if Ethan decided to break it down. "Start piling stuff up on the stairs. Anything. Bikes, hardware, boxes you can lift."

I hobbled down the stairs after Bodhi, cursing the plaster cast on my ankle for hindering easy movement. Together, we blocked the doorway with anything and everything, including a heavy-duty toolbox at the top of the steps, boxes full of Patrick's old football gear, and even a moth-bitten sofa that the Winchesters had stored in the basement. Then we huddled together at the rear of the room, near the door of the wine cellar.

"Should I call the police *now*?"

Before Bodhi could answer, the basement door rattled in its frame. I jumped in fright. Bodhi pulled out his cell out of the pocket of his sweat pants and handed it to me. "Yeah, call the police. But if he makes it down here before they do, I am not at fault for what happens then."

I dialed 911, breathing hard as Ethan thundered on the door.

"Let's talk," Ethan called, his voice muffled as it traveled beneath the gap in the door, through the mounds of the Winchesters' forgotten items, and to our ears. "I just want to talk."

"911. What's your emergency?"

"Someone's broken into our home," I whispered urgently. Bodhi searched through the items around us. What he was looking for, I had no idea. "We're hiding in the basement, but he's trying to break down the door."

"Okay, ma'am. Please stay calm. This is the Winchester house, correct?"

I guess I shouldn't have been surprised that the emergency operator knew my voice. After all, Bodhi and I had called 911 more often in the last few weeks than I had my entire life. "Yes, this is Bailey Taylor."

"Okay, Mrs. Taylor. My name is Jane. I'm going to ask you to stay on the line with me until dispatch reaches you."

"Okay, Jane."

"Aha!" Bodhi stood up, triumphantly brandishing what looked like a vintage revolver.

"Baby, that looks like it belongs in a museum," I said. "I doubt it still works."

The 911 operator sounded confused. "Sorry?"

"Not you," I said into the phone.

Bodhi checked the chamber. "It's loaded."

"Don't—"

With a crash, the basement door gave way. I screamed involuntarily as Ethan's steel-toed boot appeared at the top of the steps, but with the stairway full of crap, he wasn't making his way into the basement anytime soon.

"Mrs. Taylor?" Jane's voice was tinged with concern, despite the fact that emergency operators were supposed to remain calm. "What was—?"

Bodhi fired the gun.

"Oh my! Was that a gunshot? Mrs. Taylor!"

"Bodhi!"

He fired again. "What?"

The first bullet ricocheted off of the metal toolbox at the top of the steps, leaving a noticeable dent in the metal. The second embedded itself in the soft backing of the sofa perched haphazardly on the staircase. Either Bodhi's aim was off, or the antique gun wasn't in great shape. On the upside, Ethan withdrew into the first-floor hallway. Apparently, he hadn't been expecting a gunfight.

"Shots fired," Jane said into my ear. "Mrs. Taylor, are you still with me?"

"Yes, I'm here."

"Is everyone okay?"

"Yes, ma'am."

And then Ethan slammed his boot into the door, sending the toolbox tumbling forward with a crash, and Bodhi fired the gun again. Ethan jerked back, presumably to avoid Bodhi's erratic aim, but something odd was happening upstairs. Heavy, scuffling footsteps scratched overhead. Then a crash rang out, and Ethan yelled.

Even as Jane chattered in my ear, I forgot about her. The basement grew cold. My eyes found the patch of concrete in the middle of the room that was lighter in color. The flaw in the foundation. My body went deathly still. My vision clouded. There was something inside of me.

And then I was underground, staring up at Ethan Powell's face as he shoveled dirt over top of me. It crushed my chest and filled my lungs.

"Mrs. Taylor!"

Jane's voice jolted me from the illusion, but there was no mistaking the moment for what it was. Caroline had used me. I slumped against the basement wall, suddenly lethargic. On the floor above us, a loud bang echoed, followed by Ethan's distinctly gruff tones shouting every curse word in the book. The cacophony continued, but it faded in volume, as though Ethan was slowly but surely being driven from the house.

"Patrick?" Bodhi suggested.

I shook my head, gasping for breath. "Caroline."

"Mrs. Taylor, our officers should be there any second now," Jane reassured me over the phone. I could only imagine what was going through her head.

Sure enough, the basement lit up red and blue as a squad car pulled into the front yard, the emergency lights shining through the small storm window. The siren drowned out the noises on the first floor. Part of me wanted Caroline to drive Ethan right into the arms of the police. Ultimately, we needed Ethan to go free. Then we needed to survive his wrath until Saturday night.

The door at the top of the stairs rattled again, but this time it was a uniformed officer instead of Ethan who poked his head into the basement. Bodhi hid the antique revolver behind his back.

"Black Bay PD," the officer said. "Everyone all right down here?"

It took the better part of an hour to clear a path to the doorway, explain to the officers what had happened, and convince them that we had no idea who would've wanted to break into the Winchester house. The hallway was littered with evidence of Ethan and Caroline's fight. Broken plates, coffee mugs, and silverware—left over from the Winchesters' original kitchen—created a hazardous obstacle path on our way to the kitchen. Luckily, none of our renovation work was damaged, excluding the shattered sliding glass door. We also dug ourselves into a hole with the antique revolver. Jane confirmed gunshots over the phone, but we couldn't blame it on our intruder since there were no signs of damage on the first floor. Bodhi admitted he found the gun in the basement and used it in self-defense. After a stern talking-to about using unregistered guns without training, the officers confiscated the revolver, expressing surprise that it had even fired. By the time they explained Washington's self-defense laws, helped us cover the giant hole where our door had been, and took their leave, the sky had already begun to lighten.

"You don't think he'll come back, do you?" I asked Bodhi, securing the tarp over the open window with a piece of tape.

"Not anytime soon."

"Now he can just waltz in whenever he likes," I grumbled.

"We'll get the door replaced today," Bodhi assured me. "If I have to drive into the city to pick another one up, I will."

"Don't you think this is a bit much?" I asked Bodhi. "It's insane. We're waiting around for a guy to kill us, and in the meantime, we're pretending that we're all best buds. I don't know if I can do this."

"Hey." Bodhi detached my hands from where they were taping the black heavy-duty plastic to the wall in a haphazard fashion. "It's three more days. Who know? Maybe we'll figure this out sooner. We could evict Caroline and Patrick tonight."

"Ouch," said a voice behind us.

We turned to see Patrick sitting on the counter in the kitchen, munching on a package of mini cupcakes that we had picked up from the Sanctuary the day before.

Bodhi grinned, walked over to Patrick, and clapped him on the shoulder. "Sorry, Pat. I love your company, but you would be a lot less hassle in my book if you didn't come with a homicidal maniac. Also you eat a lot of our food for someone whose digestive system no longer functions."

"Did you want one?" Patrick offered through a full mouth, proffering the package. Bodhi snatched it away from him. "By the way, I'm not offended. I want to get out of here as much as you two want me to."

"It's not that we want to get rid of you," I said as I abandoned the tarp. At this point, there was so much duct tape on the wall, the tarp might end up as a permanent fixture in the house. "Actually, I quite like having you around."

"But I'm not supposed to be around," Patrick reminded me.

"I know," I said. "But it's like—"

"Having a son," finished Bodhi matter-of-factly.

Patrick and I both stared at him.

He shrugged, tossing a mini cupcake in the air and

catching it skillfully in his mouth. "What? It is. Watch. Patrick, catch."

And he launched another cupcake across the kitchen in Patrick's direction, who immediately repositioned himself underneath it so that it landed squarely between his teeth. Patrick grinned, but the top of the cupcake separated and hit the floor, icing-side down.

"Really?" I chucked a roll of paper towels at Patrick. "Clean that up, troublemaker."

Bodhi chuckled, shaking his head. "See? Just like a mom."

As Patrick hopped off the counter to wipe up pink icing from the new flooring, I played with the idea in my head. At first, when Patrick had been Milo, it was easy to view him as a fully-fledged adult. He was open, mature, and respectful, three things that most people well into adulthood found difficult to learn. But ever since I found out that Patrick was just Patrick, something had shifted. I felt weirdly protective of him now, like he was my responsibility. In a way, he was. Caroline, too. When we promised to help Caroline, we had signed an official contract, one that made us the temporary guardians of two teenagers in need of parents. And it just so happened that Bodhi and I were in need of children. Granted, we hadn't anticipated teenaged dead ones, one of whom wasn't visible to the physical world.

"You're right," I said finally. "And if Patrick really was my son, I wouldn't want him to suffer in a world that he couldn't truly interact with."

"Thank you," Patrick said.

"Speaking of our adopted children," Bodhi quipped. "Has anyone heard from Caroline as of late?"

I shuddered involuntarily. Caroline had been less and less active in the past few days, but there was no doubt as to what had occurred in the basement earlier. Caroline had sapped energy from me to chase Ethan out of the house, and no amount of espresso would replenish what she had taken. I was beyond sleepy, my muscles felt stiff and achy, and my eyelids were a burden to my face. Even so, I knew that Caroline had gone easy on me. If she had taken more, I would be upstairs in bed.

Patrick noticed my silence. "I, uh, think Bailey and Caroline had a misunderstanding last night actually."

"What kind of misunderstanding?" Bodhi asked, immediately alert.

I waved a hand to dismiss this. "It wasn't a misunderstanding. She borrowed some energy from me."

Bodhi's eyes widened. "From you? Why?"

"To get Ethan out of the house," I explained. "That's why she hasn't been around lately. She's getting weaker and weaker. Even the poltergeist stuff is getting hard for her to manage."

Patrick nodded in agreement. "I feel it too. It's like when you know you have a cold coming on. That tickle in the back of your throat."

"So basically we need to get a move on," Bodhi clarified. "Bailey, are you okay? How much did Caroline take from you?"

I hoisted myself onto the counter that Patrick had so recently vacated. "Enough to know I probably shouldn't handle any power tools today. What's our next step?"

"I think we've already agreed it's to find the bodies or whatever's left of them," said Bodhi. He looked to Patrick. "Any ideas?"

I took a cupcake for myself, but as soon as the pink icing touched my lips, I blanched. It was sickly sweet, although my nausea was probably a result of the day's events thus far. "Caroline was alive when she was buried."

Bodhi wrinkled his nose in distaste. "How do you figure?"

"She showed me." I sighed and passed my uneaten

cupcake to Patrick. "I'm not sure how. She remembers Ethan burying her."

"Where?" Patrick asked. "I have no memory of that."

"Probably because you were already dead," Bodhi pointed out.

"Thanks for reminding me."

I flicked Bodhi's ear. "Be nice to each other. And I didn't see where she was buried. I was too distracted by Ethan shoveling dirt on top of her."

Bodhi grabbed my fingers and cracked the knuckles for me. "Then we're still at square one."

"I say we dig up the basement," I said. "It's our only lead."

"I was afraid you'd say that," grumbled Bodhi. "We don't even know if that's where Ethan buried them."

My head swam, and dots of colorful lights decorated my vision. I closed my eyes, trying to steady myself. Caroline had had more of an effect on me than I originally thought. I swayed, nearly toppling off the counter, but Patrick and Bodhi caught me by either shoulder.

"You need to go to bed," Patrick said, studying me with a worried expression. "Recharge. Alex is working on the bodies problem today, right?"

I nodded wearily. "He was going to scope Ethan out to see if he could glean any more information."

"Then you can take the day off," Patrick said in a firm tone.

"But we're running out of time!"

Patrick shushed me. "I know that, but I also know that it's completely immoral if I let you run yourself into the ground for mine and Caroline's sake. So be quiet and let Bodhi take you upstairs."

I would've argued more—our lack of progress was making me feel overwhelmingly useless—but Bodhi swept me up in his arms and carried me from the kitchen before I could say anything else. I leaned my forehead against the crook of his neck, listening to his pulse beat soundly beneath his skin. As exhaustion engulfed me, I savored the safety I felt in Bodhi's arms. He was strong and sure of himself. His bare feet landed with precision on each step as he took me upstairs. By the time we reached the bedroom door, I was already asleep.

WHEN I WOKE AGAIN, the pinkish hues of sunset had descended upon the Winchester house. I groaned, massaging my temples. I felt as though I'd downed several bottles of wine the night before. My head dully ached, and my mouth was as dry as a cotton ball. Thankfully, someone—Patrick or Bodhi—had left a tall glass of cool water on the bedside table for me. I gratefully tipped it back, swishing it around in my mouth to get rid of the tacky texture.

Bodhi's voice floated up to me from the first floor. There was someone else here too, speaking excitedly, but the conversation was too muffled for me to recognize the second voice. It was probably the last of the construction crew, finishing up the day's work. I frowned. I had wasted an entire day sleeping. It was starting to feel more and more like Patrick and Caroline were going to be stuck in Black Bay for the rest of their immortal lives.

The thought propelled me from bed. I kicked the sheets off, chugged the rest of my water, and headed into the hallway. I paused at the top of the stairs, listening, but when I realized who Bodhi was talking to, I thundered down to the first floor.

Alex paced back and forth in the living room. His cropped dark hair glistened with water droplets, dripping abstract patterns on the wood flooring. His T-shirt and shorts were damp too, as if he hadn't dried off properly before getting dressed. Bodhi sat at the card table, rifling through a curious pile of what looked like waterlogged photographs, while Patrick tiptoed along the track of the open glass doors like a gymnast on a balance beam. As promised, Bodhi had replaced the shattered door. The tarp was gone, but remnants of my hazardous duct taping abilities remained on the freshly painted walls. I mentally added touch-ups to my to-do list.

"—and I can absolute help with that if you and Bailey aren't up to it," Alex was saying as he aired out his T-shirt, flapping it fruitlessly so that it billowed in and out against his chest.

"Aren't up to what?" I asked, padding into the room and sitting down next to Bodhi at the card table. I shuffled through the photographs.

"Bailey—" Bodhi started.

"Wait—" Alex said.

"Why?" Most of the photographs had been ruined by the water. The colors had run and bled together, leaving nothing but drooping faces and unknown locations. But when I finally came across one that had braved the damage and brought it closer to my face to study the subject, my stomach heaved. Had I eaten anything that day, I highly suspected I would've seen it again.

Bodhi snatched the photo from my hand and hid it beneath the pile. Then he reached across the table to take my wrist. "Damn it, Bailey. I wish you'd waited for me to tell you."

"What difference would it have made?" I mumbled, dropping my head into my hands in the hopes of quelling the nausea.

The photograph was of Caroline. Her face was blue. Lips robbed of color. Gold hair reduced to drenched, ratty tangles. Sopping wet and unmistakably dead.

Ethan had kept records of his disgusting deeds.

"Crap," Alex said as he wandered over to me. He smelled faintly of saltwater. "Bailey, I'm so sorry. You didn't need to see this."

"Where did you get these?" I asked him, finding his distressed expression instead of staring at the photos. Across the room, I caught Patrick pause in his balance act out of the corner of my eye. His cheeks were pale, and his jawline jutted against his skin, as though he hadn't eaten in several days.

Alex glanced at Bodhi.

"Go ahead," said Bodhi. "Tell her what you told me."

Alex pulled out the chair next to mine and sat down. He flipped over a photograph so that it was face down. I didn't want to know what was on it.

"I found Ethan's boat," Alex said.

It took a second for this information to sink in. "You what?"

"He sank it," Alex continued as he censored more pictures. "Deep enough to avoid notice. No one would find it unless they were looking for it."

"How did you—?"

"When you left the café last night, I made sure Ethan was going to be occupied for a while," Alex admitted. "Then I went back to his boathouse. There were signs he'd moved the boat. The winches were broken, and the algae had been disturbed recently. I followed the breadcrumbs. It took me forever, but I finally found it."

He shuffled through the pile of photographs, unearthing a familiar object. It was one of Caroline's leather journals. It was totally waterlogged, but whatever expensive ballpoint pen Caroline had used to record her inner thoughts had weathered the storm. The ink ran a little, but it was still legible.

"I spent the entire day diving down to it to bring this stuff up," Alex went on. "I have all of Caroline's journals. The photos were hidden in a lockbox in the cabin. And—"

"He found the rope," finished Patrick.

Relief flooded my system. This was a good discovery. This was the breakthrough we needed to make sure everything went according to plan. "Where is it?"

"Hidden," Bodhi assured me. "Locked in the wine cellar until we need it."

"That's not all," Alex said.

"It isn't?"

"No." Alex pushed a photograph my way, but I flinched, unwilling to lay my eyes upon whatever terror Ethan had inflicted upon the Winchester children so long ago. "It's okay. That one's all right to look at. Check it out."

I squinted at the picture, but the murky setting didn't seem familiar to me. "What is this?"

"It's the crawl space beneath the house," Patrick said. His voice was hoarse as though he was coming down with a sore throat, but there was no mistaking the bitterness there.

The revelation hit me slowly. "The crawl space..."

"Yes," Patrick confirmed. "The place where Ethan left me and Caroline to rot."

32

BENEATH THE BASEMENT

*P*atrick simmered with rage. I could practically see it boiling off of him. His usually casual stance was tense and stiff. The easy smile I'd gotten used to morphed into a disgusted sneer. He shook visibly, as though his temper was on the verge of spilling over.

"There's an access point," Patrick spat. "I never knew. What did I care about the house's insulation? No one's thinking about crawl spaces in high school. I was more concerned with girls and football."

There was more than bitterness in his voice. There was blame. I stood up and walked over to him, but he stiffened the closer I got. I waited a few feet away. "Pat, no one's blaming you."

"If I had known—"

"You were seventeen," I reminded him. "It wasn't your responsibility to know. Don't sweat it. We know now. That's going to help us out immensely."

"Not to mention, most houses with basements don't have crawl spaces," Bodhi said. "A basement essentially serves the same purpose as a crawl space. I wonder why your parents built the house like this at all."

"Ethan found it though," Patrick said shakily. "He barely had to lift a finger to hide our bodies. All he had to do was drag us down there."

"Wait a minute," I said, a thought occurring to me. "If Ethan didn't jackhammer the foundation, then why is the concrete in the basement all messed up?"

"We think it was Caroline," Alex explained. "Patrick said she's been obsessed with the basement ever since they died. He just didn't know why. We figured she was subconsciously trying to unearth her own body."

Another wave of queasiness overtook me. I didn't want to think about how confused and terrified Caroline must have been in the days following her death. "So when are we doing this?"

Bodhi, Alex, and Patrick all knew what I was talking about, but there was a mutual hesitation as they exchanged sidelong glances with each other. It was apparent that the three of them had had a private conversation while I was asleep upstairs.

"What is it?" I demanded. "What are you not telling me?"

"Nothing," said Bodhi. He pushed his chair back and walked over to me. "You know everything, but we were wondering if you should maybe sit this one out."

I ogled him in disbelief. "You really think I'm going to sit out exhuming Patrick and Caroline's bodies? I don't think so."

Bodhi took my hand, but I found it difficult to find comfort in the gesture. "Bailey, you saw those photographs. This isn't going to be pretty. It's going to be gruesome, and I don't want you to have to see that."

Maybe it was because I was burned out, but a familiar annoyance rose within me at Bodhi's words. I stepped away from him, pulling my hand out of his grasp. He swallowed hard as the distance between us increased.

"You think I won't be able to handle something like this," I said matter-of-factly.

"No, I—"

"No, it sounds like that's exactly what you're saying," I cut in. "You think I won't be able to deal with this because of Kali." I lowered my voice to a dangerous tone. Behind Bodhi, Patrick and Alex watched our interaction apprehensively. "Here's the thing, Bodhi. I'm not the only one with baggage. We're both digging up the past. What makes you think you're any stronger than me in this situation?"

"That's not what I meant," Bodhi insisted. "Caroline's influence has really—"

"Don't blame this on Caroline. I'm fine. I'm tired, but fine. And I'm doing this with you tonight. You can't stop me." I marched toward Patrick and Alex. "Well? What time are we getting started."

Alex blissfully did not look at Bodhi to check for permission to answer me. "As soon as it's completely dark."

We ended up waiting until midnight to get started, paranoid about unwanted visitors. Until then, we gathered what we thought we might need. Shovels, tarps, an LED light to illuminate our work space. The four of us spoke easily, defining a plan, but Bodhi and I avoided each other's glances. That was what we did best after all. I knew that we had to talk about this, but I just didn't want to. Not now, anyway. Maybe this was our truth. Bodhi perceived me as weak, but I was so far from weak that I couldn't even see it from where I stood.

When we were finally ready to get started, we assigned Patrick to patrol the area around the house. There was no guarantee that Ethan wouldn't make another attempt to taunt us, and we couldn't afford to unearth whatever was left of Patrick and Caroline without a lookout. Patrick gave a salute and jogged off, leaving us to follow Ethan's disturbing photographs to the access point for the crawl space. It was easier said than done. We had limited trouble locating the opening. It was a tiny hatch in the corner of the basement, hidden by piles of the Winchesters' leftover belongings. However, the real challenge was actually getting down to the crawl space. First off, the hatch opening was ridiculously small. Bodhi's broad shoulders wouldn't fit through it, and Alex's lanky build was too difficult for him to maneuver in the space beyond. That left the actual exploration up to me. Second, the covering was bolted firmly to the floor.

"You can't say Ethan wasn't thorough," Alex huffed. "Got a pair of bolt cutters?"

"Upstairs," Bodhi answered.

"I'll get them," I volunteered, grateful to escape the stuffy basement even if it was only for a minute or two. I jogged up the steps and found the bolt cutters in Bodhi's collection of tools. Through the glass doors, I saw Patrick making the rounds. From here, he actually looked like the ghost that he was. He was ethereal and incomplete beneath the moonlight, and his pale skin stood in frightening contrast against the wild darkness of the surrounding garden. But then he caught my eye and gave me the thumb's up, which immediately killed the creepy vision of his ghostly existence. I waved in thanks and went back to the basement.

"Here," I said, handing the bolt cutters to Bodhi.

He made sure our fingers didn't touch when he took them from me. "Thanks. Here goes nothing."

He closed the cutters around the massive bolt, and with a grunt, forced the handles together. I tried to ignore the way the muscles of his back and arms bulged. It was distracting, and moreover it reminded me that while we were silently fighting, I wasn't allowed physical access to him.

The clang of the bolt springing free jarred me from my reverie. Together, Alex and Bodhi yanked the hatch open. The rusted hinges complained, creaking until they disintegrated entirely. Accidentally, Alex and Bodhi ripped the hatch clean out of the floor, stumbling backward at the abrupt lack of resistance. Bodhi bumped into me, and I steadied him by pressing my palms to the wings of his back. He looked over his shoulder but didn't move away, and my touch lingered longer than necessary.

Alex swore as he peered into the opening. "You can't be serious."

"What is it?"

But as soon as we glanced over, it became apparent what Alex was vexed over. Mildewed, pink insulation blocked the entrance into the crawl space. I knew from past experience that it sure as hell wasn't supposed to be there.

"I'm going to kill Ethan," I said darkly. "How much of it do you think there is?"

Bodhi rooted around in our supplies, unearthing three pairs of heavy duty gloves, safety goggles, and respirator masks. "Nothing to do but find out."

So we got to work ripping the insulation out of the hatch. It was tough work. The basement was hot and humid, and the insulation made my skin itch. It expanded as we extracted it, and soon the already claustrophobic basement filled up with the pink fiberglass. Alex carried armfuls of it upstairs to throw into the dumpster, and as we continued to excavate, I wondered how much of the stuff Ethan had bothered to throw into the crawl space.

Finally, I aimed a flashlight into the opening, angling the beam to see if there was any more insulation ahead. For the moment, the passageway looked clear. "I think we're good," I said, lowering my shoulders into the small space to get a better look. "I don't see any more of it."

"Come out of there then," said Bodhi, taking the back of my tank top to pull me back. "I'll go down to check for Patrick and Caroline."

I tried to shake free of his grip. "Like you'd fit."

"If Ethan fit—"

"Twenty years ago, Ethan was nowhere near the size he is now," I reminded him. "I'm going down."

But Bodhi held me fast. The neckline of my shirt pressed against my throat. My airway was completely free, but between the stuffy air of the basement, the insulation, and the thought of inching through the limited space beneath the basement to find Patrick and Caroline's bones, my lungs felt tight. Even so, I wasn't going to admit that to Bodhi.

"Alex," he said. "Tell her it's better for me to go down."

Once again, Alex stood his ground. "I actually think she's right, Bodhi," he said. "She'll have an easier time than either one of us down there. God forbid you got stuck or something."

Bodhi glared at Alex, but I could've kissed the taller man for his common sense. Before Bodhi could protest anymore, I slid out of Bodhi's grip and lowered myself into the hatch.

"Hang on," Alex said. He pulled a box of old clothes toward him and began rooting through it. "You shouldn't go down there in short sleeves. I'll bet there's all kinds of bugs, among other stuff. Here."

He handed me a sky-blue, long-sleeved scrimmage jersey. At first, I thought it was Patrick's, but it was far too small for a teenaged boy. That and it was a soccer jersey rather than a football one.

"Who—?"

"Caroline played goalkeeper for the junior varsity women's team her freshman year," Alex said, letting the fabric slip through his fingers as if it were a memory. "She hated it. She was so good at it too. She only let one goal in the entire season *and* she was named MVP. But everyone already knew Patrick on the football field. No one bothered to know Caroline on the soccer pitch."

I pulled the jersey on over my head. Beneath the must, I could've sworn I picked up the delicate hint of women's perfume, but I figured it was just Alex's recollection messing with my head. I made sure the fabric covered as much skin as possible then attempted to resume my way downward. Bodhi's hot fist bunched in the jersey material, pressing against the small of my back. I looked up at him, ready to let loose, but his expression tempered my frustration. Bodhi's golden eyes were practically invisible in the dim light of our flashlights, but I could see every emotion in them. Fear. Guilt. Loathing. Love. It was like looking into a kaleidoscope of feelings. He needed something other than the tension between us.

"I'll be okay," I told him. "Really."

And his fingers loosened just enough for me to pull out of his grasp. At long last, I lowered myself into the hatch, holding my flashlight between my teeth, and shimmied forward on my belly into the crawl space.

"Ugh," I mumbled around the flashlight.

"What is it?" Alex called down. "What do you see?"

"Nothing much."

The space was distasteful to say the least. It was eighteen inches high, if that, from top to bottom. Termites had made quick work of the supportive structures. Mildew and mold grew in every dingy corner. In hindsight, it was lucky we had found the crawl space before Bodhi and I sold the house. We would definitely have to come down here again to do some damage control.

At the far end, something shadowy and still lurked in the darkness. The flashlight's beam reflected off the surface of the objects. They were trash bags. Big, black contractor bags like the ones Bodhi and I used for yard and hardware waste.

"I think I found them," I called up.

Bodhi's voice was muffled as he replied. "You think?"

"Give me a minute."

I shuffled forward, using my elbows and knees to propel myself across the damp, dirty ground as I tried not to think about what lay waiting for me at the other end of the crawl space. I closed my eyes and navigated by feel. The cramped space was already getting to me. The walls seemed to shrink inward, pressing against me on all sides. I took a deep breath and reached forward. My fingers connected with plastic, and I opened my eyes to find myself within inches of the garbage bags. With shaking hands, I dragged the first one toward me. It was heavy and zip tied shut. I heaved a sigh of relief. I did not want to have to open the bags on my own.

"Bailey?"

"Working on it."

With some trouble, I flipped over so that I was on my back, seized the first bag, and used my heels to scoot toward the open hatch. The walking boot scuffed across the dirt, but my method worked well enough, even if it was tedious work. Caroline's goalkeeper jersey snagged on the rough floor of the crawl space. My breaths came in short gasps as my triceps strained to keep pulling the bag toward me. After what felt like an hour, I reached the hatch.

"Number one," I announced. Bodhi and Alex heaved the bag upward. "I'm going back for number two."

"Take a sip of water first," Bodhi said. He tilted the bottle so that the cold water dribbled into my mouth and over my chin.

I coughed, but the chilly water soothed my heated nerves. "Be right back."

And before I lost my motivation, I dove back into the

crawl space and worked my way to the second bag. This one was heavier than the first. At first, it wouldn't budge. I planted my feet on the walls of the crawl space on either side of the bag and yanked it out of place.

It ripped.

"Shit."

A foul odor seeped through the crawl space, so fetid and profound that I immediately turned my head away and violently gagged. Bodhi's panicked voice echoed around me as my eyes watered.

"Bailey. Bailey! What's going on?"

But I was having trouble pulling enough air into my lungs to form words. I hacked and dry-retched, pulling the collar of Caroline's soccer jersey up over my nose and mouth. It didn't do much, but I was finally able to take a breath in through my mouth that didn't make me want to vomit. I examined the bag, taking care not to look too closely. It had gotten stuck on a protruding nail. Carefully, I detached the plastic and gave the bag an experimental tug. It released. Keeping an eye on the tear, I dragged it toward the hatch.

Three quarters of the way there, my muscles cramped up. I released the bag as my whole body tightened, letting my head drop to the dirt below me. I panted through the fabric of Caroline's jersey and tried to relax as my arms and hamstrings convulsed. To my annoyance, tears leaked from the corners of my eyes.

"Bailey?" Bodhi called. Another flashlight beam illuminated the crawl space. I tilted my head back to see Bodhi's face peering at me from the hatch. When the smell hit him, he swallowed hard but didn't falter. "Baby, it's okay. Come on. You can do this."

I shook my head and closed my eyes, hating the way my lips quivered as the moment tried to overwhelm me.

"Bailey, look at me."

I did. My vision was blurry, clouded with tears, but Bodhi's golden irises were like beacons in the darkness.

"It's just a few more feet, baby. You can do it. On three. Ready?"

I gripped the black plastic again and nodded.

"One. Two. *Three.*"

I heaved myself and the bag backward again. A feral groan of effort, anguish, and defeat ripped from my lips. It echoed back to me between the cramped walls, and I took strength from it, thrusting myself another foot in the direction of the hatch. Bodhi forced his shoulders through the opening and reached in as far as possible. With one last push, I got the bag close enough for him to grab on to.

"It's torn," I gasped, narrowly avoiding the aforementioned rip as Bodhi dragged the bag up out of the hatch. Some kind of residue remained in the dirt, but I didn't want to look at it too closely.

"I don't care about the bag," said Bodhi. Overhead, I heard Alex's heavy footsteps as he relieved Bodhi of his burden. Bodhi reappeared in the hatch opening. "Come on, baby. Let's get you out of there."

But I couldn't move anymore. My limbs trembled and shook. I was spent, sweating, and dirty, and the three feet between me and the hatch looked more like a mile.

"Give me your hands."

It took all of my concentrated willpower to reach toward Bodhi. He strained through the opening to wrap his fingers around my wrist. I tightened my grip. Then, like pulling a drowning child out of a swimming pool, Bodhi towed me out of the crawl space and into his lap.

I gasped for air, but Caroline's jersey still covered my mouth. Bodhi tugged it away from my face, cradling me on the floor of the basement. Alex was gone, as were the two bags. He must've already carried them upstairs. What an immense relief.

Bodhi pushed my sweaty hair away from the nape of my neck. He pulled his T-shirt off, poured cold water over it, and pressed the cool fabric to my flushed forehead. My eyelids drifted shut. God, the stench lingered. It invaded my nostrils. My very being had filled up with the scent of rot and decay. I turned my head and pressed my face into Bodhi's torso, but even his musky sweat combined with his lemony body soap couldn't combat the smell of dead bodies.

He didn't say anything. There wasn't much of anything to say. We just sat there, my head and shoulders in Bodhi's lap and my legs still in the hatch. I stared into the darkness below and pulled my feet out of the opening. Even though I knew the crawl space was now empty, I half-expected dead fingers to wrap around my ankles and draw me back under.

"Alex?" I muttered.

"He's all right," Bodhi assured me, wiping my face clean with the damp shirt. "Very stoic. He took the bags outside."

"Through the house?"

"Yes."

"But the new flooring!"

Bodhi chuckled. I understood why. We had just found two murdered bodies beneath our house, and I was worried about ruining the flooring. Nevertheless, I had my priorities.

"He found some of the old carpet in the dumpster," Bodhi explained. "He used that to keep everything clean."

"Thank goodness."

"Hmm."

He caressed my hair, smoothing it away from my face. I closed my eyes as the rough pads of his calloused fingers danced across my skin. He trailed down my neck and shoulders, rubbing my arms and hands between his own to calm me down.

"For the record," Bodhi murmured as he concentrated on kneading my shoulders again, "I never thought you were weak. You're the strongest person I know, Bailey. And yet there is still something incredibly difficult about letting your wife crawl underground to retrieve bags of bodies."

"I had to," I mumbled.

"I know. I'm proud of you."

I let that sink in for a moment, loving the way Bodhi's fingers separated the matted hair at the nape of my neck. "Where's Patrick?"

"I'm not sure. Outside with Alex, I think. Why?"

I shifted, experimentally stretching my limbs out. My hamstrings shook with the effort. I was going to be sore tomorrow. "We should ask him where he wants to be buried."

There was a note of surprise in Bodhi's voice. "Oh."

I pushed myself up into a sitting position with Bodhi's house. "What? Is that weird?"

"No." Bodhi pulled me to my feet. My aching legs nearly gave out under my weight, but Bodhi looped my arm around his shoulders as we headed for the stairs. "Well, yes. But that's not what I was thinking. For some reason, I automatically assumed that we were burying them beneath Caroline's plumeria tree."

It was my turn to be surprised. "Oh. You know what? I quite like that idea."

"Let's run it by Patrick, just to make sure."

33

OLD LOVE

*P*atrick was outside, kneeling in the dirt of the backyard next to Alex, whose shoulders shook with grief. Nearby, the plastic contractor bags waited for someone to tend to them. Apparently, Alex wasn't quite as stoic as Bodhi originally assumed. Bodhi helped me down the steps of the deck so that we could join Alex. Patrick stared at us wide-eyed, as if he didn't know how to calm down the man who once used to be his best friend. I knelt beside Alex, fighting to keep control of my aching joints, and gathered him into a silent hug.

"I can't do it," he said. "I don't know how you pulled them out of there, Bailey. I just… I looked inside the bags. It's horrible. Worse than horrible."

"It's them?" Bodhi asked. It was a terrible question, but we needed the confirmation. Otherwise, what was the point?

Alex nodded as he drew away from me and wiped his eyes. "It's them. God, you can't even tell, but it's obvious."

"How bad is it?"

"It's mostly just bones," Alex sniffed. "Everything else has decomposed, but the plastic kept it all together. It's disgusting. I can't believe I ever trusted Ethan Powell. This is the work of someone truly sick."

I rubbed Alex's back as Patrick inspected the bags with a wrinkled nose. All in all, he was the calmest of the four of us. He peeked inside the first bag and groaned. "Ugh. Yeah, that's definitely me. Sheesh."

Bodhi escorted Patrick away from his body before he could continue his scientific examination of the remains. "Really, Pat? Really?"

"What? It's kind of interesting. Besides, I got over being dead about fifteen years ago."

"We're so thrilled," Alex deadpanned. "But in all honesty, I can smell your body from here, and I'd like to get it in the ground as quickly as possible before Ethan decides to make another visit, so could you do me a solid and let me know where I should start digging your grave?"

Patrick revolved on the spot, looking around the backyard as if scoping out the best place for his final resting place. "Boy, I never thought this was something I'd do. There's a lot of pressure, you know?"

Since he didn't seem to be making a decision anytime soon, I elbowed Bodhi. "Bodhi, tell him what you were thinking."

"Oh. Uh, Patrick?"

"Yeah."

Bodhi pointed across the garden to the edge of the bluff where Caroline's plumeria tree was in full bloom. "I was thinking you might like to go under the tree? It's the nicest place in the garden. For now, at least. I promise we'll clean up the rest of it before we sell the house."

Patrick considered the possibility, gazing toward the pink flowers. "I think Caroline would really like that actually."

"What about you?" Alex asked.

Patrick smiled wistfully. "Alex, I just want to be with my sister and move on from whatever this is."

"Fair enough."

"Could you do me a favor though?" Patrick added, fiddling with something behind his back.

"Anything."

Patrick tossed his football to Alex, who caught it without thinking. "Could you bury that with me?"

Alex rotated the football in his hands to look it over. "Is this the game ball from our junior year championship?"

"It sure is."

Alex grazed his fingers across the laces in awe. "You sure you want it buried? I will absolutely throw it in there with you, but I'd much rather keep it."

Patrick's eyebrows shot up toward his hairline. "Wait, you want it?"

"Of course. That game was one of my best high school memories."

"All right. Take it then."

Alex grinned and clapped Patrick on the back. "Thanks, buddy. Let's get to work."

I SAT OUT THE SHOVELING. Alex and Bodhi worked side by side, each one working on an individual grave beneath the plumeria tree. Patrick and I supervised quietly. I had lost track of the time. The moon was high and bright, and the stars were out in full force. While I listened for any signs of intruders, I lay down in the grass of the garden, cradling the back of my neck in my interlaced fingers, and gazed up at the constellations. I was never good at picking the shapes and patterns out of the stars. For some reason, my imagination couldn't connect the dots or fill in the pictures. Tonight, however, something shifted.

It probably wasn't even a real constellation, but right overhead I swore I saw the outline of a plump toddler with a wide toothy smile in the sky above. I shot up from my bed of grass and stepped up to the deck.

Bodhi wiped his forehead, up to his shoulders in dirt. They were nearly done. "Everything okay, Bailey?"

"Yes," I said, slipping through the open glass doors. "I thought of something. I'll be right back."

As Bodhi returned to digging, I went upstairs to the second floor of the Winchester house and into the bedroom that Bodhi and I were sharing. My suitcase rested in the corner of the room, propped open. I had never bothered to fully unpack. It was too weird to hang my clothes in the house of a dead family. I swatted aside my belongings, feeling for a certain compartment on the side of the suitcase. When my fingers found the zipper, I reached inside and pulled out the object that I kept with us at all times. Every house we flipped. Every project we took on. Every shitty hotel we stayed at between jobs. She was there too.

It was Kali's urn.

It was impossibly small and made out of polished blue marble. I rarely looked at it anymore, let alone touched it. It just sat there in my suitcase, reminding me of what Bodhi and I had lost. Never had I considered any other options for it until now. I carried Kali down to the first floor in the crook of my arm. In my mind's eye, I could see her brown curls and hazel eyes, the round pink cheeks and fat baby arms. It should've made me cry, but instead I felt a strange sense of relief as I stepped into the warm summer night. I took a deep breath before heading over to Bodhi and Alex. They sat beside the giant piles of overturned earth, covered head to toe in dirt, while Patrick dangled his feet into the grave nearest him.

When Bodhi saw me, he hopped up from the ground and

dusted his hands. "All done. Are you ready—?" He cut himself off when he saw what I was carrying. "Is that—?"

I nodded, freezing in place a few steps away from him, suddenly unsure if this was a good idea or not. "I thought if you were all right with it, we could let her go here."

Patrick and Alex watched from a distance as Bodhi warily approached me. He offered his palms, asking silently for what I held in my arms. Gently, I placed the urn in his hands.

"I haven't seen this since her funeral," he murmured, turning the object over to marvel at its miniscule size. "You've had it all this time?"

"Of course. What else would I have done with it?"

Bodhi hugged the cool marble to his chest. "I figured you'd given her to your mom to hold on to."

"Never. She's been with us. Always."

Bodhi gazed out at the water. Behind us, the sky was just beginning to lighten. We had spent the entire night with the dead. If we were going to finish before morning, we needed to get a move on, but I didn't want to rush Bodhi's thought process. This was a joint decision. I couldn't make it alone.

Finally, he nodded. "Yes. This is the place."

While Alex and Bodhi heaved the ugly plastic bags into the holes they had dug and began to fill the dirt back in, I sat on the deck with Kali in my lap and Patrick at my side. As he watched Alex cover his body, a pinkish hue returned to his cheeks. He looked healthier, as if the simple act of burying him respectfully had already begun to have an effect on his afterlife.

"Can you feel Caroline?" I asked him, wondering how the other Winchester child fared under such unusual circumstances.

"She's here," Patrick said softly.

As if to prove it, a chilly breeze that had nothing to do

with the balmy summer air danced around me, blowing my hair around my face. I smiled. "Hi there."

"She wants to know about Kali," said Patrick, gesturing to the urn resting on my knees. "What was she like?"

I toyed with the lid of the urn, reminiscing. "Adventurous. Unstoppable. Mischievous. Quite a bit like Caroline actually."

Patrick grinned. "Like you, you mean."

I exhaled a big breath. "Years ago maybe."

"Hmm." Patrick leaned back on his palms. "She's still in there somewhere. You just gotta let her go."

"You're very wise for a seventeen-year-old."

"Technically, I'm thirty-seven."

I scoffed. "I've met plenty of middle-aged folks who are nowhere near as enlightened as you."

Patrick brightened at the compliment, but before he could respond, Alex patted down the packed dirt, surrendered his shovel, and jogged over to us.

"We're about finished," he said. "I thought we could all say a few words."

Patrick and I stood up and walked over to the graves. Bodhi lay down his shovel and wiped his hands on his shorts. I handed Kali's urn to him then walked to the plumeria tree and picked a handful of flowers. I laid three on top of Caroline's grave, three more on Patrick's, and placed a sole plumeria right in between them for Kali.

The four of us stood side by side, facing the cliff's edge. Caroline was there in spirit. I could feel her whispering around us like a light wind. No one seemed to know what to do, so Alex cleared his throat and took a step forward.

"I've done something like this every year at the Winchester Celebration," he said, his voice shaking. "But I've never done it with the knowledge that you might be listening in. Patrick. Caroline. I love you, I miss you, and I wish every day that you were still with us."

And that was that. Alex stepped back in line with us, and Patrick reached up to rest a hand on Alex's broad shoulders in solidarity. Then, to my surprise, Bodhi moved forward and turned to face Patrick.

"I want to thank you," he said firmly. "You too, Caroline. Were it not for this experience, I'm not sure where Bailey and I would be." A gust of wind tickled Bodhi's long curls. From his resulting shiver, I knew that Caroline had swirled around him. "I also wanted to say a few words for my daughter. Kali, if you're out there somewhere, please know that I have and will always keep you in my heart. I hope you find enlightenment. I love you mightily."

Silent tears made their way down my cheeks. I let them go. It was what I needed. Bodhi caught my eye. He too cried peacefully, his golden irises glistening as they reflected the lightening sky. I stepped out to meet him, looping my arm through his. Together, we turned and walked to the edge of the bluff. There, I unscrewed the lid of the urn. It was a little stiff, but it gave way eventually. As the lid came off, a dusty puff rose into the air. I offered the urn to Bodhi, but he shook his head.

"You should do it," he said.

I placed his hand on one side of the urn, leaving mine on the other. "Together."

And we tipped the small jar over. Kali's ashes billowed out like a gray sail, floating away across the water. Bodhi tucked the empty urn under one arm and me under his other. I wrapped my arms around his waist, listening to his pulse as I rested my head against his chest. He gently stroked my hair and brushed his lips across my forehead.

"There she goes," he mumbled softly.

We stood there for a while. Letting go of everything. Of

Kali. Of Patrick and Caroline. Of all that came before. It was a renewal of sorts. Another beginning. And we were facing it head-on.

WE WENT to bed as the sun crested over the horizon. Bodhi had called the construction crew and told them to take the day off. Alex crashed on an air mattress in Patrick's old bedroom after letting his wife know where he had gone. None of us were in any state to work on the renovations for the house. We needed the day to recuperate from the evening's physical and emotional drainage. It was Friday. Tomorrow, Patrick and Caroline would officially pass on to the next life. If everything went according to plan, of course.

Before turning in, we had charted out the necessary steps for what came next. There was still the matter of "recharging" Patrick and Caroline before their final confrontation with Ethan. Funnily enough, we'd used Bodhi's offhand joke about the car battery as inspiration. We planned to rejuvenate Patrick with the energy from the white rental truck that Bodhi used to transport hardware to and from town, and Alex offered to drive his SUV up to the bluff in order to get Caroline the power that she needed.

In addition, we worked out who was acting as whose energy conductor. Bodhi volunteered to be Patrick's proxy, the human vessel he needed in order to collect the power from the truck's battery. That left either me or Alex for Caroline, but before I could even open my mouth to offer up my bodily services, Alex jumped in with the declaration that he would be the one and only person to connect to Caroline. I conceded immediately. There was no arguing with old love. We arranged to perform the energy transference Friday evening.

I woke up sometime in the late afternoon. Bodhi snored

beside me. Both of us were completely worn out. My very bones seemed to ache with the aftereffect of my jaunt into the underbelly of the house. The muscles in my legs and arms felt agonizingly tight. I massaged them myself, digging my knuckles into the hard knots beneath my skin as I tried not to wake Bodhi. Then, for good measure, I checked my blog. I hadn't posted much since my last update a few days ago, but my followers were as friendly and active as ever. Their comments were uplifting and positive, encouraging me to continue living my truth. I typed up a new post.

Bailey and Bodhi: Flipping Out

HELLO, *flippers! What a crazy couple of days it's been. As you know, we've been preparing to renovate the rest of the rooms on the first floor of the Winchester house. The ballroom is going to be the biggest challenge there. It's at the very back of the house, and it has these rows of paned windows down each wall. It's gorgeous as is, and half of me is tempted to leave it, but I doubt whoever we sell the house to is going to go with the flow and heartily accept the old-school ballroom when the rest of the house is industrial themed. Who knows? Maybe we'll find a good compromise.*

In the personal department, Bodhi and I hurdled a major milestone last night. I've been carrying around Kali's ashes in my suitcase ever since she died. Honestly, I never thought I'd ever find a place that was worthy of them. Nepal, maybe, if we ever returned there. Then I realized that Bodhi, Kali, and I would've loved Black Bay together. I could picture Kali jumping off the docks in the marina. I could see all three of us playing in the annual flag football tournament when she got a little older. I could imagine walking along Main Street, swinging Kali between me and Bodhi.

She belonged here. Or at the very least, I could believe that she could be free here. So last night, Bodhi and I scattered Kali's ashes at the top of the bluff behind the Winchester house. I always assumed it would be beyond painful to let her go. Instead, it was sweet. Lovely, even. I'll remember that moment forever.

THANKS FOR READING,
   Bailey

A LIGHT KNOCK on the bedroom door stirred Bodhi from his slumber. He turned over with a groan and pushed my laptop off of my blanketed thighs so that he could rest his head there instead.

"Come on in," I called.

Alex popped his head inside, his short hair disheveled. He wore a pair of shorts and a T-shirt that he had borrowed from Bodhi, both of which were a couple inches short for his tall, lean figure. "Hey. Sorry to wake you, but it's getting late. Should we do this before we run out of daylight?"

Bodhi mumbled something unintelligible. I suppressed a laugh. "We'll be down in a minute, Alex."

It took much longer than a minute to convince Bodhi to leave the comfort of the double bed. I didn't blame him. All I wanted to do was sleep for another couple of days. Unfortunately, there was work to be done.

When I finally coaxed Bodhi out from underneath the covers and down the stairs, Alex and Patrick waited for us in the kitchen, discussing strategy for what was about to happen. Alex had already gone into town and brought back his SUV. It was parked in the front yard next to Bodhi's truck. Both hoods were propped open, and a pair of jumper cables dangled from each of the batteries over the grill of the vehicles. Something jumped in the pit of my stomach. Maybe this wasn't such a good idea after all.

"Oh, good. You're up," Alex said. He offered me a mug. "I made coffee."

Bodhi lurched over to the fresh pot to fill his own mug then leaned against the counter and inhaled the steam rising from the chocolate-colored liquid.

"Bodhi, are you going to be okay to do this?" Alex asked, raising a worried eyebrow.

"Yeah, I'm fine. Just exhausted."

"It'll be all right," Patrick jumped in. "Like I told you before, we're taking energy from the cars, not from you."

"Thank goodness," I said. "Caroline packs a punch."

Alex finished off his beverage. "Alrighty then. Should we jump right in?"

We all exchanged looks. Bodhi shrugged and tipped back his mug for another gulp of coffee. "Might as well."

The four of us made our way out to the front yard. Patrick and Alex had saved us some time and energy with the setup. The jumper cables hung loosely from each car, harmless for now, but it was hard to wrap my mind around the science, or lack thereof, behind how this was going to work.

"Bodhi, you stand here," Patrick directed, escorting Bodhi to the hood of his pickup truck. He picked up the slack of the jumper cable and handed Bodhi one of the clamps. "Hold this. I just need to be in contact with you somehow."

"Do I need the positive end or the negative end?" Bodhi asked.

"I don't think it matters much," Alex answered as he picked up the cable hanging out of his own vehicle. "If Caroline's not around, how's she going to make contact with me?"

"She'll come around when we start the car," Patrick said. He grasped Bodhi's wrist. "Who wants to go first?"

Bodhi raised his hand. "Let's get this over with." He tossed me the keys for the truck. "Bailey. You want to fire it up?"

I caught the keys, juggling them in my fingers, but I hesitated before circling toward the driver's door. Bodhi held a live wire in his hands, and I had to be the one to fuel it with power. We had only Patrick's word that the energy wouldn't harm Bodhi on its way through to the next entity.

"Patrick, are you sure this is safe?" I asked the younger boy.

"I would never even think to ask you to do it otherwise."

His promise reassured me, but I slid into the driver's seat with an uneasy feeling. Bodhi and Patrick faced me through the windshield. Bodhi's knuckles were white around his end of the jumper cable. Similarly, Patrick's grip on Bodhi's wrist tightened in anticipation.

"Ready?" I asked, fitting the key in the ignition.

Patrick nodded and closed his eyes, as if bracing himself.

"Let her rip," said Bodhi.

I turned the key, and the truck's engine rumbled to life. For a second, nothing happened, and I wondered if Patrick and Alex had connected the jumper cables to the battery incorrectly. Then, at the same time, Bodhi and Patrick convulsed.

I yelled instinctively, reaching for the key to turn off the car, but Alex bolted to my window and yanked my hand away from the ignition.

"Leave it on," he ordered, pinning my fingers to my side. "They're fine. Look."

I took a second look. Bodhi shook from head to toe, bracing himself against the hood of the truck, but other than that, he appeared to be unharmed. He even gave me the thumb's up with his free hand.

Patrick, on the other hand, glowed with an ethereal white light. His entire body vibrated as he absorbed the energy from the truck with Bodhi's help. It was like staring at a star explosion. I covered my eyes as the light brightened to a blinding force. Bodhi squeezed his eyelids shut, shuddering as Patrick took everything he could. The truck whined underneath me. With one last flare from Patrick, the engine died. The truck's rumble quieted. The light faded into the sky.

And Patrick was the thirty-seven-year-old man that he was meant to be.

We stared at him in silent awe. Like Alex, he aged well, or he would have if he had been given the chance. His hair was shorter and neater, a shadow of a beard grew on his cheeks, and his jaw and cheekbones had hardened into strong, handsome features. He appeared in tailored jeans, a collared shirt, and his signature deck shoes, as though he was ready to take the Winchesters' sailboat out on the bay for their weekly family trip. All in all, he looked like a younger version of his father.

Patrick stared at his hands, which now sported the wear and tear of years in the sun behind the wheel of a sailboat. "I'll be damned."

Bodhi dropped the jumper cable. To my great relief, he was fine, if a bit shaky on his feet. I stumbled out of the truck to meet him, but even as we caught each other, we couldn't look away from Patrick's new face. Alex was likewise dumbstruck, but he recovered first. He stretched out his hand toward Patrick, who paused before shaking it, and then Alex tugged Patrick into a hug.

"I never thought I'd get to see you like this," Alex admitted, thumping Patrick on the back. "It's surreal, man."

"You're telling me," Patrick mumbled. "Anyone have a mirror?"

Everyone laughed as Patrick ambled over to the truck, looked in the side view mirror, and traced the new lines around his mouth. He ran a hand through his hair, which had lightened in color, staring wide-eyed at the man in the mirror. He straightened up quickly, the set of his mouth solidifying into a determined smirk.

"Let's get Caroline."

Alex handed me the keys to his SUV, returned to his place near the hood, and picked up the jumper cables. "Way ahead of you. Let's do this."

With renewed confidence, I hopped into Alex's SUV, fitted the keys into the ignition, and revved the engine. Like before, a few seconds passed without action. Alex waited patiently, his arms outstretched over the hood of the car as though offering them up for Caroline to take. My breath caught in my throat as a breeze disturbed Alex's borrowed shirt. She was here.

The light began slowly this time. A tiny orb appeared between Alex's extended arms and hovered in the space there. It grew in size and intensity, gradually elongating and brightening until it filled my vision. I closed my eyes, the glow pressing red against the darkness behind my lids. The SUV sputtered out. I waited a beat, buzzing with anticipation. Then I looked out the windshield.

Caroline, thirty-five and eternally beautiful at any age, stood between Alex's arms. He stared at her, stunned, and she smiled like a radiant sun.

34

IN EXULTATION

"*Y*ou can probably set the jumper cables down, Alex," Caroline said with a smirk. Her voice was everything and nothing like I'd expected. It was a little huskier than it had been in the videos I'd seen of her as a teenager, and it also conveyed the sense that she knew more about the world than anyone else did.

Alex's lips parted as he gazed down at her in disbelief as his fingers unclenched and the cables dropped from his hands. They clattered against the grill of the SUV, but Alex couldn't care less about the state of his car. He wasn't the only one enthralled with Caroline's appearance. Bodhi and Patrick were similarly entranced, and I'd admit myself that seeing Caroline in the flesh felt like an out-of-this-world experience.

She wore a long, flowing, summery dress. It was a peachy white color, like the color of clouds at sunrise, and decorated with delicate lace trim. Her flaxen hair was pinned away from her face, but the rest of it rained down the tanned skin of her back. Her eyes were sharp, her brows defined, and her lips set in a sly, satisfied smile that I imagined was a permanent fixture on her face. Like Patrick mirrored his father, so Caroline reflected her mother. There was no denying the flawlessness of the Winchester gene pool.

Since we all were frozen in place, Caroline made the first move. She stood up on her tiptoes, steadying herself on Alex's forearms, and gently kissed his lips. He responded in kind for a short second before shifting away.

"I'm married," he told her.

"I'm dead," she reminded him with a nonchalant shrug. "It's not cheating if the other woman isn't even alive. I just wanted to remember what that felt like."

Alex continued to stare at her, unable to process her existence. She hovered there for a minute, waiting for him to respond. When he remained unmoving, she ducked beneath his arm.

"Patrick!"

Caroline jumped into Patrick's arms. He whirled her around, and the skirts of her dress spiraled like wispy clouds. Patrick set his sister firmly on the ground. "It's nice to see you," he said. "It's been a while."

Caroline playfully squeezed his shoulders. "I know. I can't believe you're real. God, you got old. Are those crow's feet?"

"Um, excuse me. Have you *looked* in a mirror?"

Bodhi cleared his throat loudly, and Caroline peeked around Patrick to get a glimpse of him. She smiled widely and approached Bodhi. "But of course. How could I forget our magnificent hosts? Can I give you a hug?"

He eyed her warily. "I'd rather have an apology."

Caroline had the decency to bow her head sheepishly. "You're right. Forgive me for the trouble I've caused you."

Bodhi nodded toward me. "Tell that to my wife."

Caroline revolved, finally finding me near the door of Alex's SUV. A hesitant smile tipped her lips upward as she walked over to me. "Bailey."

I held on to the car to keep myself from shaking. "Caroline."

"I'm so sorry," she said. She gestured to my walking boot and skinned knees. "I have no excuse for the way I've treated you other than impatience. I saw a chance to get someone's attention, and I took it."

"That's all right."

"It's not," she replied, shaking her head. She seemed hesitant to fully approach me, as if I might scold her for all the injuries I sustained as a result of her wrath. "I was immature and irrational. I should've found a better way to contact you."

I mustered my courage and closed the distance between me and Caroline, taking her hands. "Caroline. You did what you thought you had to do. I forgive you for that."

Her lower lip trembled. Without warning, she threw her arms around my neck and hugged me fast. I felt as though I was hugging both Carolines at once: the callow teenaged ghost and the corporeal apologetic woman in front of me.

"Thank you," she murmured. "You could've run, but you didn't. No one else stayed."

"You're welcome," I said back. "You deserve to be free." I pulled away from Caroline, sniffling. She smelled familiar, like the perfume that lingered on the soccer jersey I'd borrowed, and I finally recognized the scent as calla lilies. I cleared my throat, gazing around at our odd party.

"Well?" Alex prompted. "What's next?"

Caroline's demeanor changed at once. She wiped teardrops from her eyelashes and pursed her lips.

"Next," she declared. "We find Ethan Powell."

SATURDAY MORNING SAW three living people and two dead ones crowded around the tiny card table in the Winchesters' otherwise empty family room to discuss strategy. We were a mismatched bunch: Bodhi with his long hair and bare feet; Alex with his baseball cap and Lido's T-shirt; Caroline who, in a pair of riding pants and a crisp collared shirt, looked more like she belonged at the equestrian center for the day; Patrick, whose wiser and more mature face I couldn't get used to; and me, in paint-stained shorts, a tank top that hadn't been washed in a few days, and the plaster cast encasing my ankle that was filthier than a bar floor. If any of the locals walked in on us, they would be sure to wonder what an amalgamation of characters had to do with one another.

The subject of the morning was how to get Ethan Powell around to the Winchester house again. We hadn't gone into town since that night at the Sanctuary. Groceries were running light, as was our toilet paper supply, but we didn't want to risk meeting Ethan if it was avoidable. Now, our goal had flipped. We needed to locate Ethan, and we needed to lure him up the bluff before he realized exactly what was happening. The problem was executing such a plan without the locals getting suspicious. It took us two hours to solidify an arrangement, and even then, most of it relied on where Alex found Ethan, who he was with at the time, and whether or not we could get him alone.

We parted in the early afternoon to put our plan into action. Caroline and Patrick jumped the cars. Apparently, once ghosts were fully charged, they were able to lend their own energy again without much consequence. Alex got a head start, trundling out of the front yard in his SUV and down the dirt road. Bodhi and I followed shortly after. When we got into town, we drove straight toward Lido's Restaurant. As it was a balmy Saturday morning, the locals were out in full force. The park was full of families and dogs. The marina was a flurry of sailboats and speedboats trying to get out on the water. The main street boasted refreshed businesswomen enjoying their weekend freedom as they shopped at Black Bay's various boutiques. We waved and smiled at the familiar faces, doing our best to look natural. This was part of the plan. The more people who saw us driving through town, the better. It gave us an alibi.

We pulled into the employee lot beside Lido's, where the dumpsters were, and parked out of sight of the main road. The restaurant was already loaded with customers, many of which were eating their lunch on the patio out back. This presented a little bit of a challenge. If Ethan gave us any trouble at all, he would surely alert any and all of Lido's patrons to our ruse. Nevertheless, we had no other choice, so Bodhi and I settled in to wait for Alex to pull off his part of the plan. The radio played faintly in the background as the truck idled. The stale smell of the dumpsters permeated the cab. I wrinkled my nose. Hopefully, Alex wouldn't take too long.

Bodhi rubbed the corner of his eye, blinking his drowsiness away. He hadn't slept well the night before. None of us had. The weight of the day settled on my chest like an anvil. The purpose of our mission hadn't escaped me, but I tried to temper the anxiety that rose in my throat every time I thought about the fact that we were helping a pair of ghosts to murder someone.

"You okay?" I asked Bodhi, flipping up the armrest between us to shuffle over to him. The seat belt jabbed into my hip, but I ignored the nuisance as he snaked an arm around me to rub my back.

"As okay as I can be," he replied, but he stared absentmindedly through the front windshield at the part of the bay visible to us.

"Everything's going to be all right," I promised him. I didn't entirely believe it. There were too many things that could go wrong. But in that moment, Bodhi needed reassurance, and if we went into this without at least a little bit of faith, it would go much worse than we anticipated.

We could've talked through the plan again. We could've spoken about the dubious morality of what might occur in the next few hours. We could've talked about how the day's events would affect us in the long run, or what would happen if we got caught, or who might suffer if Ethan got the best of us. Instead, we waited for Alex to arrive in comfortable silence, curled up together like a pair of cats in the sunshine. At some point, I think we even dozed off because when Bodhi's cell phone rang to warn us of Alex's arrival, we both jerked out of our sun-soaked stupor.

"Is he here?" I asked, peeking over Bodhi's shoulder to see the message.

"They're pulling in now. Let's get ready."

We hopped out of the truck, opened the tailgate, and gathered our materials. Then we stationed ourselves on either side of the restaurant's back door. My heart pounded. Blood rushed through my ears. I pressed myself to the building, feeling the rough, warm bricks press against my back through the fabric of my shirt, and willed myself to calm down. Across from me, Bodhi mouthed silent words, standing at the ready.

When the door handle turned, I coiled like a spring, my fingers tightening over the rag between my fingers. As the door opened, Alex's voice rang out.

"You should see this smoker, Ethan," Alex was saying. "I can't wait to start trying my hand at smoking my own meats. The customers are going to go wild. It's just out back—"

"The customers?" Ethan rumbled with a laugh. "*I'm* going to go wild."

My breath stopped as Ethan's boot led the way through the back door and into the parking lot. Time slowed. Ethan's head turned to the left ever-so-slightly. Toward me.

The three of us lunged at the same time. Alex tackled Ethan from behind, tangling himself around Ethan's knees to send him crashing to the pavement. Bodhi rocketed forward before Ethan even landed. He kneeled on Ethan's upper back to prevent him from moving as Alex pinned his legs to the ground. While Bodhi secured Ethan's hands behind his back with a rope knot that Alex had taught him that morning, I shoved the rag into Ethan's mouth. Thankfully, he was too dazed from our sneak attack to put up much of a fight at first. Without his hands to break his fall, Ethan had smacked his head pretty hard against the asphalt. As his eyes cleared, he yelled for help, but the rag muffled his voice. No one inside Lido's or sitting on the patio would hear him over the commotion of midday Saturday.

Alex and Bodhi hauled Ethan to his feet and heaved him into the back of the pickup truck. Alex leapt into the bed of the truck, forcing Ethan to lie flat so that no one would notice him as we drove through town. We slammed the tailgate shut, got into the cab, and peeled out of the parking lot as quickly as possible.

I kept watch in the side view mirror as we rode back up to the bluff. From a distance, no one would think twice about our jaunt through town. Alex stretched out in the back, waving merrily to passing locals. We were simply enjoying the day, just like everyone else. Still, it was a massive relief to find the sanctuary of the woods at the base of the bluff. As we rode into the shadows, I let out a breath I hadn't realized I was holding. The hardest part was over. Or was it?

Caroline and Patrick lingered in the doorway of the house. As Alex unloaded Ethan, Caroline took a step inside. The siblings wore similar expressions, a balance between hate and fear, as they regarded the man who had ruined their lives so long ago. Alex forced Ethan to his knees in the dirt and ripped the rag out of his mouth.

Ethan let loose a string of expletives. "What the *hell*, Alex? Have you completely lost your mind?"

"Don't play stupid with me, Ethan," Alex spat. "I know what you did."

"And what did I do?" Ethan challenged him. "Huh? What sort of nonsense did Bailey and Bodhi put into your mind? Did they feed you that ghost story too?"

Caroline emerged from the house. The sun highlighted her high cheekbones. "It was no story, Mr. Powell."

Ethan squinted upward. "Who the hell are you?"

"You don't recognize me?"

When it finally hit Ethan who he was staring at, I could see the realization in his eyes. He gazed up at Caroline, and a look of something like horror and shock crossed his features. "No," he sputtered. "It can't be."

Patrick joined Caroline in the front yard. "Did you miss us?"

Ethan squeezed his eyes shut and shook his head. "No, no, no. This isn't real. You're dead!"

"You're right on that count," said Caroline. She knelt down, took Ethan's chin between her fingers, and forced him to look at her. "You made sure of that. But you already knew that I wasn't entirely gone, didn't you? You used to come here once a month to check up on me, but you never thought I had the ability to touch you. Guess what, Ethan? Karma's a bitch." She stood and spat in the dirt in front of Ethan. Then she looked up at Alex, who watched with uncertainty by the truck door. "You should go," Caroline told him.

"What? No!"

Caroline circled toward Alex, giving Ethan a wide berth, and took his hands in hers. "Alex. Please. I don't want you to be a part of this."

"I'm not leaving you," he insisted.

"She's right," Patrick said as he approached Alex as well.

"You shouldn't have to watch this, Alex."

Alex looked between the siblings. "You both want me to go?"

Caroline nodded. "It's for the best."

"So is this goodbye then?"

A sense of infinite sadness radiated outward from the trio. This wasn't the first time Alex had to let go of his best friends. Was it easier or harder the second time around?

"We'll always be with you," Patrick told him. "Don't forget that."

He gave Alex a hug then retreated toward me and Bodhi to allow Caroline a moment alone with him. She entwined her fingers around his neck. Instinctively, he pulled her closer.

"I'm happy you're happy," she told him in a quiet voice that carried across the front yard. "You deserve that and so much more. Live your life, Alex. Patrick and I are moving on. You should too."

He rested his forehead against hers. "I missed you."

She tapped his nose with the tip of her finger. "We'll always be best friends."

"Same here," Patrick called over jokingly. "Even though I know you like my sister better."

I made a face, knowing I'd never experience something like this ever again. The trio had momentarily forgotten about Ethan as he knelt in the dirt with a look of utter rage etched into his features. Bittersweet happiness and terror warred in the front yard, but Caroline and Patrick had no intention of letting Ethan ruin the only chance they had to say goodbye to their friend.

Caroline drew away from Alex. "Go."

"But—"

"*Go.*"

Alex hesitated, looking between me, Bodhi, and Ethan. I

gave him a reassuring nod. "We have this under control," I told him. "I'll call you when it's over."

"You're making a mistake, Alex," Ethan said.

"Shut up," Bodhi and I chorused.

Alex looked at his friends one last time as he backed toward the dirt road that led into town. "Goodbye, Patrick. Caroline."

"Bye, Alex."

"Later, man."

And then he was gone, disappearing into the trees with his hands in his pockets and his shoulders hunched in sorrow. Caroline breathed a sigh of relief, which Patrick soon echoed. Neither one of them had wanted their friend to witness what came next.

Patrick turned to Bodhi. "Got the rope?"

Bodhi nodded, jogged into the house, and reappeared with the nautical rope that Ethan had used to kill Patrick. It looked worse for wear, bloodied, frayed, and moldy from its time underwater. Bodhi handed it over to Patrick, who swung it between his fingers as he stalked toward Ethan. To my surprise, he untied the knot around Ethan's hands.

"Get up," he snarled at the older man.

"No."

I jumped away as Patrick looped the rope around Ethan's neck and yanked him to his feet. Ethan choked and stumbled upward. He struggled against his binding, slipping the fingers of one hand beneath the noose to prevent it from tightening too much. With his other hand, he wrenched the rope toward himself in an attempt to stop Patrick from leading him like a dog into the house, but Patrick's other-worldly abilities outweighed Ethan's brute strength. He dragged the larger man like a ragdoll, and Ethan had no choice but to blunder along unless he wanted to suffocate on the spot.

As Bodhi and I followed them into the living room, a wave of nausea hit me like a ton of bricks. I didn't want to see this. Yes, Ethan was a murderer, and Patrick and Caroline were doing what they had to do in order to free themselves from this life, but I had seen enough death to last me a lifetime. As Caroline restrained Ethan, Patrick swung the other end of the nautical rope up and over one of the exposed beams in the living room. It was the same place Patrick had met his own end. It was where Caroline had once hung Bodhi by a length of invisible rope to prove a point to us. That beam held more terrifying memories that the rest of the house put together.

Patrick used all of his weight to pull down on his end of the rope, the muscles in his back straining. The noose lifted Ethan to balance on his tiptoes. His face turned bright red and spittle flew from his lips as he grappled with the rope around his neck.

"No," he choked out. "I'm sorry."

Caroline frowned, regarding Ethan with her arms crossed nonchalantly across her chest. "I don't think that's good enough. What do you think, Patrick?"

"Nope."

And he wrenched the rope again. This time, Ethan's feet left the ground. The force pushed his breath out with a grunt, and his head looked as though it would pop right off his body. I turned away, hiding my face against Bodhi's chest. I couldn't watch this. But a second later, a loud thunk made the floorboards shake.

Patrick had dropped Ethan. The rope slithered off the beam and fell to the floor in a heap. As Ethan heaved for breath, Patrick fell to his knees, covering his head with his hands. Caroline rushed over to him.

"What is it?" she asked in a hushed tone.

"I can't do it," Patrick said, his voice shaking. "I can't kill him. It makes us just as bad as he is."

"Patrick, he murdered us—"

"I *know* he did."

"We have to move on."

"I know we do!"

Out of the corner of my eyes, I saw a flash of movement. I was so focused on Patrick's grief that I hadn't noticed Ethan slowly removing the rope from around his neck and inching toward the sliding glass doors.

"No!" I shouted as Ethan shot to his feet and slipped out into the backyard.

Bodhi was the first to follow him, throwing the glass door wide. He plunged into the wild rose bushes where Ethan's enormous form had already trampled through the plants. I ran after them, ignoring the thorns that bit and tore at my skin. I could hardly see through the thick foliage, but when I emerged on the other side of the garden, I slammed into Bodhi's broad back. He had stopped short, breathing hard, and stared across at Ethan. When I looked over, I realized why.

Ethan stood at the edge of the bluff with only open air behind him. In his hand, he held a small gun, and its muzzle was pointed straight at Bodhi's chest. A harsh red line encircled Ethan's neck, the leftovers of Patrick's attempt on his life.

"Did you think it would be that easy?" Ethan asked hoarsely. The gun traveled to point at me. I shook from head to toe but held on to my composure. "I don't think so. I didn't work so hard for what I have for two insignificant out-of-towners to come along and ruin it all."

"Ethan—" Bodhi began.

Ethan brandished the gun. "Shut up! I'm not going to shoot you. After all, why condemn myself?"

"How heroic of you," I spat, taking Bodhi's arm.

"Shut up," Ethan growled again. "Here's what's going to happen, morons." He gestured behind him to where the cliff dropped off. "You're going to jump off together. A nice little suicide pact between the two of you. It'll be an easy story to sell. The tragedy of the Winchester accident and the death of your daughter finally caught up to you. You couldn't take it anymore. Black Bay will forget about you, and I'll go back to the peaceful way of life that you ruined with your existence."

"Like hell you will," said a voice.

Patrick and Caroline had caught up with us. Patrick planted himself squarely between us and Ethan's gun, but Caroline marched straight across the garden to Ethan's side. He pulled the trigger. I flinched as the bullet embedded itself in Caroline's torso, but instead of falling to the ground, she laughed.

"Oh, Ethan," she said, giggling. "You can't kill me twice."

And before anyone had the chance to react, Caroline pushed Ethan off the rock face.

I let out a shocked shriek as Ethan disappeared from view with a garbled yell, but Bodhi held me back from rushing to the bluff's edge. A few seconds later, a terrifying thud echoed up from the rocks below, followed by a splash that was swallowed by the sound of the waves.

Almost immediately, Caroline and Patrick exploded with the same white light that had surrounded them during the energy transference. A rift opened between them, a doorway of sorts that neither Bodhi or I could look directly into or risk frying our corneas. At first, I wondered if this was what was supposed to happen, but a look at Caroline's awed expression confirmed this was what she and Patrick were waiting for. Then, with one eyebrow raised as if to ask a question, Caroline glanced my way.

I gestured toward the ethereal doorway. "Go on."

But Caroline bypassed the doorway and rushed into my

arms instead. I hugged her tightly. Then Patrick gathered us both up, waving to Bodhi.

"Get over here, Bodhi."

Hesitantly, Bodhi joined our group hug. The light of the doorway shined down on us, brightening with every passing moment, as though impatient for Patrick and Caroline to walk through it.

I pulled away from the siblings, wiping my eyes, and shooed them toward the doorway. "Get out of here, you two."

"What about Ethan?" Patrick asked. Worry colored his tone. He was genuinely concerned with our well-being. "Won't people ask questions?"

"We'll handle it," Bodhi reassured him. "Go."

Caroline squeezed my hand. "We can't thank you enough."

The doorway flickered and dimmed. It was a sign. It was officially time for Patrick and Caroline to go. Gently, I pushed Caroline in the general direction of her afterlife. She grabbed Patrick's hand and pulled him toward the doorway. Right before they stepped through, both of them turned to look at us.

They'd returned to their teenaged selves again. Seventeen-year-old Patrick grinned at us from beneath the brim of his Black Bay football cap, while fifteen-year-old Caroline smiled and waved excitedly like a happy baby.

"Don't forget about us," Patrick called.

"Are you kidding?" said Bodhi. "How could we?"

And then they waved one last time, rotated toward the light, and stepped through the doorway. Bodhi slipped his hand into mine, holding onto my fingers tightly, and we stood like that as the otherworldly light swallowed up Patrick and Caroline and began to fade. Soon the doorway closed completely, leaving Bodhi and I alone on the bluff. All that was left was sunshine.

EPILOGUE

Bailey, Bodhi, & Baby

aby number two makes four! Yes, that's right, ladies and gentleman. I will soon have to change the name of this blog yet again because we are expecting a little girl in addition to our handsome man, Winn. By the way, today is his fourth birthday, and he is pumped, but more on that in a minute. I want the amazing news to sink in with you. A girl! We get a girl!!!!! How many exclamation points are applicable for a scenario like this?!?! One may never know!!

If you couldn't already tell, I am beyond excited. So are Bodhi and Winn. Well, actually, I'm not sure if Winn has grasped the concept that he won't be the only little bean begging for our attention anymore. Not that he has to beg, of course. He's spoiled rotten. Anyway, you all should've seen Bodhi in the doctor's office. He was practically doing backflips. I would've actually done backflips, but unfortunately I was never much of a cheerleader.

So! This year, Winn's birthday falls conveniently on the same

434

day as the summer festival. It's his favorite town event, so it works out well. He's dying to play in the flag football tournament with Bodhi and Alex, but he's not quite old enough. God help me when his tiny fingers grow big enough to actually throw a full-sized football. He's trouble enough with the miniature foam one that Alex bought him. I've already kissed a table lamp and a decorative clock goodbye.

The only bad thing about being pregnant around this time of year is that I must regretfully abstain from Ava's famous party punch. It figures because I had totally planned to swipe a cup of it in order to analyze the contents and put together a recipe for you guys. Oh well. Maybe next year! In the meantime, you'll have to settle for this amazing lemon cake I whipped up. Pictures and instructions under the recipe tab!

Naturally, I plan to take a ton of photos today. Talk to me, people! What's on your agenda for this beautiful afternoon? Going to the beach, hanging out in the park, adventuring through the backwoods? Let me know!

With absolute love,
  Bailey

"Babe!"

I glanced up from the desktop computer in my office. Bodhi stood in the doorway, dangling Winn upside down from his ankles. Our little boy laughed raucously, his pristine baby teeth visible from across the room, as his light brown curls—naturally highlighted by all his time in the sun—bounced around on his head.

"I caught a monkey," Bodhi reportedly breathlessly. He pulsed Winn up and down, causing him to squeal with delight.

"Put him down," I ordered with a smile.

Bodhi dramatically rolled his eyes. "Fine. Release the beast!"

He lowered Winn to the floor. Winn somersaulted to his feet, sprinted toward me, and climbed up into my lap to try and read my latest blog post.

"I know that word, Mama," he declared, pointing at the screen. "But not that one. Or that one. Or that one. Or that one—"

"Alrighty," I interrupted, swinging Winn up onto my hip as I stood up. I groaned. "Sheesh, kid. You're getting way too big for this. What have you been eating?"

"Whatever you feed me."

I laughed. "Touché."

He wriggled to get down so I set him on the floor and he shot off like a wind-up toy. As he rounded the corner, his bare feet working like overactive windmills, I paused in the doorway next to Bodhi.

"Hi," he said.

"Hi."

He pulled me toward him. Our hips pressed together as he wrapped his arms around my waist and bent me over backward to kiss me. I smiled into it and felt his warm lips respond in the same way. When he righted me, he grinned.

"Are you ready for this festival?"

I nodded. "Let's do it."

AFTER CONVINCING him to put on his shoes, Winn led the way out, bouncing on the soles of his feet as Bodhi and I trailed along after him. I looked back at our house from the sidewalk. I would probably never get tired of coming home to it. After we had finished renovating the Winchester house, the smaller home had gone on the market in the middle of Black Bay's cozy little neighborhood. It was just big enough for the three of us, and it had an extra bedroom to convert into a nursery. Not to mention, the front windows boasted a beautiful view of the marina. Bodhi and I had fixed it up and moved in all within months of selling the Winchester house. Out of every house we ever flipped, this one was my favorite, because for the first time in so many years, we had a place that felt like home.

The Winchester house had been sold to a family of five for a price that would allow Bodhi and I to live comfortably in Black Bay for quite some time without having to worry about our finances. The new family was lovely too, and the locals of Black Bay had welcomed them with open arms. Steven worked in IT for a private business, and his wife, Lena, was an artist. That was why they had wanted the house on the bluff. It was a perfect place for Lena to set up her own studio. Winn was friends with their youngest daughter, who was the same age as him, and their eldest daughter babysat for us on a regular basis. We visited the Winchester house often for playdates or dinner parties or art lessons, but we never filled in the new residents on the details of their refurbished home.

With our nomadic phase finished and no other houses to flip in the area, Bodhi and I refocused our attention on other hobbies. Bodhi had established his own business and contracted himself out to work at sites all over the country—and occasionally some overseas—in order to fulfill his wanderlust. Sometimes, Winn and I went with him. In the past five years, we had explored New Zealand's coastlines, Italy's various vineyards, and South Korea's spiciest cuisine, among other adventures in between. But when the travel wore me down, I felt safe and comfortable with Winn in our new home in Black Bay. Bodhi always returned from his jobs happy and rejuvenated, and for me that was more than enough.

Flipping Out morphed into something else entirely. It was now a collection of our daily adventures in Black Bay and the surrounding area. At first, I wrote mostly about the hilarity that came with having a toddler, and my followers ate it up. The site attracted so much traffic that I eventually had to upgrade my overloaded server. *Bailey, Bodhi, & Baby* became so popular that I was getting calls from big name publishing companies asking me to compile my blog content into a parenting and family book for them to sell. Little did they know, I was already cooking up something along those lines. While my first draft covered the fun of raising a child all over the world, I also wrote it with the intention of helping other mourning parents to cope with the loss of their children.

These days, no one even thought about Ethan Powell anymore. Shortly after Caroline and Patrick's final disappearance, everything magically fell into place. A piece of Ethan's sunken boat surfaced in the bay, leading the police right to it. Bodhi and I turned in the evidence in our possession, claiming that Ethan had attempted to frame us for withholding it. The Coast Guard found Ethan's body in the rocks below the bluff, but since everyone in Black Bay had seen us in town that Saturday, the police ruled his death as a suicide. The lumber mill was renamed and the town collectively decided against burying Ethan in the local cemetery beside his parents. The *Black Bay Banner* published an article to clarify what had really happened to the Winchester family, Bodhi and I were heralded as heroes for discovering the truth, and Ethan Powell got the ending he deserved all along.

A wolf whistle woke me out of my daydreaming, and I looked up to see Alex's son Anthony skipping toward us as we neared the park for the summer festival. He was fifteen now and had grown to a whopping six feet already. Alex and his wife, Julia, often commiserated about how much he ate.

"There he is!" Anthony announced, kneeling down to Winn's level. Winn rocketed toward him, yelling like a madman, until Anthony swung him up in one fluid motion so that Winn sat on his shoulders. "Winchester Taylor, front and center!"

Winn drummed on Anthony's head. "Tony, Tony, Tony!"

"Easy, kid!"

"Sorry about that," Bodhi chuckled as we walked toward Anthony. Bodhi kept one arm slung across my shoulders. "Are your parents around?"

Anthony pointed across the park where freshly painted white lines marked the edges of the flag football field. There, Alex tossed a football to Julia, who threw it back with just as much force and spin.

"They're warming up already," said Anthony. "Wanna join?"

"Heck yeah."

It was a perfect day for the festival. The sun was out but not too hot, a cool breeze floated in from the bay, and the sky was an impossible shade of blue. As we jogged out to meet the rest of Anthony's family—we played on the same football team and with Alex's prowess we reigned as back-to-back summer festival champions for four years—Alex and Julia waved.

Alex relieved Anthony of his burden, flipping Winn over to hang him upside down. "What's up, little man?"

"Do all husbands do that?" I asked Julia as Winn fruitlessly wiggled his legs in an attempt to escape.

"Pretty much," said Julia. She reached out to tickle my belly. "So? Which is it?"

I beamed happily. "It's a girl."

She squealed with delight, twirling me around beneath one of the big oak trees in the park. "I'm so happy for you!"

Alex released Winn to clap Bodhi on the shoulder. "Congratulations, guys. An older boy and a younger girl. Just like Patrick and Caroline."

"The coincidence was not lost on us," said Bodhi, grinning.

Winn marched over to Alex and stole the football from between his hands. It was far too big for him, but that didn't stop him from throwing it into Bodhi's shins. "Let's play!"

"You heard the man!" Anthony shouted. He picked up the football and tossed it gently enough so that Winn could catch it. His voice shifted into a deep commentator's tone. "Ladies and gentlemen! The Lido-Taylor flag football team is looking flawless! But can they bring the championship trophy home for the fifth year in a row?"

"No doubt," Bodhi declared, high-fiving Alex. "Let's do this."

Everyone loped toward the field, tossing the football between them. Winn raced along behind them, his feet carrying him as fast as possible. I smiled, shaking my head as I watched my little family sprint off. Sometimes, I couldn't believe how much my life had changed in the past five years, but I was eternally glad that it had.